A Lifetime In Time

A Lifetime In Time

Written and Illustrated by

Timothy John Vaulato

LoKANTE & MOSHLOCK PUBLISHING

ISBN 978-0-9798981-0-5

LCCN 2008901435

Dedication:

To my family and friends who gave me both time and wisdom.

To the lost student who said, "What if you die first?"

Prelude
Birth and Other Ugly Truths

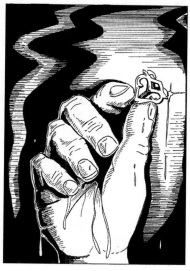

It was the last class of the day as he sat daydreaming at his desk. Announcements were passed out by an annoyed student that the teacher had made volunteer. As the papers hit his desk with a forceful shove he glanced at them long enough to get the idea of the information, and then quickly turned them over and used them for sketch paper. On the back of the announcement for the school's Sadie Hawkins dance, he drew a picture of a guitar that existed no place else but in his dreams. The dance was far off, a couple of months at least, but he knew no girl would lower herself to ask him, or maybe she would as a part of a cruel joke, only to laugh at him in the halls and point in disgust with her girlfriends. When the bell rang releasing the students into the world, he assessed his drawing, deemed it good enough to keep, folded it, and stuffed it into the lining pocket of his jean jacket. Weaving through the crowd that was either escaping, or blocking the hall to chat with their friends he picked up speed. Always the last one picked for any team he still prided himself on his ability to dodge just not the projectiles of the everyday gym class, but the traffic of people to who the words, "excuse me," would be meaningless. He was twenty feet from the door when he felt the push and his body slammed into the side lockers with a boom. Before he even turned he knew who it was.

Jim Salante's claim to fame was the unexpected attack. He never did it without an audience, he never did it to someone bigger, he never did it without his friends around as back up. His sense of humor consisted of violence, and the use of poorly constructed obscenities that usually questioned his victim's sexuality. Since he had joined the football team his random attacks had been worse. The boy didn't even stop long enough to understand the insult being hurled at him. As the crowd laughed he slipped through the door.

The laughter was fresh in his ears as he checked behind him to make sure he wasn't being followed. It was high summer right in the middle of March, 1985. Everyone knew the winter wasn't over, but for at least a day or two, the snow had melted and it was warm enough for the boy to wear his jean jacket and a down hunting vest on top of it. Ripped jeans and a bandana tied around his wrist was his attempt to be stylish. His hair was his attempt to be a rebel. It was long enough to annoy his parents, but not enough to be considered a threat by anyone else. Every time he'd try to grow it out, it fought gravity and made him feel as though he had a reddish brown Q-tip on his head. Puberty had been kind, at least to his chin and gave him a "hey, I'll have a beard someday," look which he shaved into a weak goatee which he wore proudly.

Like most teenage boys, he spent more time thinking about girls than having the courage to talk to any. Most of this was from shyness. He had no problem talking at length to anybody about anything, but talking to girls of his own age without the safety of his group of friends was another matter. This problem could have stemmed from the time he was beaten up in junior high by a very large girl. It was a complete misunderstanding, a playful insult fight that the girl had taken rather seriously.

A Lifetime In Time

In the end, it left him holding his crotch while she lifted him off the ground by his hair. The onlookers cheered. To say the least, it did nothing for his self-esteem. Though by high school the event was almost completely forgotten by everyone, it was still fresh in his mind and one of the reasons he considered himself a loser in the eyes of others. There were others that got it worse than him, students whose names had become synonymous with being uncool, students that were ignored, or, worse yet, sat alone at their lunch table whose only interaction with others was when Tuesday's luncheon special connected with their faces. He felt sympathy for them knowing the wrong move, wrong act, or another kick to the groin and he could very well fall into that same category. When the other bullies came to make their rounds he was relieved to be passed over for the geekier targets. He had just turned seventeen years old.

His feet shuffled through the worn gravel on an old road that ran along the back of his house. It's ever widening potholes threatened to become clouded gray lakes that reached to join the swamp of dried and brittle cattails. Somewhere deep in the reeds was a large wooden box that he and his friends had once used as a fort. They had found it one afternoon and it had become their private hang out till the day much larger kids found it and claimed it as theirs. The smell of cigarettes would always bring him back to that moment. The older boy's cigarette had been his clue that something was wrong before he had even gotten inside. The smoke was followed by a black eye that told him not to come back. Still, he felt the road was safe enough. He had traveled it many times since the record shop near the local grocery store opened. Nearly everyday since it opened he had been there, thumbing through the records, flipping through magazines, and spending his allowance on the music that graced the budget bins where the albums of choice received a deep cut in their cardboard housings to deem them fit for those on a budget. He felt that most of this decade's music was pathetic and searched the store for those rare gems of hard rock. He spent more time there than money. All the employees knew him by name, and if he was any other loiterer he would have been told to leave. Instead, on many occasions he told customers what album contained the song they were looking for, and informed employees what was in or out of stock. There was nothing special about this record store that compelled him to visit everyday, other than it was in walking distance from his house and that he had the time.

Most of his friends were seniors. Considered losers like himself, they accepted him because he was funny and he could draw well. Most of them had after school jobs, so when school let out he spent his time at the record shop, or when he felt the employees were getting annoyed with him, at the grocery store looking through cheesy guitar magazines the record store didn't lower itself to carry. He wanted to be like his heroes, Alice Cooper, Black Sabbath, Rush -- he knew all their albums, all the lyrics, and who played what instrument on each song. He spent more time reading about the bands than practicing guitar, but still he dreamed of joining the ranks of the Rock Stars.

Home was comfortable. Middle class, suburban ranch with attached garage, and two parents with heavy work loads. This left him to his drawings and the television. The wonder of Cable T.V. had come out a few years before. To his dismay, his father deemed that spending money for what was already free would be foolish at best. This left him to the mercy of regular programing and most of the time he would find himself lost in old black and white horror movies or rerun comedy classics like the Marx's Brothers and The Three Stooges. The public broadcasting station also grabbed his attention from time to time, leaving him practicing his British accent and trying to understand the surreal humor of Monty Python's Flying Circus.

He sent a discarded can flying across the puddles with a kick from his very comfortable, but half rotten tennis shoe. The can landed in a puddle of snow-melt with a splash, and he made a game out of jumping over one puddle to the edge of the next. On his finger was a silver Indian ring his mother had given to him.

A Lifetime In Time

The reasons she had it were unclear, but he thought it was cool, though still a little big for his hand. After today, it would only come off one more time. As he leapt between puddles, the ring slid off his finger into the bottom of a muddy hole. In a panic, he shoved his hands into the puddle drenching his sleeves and, after a few creative swear words, retrieved his valued piece of silver and held it up to the rays of the sun. Parts of it gleamed in the daylight as he tried to scrape the mud away. He was so relieved he didn't even hear the old truck bouncing toward him, splashing, and honking, until it sprayed him with a cold dirty wake up call. Opening his eyes, he wiped the mud from his forehead and turned in the direction of the laughter speeding away in the truck. As he turned back, something was wrong. It was like cranning your neck around a corner and spying into a room; try as he could, he couldn't pull his vision back to the road, and before he could understand what this visual anomaly was, he was no longer on Earth.

He looked around and, to the best his eyes could tell him, he was in a clear room. There were no floor lines, no horizon, just two large comfortable chairs. Sitting in the larger chair, a man dressed in black, waved him over. He guessed the man was probably in his late thirties. He had short stylish black hair and was dressed in a 1920's business suit as if he was in one of the old movies the boy had seen. Carefully watching his step and almost expecting to free fall into oblivion, he made his way over and nervously sat down across from him.

"Huh... hello... am I dead?" the boy asked. "Did that truck... hit me? I don't remember anything that felt like a hit. Well, I remember the hit from the water, and that was wet, but was that just..."

"No, no, my young friend," smiled the man, "you're fine, quite healthy and intact."

The man eyed the boy quietly, as the boy felt the cold dampness from his sleeves.

"Oh," he said, looking around the room as if expecting something more sinister to appear.

"The room bothers you doesn't it?" asked the man, breaking the tense quiet.

"Yeah... well it's kind of freaky."

"Well, then think of a place, any place, you'd like."

The boy thought for a moment and the room started to flow and change form, like the colors pouring from a paint tube. He grabbed the arms of his chair tightly for security.

When the room stopped moving, the two where still sitting, but in the middle of a large field.

"I take it back," he said, "this, is freaky. It looks just like my grandfather's corn field."

"It is, or at least a facsimile of it," said the man. "That is what your mind remembered on the surface."

"Are you sure I'm not dead? Grandpa's field is now surrounded by racing tracks."

The man studied him for what again seemed to be a very long time. It had made him uncomfortable, like the pause in a parent's voice when you are about to have a serious discussion that will somehow wreck your plans for the next couple of weeks.

"I'm sorry," said the man tiredly. "My name is Docheen, and I am the Keeper of the Gateway." As the man spoke, he straightened his tie.

"What's the gateway?" the boy asked.

"Well, on your planet..."

"Planet!?" exclaimed the boy cutting him off.

"Yes," the man replied, clearly annoyed at the interruption, "I said planet."

"Oh..." the boy mumbled, feeling the uncomfortable knot in his stomach growing and thinking, *Ok, I'm not dead, I've been abducted by aliens.* The man continued.

"A gateway is an opening that leads to another place. This Gateway leads to every place."

"Every place?" he questioned, running his fingers through his hair and flicking the remainder of the mud off.

A Lifetime In Time

"Every place in time, space, and even other realities and dimensions. With her I travel anywhere, or in any time I feel the desire to. I created her over a million years ago as you would perceive time, and now I am ready to move on."

"Look, I hate to keep repeating everything you say like someone that doesn't get the point, but I'm really someone that doesn't get the point. How can you be a million years old?"

"Time passes differently in the Gateway, and I've had a little help as well. Things don't decay here for we are literally outside time, and space, in a place called the Webs." Noticing the expression on the boy's face was strained, he explained. "The Webs are the life force of time and reality. They are outside time and space, and are reality's body. They allow us to instantly open a door to any point we like, for here all places are one as are all times. Outside of the Gateway we age. After the first 100 years of time accumulated outside, I was looking and feeling a little ragged. Thus, the heartstone. The heartstone is a large emerald egg the size of your fist. Once you replace your heart with it you are as near to immortal as a once mortal being can come."

"So, you're immortal, and now I'm either stuck in some sort of science fiction movie or crazy? You know," the boy started to rant, "I watch a lot of movies and it's not that the concept of time travel is beyond me, or any of the other concepts. Aliens, other realities... I mean I've read a lot of comics, it's just there are a mess of things that you're hitting me with. Gateways, webs, time travel, a green egg being shoved into a body and taking over the place of your heart, and now you're claiming to be immortal on top of all this."

"Yes, and after a million years I am ready to accept death and move on."

"If you are immortal, how can you die?" he asked, fidgeting in his chair and trying to wipe his face, feeling the mud that the truck spashed as it dried on his cheek.

"Well, it takes great effort, but the heartstone can be cracked, and once it does, it becomes dust and that's the end. Well, the end to this existence," he said, placing his hand over his heart. "I believe that it is only the beginning to the next chapter." With that he gestured to a spot in the field and a small stone table appeared with a large greenish egg on it. He got up and addressed the egg, and with a gesture of his hand stated. "This is me."

"I thought that was supposed to be in your chest," the boy said, walking over to the green stone and giving it the once over.

"It was," he replied, with a strange ring of pride in his voice. "With a heartstone, you age about one year for every thousand you live. When you get too old, you usually put yourself in a trance or coma, if your body hasn't already made the decision for you, and the egg goes dormant. Then after about hundred years it activates, and regenerates a much younger body and the process starts over again. Right now I am dormant." He turned and scanned the horizon as if this common setting had started to become entrancing. As the breeze mussed his hair he continued talking though his voice drifted as if his mind was far away. "This body you are talking to is a creation of the Gateway, and in truth doesn't even look like my real body. I decided that my real appearance might disturb you, so I picked something that you might find more comforting."

The boy stared at the egg almost as if he was hypnotized. At first glance the stone appeared to be nothing more than a shiny, brilliant green. The longer he looked the surface took on patterns and patterns within patterns. It's layers seemed to peel away revealing its never ending depths, as if he had the ability to stare through a building and allow his eyes to search the rooms and the world beyond. Patterns gave way to textures, textures gave way to forms, and then sound. For a brief moment he felt like the egg might just suck him in and he closed his eyes to regain himself. He realized that the man had stopped talking and a strange fear started to build in him. The quiet wasn't helping.

"What if you get hurt before you go dormant?" he asked, while restraining his urge to poke at the stone the way children play with fire.

A Lifetime In Time

9

"Well if you lose a limb, it stays lost till the end of your next dormancy, at least outside of the Gateway. Aside of the destruction of your body you heal pretty quickly, though you do get to keep some of the scars. The Gateway has the ability to fix most of your injuries, and can even create replacement limbs."

"What do you really look like?" the boy asked, with a tinge of curiosity in his voice.

"Do you really want to know?" smiled the man.

"Uh sure, I guess, how bad can it be, after all, I am an Alice Cooper fan."

Without a word Docheen's form flowed into a large, old, three hundred pound salamander shaped creature, with heavy string like eye brows, and a fleshy goatee. His skin was a shiny black as if it was wet with large yellow markings that made him resemble the salamanders that the boy use to catch in window wells when he was younger. In his true form his mouth was toothless. Whether this was due to his age or his species was beyond the boy to comprehend. He then climbed around in the chair trying to make himself more comfortable and grabbed the chair firmly to insure his stability. With his body pressing hard against the padding he turned his head completely round to gaze at the boy. His eyes were black and transparent and, for a moment, the boy gasped and wondered how well the Keeper's eyes could see without a pupil.

"Wow, you could be like in Star Wars, or a BBC sci-fi show or something."

"I found out early on that in traveling to different places it was best to look like I fit in, so shape-shifting was something I had to learn. It was always fun around the hippies, and at the witch trials," he said nostalgically.

"Wow, that is totally cool... I mean, can you teach me to do that?" the boy asked excitedly, momentarily forgetting his fear.

"Oh, you will learn how, but not from me. My time is short."

Sensing something was wrong the boy took a few steps back and squinted at the old reptile.

"Why am I here?" His voice seemed very loud to him and he suddenly felt very cold.

"Can't you figure it out?" questioned the man. "You're going to be the next Keeper."

"No way, I'm not putting one of those things in my chest," he yelled. "That has got to hurt like hell."

The boy jumped away from the heartstone as if it were a rattlesnake. In the back of his mind he thought about running, but to where? The end of the field he thought, but what then? Then he realized the old lizard was ignoring his panic and continued talking to him, knowing the boy had no option of escape.

"Oh, you don't get a heartstone until after you master shape-shifting or your body won't be able to do it. I never quite figured out why," Docheen said, gazing up toward the sky as if the clouds had distracted him. "I think it has to do with the heartstone wanting to keep the body in its true form. Anyway," he smiled sadly, "it's too late for that kind of pondering."

"Well, what if I don't want to be a Keeper?"

The creature turned back into the previous human form, but now his expression became almost evil.

"Why in heaven's name do you think you have a choice?" He tilted his head upward and spoke a one word command to the air, "Proceed."

Tentacles of steel formed like hot plastic from the ground, securing the boys limbs and lifting him off the ground. He felt like a thousand needles had all tried to numb him at once, and his head seemed to swim in a thick kaleidoscopic paste. His body stiffened; he blacked out.

***

Slowly, the boy awoke with a pounding in his head and a tingling in his body as if all his limbs were still asleep. He remembered something like all the colors of the color wheel spinning and focusing into a bright white light that became an all enveloping gel. Images of the Keeper kept popping in and out of his head as if someone had taken a razor blade to a film real and spliced it together in the wrong order. As the pounding in his head lessened and his tingling subsided he realized he was both naked and very cold. Then a familiar voice startled him.

"Thir," said the voice in a lisp. "Thir, pleath get off the floor and we will find thomething to make you more comfortable."

He jumped to his feet and tried to cover himself the best he could with clenched knees and two hands. His legs were wobbly and it took several attempts to achieve a standing pose.

"HEY, I'M NAKED HERE! WHERE'S MY DAMN CLOTHES?"

"I'm thorry about that Thir, but the Gateway is a little upthet about the loth of her former Keeper. All thingth conthidered, thee wath quite fond of him."

The voice was coming from a silver soccer ball floating in the air. In the middle of the ball was a glass circle that seemed to function as an eye. It whirled left to right, and would blink as if it was a camera's aperture in the hand of a very indecisive photographer.

"Who are you, and where's my damned clothes?" he said, still hiding himself.

"I wath programmed by the former Keeper in cathe the Gateway was stubborn. I'm to be your athithtant until thee warmth up to you. The lath time, thee didn't talk to the new Keeper for over a month."

"Could you just get me some damn clothes?"

"Thertainly."

A person sized hole opened on the wall leading into an empty mall. The boy quickly ran through and was grateful that the temperature was warmer, although he was now nervous about being naked in a very public place. He kept trying to replay his recent abduction in his mind. He could remember clearly his talk about being the new Keeper, and even things about the Gateway and the heartstone. When he tried to push his memory to what happened after the steel tentacles grabbed him it was a sketchy mess at best, and part of him just didn't want to know. He remembered something heavy in his hands, a loud cracking sound, faint sobbing, and then nothing.

"Where the hell am I?" he asked.

"Oh, you're in the Gateway," said the ball. "It can recreate a verthion of anything that exithtth or ever did, and thingth that never have been. It can even play back eventth throughout hithtory or things to come. I chothe this mall because you requethted clotheth, and from our data this is the plathe where you've acquired motht of your clothing, up to this point."

This was true, the boy and his friends never let a weekend go by without a trip to the mall. It was one of the few places they could hang out without the interference of parents. It contained clothing stores that carried the latest fashions, which they couldn't afford, a food court, and the only movie theaters in the area. In the fall and spring it seemed to be the one place his mother enjoyed dragging him the most, if only to buy clothes he would rarely wear. The ball followed the awkwardly running boy into a hip store. Hiding himself behind a rack of pants he pulled on a pair of men's zebra print trousers, something that any metal god from 1985 would be proud to wear.

"So there's nobody here, right?" the boy asked nervously.

"If you like I can have anybody you want created. I can even make it appear ath if the mall ith at the height of its thale theathon."

"No... No, that's quite all right," he said, grabbing a black t-shirt. "What just happened to me?"

"Well the former Keeper tranthferred the power to you. I apologize for the intenthe pain it caused."

"What pain? I didn't feel any pain," he said, as he walked into a leather store.

"Oh, you did, but I thuppose it'th like birth, one doethn't remember that do they?" said the ball, "or tho I am told."

The boy put on a pair of black Cowboy boots and stomped them down.

"Then what?" he asked.

"Then you killed him."

"Excuse me?" the boy said in shock, trying to desperately search his memories for such an event.

"Well, the only way for him to path on wath for you to break the hearthtone. You were pretty out of it and open to thug-gethtion. He told you to pick up a big hammer that he had acquired on hith travelth. It was created by an elder god. He thaid good-bye to the Gateway and you hit it."

"I killed him?" The boy's already pale face turned whiter.

"Nothing but dutht. That ith one of the reathonth the Gateway'th not talking to you."

The boy put on a black leather jacket with fringe and slid down to sit on a display stand.

"Great, just great. I started out today as a loser, and now I'm a loser and a murderer. I don't remember killing him, not really." His head started to pound.

"Really Thir, the choithe in the matter wath not your own. Without a lifeline to link to the Gateway, thee cannot keep time flowing forward in here, and would ceathe to exitht. I believe that ith the reathon you are here. He did not want her to die."

"Who?"

"The Gateway. Without your life thee couldn't function linearly and would ecthplode, for outthide of her all time ith the thame time and..."

"And yadda yadda yadda," he interrupted, as his headache had become too much to continue on this course. He took a deep breath. "Do you have a name?"

"I am yet to be named. It ith your job."

"Your voice sounds familiar, but I can't place it."

"The former Keeper programmed me with the voithe of Larry Fine of The Three Thtooges. Our records thow that you rethponded favorably to that program. In fact I altho have been made aware of all your favorite pop culture trivia."

"Well I didn't think I watched the Stooges that much. All right, I guess your name is Larry, but could you cut down on the lisp a little."

"What lithsp?"

"That one."

"At your command, Thire."

"Thire?" said the boy with a grimace. "You mean Sire?"

"My Lord?" Larry said, trying to appease the frustrated teenager.

"My Lord? I'm not Jesus, Larry."

"My Lord wath a common greeting during your world'th middle ageth. The term wath uthed to thignify the owner of the land. The peathant'th paid their taxth to their landlord."

"Well, you're not a peasant," the boy pointed out.

"But I am, Thir, your thervant, and the Gateway ith now your land, and tho much more."

"My Lord, Sir, and Servant, don't quite sound right for Larry Fine's voice. What else are my options?" He buttoned the coat realizing that he was shirtless, and to his memory most stores didn't allow that. "Hey, here's a brilliant idea, why not call me by my name?"

"The former Keeper thought it wathn't the betht practithe to be called by name. He believed that it wath important to keep your life in the Gateway theparate from your life on your home planet, or whatever platheth you call home. Tho, he had many different nameth." Larry could tell that he was rapidly losing the interest of the boy. "Until you choothe a name how about I call you Bawth."

"You mean Boss?"

"That's what I thaid."

"Yeah sure, whatever," he said giving in. "Did I really kill him?"

His expression pleaded with Larry to give him a different ending to the story.

"This time he is truly dead," Larry momentarily lost his lisp and sounded rather electronic.

"I don't feel so good."

"It'th not thurprithing, you've been in a coma for three dayth."

"Three days! My parents are going to freak. My dad goes out looking for me if I'm twenty minutes past curfew. I am soooo dead."

"Bawth, you can go back to your timeline even before you left if you like. But I wouldn't recommend it. You might run into the former you. Being the Keeper you now have almotht complete control over time."

"Oh, yeah," he lied, feeling like he somehow should have known this, but was unsure wondering if he had missed it in all the excitement. "I guess there is a bonus to being the Keeper. Even if you have to run around naked in a mall."

He was relieved to know at least he didn't have his parents to contend with and with luck they wouldn't find out he was a murderer. *Was he a murderer?* This question seemed surreal. Without any memory of it, how could he know for sure? Maybe he was just an accomplice in an assisted suicide? That thought wasn't much more comforting than the first. Larry's voice broke into his private ramblings.

"If I can make a thuggestion, there ith a food court around the corner, and I'm thure that you are hungry. Maybe you will feel better after you eat."

"I'm not really hungry," he said, fixating on the murder he couldn't even remember.

"Maybe once you thee the court?"

The boy gave him a weak nod, as he realized he was starting to chew on his fingernails.

"Yeah, fine... whatever."

The two headed off to the food court. Everything about this felt wrong. He felt like he was wearing stolen clothes. He also felt like, at any moment, the police were going to suddenly appear, pull their guns on him and arrest him for breaking and entering. After the first two attempts to find his misplaced wallet and pay for the food that he wanted, he decided to take advantage of the moment. The food would magically appear from one side of the food line onto his tray whenever he asked for something. Talking to the air felt strange, but within seconds, he had become like the little kid in a candy store, and in a short time he had ordered everything he could stomach. Larry had to help him balance the tray to the table, and they only lost one order of french fries with gravy. As soon as it hit the floor a small cinder block sized robot had managed to clean it up and fetch him another one. He sat for the longest time in silence, just staring at the food that would have normally have been a treat. He wondered if this was a dream he would wake from or, if he would find himself, at any moment, in a straight jacket being fed his daily meds in a cup of applesauce. He knew one of his grandmothers had electric shock therapy and though all his family said it helped her, he now wondered if she had had delusions of being a Keeper. She always seemed sane to him. After playing with his mountain of food and only taking a few bites, the silence became too much for him. He looked up at Larry who was waiting like a loving dog.

"Now what?" asked the boy, who had started to stack his fries to create a miniature log cabin instead of eating them.

"Whatever you'd like Bawth."

The boy, who was very tired replied in a half sob.

"I just want to go to sleep."

"Would you like to dethign your bedroom now."

"Just a bed and a dark room, Larry."

And in the middle of the food court grew a ten foot cube with a door and a comfy bed. When the boy's head touched the pillow, he was asleep.

Timothy John Vaulato

Chapter One

House Warming, A House With Warning

His sleep was restless. Visions of smashing the former Keeper's Heartstone made him toss and turn until he was tied up in sheets and damp and sticky with sweat. When his eyes opened, the complete darkness set him in a panic. He bounced from his bed and fell onto the floor frantically searching for an opening in the light-less box that had become his room. Finally, after so much thrashing around, he found the door by falling through it. Unfortunately, he had used the side of his face as the tool to open it. He fell into the food court screaming. Breathing heavily and rubbing the reddening side of his face, he looked around and was almost comforted by the sight of Larry, who had never left the side of his sleeping box.

"Crap," he said under his breath, thinking this might have just been a twisted dream.

"If you would like a bathroom, Bawth, I believe one ith jutht patht the cookie hut."

"So, even a good night's sleep is out of the question in this place?" he griped.

"It could be your choith of accommodations Bawth, they're not very accommodating. How about a better room?"

"Not now," he said considering the offer, "but a cookie would be good."

"You're the Bawth."

Within minutes he had picked out the birthday sized cookie with frosting and a diet Coke. He ate his breakfast mechanically, not tasting it at all as his mind kept telling him that he had taken a life.

Maybe, he thought, *that's the way it's suppose to be. Maybe Keeper's have to go into the next life at some point, and the next one had the crappy duty of assisting them in that journey. Maybe that was just the circle of life in the Gateway?* The thought brought little comfort. Would someone someday take his life and his new position. *What is this position?* he thought, being he didn't even know what the position meant. He needed to clear his mind and knowing there must be a record store somewhere, the boy headed off through the mall.

"Bawth, do you want to keep the mall, or should we erathe it?"

"I guess keep it for now," he said, brushing the cookie crumbs from his mouth as he took a swig from his diet Coke. "I mean, it's not a problem is it? I will need different clothes when I go home. I don't have much of an allowance or a car to get to the real mall, so explaining different clothes might be difficult."

"No, we have no problem keeping it. You can recreate jutht about anything for long term thtorage, ath long ath it's not bigger than Jupiter."

"You mean the planet?" he asked in amazement.

"Yeah, if it'th bigger than Jupiter we'll have to create a dimenthional anomaly, though we've only had to do that oneth. "

"Get out of here! How big is the Gateway?" he asked, passing the record shop and abruptly dashing into another clothing store.

"About the thize of Jupiter," Larry said, following him. "It didn't thtart that way, I can athure you. When the Gateway wath created it wath no bigger than a room like the one you thlept in. It wath only after its thentient mind wath created that it thtarted to grow. It ecthpanded at an incredible rate. Thee could tholve all the problemth that Docheen had with repairing the webth that he journeyed in, but it took a great deal of power and room to work. We're really in kind of a great big machine, or like blood thell's flowing in a giant body."

In the boy's mind he only half heard what was being said, losing Larry almost entirely around the heavily lisped word, "problems." Most of his brain played a distant echo calling him a murderer and the rest was diligently picking through the store's clothing to find his correct size.

"Hey, can you carry this?" questioned the boy, handing Larry a pack of underwear and trying to keep the frosting from his cookie off of them.

"Oh thankth," lisped Larry sarcastically, and a metal arm quickly sprouted from the side of the robot's body.

"Hey, if this is the size of Jupiter, what else is here?" The annoyed tone in the boy's voice changed showing his interest, as he found a large black t-shirt. "I mean, if this mall is made for me, what was made for the other Keeper?"

"You mean Docheen?" asked Larry.

"Who?" asked the boy.

"Docheen wath the former Keeper'th name," stated Larry, as if the boy should have been paying attention.

"Oh yeah, Docheen. Is his stuff still here, or was it erased?"

"No, It'th all here. Would you like a tour?" Larry's voice had the faint element of excitement to it.

"Yeah," he replied, tossing the rest of his cookie in a nearby trash bin, "let me see how the other half lived."

As they traveled down the endless hallways the boy noticed that the walls seemed to be alive in colors of dark blue and gray that would occasionally pulse with sound or faint ghost like light. White lights appear every six feet or so, and turned themselves off as they moved away.

"A little dark in here don't you think?"said the boy, with a sense of foreboding. "It feels creepy."

"Brandy," Larry said addressing the air, "a little light down here would be appreciated." With that the light brightened and so did the walls. The halls now seemed to have the feel of a giant vein of light blue.

"Who's Brandy?" the boy asked.

"That'th what we call the mind of the Gateway."

"Oh..." was the only reply that the boy could come up with, though the question as to why they named her Brandy was almost on his lips as they arrived at a door which seemed to grow from some metallic plant which had taken up residence on the sides of the wall.

The door slid open as they approached stopping the question the boy was about to ask. As they stepped through, the light brightened.

"Thith ith our zoo." There was an underlying tone of shame in his electronic voice.

The boy peered down the long tall hallway lined with thick glass. They looked like holding cells for criminals and not at all environmentally friendly zoo cages. As he hesitantly looked into the first cell an enormous blue slime slammed against the glass with a sticky splash causing him to jump back to the safety of the entrance.

"What the heck is that?" he yelled in shock.

"Thorry," said Larry, "that'th a Bungouth, iths a creature from a planet called Brianth."

"Do you mean Brian's?" he questioned.

"No," replied Larry seeming a bit perturbed, "I mean Brianth. Iths rather a nathty thing, it envelopeth ith prey and drainth it of all bodily fluid and then eatth the remains. Ith a bit clothe to feeding time. When they're hungry they get cranky."

"Can it get out?" The nervousness in his voice betrayed his emotions.

"Don't worry nothing in here hath ever gotten out unleth the Keeper wanted it too."

"Well I definitely don't want that thing out."

A Lifetime In Time

"You know Bawth, maybe thith ithn't the betht room to thtart with. We can come back after feeding time."

The boy looked up at the silver ball with suspicion.

"No," he said, "it's ok. I like creepy things as much as the next movie buff."

Slowly he started to walk down the hallway keeping himself to the center and away from the glass. The next cell had large worm-like beasts boring into a carcass of something that resembled a dead whale. They made quick work of their meal and then formed into a group ball to aid their digestion.

"Well that's gross," he commented.

"Oh you thould thee what they can do to non living material. We only feed them meat because it make'th them more dothile."

"That's docile?" the boy said in shock.

"Yeth, they can eat an entire thity in about an hour. They were created by one of the elder rathes for war. Thaddly they found out that when their food of choithe runth out they will conthume flesh too, though it taketh them a while to adjutht."

As the boy turned his mouth dropped open. Across from the worms cell he found himself face to face with a T.rex. If it wasn't already engrossed with its dinner the boy would have made a bee line back to the doorway. Instead, he found himself marveling at its size and color which made his mind wander back to every tye dyed shirt he had ever seen.

"That's a... a... a..." he stuttered.

"Yep," replied Larry, "that'th a T.recth."

"It's... really... colorful."

"Oh yeth," Larry confirmed, "in a couple of yearth your people will figure out that they weren't all flat, green, gray, or brown."

"Amazing."

He stood transfixed in awe of it's majesty as the king of the dinosaurs tore at the flesh of its dinner. As it started to look up the boy became afraid. It was one thing to watch it eat, it was another to look it directly in the eye. As he pushed himself toward the next cell for a hopeful break, his heart turn to utter fear. Giant bug-like monsters with bodies like millipedes climbed on the walls of the cell. The feelers on their heads searched out their next meal and as they lifted up, their undersides resembled large slimy newborn human babies with dastardly sharp teeth. The bugs stopped swarming only to eat the people that were screaming in the bottom of the cage.

"Ahhhhhhh!" screamed the boy as he ran out of the room and back toward the mall.

"Bawth, Bawth, wait a minute, you don't underthtand!" Larry pleaded, trying to follow after him.

The boy ran hard, harder than he had ever run before. As he left the hallway and broke into a slip sliding run through the mall, he searched his head for a plan. He ran straight into the first sports store he found, and smashed open the rifle case with a kick. The weapons seem too small for the amount of fear that now raced through him, and he quickly made his decision; shotgun.

"Damn it," he mumbled, "I knew this had to be one of those bad sci-fi movies, just a matter of time before they gain your trust just to kill you. To serve man kind, it's a cook book," he said out loud, quoting of the old Twilight Zone episode.

By the time Larry had caught up to him, he had loaded a shotgun and aimed it at Larry's eye.

"Whoa, Bawth look I know the bugth are a little intenth, but they can't get out of their thell, and..."

With a giant boom, Larry's body scattered all over the mall, his shattered pieces melted into the floor. The boy reloaded as another Larry flew up to take the old one's place.

"What I wath thaying ith that the people aren't real."

Again the boy took aim and destroyed the second Larry. The third time, Larry appeared in a slightly darker color.

BOOM!

The darker Larry smashed through a display window and screamed in an electronic and out of character voice.

"Bawth, would you pleathe thtop thooting me!"

Larry flew up hesitantly as the boy kept the gun locked on its target.

A Lifetime In Time

"What I wath trying to thay before you blew me up ith that the people that you thaw in the cage are made by the Gateway. They're not real, they're not alive, they don't think unleth you want them to, and the thcreaming and the thrashing ith the only way the bugth will eat their food. They're thaped and act like humanth, but their made of plant thtuff. They're kind of a thoy thubtitute."

The boy's voice broke under his strained breathing.

"W, Why p... people!?" he yelled through gritted teeth.

"That ith their natural food thource."

"Are the bugs real?"

"Yeth, the bugth are real," Larry confessed. "The Keeper uthed them if he had problemth with, uh... humanth."

"This place gets better and better. What did I inherit, Hell?"

"Bawth maybe you thould thet the gun down and..."

"No way!" he spat. "What kind of problems with humans did the Keeper have?"

The fear in the boy was growing out of control. From the corner of his eye he looked for more weapons only to realize that he had the biggest one in the store.

"Not everything in time ith cut and dry," Larry said quietly, trying to calm the boy. "There'th good and bad in all rathes. Docheen had a number of humanth that wanted control of time. Rather than rithk that, he felt that time would be better therved to eliminate them."

"Great, I did inherit Hell," the boy barked, "and now I get my own personal petting zoo of the damned. This sucks!"

"Look Bawth, you are in control here. They exitht on your thay tho. If you want them gone, moved, killed, or releathed ith your call."

"I want the room sealed," he commanded, surprised at the tone of his voice.

Larry tilted toward the ceiling.

"Brandy," he said, "lock down of zoo number twelve, by command of the Keeper."

"There's more than one?" the boy asked, trying not to let his mind wander to the countless other nightmares that might exist in this realm.

"Yeth, but their not all that bad," Larry assured him.

A Lifetime In Time

"Lock them all."

"Brandy, lock all zooth pleathe." Once again he voiced his request while peering up and then turned to the boy. "You can put the gun down now, Bawth."

"No!" he said firmly.

"Ok, maybe you thould keep the gun and get thome more ammo tho we can thoot everything we thee."

The boy lowered his gun, but grabbed more ammo and a pistol.

"All right, Larry," the boy said loading the hand gun and nervously stuffing it in his pants. "Let's go on with our little tour."

Larry paused for a moment and tried to understand if this was sarcasm. Assuming it wasn't they continued onward. They skipped the bug room and went to the next door. They found themselves in a small room with what looked to be a highly electronic vault door on it.

"Bawth, the lock ith hand activated. It changed to your imprint when you became the Keeper."

The boy slowly and cautiously put his hand on the panel and aimed his gun at it as well.

"What, you're going to thoot your hand?" Larry asked, but before the boy could answer the door opened and a football sized stadium loaded with treasure appeared.

The ceiling gave off light through an art nouveau styled grid work high above them. The boy's mouth dropped open as Larry flew about pointing to different Earth currencies and riches from other worlds. The boy had a strong desire to play in the stacks of gold or dive into the piles of paper money, but the fear of letting himself go was too strong. He moved cautiously into the room, as if he was the lead actor in one of the many bad "B" movies he had seen. He never stopped to focus too long on any one object, and scanned the sky for predators.

"Thethe are leftoverth," stated Larry, "the former Keeper kept them ath thouvenir'th oneth he figured out how to get the Gateway to reproduthe other worldth' currenly. Perthonally, I think he uthed it to impreth the ladieth."

27

The boy recognized the mountain of gold, the hills of dia-
monds, and haphazard stacks of paper money. Even the plastic
cards of different colors he assumed must be money somewhere,
but what he couldn't figure out was what the lumpy white stuff
in the glass freezer.

"Hey, what's the stuff that looks like cottage cheese?" he asked.

"Cottage cheethe, or clothe to it. Ith worth a lot depending
where you are in the univerthe."

Larry circle around him appearing to also take in the view.

"Could you stop that?" the boy asked.

"Thtop what?"

"Stay in my sight," he commanded.

"Yeth Bawth," and with that Larry took up a position in the boy's
sight line. "You don't think I'm going to attack you, do you Bawth?"

"It thoulnd't matter to you what I think," he replied, mocking Larry's speech and then something caught the boy's eye.
"Hey, is that a Van Gogh?" He rushed over to a painting left
carelessly on the floor.

"Yeah, the real Van Gogh, *The Loom*, from 1884. The one
on earth ith a Gateway reproduction. You'll find a lot of Van
Gogh'th around here, and a lot of Gateway reproductionth on
Earth. Docheen was a big fan."

The boy was tired of asking questions and the container of
dancing cockroaches was just too bizarre to consider money.

"More damn bugs," he said under his breath. "Lets keep moving."

As they left, the boy slipped a stack of twenties into his jacket
pocket, fumbling to move his ammo to the back of his jeans.

As time went on, he became more relaxed and even took his
aim off of Larry. In the next two hours, they saw twenty-seven
bedrooms, if you could have called them that, seven bathrooms
(some with toilets that would have required a Yoga master to
navigate,) and five wilderness areas. Two of the areas came from
Earth, but the other three were anyone's guess. The weightlessness one was his favorite though he wouldn't have admitted it to
Larry. He spent a solid ten minutes trying to get back to the door

and spazzed when his ammo went in one direction and his shotgun in another. Every horror flick he had ever seen kept playing through his head and he was sure at any moment that someone or something would kill him or try to feed him to some baby bellied bugs. As he grabbed his weapon he was just happy to still be alive and grateful that Larry didn't laugh.

One room was decorated in dark red satin and was full of girls, or females from different planets. They all were very distant and cold and none of them spoke. They had the look that zombies carried in their eyes and this was almost as unnerving as the zoo. Larry assured him that they also had been created by the Gateway and were not real or being kept prisoner.

They stopped for lunch in a room that seemed like a section of a Chicago city street. Larry told him that Docheen loved good pizza, and out of all his travels, Vinney's Pizza, June of 1972, on Clark street, Chicago, Illinois, was exceptional. So this room had been created to satisfy his cravings. There were other storefronts that were restaurants, or coffeehouses from different times, and even an ice cream parlor from the fifties.

"Why not just keep going back to that time?" he asked Larry.

"To keep dropping into the eggthact thame point in time repeatedly weakenth the web and the thtructure of that reality. It can leave a thcar in the webth that help uth travel through time. Altho you keep running into yourthelf. Pluth, when the thame guy buyth pizza all afternoon, people tend to notithe that kind of thing."

"Did you mean scar?" the boy asked, more out of an attempt to slam Larry than clarification.

"Yeth, I thaid thcar," said Larry unaware of the insult. "Think of time ath a cathette tape. If you keep recording over the thame tape and the thame thpot, the thound lothes clarity, and eventually the tape will break, or become worn out. Docheen had a rule of three that he followed. He felt that time could be broken into the thame plathe three timeth without long term effect. No more than three times in an hour period, in a chothen time thtream. Eventually, he wouldn't go back to the exact thame landing thpot more than twithe jutht to be thafe."

Larry flew to the other side of the table as a vacant eyed girl placed a large pizza in front of them and left without a word.

"Why go at all?" questioned the boy.

"What do you mean?" Larry asked.

"Well, Docheen could have created anything, or anytime he wanted inside of the Gateway, why bother to travel? I mean the pizza's great, the street would have fooled me if I didn't know better, why travel?"

"Look at the waitreth," he said, and the boy studied the girl.

"Yeah?"

"Would you date her?"

"No," he replied in disgust.

"Why not?" Larry asked. "Thee wouldn't thay no or no to anything you athked of her."

"She's kind of creepy," replied the boy, "and creepy with a capital C."

"That'th the differenthe." Larry turned to the waitress and scanned her form. "Thee's pretty, willing and won't athk anything of you, but it wouldn't be real. Nothing in the Gateway ith a complete replathement for a real life."

"Do they have emotions or feelings?" he asked, pointing at the girl while trying to pick up a piece of pizza that left part of its cheese in the pan, and part on his new leather jacket.

"Not unleth you program them to act like they do and even then they are not real. They are bathed on a thubthtanthe that ith very much like plant thells. We call them AODs. Artificial Organic Drone'th. They look real, can react in a real manner, bleed real and can pass for meat, but on the atomic level they are bathically plant. They can't reproduthe, age or learn. They only react in the manner they are programed, but they are utheful for thertain comfort interactionth and projection."

"Projection?" questioned the boy, trying to clean the cheese from his jacket, and almost knocking over his drink.

"When Docheen talked to you he truly wath dormant in his heartthtone, but hith perthonality and character had been programed into the AOD. To be truthful, hith AOD wath the thecond most complicated program outthide of Brandy herthelf. Thee ith truly a thinking and learning program."

"Wait a minute," the boy eyes widened, "are you saying that I've never really met Docheen, and why can you say his name without a lisp?"

"Not allowed, ith dithrethpectfull, and no, in truth you never met him, just his Heartthtone."

"Then what's to stop me from pulling up that program again, and asking him for the tour of the Gateway?"

"Nothing, other than each time you pull it up you pith off Brandy. They were very clothe."

The boy's face squinted at Larry and he was about to say something, but stopped himself. He sat for a moment and then smiled.

"If he is a copy of himself, would he answer my questions truthfully?"

"Ath much ath he would if he were alive," Larry replied.

There was silence again. The boy said nothing, but he intentionally made his chewing of the pizza loud, almost as if to indicate that he had become bored with the topic and the answers.

"So... what other fringe benefits do I get from being the Keeper?" he asked, making the imaginary quote signs in the air after saying the word Keeper.

"The powerth of the Keeper are lengthy. Where would you like to begin?"

"How about shape-shifting?"

The eagerness in his voice betrayed his desire to know more. To him the idea of shape-shifting was a sure route to becoming a super-hero, and what teenaged boy doesn't dream about that? Besides, from a very young age he loved werewolf movies so the choice of what to change into first wasn't going to be a difficult one.

"Well, thape-thifting is a learned ability, not one you get automatically. It takes yearth of prathtice and thtudy, if done right. What you do get immediately, ith the ability to thpeak, or rather be heard in other languageth, and to underthtand those languageth.

In the Gateway all beingth can underthtand each other ath you underthtand them.

"Choice... what else?"

"Well, there'th the traveling in time, thpace and other realities, though the latht one is a bit more tricky. Other realitieth are interethting, but they're not your true or current life. When you think of the Gateway and wave your hand in the air, in a thircle, you create a doorway into the landing area."

"Landing area?"

"You haven't been there yet. Think of it ath the airport terminal. Ith the only plathe one can depart from or arrive to the Gateway."

The boy waved his left hand in the air and nothing happened.

"Well firthly Bawth, you leave the Gateway from the landing area, which meanth you just walk through the doorway at the far end of the room. Outthide the Gateway, and you have to use your ring hand. The ring ith the antenna that thignals the Gateway to open a portal for you to come back. You have to conthentrate, wave your arm in a great big thircle, and then thtep through. Anyone that you want to take with you hath to come firtht, because when you've thepped through, the porthole clothes."

"What if I lose the ring?" he said, checking for the ring and noticing that it no longer felt loose. This prompted him to start trying to pull it off, first hard, then harder, but to no avail.

"You can't take it off, ith now bonded through your thkin to your bone. The power ith in you. The ring ith jutht what thends the thignal."

Even understanding Larry's words, he still kept trying.

"What if someone cuts off my finger to get the ring?" he said, finally giving up.

"Well that'th an ugly thought. I thuppose you'd have to cut away thome other part of your flesh until the bone is showing to act ath an antenna."

"What if I'm knocked out?"

"You would find it difficult to cut away the proper amount of thkin."

A Lifetime In Time

The boy finally pushed the pizza away.

"That bringth me to another thubject," Larry said cautiously. "Your thafety is key to the Gateway's thurvival. Thince all the plathes you go may not be friendly, you will thtart defence clathes in the morning."

"Oh, you have to be kidding me," he moaned.

"We could thend you out with an ethcort each time, but armed guardth tend to attract attention."

By this time the boy was pouting.

"Listen, I know I'm no Bruce Lee, but I've had fights and I've managed."

"You've had thchool boy thcuffles. I think you'll underthtand better after we vithit the training area."

The boy followed Larry out of the Chicago room and down several hallways and through a large hole in the wall. Larry went in and immediately dropped into darkness. The boy stood there confused, and then heard a faint voice echo.

"Are you coming?"

He stepped in and fell what seemed to be ten stories, straight down, screaming and swearing as his body flipped end over end. It was at this point he realized he had left his shotgun at the pizza place. The panic made him search for the revolver as his mind told him that it wasn't going to do a damn bit of good if this fall killed him. Gun clenched tightly in hand, his body slowed and he was set gently on the ground.

"What the hell was that?" he said, breathlessly pointing the gun at Larry who took no notice of the weapon.

"Our verthion of an elevator. The quicketht way from one point to another under your own power ith to fall. We did try to thpeed it up, but people thtarted getting thick. Don't worry, no one'th ever gotten hurt."

"I'll try to remember that. Next time, I won't eat lunch first," he said holding his stomach.

He walked into the darkness and the room brightened as if the walls were giving off light. In front of him was another stadium sized space blank as a sheet of fresh paper with the exception of a waist-high pillar with buttons and a set of headphone shaped controllers. Larry flew over to the pillar and a long metal pole came out of his body and went into it.

"You're not getting excited, are you?" the boy laughed.

"Hardly. The prathtice room ith locked becauthe it ith dangerouth. I am calling up one of the battle programth that Docheen favored."

The room transformed itself into an alien landscape. Tall columns of black rock that shined like glass jutted into a crimson sky. Each column dripped with a red lava-like substance that seemed to make the columns glow and the room considerably warmer. Figures, twenty in black and silver armor, surrounded a single figure in blue and gray. The armor was organic and sleek and not at all like the armor the boy had seen on the knights of old. It form-fitted each warrior and spikes sprouted from the coverings that protected the joints of each creature. All the figures were at least human in some respects. Something was where a head should be and there were two legs. The two legs looked like they belonged on a velociraptor's body. The central figure's lower body was made even more dinosaur like by the addition of a long tail. Where there should have been two arms there were four. Two of the arms were longer and sprouted from what would have been shoulder blades on the back of a human.

"Thtay behind the pillar and you will be thafe," Larry advised. "Jutht preth play to thtart, the yellow button."

"So your date will protect us?"

Larry said nothing to the boy's sarcasm.

The boy tightened his grip on the revolver and pressed the button. The drama that unfolded in front of him was two and a half minutes of the most gory scene he had ever seen. Arms flying, heads rolling, and at one point the center figure took out five of the black armor attackers with an almost graceful dance move, sticking four with different sized swords in each of his hands and one with a blade attached to his tail. It could have been a scene from a dark comedy; body parts flying through the air like tossing pies or water balloons. When it was over only the blue and gray figure remained standing. The figure removed its oversized helmet and it looked vaguely like Docheen, but in a really buff version of his lizard form. The boy had been so shocked by the violence that he forgot he was even holding a gun.

"Can you do that?" questioned Larry.

"No." The boy said flatly.

"That'th why you need training." Larry turned off the program.

"Wait," said the boy, as if he had figured out the answer to a perplexing question, "was that Docheen?"

"Yeth, that wath the form he took into battle. The form he felt motht comfortable in when thingth got ugly."

As they left the boy wondered what his fighting form might be one day. Werewolves were cool, but he had a feeling that anything from his favorite monster movies wouldn't have lasted long in that arena.

The rest of the day became a blur, like the first time listening to a new band, you knew was cool but couldn't remember most of the songs. As they explored more rooms they came across the one that was for creating the AODs. It was the size of a factory though its lack of noise and green glow made it feel very eerie indeed. Larry informed him that most of the rooms in the Gateway had a link to this room and that's why AODs could pop up when requested. A green syrupy gel poured down from a tube in the ceiling and into a mold that would change its shape as the boy requested. The boy created two girl figures resembling TV stars that he had crushes on. They were taller than the boy, so Larry suggested he shrink them. This took nothing more than putting them back in the mold, and squeezing out some excess goo. After experimenting with hair color and body type their lifeless eyes made him feel uneasy. Still, they were both attractive and far better looking than anyone he had ever hoped he would have a chance with, and now he had just created them with a thought and a word. Larry's words rang in the back of his head, *they would do anything you want.* At that moment Larry seemed to read his mind.

Timothy John Vaulato

"Would you like thome time alone Bawth?" he asked as the boy gave him a questioning glance.

"Not if this is the moment you and the Gateway are going to kill me," he returned while checking his gun to make sure that it was still there.

"I promith that no harm will come to you inthide the Gateway, you are the Keeper."

The boy looked back at the two girls and nodded hesitantly that Larry should leave. Once the door shut he assessed his creations and questioned his desires as his mind entered into a heated debate.

You're an idiot, one voice said.

Oh, like he'd have a chance with any girl this fine in the real world, argued another.

Their not even alive, how gross is that?

Dude, they look totally real.

They're not!

The eyes, they're just like the ones on that creepy pizza girl.

You know some freaks date inflatable girls.

That's sick.

So's this.

If all inflatable girls looked like this... started one.

The population problem would be solved, finished another.

Chalk it up to practice, laughed the calm voice, *after all, not a single breathing girl is going to ask him to the Sadie Hawkins dance, but let's say one did... he's never even had his first kiss. He should at least get that down.*

The last voice seemed convincing, and the boy moved in to the closest AOD. He was just about to kiss her when he stopped.

"Is it..." he struggled to say, "is it all right if I kiss you?"

The AOD's blank eyes looked straight ahead as it answered yes. He pressed his lips against hers only to receive no response. The harder he tried the worse it made him feel though she did nothing else but stand there passively. In a desperate attempt to draw some sort of reaction his hand slid upward toward her breast. It surprised him. After looking at stolen copies of Playboy since he was in third grade he had always assumed the breast to be hard like a muscle. This was not only soft, but the shear coldness of the AOD's flesh made him pull away as if he had touched a cadaver. It took several minutes of mentally screaming to himself that he was both a pervert and a fool before he could lift his gaze back up to look at the AOD. She still wore no expression and looked out blankly as if nothing had ever happened.

Feeling guilty and stupid, he unmade them, and back into the gel they went. Unmaking them made him feel even more dirty than when he had touched the breast because now he felt like he was trying to get rid of a body to hide a crime. In his head a lone voice asked a question. *Murderer and molester of the living dead... my oh my, what's next on your agenda?*

Timothy John Vaulato

Chapter Two
Rock, Paper... Name

His dinner was in a restaurant that could have been called, "a galaxy far far away." This room was different from the other places he had seen to eat in the Gateway. He couldn't believe that there were background people, and aliens, set in the room just to make the restaurant seem alive. These AODs were different, they laughed and made small talk to the others. He asked Larry why they weren't speaking their own languages? Larry reminded him that they were, his powers were working as were the Gateway's and everyone he would hear would speak in his native tongue. The boy decided he wasn't fond of alien food, but the clothing styles with the plunging butt cleavage he thought was a good idea. That is, at least on the human girls.

In frustration he made a McDonald's so he could order his standard two cheeseburgers, fries, and a large Diet Coke. Every Sunday since he was little, his family had McDonald's for dinner and he found the taste comforting. He realized his future diet might just consist of pizza, burgers, and really large cookies.

Since it was getting late for his internal time clock, Larry suggested that he might want to create better sleeping quarters than he had the night before. They went into a room that was filled with antique cars and Larry commanded the room with the word "new." The cars flowed into the walls and the space was left with the same kind of clear and seamless room that bothered the boy on his arrival.

"Thpeak your mind and you thhall retheive." said Larry.

The boy felt like he did in school. He usually couldn't shut-up, but when told to say something relevant, like in speech class, he choked. Then an idea from his tour worked its way into his head.

"Can I make it like one of the environment rooms?" he asked excitedly.

"Anything you want."

"Well, the last couple of years, my family has been going to the Rocky Mountains, and there's this spot in Colorado."

A pillar similar to the one in the practice room appeared.

"Plathe the headphone looking devithe over your head. Jutht think of what you want, but think very detailed, in this way your thpace will be the thame ath in your mind."

The boy gave him a confused look.

"Can't I just ask for what I want?" he asked, "like in the food court."

"If you jutht athk the Gateway to create thomething it will create the motht common of that object with your experienceth ath the guide."

Larry flew over to the side of his shoulder and waited. The boy put on the device and almost instantly the room tuned into a clearing in the middle of Rocky Mountain National Park, where he had once pitched a tent. A small creek ran through the center of it.

"Choice," he said with a broad smile. Suddenly the creek widened at one point and created a large swimming hole. A giant oak tree grew near the pond and a tree house changed shape rapidly

within its branches, never settling on one true form. The boy threw off the device and rubbed his temples.

"That was too much too quick. I guess I'm too indecisive. I need to be able to plan. Can I get a sketchbook and some pencils?" Before he could finish, the items he requested were on the ground in front of him, "and a drafting table?" An old oak drafting table grew from the ground. The boy picked his sketch pad off the grass and leaned it on the table.

"Chair," he said with a sly smile.

The next few hours he drew like a mad man stopping only to ask that Alice Cooper's, *From the Inside*, be played loudly. This was truly the happiest he had been since he arrived in the Gateway. Every once in a while, when he thought he had gotten the idea down he'd put the device back on his head, imagine, run around or through what he had created and then return to the sketch book.

The tree house looked as if it was part structure, part tree. He could enter at the base of the trunk, climb the stairs and enter into a drawing room; drafting table, pencils constantly sharp, and erasers, with a clean paint brush to whisk away the eraser crumbs. Bookshelves appeared that sat deep into the body of the tree, in both the drawing room and his new bedroom. His favorite books instantly filled them, which caused him to pause when he realized that some of them weren't even books he owned at home. He created a stereo out of habit. He wanted some physical control over the sounds that he chose, and his favorite albums followed. Dresser drawers that came out of the walls, closets, and a sky light above the bed, which allowed him a spectacular view of the sky.

Larry suggested the room be linked to the boy's biological clock, so that day looked like day and night was night. When he was too tired to continue, he slept in his first king sized bed, though his dreams left him shaken in the morning.

The days lost their numbers inside the Gateway. He loved the ability to draw something and make it become real. He would

A Lifetime In Time

spend hours creating spaces that he could only have dreamed of before. Some were sets of his favorite movies, some came straight from his mind via his sketch book. He started to become good at designing, and was so happy about his creations that when they went to refurnish the Landing area, he felt confident that he could change it without insulting the former Keeper's taste or memory. He changed what once looked like an airport terminal into a futuristic clock shop. He had a large clock that showed the time he had spent in the Gateway installed on the ceiling, another on the floor under thick glass, and several on the walls around the room. Each clock gave off a low level of light which lit the room, and each was slightly different. Some had basic numbers, others had Roman numerals and still others were graced with strange symbols that he had found on several clocks in the Gateway. Other items were placed near a wall, a coat rack, earth calendar, an old style accordion camera, mirror and a bulletin board with a comfortable chair in front of it. He hoped to use these items soon to record his arrivals and departures and to remind him what he was wearing when he came through a portal.

He felt that he had been away from home too long. He started to miss simple things like his ritual of watching late night talk shows, and even having conversations with his friends about bands or girls that they didn't think they stood a chance with. Larry assured him that he would return home soon, but only when he had a better grasp on what he had now become. He also told him that if it was late night talk shows that he craved they could be provided.

The boy met his trainer every morning, but it didn't seem like a defense class to him. They would spend hours meditating, and doing something that was like Yoga mixed with Tai Chi. His trainer was a dark brown skinned older man in his late sixties named Mo-pa. His clothing was a simple thick woven material that the boy thought was very close to his Senior Lopez pull-over jacket. The man had a strange almost philosophical way of speaking and the boy thought that even though he looked human, he didn't seem to know much about Earth. His voice was calming and yet still forceful. The boy's interaction on a friendly basis was met with questioning glances. Mo-pa didn't laugh at his attempts to make jokes, and sarcasm was almost completely lost on him.

What Mo-pa did seem to know about was a softball sized ball called a Calleash. He could throw it from any angle and hit not only his target, but three to four targets after each other and always with the ball returning to him. Mo-pa's ball was a brilliant blue with thin yellow stripes and orange markings that looked like bass clefts. The boy got his own ball, it was wooden and a solid dark brown. It was bigger than Mo-pa's and heavy. Mo-pa said that to begin to learn to use the Calleash, one started with wood. Wood was of nature and being that it was once living it would bond with the user and remember. The Calleash made him feel stupid. He was happy just to hit the one target with any accuracy, and Mo-pa would always profess that the user must become the target. The boy thought this too was stupid, why would you want to hit yourself?

On their first meeting the old man told the boy to throw the wooden ball. It flew through the air like a baseball and missed the target completely. The old man shook his head and sighed heavily. They stood there for an uncomfortable few moments when the boy turned and said, "Now what?"

Mo-pa looked at him in a way that made him feel small and rather silly.

"Now," said the old man, speaking very slowly and with purpose, "you go get it." He gestured at the ball that sat like an ugly wart on the clean white ground.

The boy's tours through the Gateway continued. He visited more strange rooms, more environments, and they even passed through a room known as the Library. Larry told him that it would be a while before he was ready for this type of library. The room looked like a television editing room with screens everywhere and a beastly metal chair that allowed you to completely recline. Larry called it the ultimate Lathy Boy.

A Lifetime In Time

His clothing choices became less flamboyant, since there really was no one to see them, and blue jeans and black shirts became his comfort zone. He liked to wear a gray hooded zip up sweat shirt just because it was comfortable, and it reminded him of the one he had on Earth. There were moments when he even wore black button up shirts just because he didn't have to iron them.

One day he found the remains of the clothes he was in when he entered the Gateway. They were neatly stuffed into one of the dresser drawers in his tree house bedroom and appeared shredded and even a little singed. Though they were beyond use, he still rifled through the pockets to find his house keys, wallet, and the school announcement that he had drawn the guitar of his dreams on. It was at this moment it dawned on him that he could create guitars. He quickly made his dreams a reality. The standard guitars that were beyond his budget at home appeared first. With fresh catalogs in his hand it was only a matter of choosing the color and how many of them he would like. He then started to customize them. Some became hollow bodies, some became twelve strings and most were either a beautiful wood grain or his favorite color, green. Days later when he returned to his sketch from the pocket of his jean jacket the reality of this new power hit him in the face. The guitar that formed from his mind was the drawing of a double neck with one neck being a six string and the other a twelve. It had the look of two Gibson flying V's melted together at the wings. He dubbed his proud creation, "The Flying W." Then he created one in black, one in white, one in maple, and the last one an emerald green over a flame maple top.

He also realized he could create his own band with the AODs. After this Mo-pa would have to chase him out of his bedroom for his practice sessions. He tried to play with the band Rush and felt completely outclassed. He even believed that the AODs he had created as the band members might have been looking at him as if he were a fool. Eventually, after going from difficult music to less difficult music, he felt some success playing some of the Simon and Garfunkel songs, mostly hits like *The Boxer* and *The*

Sound of Silence. Other Paul Simon songs had a lot of chords that moved pretty quickly, but he kept practicing till his blisters made him stop. He knew that his friends didn't like this type of music, but at least when he played it, it was recognizable as a song. Deep down, he really did think the music was cool. One day Larry informed him that he was ready to visit his first life.

His trip home felt weird. He wondered if anyone could tell he was hiding a secret. He wanted so badly to just turn to his friends and blab everything about the Gateway and what had happened to him, but he couldn't. He wondered if he would be putting himself or his friends in danger. In the movies, the bad guys used the ones that the hero cared about against him. Would this bad movie plot be reenacted in his life? He also wondered that if he had this secret, could there be others out there that had been given powers over time and reality? If there were, would they look at him as a friend, or would they come after him to level the field of competition? He chuckled at his paranoia. He hadn't even traveled in time yet, and now he was considering himself a marked man.

Nights in the Gateway felt safe. Nights at home were restless. His mother kept asking him if anything was wrong, if he needed to see a doctor. She had acted this way as far back as he could remember, but when she sat him down to ask him if he had a drug problem all he could manage as a reply was to ask about the time his Grandmother had shock treatments.

"Grandma had a hard life," she stated, "though we loved your grandpa, he had many problems. His drinking was the worst."

The boy just bowed his head in a moment of silence knowing his role as spectator in this up coming monologue. His mother surprised him by not launching into the sordid acts of his grandfather, but hit him with an unexpected question.

"Have you ever drank?" she asked, feeling like the progressive mother that could understand her child.

"No, Mom," he replied, with a bit of shock and truth, "I don't drink."

A Lifetime In Time

"What about the drugs?" she asked, pressing on as if they were sharing a special mother son moment, "do you do the drugs?"

Her eyes were wide open and he gave the truthful answer she was hoping for, he wondered for a brief moment what would have happened if he lied and told her that he was a full-blown coke addict. Though he thought it might be entertaining to see her squirm only to throw the words Diet Coke at her after she was in hysterics. He opted for the road of less resistance, truth, and no entertainment.

"No, Mom, I don't do drugs. Well, I did do the ritalin, but you gave me that."

"The doctor gave you that," she pointed out, removing herself from all blame. "It was to help you focus. I mean, my God, all those drawings you do with the monsters and the comic book characters, can't you draw something nice?"

"Sure, Mom," he said rolling his eyes, "what's nice?"

"Flowers or a pretty landscape," she suggested. "Why does everything have to be blood, gore, or guitars?"

The question was the same one he had been asked since he was in second grade when a baby-sitter had let him watch his first werewolf movie. This time he decided with his bag of secrets rolling round in his head that if he didn't placate her, he might end up in shock treatment.

"I was just heading off to draw a pretty landscape, Mom."

"That's nice dear, but remember, don't do the drugs."

"Yes, Mom, no drugs, just pretty flowers."

After this encounter he decided he needed to be more careful with what he said and how he acted around her, or he just might find himself drawing flowers till he threw up rose petals.

One day upon entering the Gateway, Larry floated with excitement, as much as anybody can float with excitement. He seemed to dart from here to there more than usual.

"Bawth, I have a thurprize for you," he beamed.

"Define surprise," said the boy, worried that it might be one of those surprises that one doesn't really find all that pleasant.

Timothy John Vaulato

"Come thith way." Larry managed to beep and lisp at the same time.

The two traveled down three halls, two elevator tubes and eventually came to a door.

"What's behind the door, a tiger, or a lady?" the boy asked, remembering the story from seventh grade English class.

"Open and you'll thee," Larry said, so he did.

The room appeared to be an art gallery with sculptures that looked as if they were from the Renaissance with large paintings tightly packed all over the walls. Greek columns held up a ceiling pointing up to Michelangelo's "*Sistine Chapel.*"

"That one ith a copy," said Larry. "Thome thingth Docheen didn't feel right about taking."

In the middle of the room was a smaller Greek column, waist high, with a bowler hat upside down. The boy didn't notice the hat, and proceeded to marvel at the art.

"Wow, this is cool... copy, or not."

"Over here," said Larry nudging him toward the hat.

"It's a hat," he stated, as if it were a big surprise to both of them. "Kind of doesn't really fit the decorum," he said unimpressed, with his eye's still darting from art work to art work.

"And a thigar ith jutht a thigar. Look, ith what'th inthide of the hat that matterth."

The boy moved over to the hat hoping that it wasn't more bugs and saw that it was full of folded pieces of paper.

"What, are we playing charades today?" he asked sarcastically.

"No, we are picking your name."

"What do you mean we're picking my name?" His voice had become cross.

"Well, if left to your own devitheth the Gateway calculated that it would take you 50 of your Earth yearth to thettle on one, and that you wouldn't really be pleathed with it."

"And why not?" he asked, becoming even more irate.

"It would be thomething we'd call you behind your back. Thith way ith left up to chanthe. No futh, no muth."

48

A Lifetime In Time

"Why do I need a new name, you don't even call me by my name, you call me Boss, or should I thay Bawth."

"You would be amazthed at the problemth uthing your real name can cauthe. Even human'th are bright enough to track down thomebody by their name."

"Hey," said the boy clearly insulted, "human standing here."

"Let'th jutht thay that ith dangerouth to uthe a real name, Bawth. We don't want any rithk here, for you, or the Gateway."

The boy peered into the hat and thought for a minute.

"Well, my parents picked my real name, and I've been ok with it, how bad could it be."

He dug his hand deep, fished one off the bottom, held it up and questioningly read allowed.

"Traven," he said. "Traven... What kind of name is Traven? Is it another name for a bar that can't be pronounced correctly because of too much whiskey, or a drunk with a speech impediment trying to say his favorite bird? Wait, I got it, it's where birds go to get drunk?"

He was so pleased with his little rant that he wasn't paying attention as he stepped backwards and knocked the hat off its pillar. Hundreds of little white papers scattered on the ground. Out of habit, he started to bend over and pick up the pieces of paper when Larry flew in front of him distracting him.

"Look, at least you pronounced it correctly, and bethideth what'th in a name? Alithe Cooper thounds like a PTA chair woman. Ith what you do with it that'th important," Larry said excitedly.

"Look, I really don't care, call me whatever you want, but is this really the best name in this hat?"

He started to dig as Larry once again blocked his attempts.

"Ith a fine name, you'll do well with it, and bethideth, it hath to be better than Mo-pa calling you Boy," Larry said, ushering him quickly to the door leaving the papers where they lay.

Mo-pa had refused to call him Boss, and he didn't really feel secure enough with even that weak title to ever force someone to call him that.

Timothy John Vaulato

"Well that's true, I hate that..." he considered. "Traven huh? All right, Traven needs a cookie."

The name felt strange on his lips.

"And a pop?" Larry questioned.

"And a pop." Traven agreed, as he walked through the door.

As they left, cleaning robots quickly dispensed of the mess of little white papers, each of which had the name Traven on it.

Chapter Three
Lunch And Other Near Death Experiences

Traven found school even more dull after the time he spent in the Gateway. Lunch was one of the worst periods of the day. Not only was the food awful, but the food in the Gateway came the moment he asked for it. Waiting in lines really started to bug him. The cafeteria seemed so loud in comparison to the Gateway where the only loud sounds were the music he requested and a Calleash hitting or missing a target. Lunch itself was the same, only his outlook had changed.

The only part he enjoyed, was sitting with his friends. His closest friends were Matt, Brian, and Willie. They too were outcasts and, like him, they shared his despicable taste in clothing. They wore purposely aged jeans, ripped tennis shoes, and flannel shirts that covered whatever black concert shirt they had picked up over the last few months. They tied bandanas of different colors on their wrists or around their pant legs, but would be asked to remove them if seen by a deans' assistant. The deans' assistants were wrongly informed that it was a sign of gang involvement and not just a fashion nightmare. Jean jacket's were also popular, though if he didn't keep his eye on the new one the Gateway had created Brian would try to walk off with it.

Brian was the comedian, he could make even the toughest school punk laugh. He was tall and thin, with the face of Jim Morrison, and the lips of Mick Jagger. He hated when people talked about his lips. He was popular, but never enough to be in the "in crowd." In the party scene he was invited as entertainment, which was more than anyone else in the group could say. He never really made any strong attachments to the people he partied with, and in the back of his mind he hoped to draw like Willie someday. At this point he was having a tough time even keeping up with Traven's skills, which, though very good were not like Willie's. During lunch Brian would run a play-by-play commentary on every girl who walked by, and even gave them nicknames only known by the people at the table. Minnie Mouse was a table favorite with her big blue eyes and larger than possible brown hair. Another girl was known as Lower Mandible. She was also a hit, a perfect body for a seventeen year old, but a somewhat larger than normal jaw. Lastly, there was Jugs, whose bodily blessings would enter the room before she did. To these, and many others, Brian provided the dialog that he believed them to be having in their heads, and shared it with the table.

Willie was the artist and the best in the school. His reddish-brown hair was much longer than the rest of theirs and cut as if he was trying out for the role of squire for a knight in the middle ages. He hid behind it most of the time, keeping his head pointing toward the ground with only his large nose peeking through. The art teacher, Mr. Klang, would give him assignments that he deemed not worth his time to do, usually for really low pay or just as Mr. Klang would say, "For the experience." The counselors had a file on Willie three inches thick. He always had weapons on him hidden within his loose clothing. In his mind he saw himself as a dark warrior of old but, in truth, he was a really nice guy with an arsenal. His hidden armaments consisted of throwing stars, chains with weights on the ends of them, small hunting knives and on strange occasions a fifteen inch bowie knife that his father had left him when he died. No one said anything about these weapons, not the students, and not the teachers, and for some reason they even let him make his own broad sword in metal shop. It impressed everyone, and he even cast the pommel with a killer looking dragon head he himself had sculpted. Traven would look back at this in later years and wonder how he got away with it, but in the end he would chalk it up to it being the 1980's, where being drunk and behind the wheel of a car would only get you a slap on the wrist and the warning to drive home carefully. Willie's ability with a bow was far greater than any of the teachers, and when asked to teach the archery class he took it with great pride. He made sure that all the students held the bow correctly, not just the girls, and he made sure they sighted the target in the proper manner. He was generous with his drawings, giving them to whoever had an interest, and rarely was he the cause of any real trouble. Still, the office watched him as one of those students who might, at any moment, go over the edge.

Matt was quiet and funny although he always took a back seat to Brian's rule as class clown. He too was a "want to be" artist that did quite well though it would take him months to finish a single drawing. A comic collector and music fanatic, whose parents were out of the house most of the time which made it convenient to hang out at his place, listening to tunes and drawing. The house was always slightly chaotic, with inventions his father had started and forgot about, or ones that momentarily had, become an obsession. No one had ever asked his dad what he was working on for fear that the question would give him the format to talk at length. Matt also was the man with the wheels, a mid-sixties Buick that his dad had kept in pristine condition. It was a boat that bordered on being almost cool. Matt was the mastermind of group activities and the organizer of most concerts.

"Hey B., here she comes," Matt pointed as Lower Mandible walked down the middle aisle of the cafeteria. Without missing a beat, Brian switched to a squeaky voice and began.

"Oh look at me, I woke up late from my exciting evening of self gratification... my rubix cube gets me so hot. Is my make-up on thick enough? If I eat one more peanut butter fudge square my pants will burst. I wonder if people can see my panty lines? Oh tee hee, I forgot to wear any."

As she passed the table the boys eyed her like jackals. All heads were turned when Matt said. "Nope, she's got her panties on today."

Unfortunately, Matt spoke louder than he had intended. She stopped and turned slowly, flicking him off and mouthing the words "up yours."

In his mind, time slowed, and this gesture took forever, and sadly would be replayed during most of Matt's future attempts to talk to girls. He dropped his head to the table and tried to hide within his folded arms while turning beat red. Brian pointed at him and yelled.

"Busted!"

The whole table broke out laughing, until Matt finally raised his head to watch her strut away. He put his head down until another girl passed and would quickly lift to allow him to focus on her form.

"Look at him," said Brian punching Traven's arm, "he's got built in radar."

Willie didn't eat lunch, not really. His head was down toward his sketch book drawing away, stopping only to look up when a girl was pointed out by the others. The truth was that his ability to draw was the only reason girls ever stopped by the table; usually, to request that he draw a heart with an arrow through it, with the girl's name and whatever the girl's current boyfriend's name was. This day he was fed up with the requests and when the young blond stopped by to pick up her drawing it was a drawing of a real heart with a bloodied arrow ripping through the tender flesh. The names looked as if they were carved in it with what would have had to been a dull knife. "Gross," she yelled at him as she stomped away.

"What?" he said, "I got the ventricles right."

Again the table burst into laughter. Finally with no females in Matt's sight he looked up and said. "Hey, I'm picking up tickets for the Dio/Twisted Sister concert. Who's in?"

"In," said Brian.

"Me too," said Traven, pushing his unsatisfying cafeteria cookie away.

"Nope," said Willie, and he went back to drawing.

"Come on man," said Matt, "Holy Diver, Last in Line, Rainbow in the Dark, not to mention Sister."

With that, the table started singing in a deep voice the words to *Captain Howdy*. They didn't stop until someone screwed up the words.

"Why not?" asked Matt.

"Got the cassette," Willie replied.

"Not the same," said Traven.

"Look, the lawn seats will be cheap," said Matt.

"Nope," Willie replied, not looking up from his sketch pad.

"All right, I'm buying an extra ticket, if you want it it's yours," said Matt.

"What are you going to do with an extra ticket?" asked Traven. "You know he won't go."

"He's going to give it to Lower Mandible," yelled Brian. Again the table burst out laughing.

"Screw you man," said Matt, giving him the one fingered salute as the dismissal bell rang.

As they walked through the halls, Traven wanted to tell his friends what had been happening to him, but he wasn't sure if he believed it himself. Having power over time, was an insane thought, and he wasn't a hundred percent sure that it wasn't just going on in his head. He had checked a few books out of the school library to try and read up on these kind of delusions. Mostly he just looked at their covers. In the pocket of the jacket the Gateway had provided him, he discovered the stack of twenty's he had taken from the treasure room. This proved something had happened. He just hoped that he wasn't stealing and crazy too.

His next class was Earth Science. He had the choice of taking it or Biology and the thought of cutting up animals didn't really appeal to him on any level. The classroom was laid out in long horizontal rows of tables that faced the board. "Bored," was the key word. He spent most of his time drawing doodles instead of taking notes. The teacher was a middle-aged man named Holtz. He had a son that was a fantastic drummer and Traven always wanted to ask if his son would be interested in forming a band with him. But in his heart, he knew that Holtz's son was much better than he was, and making a fool of himself in front of real people would make him never summon up the courage to ask. The one thing that made today different than most days in class was the topic. Holtz was going on and on about what their hometown looked like during the ice age, before the white man had invaded and before people had ever set foot on the country known as America. Traven always perked up when Holtz talked about the past. The man seemed to have a true passion for what the world used to look like. Sadly that did not apply to most of his lectures on the state of the flora and fauna. In his head Traven thought, *This guy would die to see the world back then like I can. Hey, I can!* The realization was like a quick push into a swimming pool when you really had just come for the food, and suddenly you remembered that water is wet. *Why don't I?* He thought, *Why not actually travel in time rather than sitting around staring at a wooden ball?*

School passed quickly and when it was over, he headed home to his room. He made sure that his mother was involved in a deep phone conversation, this was never hard to do. When he heard her use her friend's name he knew that it was about her work and nothing less than a bomb would have distracted her. He checked his watch, waved his hand, and stepped into the Gateway.

Larry grilled him on the day's events and took long electronic notes to allow Traven not to seem like he had been gone any real length of time. A camera on the tripod scanned him for hair length and the clothes that he arrived in. He went to the wall and wrote on the calendar his arrival time which seemed primitive when compared to the Gateway itself, but at least it let him feel involved. He turned to check himself in an old fashion mirror. The funny thing is his hair and finger nails seemed to grow even though he didn't age. He did leave his hair a little longer when he left, but somehow it was as though his mother could almost tell.

"Hey Larry," he said, as soon as Larry finished his interrogation, "I have an idea."

"That doethn't thound good, your latht idea wath with the tubeth of water to ride in. That idea flooded levelth ninety and ninety one," Larry buzzed.

"I'm thinking of taking a trip," Traven said.

"Dithney World?" Larry asked tentatively. "I hear 1987 might be a good year, very short lineth. Next to no thtaff though."

Ignoring Larry he continued.

"No, I'm thinking more like the ice age."

"It wath very cold," Larry said dryly, "and no adventure rideth or mouthe ears."

"Come on," Traven wined, "I haven't traveled in time yet and besides, we were talking about it in school. Don't you want to further my education?"

There was a long silence. Larry turned away and flew into another room. It appeared that he was having an argument with the wall, at least from what Traven could see through the door. Larry flew back.

"You are the bawth, Bawth," he stated flatly.

"What was that about?" Traven questioned.

Larry was silent.

"Well?" Traven tried to push harder.

Larry avoided the question all together and two other Larry type robots flew up holding a jacket and boots.

"The jacket lookth thin, but ith incredibly warm, ath are the booth." Larry's voice always became more robotic when he was upset, and Traven's idea had definitely made him upset. "Walk toward the doorway at the end of the room when you are ready. Think of the Gateway and wave your hand in a thircle when you want to return."

Traven looked at Larry for a moment, wondering what he wasn't telling him, but then he walked toward the big doorway and for the first time stepped into the past. The passing into the past surprised him, for it was no different than walking through one room into the next. It felt like stepping onto a never ending movie set.

Larry was right, it was cold, but the air smelled different than any other cold day he had ever spent on Earth, and for a moment he did nothing but breathe deeply. He realized that the world was quite different before the use of fluorocarbons and wondered if mankind had any knowledge of the abuse that they had placed upon the earth. Even in the biting cold the land before man had almost a green house smell to it. It seemed as if every plant had its own perfume and for a brief moment, he wondered how out of place he smelled in the scheme of things. He took his Blues Brothers like sunglasses out of his pocket and placed them over his eyes. Though it was almost dusk the snow was untouched by any tracks and the sun reflected brightly.

"Now what?" he mumbled. "Not really much of a plan I guess. I could build a snowman just for the surrealistic quality of it," but instead he took his first step. "One small step for man," he muttered. His leg went deep into the snow, and though his feet were warm he noticed the incredible cold through his jeans. "Jesus, this is unpleasant!" he barked, and tried another step and only managed to plunge his other leg into the primitive refrigerator. "All right," he said to himself. "I'm pretty sure I'm done. I mean there has to be better places to go than this."

He started to wave his hand in the air and from behind him came a low, distant, almost silent growl which he could almost swear said the word "food." This distraction stopped him from completing the circle with his arm and he jerked his

A Lifetime In Time

body toward the sound. He found it wasn't easy to turn, or do much of anything with his thighs firmly buried in snow. Far away a large shape was moving quickly toward him. Snow was flying up from the creature as if someone had taped snow blowers to its body. Traven froze seeing the creature coming closer and closer. It looked like a cross between a bear and a wolverine except the wolverine had been on steroids, and it was running as fast as a horse in the Kentucky Derby.

"That's got to be my cue to get out of here." He waved his arm again but his concentration was poor due to the approaching growls and nothing happened. "Larry!" he yelled, "I did the hand thingy, how about a little help here!" The non answer made him frantically try again, and again, but to no avail. "I'm going to die," he screamed like a little girl, and this one thought was enough to awaken him to action. He first tried running but after five unsuccessful steps and a face full of snow it dawned on him that the only way back to the Gateway was in his hand. He completed the circle but again nothing happened and the thing was getting closer. "Clear your mind," he heard Mo-pa say as he tried to summon the wisdom from all the lessons he had to endure. Again he tried, again he failed. The sound of the beast's paws breaking the snow could be heard. "Damn it, concentrate," he muttered, and for a brief second all the meditation Mo-pa had taught him cleared his mind and he could see into the landing room.

Before he could make a single step he felt heat from the "thing's" breath on his neck as it bit into him and started to thrash. His body left the ground and his vision blurred like a cheesy carnival ride. He thought of his seventh birthday, holed up in his bedroom and crying as the party went on without him till his mother coaxed him back to the festivities. Why did he leave? Why was he stuck in the corner of his room crying? The reasons why his mind was even there caused him to become frustrated until a stronger bite brought him back as his collar bone snapped. Its claws tore into his side and thigh as the beast steadied his dinner. *I'm dying,* thought

59

Timothy John Vaulato

A Lifetime In Time

Traven, *this is it*. With the metallic taste of his own blood in his mouth he blacked out.

He awoke in the Gateway's medical lab. Little lights flashed in blurs and then came into focus. Larry floated above him, and Larry doubles zoomed around the room doing things that seemed incredibly important. As he looked around the room he noticed Mo-pa sitting next to him and groggily Traven tried to speak.

"I didn't know you had family," he said, trying to focus on the Larry doubles and feeling very drugged. "Am I dead again?"

"Almotht," said Larry, checking one of the machines that Traven was hooked to.

"Why didn't you get me... you... round bastard!" Traven's head wove back and forth as if his eye's were beyond his body.

"We did Bawth, thaddly there'th nothing we can do till you open the portal."

It was as if the answer never quite made the impact to Traven's brain and then it became hard for him to remember the question he asked. He turned toward Mo-pa in confusion.

"I never asked if you're real or some kind of plant AOD thingy," he said weakly.

This was the first time he had ever seen Mo-pa smile and the old man just patted his hand.

"What... the hell happened?" Traven said, to assemble his thought pattern and then a coughing fit hit him making him aware of the pain in his limbs, neck, head, and chest.

"The pain will thubthide quickly," said Larry, and it did. "What you are feeling are phantom painth. Your body hath been repaired but your mind holdth an imprint of your trauma. You thould be back to normal in about a day."

"Do you ever notice how you don't answer the questions I ask?" Traven said closing his eyes. Mo-pa placed Traven's Calleash in Traven's hand.

"For strength," he said, and with that he got up, nodded toward the boy and left the room.

"Great, one barely talks and the other withholds information."

Traven surprised himself by hitting Larry square in the middle of his eye with the wooden ball. Larry somersaulted and flew back to Traven's side.

"Ursus Spelaeus," Larry said in a moment of correct grammar. "From your period 25,000 B.C., the measurements, 6 foot 6 in height, 18 feet in length. In short, one really big bear with bad attitude. We had to pull you into the Gateway because you couldn't do it on your own."

"What about the bear?" asked Traven.

The question seemed strange to him, but up till now he always liked bears. He even had one on a belt buckle at home. He was never brave enough to wear it past sixth grade. Bears were his second favorite animal next to the wolf.

"Ith on a wall in the banquet room level nine." As Larry talked, Traven shut his eyes. Sleep was quickly taking over him and as he drifted off he heard Larry say. "Thee wanth to meet you. Tomorrow when you are feeling better. Thee'th willing to talk."

If Larry said anything else Traven couldn't remember, he had fallen back to sleep.

Chapter Four
The Meeting

Traven healed quite nicely. In the morning he felt as good as new. He marveled at the abilities of the med unit and though he felt some phantom pains early in the day, by the afternoon they were almost completely gone. An attack like that on earth would have left him dead or crippled for life, but thanks to the Gateway he found himself walking down the hall with his biggest concern being that he didn't say anything stupid while under sedation. Even Mo-pa allowed him to start training later than usual. They had gone through training movements for about an hour. This was the time where he usually started to let his mind wander and Mo-pa corrected him with a quick slap to the back from his bamboo cane. The cane was clearly not used to help Mo-pa walk, and it seemed to appear from nowhere the moment he needed it. Today was different. Instead of a hit to the back Mo-pa suggested they take a break. The boy looked at him strangely and glanced side to side for the cane as if he was awaiting his punishment. Mo-pa looked back at him with a rare full smile.

"What, no smack across the back?" Traven questioned. "Isn't that standard practice?"

"Yes, pain can help one focus," Mo-pa agreed, "but not today."

They both took their seats on the floor.

"You seem preoccupied," stated the old man.

"Well the almost dying thing did put me off," he said, starting to realize that he was not as focused today as he usually was. "I mean, I'm supposed to be learning to defend myself and I almost end up as bear carry-out."

"You did well for your limited training. If you had met the bear before your training, he would have eaten you without you opening a portal to the Gateway."

"But, I would have liked to have not been snacked on at all. Isn't that what learning to fight is all about?" he asked, hoping for an answer from his usually distant trainer.

"I see," said Mo-pa, "you are under the impression that I am teaching you how to fight."

Traven's surprise overtook him and he jumped to his feet.

"Well, what the hell have we been doing here?"

Mo-pa got to his feet and pulled his Calleash from his nap sack.

"Child," he said, "we have been opening your mind and your senses."

Traven looked utterly confused as Mo-pa allowed himself a silent chuckle. "Pillars," he said, in a soft but commanding tone. The standard target pillars rose from the floor of the room. "Close your eyes, sense the air, feel the vibrations on your skin. Without the use of sight point to the path that the Calleash takes."

Traven stood still as Mo-pa's ball took to the air without him even seeming to throw it. It bounced from one pillar to the next, and though the sound of the impacts were a dead give away to when it contacted the posts, the boy realized for the first time he could sense it as it moved. In his mind he saw a shadow shape moving through the air, like watching a child's toy move through water. This sightless vision was in half-time while his body functioned in the present. He pointed his finger and traced the path that it had made. It's last turn sent it hurdling at his face and with reflexes he didn't know he had, he snatched it out of midair.

"That is what you've been learning," Mo-pa stated flatly.

Traven looked at Mo-pa and then the ball. He was amazed that he had plucked it out of the air without as much as a second thought.

"Killer," he chimed, as Mo-pa was once again confused by his unique vernacular. "But, what do I do when I have to fight. I mean I can't keep ducking and blocking forever."

Mo-pa took the Calleash from his hand and turned away.

"Another," he said, "will teach you what you need to know."

"Who?" Traven asked with surprise.

"I... am not sure, but if it is as it was before, your trainer will be very interesting." With this statement Mo-pa started to leave.

"Wait, we still have another couple of hours." Traven almost hit himself, he really didn't enjoy practice at all but this was the first time that he could see a purpose to this strange ballet they had been doing.

"Today we need a break. Even the wind becomes still from time to time," said the old man, "and you have someone to meet."

Suddenly it all came back to Traven like a forgotten dream. He remembered yesterday's fuzzy conversation with Larry. Though the talk was limited, because he was stretched out on the med unit bed, he was almost sure Larry said he was supposed to meet her. That must have meant the Gateway was ready to talk to him.

"Mo-pa, before you go, yesterday I asked if you are real?"

"Yes, I am very much real."

"Where do you go when we finish?"

"The Gateway has provided me with comfortable living quarters, if I am not there, I am in my garden, or I am eating pizza in the Chi-ca-go room."

Traven laughed thinking of the old man eating pizza losing his cheese on his shirt, just as Traven did every time he ate there.

"Do you live in the Gateway all the time or do you go home?"

"The Gateway is now my home and has been for a long time."

"Don't you have any family or friends that you'd like to hang out with?"

This was the first time since Mo-pa had decided to cancel practice that his appearance became somber. He walked back into the room and called for a simple wooden chair.

"I have lived a very long time, though my youthful appearance might deceive you. When the former Keeper found out I was dying, he offered me a deal. In the Gateway we do not age. I use my little time left outside the Gateway to fulfill a promise to be with my children on their birthdays."

Traven was shaken by this, and for the first time he felt as though Mo-pa was not just some sadist drill instructor.

"But can't the med lab fix your problem?" he asked, as if the idea had never been asked before.

"It has fixed my pain and has slowed my death, but the end is inevitable."

"But..." Traven tried to interject, to lodge a protest to the outcome of this story, but was cut off.

"No more words, you will be late." As Mo-pa left the room, Traven thought how odd it was that someone who had control over time was being told he was going to be late. He went back to his room, bathed off his sweat in the heated pond and made himself presentable for the meeting. He picked out his sharpest black button down shirt, but the idea of finishing the look with slacks was almost unthinkable to him. He settled on black jeans and even had a black suit jacket appear. A tie was the mark of adulthood and he couldn't, being himself, go that far, so he chose a bolo tie as if he was a confused cowboy. With a color change to his sneakers he looked a little like Johnny Cash. He paused for a moment to view himself in the mirror and by his standards he felt very dressed up.

Traven went into the banquet room and was greeted by the shock of a large bear pelt. The same bear who only yesterday had almost ended his life. It was massive and the mere sight of it made him both cringe and feel sad for the bear. The room looked like it came from Norse Mythology, with large wooden beams and thick heavy wooden tables with assorted bronze and iron aged weapons on the walls. He scanned the room for any sort of figure and wondered if he should call out for her. Instead he said, "Diet Coke," and one appeared. As he sipped on his 32 ounce beverage, she appeared. It was almost as if she had stepped out from a rather enjoyable dream and unlike the AODs this girl smiled. She was taller than him. Her stride was regal and flowing as if the effort to walk took no effort at all. Against Traven's character he pulled out the heavy chair for her to sit in. She acknowledged his chivalry with a nod and sat. There was an angelic innocence to her young doll like face that was only contrasted by her eyes rimmed with thick eye liner. Her long, sandy hair seemed to glow with golden highlights and cascaded down thin tan shoulders in waves and loose curls. The dress she wore was a light gauzy blue. Not the clothes one would guess to be worn by a being of great power, but a renaissance style sun dress, something that you'd see dancing in the parking lot at a Grateful Dead concert. Oddly, her feet were bare and the bottoms would faintly glow as they were lifted from their silent contact with the floor.

Traven's jaw dropped and he found himself unable to speak.

She clasped her hands under her chin and smiled confidently, amused at his expression.

"Put your tongue back into your mouth boy," she joked, as her words dripped with a southern accent.

"Sorry," he said nervously and surprised at her voice, "I... uh."

"Not what y'all were expecting?" she winked, as she played with one of her many necklaces. Each one seemed to have a different origin. The choker around her throat was made of simple black and white coral while the three long necklaces on plain silver chains had unique and different ends.

"No, I thought... that you'd be more like... Larry."

She laughed and leaned back in her chair.

"Well if you like, Ah can appear any way you want."

"No, no this is fine," he said, painfully aware that his voice had just cracked.

"Good," she replied, both as affirmation for her current form and an underlying tone that suggested that she may have not been willing to change her form for anybody. "Ah figured it was time for you and Ah to make conversation, face to face. Though Ah can hear and see all that goes on around here, so a form is just, shall we say, a formality."

The boy felt nervous, remembering his recent bath, and counting all the other times he had been naked, as well as other, shall we say, highly embarrassing personal moments. He regained his composure and concentrated on his speech so it would not betray him again.

"I'm sorry," said Traven, suddenly very aware about the informal way he had been talking to her, "I wasn't told how to address you, or any of the protocol thingy's I should do in meeting you."

"Protocol?" she said with a slight snicker, "ya mean like on bent knee and all?"

"Am I suppose to?" he asked nervously.

"Well it does do a girl's heart a world of good," she replied, giving him a suspicious look, "but it is unnecessary. You are the Keeper, Ah am the Gateway." Her eyes focused on him as if she was dissecting him.

"I'm sorry if I sound forward," he said measuring his words carefully, "but what does that exactly mean?"

"Not the ripest apple in the bushel, are ya?" She stated as a matter of fact, and tossed her hair to one side as if she was going to be bothered by having to explain to him what he already knew.

"Well... I mean I understand that I'm the Keeper," he said, trying to recover, "and that I can travel in time and space and that thing about other realities."

She winced ever so slightly at the words "other realities."

He continued, "and I get the part about you being the Gateway. As Larry explained, we live inside of you, and as you have said you are now a part of me and I you."

She bit the end of her lip as if she was going to say something or correct him and then chose not to.

Each word that came out of his mouth seemed very loud to him.

"But... do I work for you?" He tensed, hoping that he hadn't made a gigantic blunder or had overstepped his bounds.

She through him off by stretching her arms in the air and thus displaying a perfect body.

"No," she replied, squinting her eyes and staring deeply into his, "Ah work for you."

The eye contact made him painfully aware that at this point she could control him if she took the notion. He also questioned if she was telling him the truth anymore than Docheen had. He decided he had better change the questions before he said something truly stupid.

"Why do you want to talk to me?" he asked, taking a sip of his Coke and thinking, *Toaster, toaster, why the hell am I thinking about a toaster?* It was the first thing his mind could come up with to divert his teenage urges.

She watched him with a slight smile almost reading his internal monologue and decided to interrupt him when he shook his head in confusion to the workings of his own mind.

"Well, to go an' whack the nail on its head, I don't know how much longer y'all have to live. I mean after the bear attack and all." She glanced over at the skin on the wall. "Though it's against mah better judgment, Ah reckon Ah should give you a chance." Traven's heart sank. If the Gateway didn't think he had much longer to live, what kind of chance of being the Keeper did he have? "Don't misunderstand me," she said pinching the end of the necklace with a split triangle. "I am still furious about Docheen, he may have pulled the trigger but y'all were the gun."

"Look, I'm sorry," he pleaded.

"I know ya are, but sorry doesn't change the timeline in here."

"What if I could?"

"Could what?" she asked.

A Lifetime In Time

"Why don't I go back in time and stop myself from smashing the heartstone? I mean, don't get me wrong, these abilities are very cool, but I don't really think I'm the guy for the job." As he gestured with his hand he almost succeeded in knocking over his drink. Small puddles of soda now dripped from the table. He finished his thought's while being consumed with the mess that he was wiping with his jacket sleeve. "I'm not even a good student and yesterday may have proven that to everyone."

She looked at him questioningly, almost as if he was partly naive to the workings of his new position and partly selfless. She snapped her fingers and pointed to her face to redirect his attention from his frantic cleaning.

"Y'all can't change what has been done in here. It doesn't work that way, Honey. In here the timeline can only move forward cause now it's yours. Besides," she said, as a look of sadness came into her face, "the old fart wanted to die, he had been through too much. We all have been through too much."

"Please tell me you're not suicidal too," Traven said in a worried tone.

"No," she laughed softly. "Just sad." She started to rub the end of the necklace that seemed to be some sort of abstract lady bug in the same way someone would use a worry stone. Not knowing what to say he awkwardly stumbled into another question.

"Why me?" he asked, as she dropped her necklace and cocked her head in the other direction. "There has to be people or beings that are better suited for this than me."

"Y'all mean those that do not require babysitting?" As she said this he felt very small and slumped forward again staring down at the wood grain of the table. "It was random."

"Random?" he said looking up. "You mean I'm..."

"Not special in any way," she twirled one of her long curls around her finger. "Sorry, maybe to your parents you are, but not in the cosmic talent line up, no."

"Why random?" he asked, trying to make sense of his appointment as Keeper.

"Ah didn't see it as one of his better decisions either." She paused and took in a deep breath. "The power that y'all possess would corrupt the noblest of hearts. If we would have looked for a volunteer we would have had those that searched for power as the main goal of their lives. Those who seek power can rarely be trusted with it because they are self serving. Think of your presidents, the highest office in your land and only a few have had the best interest of your people in mind. Plus, Docheen was rather taken with the human race, the reasons why are beyond me."

"Then am I suppose to be some kind of servant of the people?" Traven felt a fear of responsibility build deep inside of him.

"Y'all can be whatever you want, Honey." She smiled with a laugh, "Savior, destroyer, or coach potato, or perhaps some dastardly mix of all three."

Traven just sat in silence for a moment being overwhelmed by what she was telling him. He took another nervous sip off his Coke and cleared his throat.

"Will I become evil?" he asked, as she leaned back and knowingly started toying with his head, knowing that is was already a mess.

"True evil is an option, even though you may struggle against it, but it is not a certainty. The things y'all will do will greatly affect the lives of everyone throughout time. For better or for worse those choices are now up to you. Evil can also be a perception. Do people make hard choices that wreck the lives of others to serve the greater good? They sure do, everyday, on every planet and in every time."

"So... you're saying make good choices?"

"On your world people make choices good or bad every moment of every day, same here. What you choose to be as the Keeper is like what you choose to be on Earth, but with far more temptations and consequence than y'all can ever dream."

His mind raced with the fear and trouble of responsibility and several stirring speeches made on the pages of his favorite comic books. This seemed all too much for him. In his head he was still the kid who caught the frogs from the window well and forgot to feed them. Sure they were just frogs, but now all reality was in his aquarium. One slip and he could be viewing the skeletal remains of people, not amphibians. He wanted desperately to resign, but Docheen hadn't given him an out and, from the sounds of it, neither had the Gateway. He decided to switch this topic before his head exploded or he curled up into the fetal position and started sucking his thumb.

"So... can we talk about you?" he asked, hopeful for any diversion he could muster.

"Mah, oh Mah," she smiled, "y'all do have the ability to understand what is important to a girl. There may be hope for you yet. Well," she crossed her arms and began, "Docheen created me and then one day he had the notion to give me a brain. One of his better idea's, though Ah am sure he regretted it from time to time. As to my current form it evolved over time and his travels. One of the first places Docheen went after exploring his planets timeline was the American South. He took quite a liking to it. The moist heat and swamps reminded him of his home as it was meant to be. I reckon it was the reason that he learned to shape shift, that is after he had been shot at for being a swamp monster. He spent a mess of time there. After he took a shine to a little miss from Georgia he came back and changed my voice."

Traven shuttered at the thought of a 300 pound lizard and a human girl making out. He wanted badly to ask more about it but decided to leave it for another time.

"T'was bout that time, in the Gateway's time-stream that he started calling me Brandy as well."

"Why Brandy?" he asked, hoping she would continue down this more pleasant history lesson. "It's not a very southern name."

"He also liked California in the early 70's, there was this song."

Traven was caught off guard and for the first time in the conversation laughed. He knew the song well.

"Oh Ah see," she pouted, "y'all heard it. Well that's why the name Brandy. He used to play it incessantly. Seemed to give him a fair amount of pleasure to tease me with it."

"I've got it on a tape at home," he chimed. "I'll bring it in for you, if you like."

"Oh, we have it, believe me, but Ah am not sure I ever want to hear it again."

"I'm not sure you do either."

They both laughed, which he found comforting.

"Look I don't care what you call me," she said looking at the floor.

"Do you like your name?" Traven asked.

"It's comfortable, as is this form that I have worn for thousands of years," she said, looking deeply at his eyes as if to imply that she had all intentions of keeping the name.

"Well then, far be it from me to change it," he said quickly. "I had to pick my name out of a hat." Though she knew this too, it struck her as funny.

"Thank you," she said, more out of habit than politeness and she got up to leave. It seemed abrupt, as if she had just stopped by to declare that times would run as usual and that him becoming the Keeper was just another appointment. Before he could stop himself the words fell out of his mouth.

"Did you love him?" For a panicked moment he knew that it was not an appropriate question. She merely turned to him and said flatly. "Ah suppose I did. In my own way," and then quickly changing the subject, she warned him very calmly. "But now I am stuck with you, and I believe you need less dangerous trips through the webs if we are both going to survive. Larry has a schedule for ya. Y'all will find the next week to be interesting." Her body melted into the floor without a trace. She was gone.

He sat on the heavy wooden bench and thought about responsibility, becoming evil, and his actions affecting the whole of time. He had barely gotten through his math class last year with a passing grade. What kind of Keeper would he become?

Chapter Five

So This Is The Universe

Things went swimmingly for the next couple of months in the Gateway. For everyday the boy spent on Earth, he spent two, or three in the Gateway. Twice, he spent an entire week. He was starting to miss his friends and realized that the summer vacation on Earth was getting farther away the more time he was in the Gateway. His grades did pick up, Brandy insisted on it. She provided him with AOD tutors so that when he got back he was more than up to speed with his classes. This made his parents happy and at least they stopped asking if he was on the drugs.

The trips through time and space that Brandy allowed him to take were safe, and even fun. He visited Italy when his grandparents were young. Brandy said that it is important to know where you came from so that you could see where you are going. While this sounded like she had been talking to Mo-pa too much, the experience made a deep impression. He always wondered why his grandparents left their home, and now he understood why they left. Everyone was poor and struggling. America seemed the land of opportunity. He even got the chance to drink espresso with some distant relatives, but realized he shouldn't meet his grandparents at least directly. He was afraid he'd alter time in the present, which could mean different grandparents, or none at all.

Would different grandparents mean a different him when he returned home, or even gender? Was that possible? Was it possible that he could mess up his existence completely? There were so many things that he was unsure about with time travel that he started writing down his questions in his sketch book for future clarification. He decided that spying on them couldn't possibly have any long term effects on his life so he worked on both his hiding in trees or bushes and not making a sound skills. He found that he wasn't that bad at either and laughed silently thinking that sitting still and being quiet were the skills that his teachers prayed for him to master. He also found to his surprise that his grandfather had a pet goat that would follow him to and from school. Traven thought of the children's poem, *"Mary Had a Little Lamb,"* and laughed thinking that if Mary had a goat it would have been more interesting because his grandfather's goat acted more like a watch dog. It would even chase his grandfather's friends away to protect him if there was too much horseplay and the goat thought the situation was unsafe for its master. Traven really wanted to ask his grandfather about the goat, but how would he phrase the question? "Hey Grandpa, I was messing around in the fabric of time spying on you and you had a goat. What's up with that?" He decided that probably wouldn't go over well. Later, to his dismay he found that when things became bad enough that the once lively goat became dinner.

His grandmother lived on the other side of the mountain range in a village known as Canischio. Her childhood home was a small stone house which had a milking cow on the first floor while the people slept on the second. Aside from the cow, which Traven found strange, he also was bewildered that the small building's roof was made of impossibly large, somewhat flat, chunks of rock. While the roof functioned well enough to keep them dry it had the added bonus of making a wonderful home for furry critters. His grandmother was a young girl at this point with dark, ankle length hair. She had told him once that as she got older she cut off her hair to sell to a wig maker because they needed the money. As he watched her play, from the safety of a bush, he felt sad that one day she would lose this enchanted mane. This moment made him realize that even his grandmother was once young and spent her time playing games instead of cooking or canning the vegetables from her garden.

He made a girlfriend in China; well, at least he made a friend. It was 217 BC and while she thought he was both strange looking and acting, she seemed to enjoy their conversations, so in his mind it was a heroic start. At one point she even asked him if he was a spirit. He laughed and told her not really, but even this made her unsure if he was or wasn't. Every couple of days in Traven's timeline he would go back to see her. One night she overstepped her bounds and showed him the project the Emperor had decreed be built for which it was her job to fetch water. It was thousands of terra-cotta warriors that would protect him in death. They snuck past the drunken guards and, in the light of the moon, Traven stood face to face with a brightly painted soldier of clay. It was taller than Traven and in its hand it carried a real sword. It was almost hypnotizing in its own intense way and the craftsmanship of the sword called to Traven to reach out and touch it. His friend's eyes grew large in horror as she silently admonished him with lip curls and hand gestures that this was a disrespectful act. Traven withdrew his curious hand and tried very hard not to laugh at the faces she had just made. She grabbed his shoulder tightly and guided him along. Her hand slipped from his shoulder to his hand. The gesture of hand holding was not lost on him, this was the first girl's hand he had ever held. Normally he would have been overjoyed at even this small accomplishment, and would have been, if he wasn't certain that she wasn't only trying to stop him from damaging the rows of warriors or bring attention to the two of them. Each warrior had carved armor and sculpted hair that was pulled up in a top knot. As they crept quietly from section to section it seemed like the sleeping army went on forever and that they were the strange ones for being able to move in this city of frozen citizens. The scene even felt creepy, not only with the threat of being discovered by the guards, but the slight fear that the soldiers might just come to life. There were foot soldiers and archers, but the thing that impressed him the most was the fact that some of these warriors were on life-size clay horses and some horses stood waiting to pull chariots and wagons.

"Yep," he whispered, "if they come to life we are totally dead."

Traven couldn't understand why an Emperor would be so afraid of the afterlife that he would go to such measures. Later, upon voicing his thoughts she warned him that to talk in such a way and not be a spirit would surely get him killed.

It was shortly after this that Brandy warned him he was getting too close to the girl and should cease traveling there. Traven, fearing that he would lose his only human friend he had made while in the Gateway, replied bluntly, "I thought you said I could do what I want as the Keeper?"

The moment the statement came out of his mouth he knew that it sounded too forward and wished he would have rephrased his question better.

"Y'all can certainly do what ya want," she said, stomping her foot, which Traven noticed that the light from the bottom of her foot became brighter when she was angry. "But y'all might want to take a little time to learn how to act as a Keeper before you make any more mistakes."

This wasn't the first time Brandy had purposely used his last mistake with the bear to remind him that while he was the Keeper, he wasn't beyond making life-threatening blunders. Being almost eaten would have been reason enough to listen, but he was also afraid of upsetting Brandy. He apologized and left for his practice session with Mo-pa. Larry caught up with him on his way and stated that while he agreed with Brandy it didn't mean that Traven couldn't visit the girl again when he understood his new found powers better.

The word responsibility kept replaying in Traven's mind and he wondered what a long-term contact with someone from a different time line might do to history. Trying to figure out the outcome to this question was abruptly halted as the door to the practice room opened. Though he felt like he might be losing his friend, he was glad just to be clearing his mind and focusing on his lesson.

France during the Impressionist movement made as big of an impression on Traven as it did history. He though that perhaps he would study history when he got older because now he could live it and understand it from more than just silent pages and dry lectures. Plus it would give him a reply when his parents asked that age old question, "What do you want to do with your life?" His standard reply was stolen from a Twisted Sister album, "I want to Rock!" which was followed by energetic air guitar and head shaking in different directions from both he and his parents. While the Impressionists knew nothing of rock'n'roll they knew quite a bit about rebellion. They had gone up against the norms of their time and carved a great big spot for themselves in history. Their paintings changed the way art would be viewed forever. While the back story was impressive, Traven found it hard to wrap his mind around the concept that this type of painting was rebellious. Why even his mother had an Impressionist painting in her living room, well, a copy that is, and how rebellious could it be if your parents liked it. Nevertheless, Traven got to meet some of the greatest painters of that time, and felt honored just to have the experience.

Monet, Degas, and Toulouse Lautrec, were party animals by any standards, though Degas was a bit of a grump. They all called him the Funny American and were amazed at how well he spoke French. This made him laugh, because his father had an obsession with languages that Traven had never shared. Hanging out with them made him take up painting, though only while he was in the Gateway. He would never be brave enough to show the masters of Impressionism his weak attempts with the brush. One day they managed to pry Traven's sketchbook from him and started to critique it. Monet told him that he too had started drawing cartoons in the beginning. While Traven was trying to decide if this was a compliment, insult, or just a statement Degas launched into his beliefs.

"The masters must be copied again and again," he offered sternly, unimpressed by Traven's sketches, "only after given every indication of being a good copiest can you reasonably be given leave to draw a radish from nature."

Traven took the advice hard but tried to tell himself that he was both young and had a long way to go in his art. He also tried to remind himself that Degas was very opinionated and was not beyond starting an argument just to get up and leave in the middle of it. Traven loved to watch them paint in Monet's garden. Monet said that he was good for only two things in life; painting and gardening. From looking at the garden it was obvious that the old master could easily combine both his skills, and many of his paintings were emotional records of the things he loved to do best. One of the best parts of these days came when the painting was over and Monet started to cook. While Monet said he was only good for two things it quickly became apparent to Traven that he cooked just as well as he did the other two.

After they were stuffed and almost sleepy from food, cigars would be lit and the painters were hit with their second wind. While Traven declined both the cigars and drinks that they constantly offered him, he was not beyond tagging along for a night on the town. Cabarets and dance halls became a blur as one turned into the next and night usually ended with Traven escorting them back to their homes at the crack of dawn. The painters tried to keep a low profile on their less honorable activities, that is with the exception of Toulouse.

Toulouse was constantly trying to persuade Traven to venture with him into the bordellos under the pretense to draw.

He said that drawing from a professional model was like drawing a dummy and that these women were real. On his advice Traven did follow Toulouse once, but found the women to be more hormonally interesting than artistically. He bowed out halfway through his drawing worried that the women might just convince him to do something other than draw and that they might just possess traits that couldn't be cured, even in the Gateway's med lab.

One morning he arrived in the landing area after a long night in Paris. He was greeted by the image of Brandy forming from the floor. She looked very cross and tilted her head to the right with a pout. Under Traven's arm was a small wrapped painting that Monet had given him.

"What?" he said, appearing clueless to her incriminating look.

"Y'all going to put that painting up where your mama's use to be," she stated, in an accusing voice.

"I was not," he replied, in an almost believable tone.

"Were too."

"Hey, he just gave me a painting, what was I gonna do? Say no thank you, Monet, my mother has this one."

"You could have declined."

"It's a Monet!" he stressed. "Besides, from the looks of it Docheen nabbed quite a few Van Gogh's," and then as if realizing that he now owned some of the most expensive paintings on Earth quickly asked, "Hey what levels are they on again?"

"Docheen replaced what he took, even if they were copies from the Gateway they still effected how others viewed the world. The moment you accepted it and brought it here it ceased to exist on your planet."

"What do you mean?" He asked in confusion.

"Because it fell into your arms, your planet's current timeline has no history of it. In fact, as we speak your mother has a different painting over her couch and has never seen the one you are now holding. Y'all have made it so your little private joke taint even funny no more ."

"Ok," he replied, "I wasn't trying to make a joke, but I'll sell a copy to whoever was going to buy it." The look in Brandy's face softened. "I can keep it, right?" His tone changed as if he was the little kid with the puppy that followed him home.

"Of course ya can," Brandy stated slowly melting into the floor. "You're the Keeper."

As her body disappeared without a trace, Larry flew up and took his place at Traven's side.

"You were gonna plathe it over your mother'th couch, weren't you?"

"Would have been damn funny," he stated as they headed off to find the Van Gogh's.

As if Earth's past wasn't amazing enough, other planets were mind-blowing. Fujitor was a planet of breathable water with people that lived both on the small land masses and in the sea. They had the ability to form legs on the land and a single fin-like tail when they took to the water. While he wondered if they were the reason that human's had stories of mermaids, their beautiful markings looked like no drawings he had ever seen. They also informed him they had never heard of a place known as Earth. Traven, who had always considered himself to be a decent swimmer realized that to travel underwater took a lot of effort, and in comparison to just about everything on the planet he was really slow. The people were very generous with their food and their help with his travels from one part of their planet to the other. They would literally let him grab ahold of their shoulders and hitch a ride. While the raw fish repulsed him at first, he ate it out of respect and realized that it was quite tasty, in its own way. The only drawback to these trips to Fujitor were that he always had to shower when he returned as he smelled of fish, and the hanging upside down till the breathable water drained out of his lungs was really unnerving. Traven asked Brandy if there was an AOD that could teach him how to swim better. She said there was, but that you could only do so much with human limitations.

A Lifetime In Time

Topacies was a beautiful, unspoiled planet with rock formations that floated in the sky. Larry told him that this wasn't as strange as it appeared and was common on planets that had large amounts of metal and had big electrical storms, though it was usually in just a few areas of the planet where the rock formations occurred. The creatures on Topacies were like none he had ever seen. Big frog-like beasts with three eyes roamed the wetlands and giant fruit bats with pancake-like heads littered the skies and nested in the floating rocks or giant trees with multi-colored leaves. Traven would often find himself staring at the clouds as they formed images in his head of dragons or cartoon faces of old men. He hadn't looked at clouds for years and the peacefulness of the planet always left him feeling rested and relaxed. Mo-pa even allowed them to conduct their practice there. Well, Traven practiced to a holographic image of Mo-pa from a high tech gadget that he found hard to pronounce. He found it strange that the old man would decline a vacation, but he wasn't about to question him for fear of a long and incomprehensible explanation. Then he remembered that his teacher was existing on borrowed time.

The sunsets on this planet were unbelievable in warm rich colors that made him reach for his paint brush on many occasions and left him playing with the idea of bringing the Impressionist masters to see what a real painter could do. Before he could start the sharing of his idea with Brandy she told him, "No, you can't take the Impressionists." It was as if she read his mind again. Even after Larry had assured him that it was not within her ability to perform that carnival trick, Traven still felt skeptical. He knew that being the Keeper wasn't going to be easy with Brandy playing mother hen, and hoped that she would loosen up once he got a few more trips under his belt.

If his training and studies went well, the fifth day of each Gateway cycle he would be allowed to go to a planet called Dirgewhere. He kept wondering why it was a matter of being allowed, after all, wasn't he the Keeper? Shouldn't he get to choose when he wanted to go to places? He understood that Brandy wanted safe trips, but now she was telling him when he could go as well. Mo-pa explained it to him like this.

"If a child picks what he wants to eat, he eats sweets. Sweets will not make him stronger, it will not provide what that child needs mentally or physically. When the child is grown he eats as he wishes, but his wishes will not be for sweets if he learns the importance of all food."

Dirgewhere was Traven's candy. It was unlike anything he had even dreamed of, for these beings form of communication was music. Sadly, he was told that he couldn't sing that well, though they were impressed that he would try. His lack of singing skills didn't stop him from going to the concerts. They were an advanced race of tall thin people with incredible lung capacity. Being an advanced race with a flair for entertainment they had become a magnet for beings from all over the galaxy. A Vegas in the stars without the gambling. Millions would come to hear the concerts. During intermissions Traven spent his time watching the people and buying concert shirts that he could never wear on Earth, at least without drawing questions from his friends. This was one of his favorite planets, not just for the music, but because no one thought twice about Larry accompanying him. At least on this planet he didn't have to be alone. It turned out that Larry sang worse than he did, the Dirgeinites said that it was because he had no soul, though Traven blamed the lisp.

While it seemed to Traven that Brandy was really the one in command, they had started to fall into a comfortable routine. She would meet with him once a day, usually as he ate dinner unless it was the pizza place. Traven couldn't understand why she didn't like the pizza place, she never ate anyway, but he wasn't about to make an issue out of it. He really just enjoyed looking at her, all of her bossiness aside she was beautiful and he was a teenage boy. Unlike the AODs, Brandy was brimming with personality even when it was a grumpy one. He tried to question her about Do-cheen and she would reply in quick short answers as if she didn't

really want to talk about him. This made him wonder what had happened between the two of them. Was she mad at Docheen for dying, or that he had left a teenage human in charge? It was safer asking her about his role though even then she would sometimes make her answers abrupt. To the questions in his sketchbook he wrote the answers she provided, while it always appeared that the answers gave her a headache.

"No, ya will not turn into a girl if y'all change the events in history and no longer have the same parents or grandparents."

"No, ya cannot cease to exist if you accidentally run over yourself with a truck at age two."

"No, if ya gave yourself a scar as a child one would not appear on your forehead at any time."

" No, the Keeper is the head of his time flow."

"Yes, if y'all cut yourself on the forehead outside of the Gateway the cut would be on your forehead tomorrow unless ya sought medical attention. Even if you stepped out of the Gateway to a time before you cut yourself, the cut would still be there. The present only changes once y'all step back into it from making a change in the past. Otherwise, whatever time line ya walk flows at your rate and would continue to flow at that same rate as you perceive it while y'all are in it. Ya can not know what the future of any action was until y'all came back to the Gateway."

"No," she said in a completely frustrated tone, "stuffing the ballot boxes with Walt Disney as a write-in presidential candidate isn't funny, even if he has been dead for twenty years!"

"No, he is not frozen, not even in other realities!"

He also learned that asking about other realities was a topic that she didn't enjoy or felt he was ready for. She would flinch at these questions and would quickly redirect the conversations with words or a stern look. For the most part he tried hard to end their meetings with talk about her or less dangerous topics like music, which she seemed to both enjoy and know quite a bit about. After his nonstop raving about the concerts he had been to Brandy took pity on him and introduced him to the music library. He refused his deep urge to play the song of her namesake knowing that it would most likely make her upset. Because of this discovery the Gateway had taken on the feel of an eclectic radio station. Oh, he tried music from other planets, but the sound track of Earth was the main format, with an occasional tune from Dirgewhere. Earth music that he never would have listened to before now reminded him of the places he had been. These pieces were also in rotation though usually followed by Black Sabbath as a pallet cleanser. The only time music would stop is when he tried to sleep or during practice with Mo-pa. Mo-pa said that music was distracting and caused the mind to focus only on it, but in Traven's spare time he turned the old man on to the band Quiet Riot. He found it hilarious to hear Mo-pa humming *Cum on feel the noise.*

The thoughts of his responsibility to time would creep in now and again and even into his dreams. One repeating dream had the image of Docheen's heartstone being smashed and as it erupted light became sound and the sound became a warning. *It's all in your hands,* followed by a strange chorus of, *the universe is screwed.*

He hated this dream with a passion and even more so when it came in the middle of the night and he had to fight his thoughts to rediscover the land of sleep. Brandy had said he could be whatever he wanted, good, evil or a smorgasbord of both. He wondered why she wouldn't care if he was evil or if the need for evil was inevitable. His parents had raised him to do what was right, he just hoped that he would be able to tell what right was.

One day after what seemed like a long day at high school, he stepped into the Gateway to find that Larry, Mo-pa, and Brandy were waiting for him. He had just picked up the latest Alice Cooper album, and was hoping to get them to give it a listen. Brandy would point out later that the album was already in the music library and had been before Mr. Cooper had even been born in Traven's timeline. A greedy look came over his face. He hadn't even thought to check his favorite artist section because he figured he had bought everything that had been released.

Today with their static body language they appeared as if music was the farthest thing from their minds. Larry held in his robotic hand a long woven cloak and a face mask that obstructed most of the face except the eyes. Traven glanced at the population of the Gateway and in a worried voice asked, "What's going on?"

"Today Dearheart, y'all get to meet your new trainer," Brandy said, her accent becoming thicker when the mood struck her.

"What... where is he? Should I meet him in the practice room?" he asked, looking at Larry for an answer.

"No," said Larry. "Ith not a he, but a thee, and you have to go get her."

"Well, its gonna be more than just getting her," said Brandy. "Y'all have to convince her."

Traven looked worried.

"What do you mean I have to convince her?" he asked.

Mo-pa stepped forward and spoke.

"She will want something in return. She is one of the best. More importantly, she can be trusted to keep your secret. Whatever her price, you agree to pay." Mo-pa had a nervous look on his face.

"With money?" Traven asked, feeling very confused.

"Most likely she will want a favor," said Brandy, trying to calm Traven's uncertainty. "Honey, the skills she will teach will keep you alive, just be agreeable. You reckon you can manage it?"

"Yeah, I suppose," Traven agreed, painfully aware that Brandy was talking to him like a child. "But what if she is like in the Mafia and wants me to whack someone?"

The three looked uneasily at each other and then said in unison. "Do it."

"Wait a minute, I can't kill somebody." Traven laughed nervously.

"Y'all did before," Brandy said.

A Lifetime In Time

"That's not fair," said Traven, who was still having many, many bad dreams reliving that moment of semiconsciousness. "I never wanted to kill Docheen and didn't really have a choice."

At that moment Larry interrupted.

"What I believe thee ith trying to thay ith that the power you are in charge of ith tho vatht that you have to weigh your importanthe over the cotht of otherth thurvival."

"What makes my life more important than anyone else?" Traven said angrily.

"We have been over this," Brandy reminded him, in one of her sweeter tones. "While most people's lives affect others, your life can affect everyone's, not just little ole me, but the whole of time and space."

This stunned the boy as it always had and unthinkingly he took the garment Larry was holding. As his brain tried to mull the concept over, he thought, *It's going to happen, I'm going to have to start weighing the lives of others. I might have to kill someone. I'm not ready for that.*

"H... how will I find her?" he stuttered.

"Thee'll find you," said Larry. "Her name ith Thealand, thee ith from the planet Fecha. Thee ith an Atrill, and like all of her people, thee will look like thee belongs in the muthical *'Cats'*."

"So... her name is Sealand?"

"No," said Larry a bit confused, "her name ith Thealand."

"Thealand?" he questioned for the second time.

"That'th what I thaid."

"Just find an access to their underworld," Brandy interrupted, hoping to stop this sad poor man's version of *Who's on first*, and reassured him with a smile, "it will look like a square manhole cover. Pry off the grate and go down as far as the shaft takes you. She will spot you from your body language. Oh, and before she hits you too many times, Dearheart, tell her that you're the Keeper."

Traven did not like the sound of that at all.

"The Mathk," said Larry, "ith to make your breathing eathier, you won't need it in the underworld, but it will keep the other Atrillth from thpotting that you're not one of them. Keep it on ath well ath the hood on the garment."

Mo-pa slipped Traven's Calleash in his hand and nodded as Traven realized that the Calleash might be his only way to avoid a beating and nodded back. He tucked it into his sleeve finding that there was no possible way to get to his pockets in this outfit.

The doorway opened and giving his crew one last look, he stepped through.

Fecha was a mess of a planet. There were no plants just endless rows of giant block buildings reaching to the sky. Traven thought it was night, but in reality it was the middle of the day. A thick red-gray haze blocked out most of the sunlight and left the world with two dim orbs in the sky which long ago were seen as beautiful suns, but had now taken on the appearance of dirty moons. A gray-brown soot fell from the sky and left the equivalent of dust drifts in the streets. Tracks from large public vehicles cut deep paths through the drifting mess and a few figures dressed as he was wandered through the street and disappeared into the shadows. What light there was came from vertical poles that must have been streetlights. The damaged lights gave little or no illumination, but luckily for him there was just barely enough light present from his mask to make out an entrance to the underworld that had been uncovered by the winds. He looked in both directions to make sure no one was watching, removed the cover and climbed down.

The underworld was really a sewer system, the biggest one Traven had ever seen. It was large enough to comfortably race semi's through, that is, if they had the trucks to race. The walls were lined with a strange material that Traven had never seen, and when he pushed against it there was a faint clicking sound. It felt like he was pushing thousands of paper-thin tape cassette buttons though it was a solid plastic-like sheet. Lights from the top of his mask grew brighter when he thought he needed more light and brought clearer vision to the darkness. The lights in the sewer were few and far between which made everything look like a black and white movie that had been poorly colorized with a dingy yellow glow. He backed away from the entrance and just stood for a little while, tense and waiting to be attacked. After what seemed to be ten minutes he decided to start walking. At least while walking he felt he was doing something other than just being a target. The sewer seemed free of debris but this didn't help it to smell any better. He then thought about his hand touching the wall and wanted badly to wash it. He had almost started to laugh at the fact that the place smelled like a cat box when he realized something was coming at him from behind. In the same way that he had felt the Calleash Mo-pa had directed at this head during practice he sensed something even less friendly than that was about to hit him. He moved and the figure landed with less sound than a ghost. It pivoted instantly and he was caught in the face mask by an elbow and then in the stomach by a fist with the turn of the same arm. Bits of broken mask and light fell to the ground in random dance of percussive patters. Falling back in pain he sent his Calleash flying. The figure caught it the second before it hit her in the face. This stopped her for a moment which was enough time for Traven to suck in some breath from his wounded stomach.

"What the hell... this is a Calleash!" she yelled. "Who are you?"

"I'm... the Keeper," Traven struggled to say. "You... must... be... Thealand."

"You're not any Keeper I've ever seen," she said, giving him the once over and rolling her eyes. "At least you don't move like one."

"I'm the new guy," he said, as he tried to stand.

She abruptly knocked him back onto the ground with a kick he didn't even see.

"Hey, would you... stop... kicking my... ass!" he yelled.

"Why?" she asked, pacing around him as if he were a mouse having a really bad day and a bleak future, "I don't know you."

"I'm Traven, pleased to freaking meet you."

She threw another kick toward his head. He surprised himself and her by sensing it and blocking it. The force of the kick caused him to roll into an upright, but painful position. Suddenly there was a loud distant rumble with the sound of a million clicks. She looked at him as if deciding what to do. She then threw a wrestling hold on him and lifted him easily into a small hole in the wall. The hole that was clearly designed for one person, there was a control panel with a single red button with symbols that he couldn't understand. It was all he could make out from his one working headlight, the only headlight that she had not smashed in their fight. As she pushed the button, a clear shield rolled up over the hole pinning them both very tightly together. Her body was soft and warm against his and while he definitely didn't like girls that beat him like a geek school boy, this moment was the most erotic encounter he had ever had in his short life.

He shook his head as a brief chill went through his body. His already damaged face mask broke free from his head and wedged between the top of his arm and the door. A mammoth flood swept through the sewer shaking the foundation and their bodies as they touched. He wanted to wave his hand, to appear back in the safety of the Gateway, but his arms were pinned by the lack of space. Their legs were intertwined and her muscular legs pressed against his almost as if she was trying to best him in a wrestling match. Her chest on the other hand did not feel at all like it was trying to subdue him, at least not aggressively. In fact, it was soft and he could feel her heart beat in unison with his through her clothing. They held each other closely as the watery sludge ripped its way past the questionable safety of their cocoon which heaved under the pressure of the sewage.

I don't want to die! his mind screamed, *I really, really, really, don't want to die in an ocean of crap.*

When it was over he breathed a sigh of relief as a flood of air flowed through the tunnel blowing the majority of the moisture away. He looked deeply into her eyes. They were bright green and rather human for a cat person, though the pupils were only

slightly vertical. Her skin was a golden yellow, and her hair was a light sandy brown feather cut, that reminded him of how the girls wore their hair when he was in middle school. From the lobes of her large pointed ears hung two large brass earrings that caught the beam of light and glimmered. She definitely had the cat-like nose, although it seemed to be more of a discoloration, like the way Peter Criss had his nose painted for the band Kiss. She definitely didn't have a muzzle and with a little make-up and an ear tuck, could have easily passed for human. Over his current fear for his life his eyes and other parts of his anatomy agreed that she was very cute. He felt this strange insane urge, like he should kiss her, but before he could do anything stupid, she pressed the release button.

The door opened and she sent him flying into the sewer with a knee to the groin. Any romantic thoughts he might have been having were now gone and he cursed her with a string of swear words that neither fit together nor made sense. She laughed as she walked circles around him, toying with him as if he were a mouse.

"Well, aren't you the brave pup," she said almost sensing his thoughts. "Why are you here?"

"I'm supposed to be offering you a deal," he moaned.

"The last deal I made with a Keeper helped lead to the mess Fecha is in right now. I'm not very keen on repeating my mistakes."

She aimed her foot at his head and pulled it away missing him, but causing him to twitch the way the school bullies always did.

"Look, damn it," he tried to stand, but slumped down into the dampness of the sewer floor. "All Brandy wants from you is for you to teach me how to fight."

"The story is always the same," she said. "I must say you're in even greater need of my talents than the last Keeper was." She continued pacing. "But the real question of the hour is what do you want pup? Do you want me to teach you to fight?"

"I want to kick you in the head," he said, causing her to laugh.

"Not much chance in that pup." She stopped pacing and stooped down to look him in the eyes.

He felt as if this might be the moment that she would kill him, but instead her voice changed slightly.

"What's in it for me?" she asked, as if she just might bargain, but then threw another fake kick toward him.

"Why the hell do you keep doing that!" he screamed.

"Oh," she said doing it again, "That's just for me. I'm just amusing myself." A dark smile of satisfaction spread across her face. "I'm sorry, I got a bit distracted. Where were we? Oh yes, what's in it for me?"

"Whatever you want," he coughed.

"Well, well," she said, starting to pace again. She played with her long hair. "I want..." Then she paused pretending to try and decide on her reward for her future services. "I want you to save my people."

"How am I going to do that?" he asked, wondering what that meant or why they needed saving aside from really bad housing.

"Oh I'm sure you will figure out something, after all pup, you are the Keeper, such as you are, and we have lots of time outside of time for you to work your miracles." She roughly helped him to stand. "Come on," she said. "Open your door."

Within the few moments it took him to stand and focus, they were gone.

Timothy John Vaulato

Chapter Six

Masterpieces And Other Beatings

Week after week passed in the Gateway, quickly becoming months. This was the longest time Traven had been away from Earth and, in truth, he started to lose count of the days since he had last set foot on his home planet or heard his friend Brian make lewd comments about passing girls.

The lessons with Mo-pa continued, and since he saw a point to them, he was starting to enjoy or at least tolerate them. He was even getting his Calleash to hit one target and then hit another on the same throw. It worked every third or fourth time. Once in a great while it would return to him as it did to Mo-pa. Just as he was starting to feel proud of himself, Mo-pa showed him that a true Master could hit twenty-one targets with two Calleash, throwing them at the same time and getting them to return to his hands. Traven stood there dumbfounded. Mo-pa told him again it was all about freeing your mind and for the first time added, you also need a bit of geometry and luck. On a whim Traven made Mo-pa follow him to the Gateway's game room and introduced him to the game of pool. Mo-pa found the game too simple and after clearing the table three times in a row on the break shot Mo-pa was bored. Traven was entertaining the idea of using his training to become a pool shark. He wanted to have money like his friends with jobs. The truth was he had access to an immeasurable fortune due to the Gateway, but how would he explain his sudden wealth to his parents? They watched him like a hawk, and since he earned most of his money from doing chores around the house, they had a pretty good idea of his income. He had already brought back most of the stack of bills he had snatched from the Gateway. Oh, he kept about a hundred dollars, but quickly spent it on comic books and future concert tickets. He had been collecting comics since second grade and with his massive collection a few more wouldn't be noticed. It was like hiding a tree in the forest. Comics had been his refuge since he was very young, constantly designing new superhero's and short stories about their adventures. Now he was living an adventure. Still, most superhero's had some sort of income and he had next to nothing in the way of explainable cash. No, the thought of being a pool shark was really out of the question, it wasn't something his parents would look upon fondly.

Though training with Mo-pa was beginning to take off, his training with Thealand was abysmal. At the end of the first day of punching and kicking, he was so sore that all he could do was crawl into bed and sleep. The day after that, there were lessons on blocking punches and kicks. This day ended with Traven in the med lab. By the end of the first week he was fighting AODs that were programed by the practice room to hurt him severely. They were mostly human thugs, and Thealand said that in the upcoming weeks he would have to fight multiple attackers with various weapons. She constantly told him that long hair was a disadvantage in a fight, and on occasion showed him why. Yes, being thrown by your hair was definitely not an advantage in any fight, but it didn't change Traven's want of long hair. When he asked Thealand about her long hair and over sized earrings being a disadvantage, she replied that she was good enough and that for her they were not.

The only time that he came close to enjoying training was when they trained on the planet of the floating rocks, Topacies. Topacies was quiet and the scenery was always breathtaking. She used this time to teach him how to track animals. She said it was a lot like tracking people, though people tended to leave bigger clues. She reveled in hunting wildlife. This was the first time he was made to kill anything, other than Docheen. At least with Docheen the memory was mostly blurry, with these creatures the image was crystal clear. He felt a compassion toward the weird creatures they would hunt. He didn't like this experience at all, and even less when she made him clean the animals for dinner. The creatures that they hunted were the smaller three eyed frog beasts from the edges of the swamp, the bigger ones were far too fast for Traven to even get close to. Seeing the insides of the once living creatures left him unable to eat. She called him weak.

Brandy and Thealand seemed to get along as old friends do. And being friends meant that Brandy was around more of the time as a physical form and spent less time playing the all seeing ghost. Traven was glad to see her, but was ashamed that almost every time she saw him, he was being beat up or rushed to the med lab on a stretcher. The two girls were always chit-chatting about something, but Traven could never make out what the conversation was, mostly because it seemed they only talked when he was in pain. In his mind they were sharing a secret or talking about how pathetic he was. He turned away and took another dive deeper into depression as Larry's med-doubles mended his bones with expert care.

At least the Gateway had what he considered real food. As the training continued over these long months Traven fell into a routine. He would take a couple hours off each day to play his guitars. Sadly, he found that his swollen hands had trouble finding their way around a fret board. During these times he would try to watch old movies, but he found that it was hard to get involved with the stories. The training was so painful and he was so bad at it, that it left him dreading the next session. When he thought about it too much he'd find himself on the verge of tears. He didn't understand how he could have so much power and still be so powerless.

When he wasn't feeling sorry for himself he would paint. This was the only time his mind could concentrate on something other than training. His painting took a completely different direction than he had started with the Impressionists. Tranquil scenes of daily life or pretty girls playing instruments were replaced by abstracts of dark colors and violent brush strokes.

His body started to change as well. This was the first real muscle definition that he had ever had and it seemed to come from nowhere. When he thought about it he realized that this was the most physically active he had ever been in his life. The swimming, the training, and even his workouts with Mo-pa had gotten him to use muscles that no couch potato would have ever used. *At least this summer I won't have to go to the pool with a T-shirt on,* he thought. He normally was ashamed of his chest as it had always appeared as if it was in search of a gender. This made him feel better about his body, especially since he considered himself a leader in the dough boy club. He would catch quick glimpses of himself in the mirror, but wouldn't look too long for fear that the ever present Brandy would be watching or worse, form out of the floor with some sort of comment.

Thealand and he would never talk unless it was about training. He would look at her and feel stirrings that any teenage boy would have for the opposite sex, but he hated her for the way she treated him. She was strong and muscular beneath her skintight, gray training outfit which left little to the imagination. She would constantly wear an off-white turtleneck, which he found strange because he himself had asked Brandy to control the temperature; he liked it warm. He had wanted to ask her about the shirt, but every time he had a question she made him feel like an idiot. Larry said that turtlenecks were the shirt of choice on Fecha because they kept the planet's ever present dust off one's neck. Like cats, Atrills were rather finicky about hygiene.

A Lifetime In Time

When she would demonstrate a move he watched her intently. Many times his mind would wander to when she had saved him from the flood back in the sewers of Fecha. Well, at least the moment before she kicked him in the groin. As a gesture of friendship he tried to introduce her to some of Earth's music. She just stared at him angrily and said that she was not there for entertainment. If there was anyone colder in the universe, Traven had not yet met them.

One day she came to drag him away from his painting. He had set up a separate room just off the stage in his bedroom so that he could paint if he didn't want to play music or sleep. He was so engrossed with the image that he had lost track of time. The music was blaring as he hit the canvas with a six inch wide brush of brilliant blue. He didn't even notice Thealand walking behind him as the song climaxed. He screamed almost in key with the lyrics. Traven was so into the flow of what he was doing and the music that when she tapped him on the shoulder he spun around instinctively and smacked her across the face with the wet brush. The left side of her face was completely blue, as was some of the right. She crouched down to try and wipe the stinging pigment from her eyes, but only managed to make it worse by smearing it across the rest of her face. In a panic he tried to apologize over the blaring music, but when her green eyes opened in the middle of an impressionist seascape he knew he was in trouble. She sprang at him knocking him into his large canvas, and spilling his supplies everywhere. As they landed on the ground in a splash of paint his knee came up to block her attack. His arms countered her blows and with every bit of strength he could muster he amazingly pushed her way. As they stood both canvas and floor were coated and she slipped. Though flailing wildly, she couldn't regain her balance and crashed back to the ground. In a moment of complete defiance he took the opening she had left him and whacked her with several open gallon cans of white and gray paint. Her lighting fast reflex's slowed due to a lack of steady footing that made her question each movement as she tried once again to stand. As her last option became clear she jumped at him again. They slipped into a wrestling match that covered them both with paint leaving an image of the fight where Traven's masterpiece use to be. All of the holds she tried to place on him were useless due to the paint and Traven wiggling like a greased pig, which only served to make her more angry. As the music ended Thealand gained the upper hand and straddled his chest, pinning his arms with her knees. At that moment he truly believed that he was going to experience the most painful painting session he had ever had. One strange thought popped into his head and as it did it also came out of his mouth.

"Is this..." he questioned, "suffering for your art?"

For reasons beyond him Thealand froze. She stared at him for a moment, and then at her hands. Her long hair fell in a blue-gray mess in front of her face, and her body started shaking. He thought for a moment that she was either going to cry or explode. It soon became clear that she was fighting with herself not to laugh. The harder she tried the more her body shook till finally she fell off of him, laid back on the canvas and burst out laughing. The laugh came like a tidal wave, first loud and then even louder. Her high pitched laughter inspired Traven to do the same, and soon they were both doubled over holding their stomachs with tears in their eyes. When the laughter would start to subside one of them would snort and the whole thing started over again. Finally, when it had finished, when the moment had run its course, Thealand carefully rose to her feet and walked to the door. She turned to him and said, "I don't know what you've learned pup, but you've learned something."

The door opened and over her shoulder she yelled, "Practice will start in an hour if I can get this damn paint off." Peeling a thin paint brush from her earring, she threw it to the floor and left.

Traven didn't really know what to make of their fight. She left his room almost smiling and this new look on her face almost disturbed him. If she wasn't angry now he thought that could very well change when she tried to get the paint off of her. Even with the Gateway's advanced cleaning methods, getting the oil paint off of himself wasn't fun. The solvents left his eyes red and his skin raw. He pictured her cursing the paint on her skin and then cursing him. He thought about going home to Earth and hiding out for a while, but as his time went forward so did the time in the Gateway, and he knew that she would figure out he had fled. His only choice was to face her. As he went back to the scene of the fight it had already been cleaned and the canvas gone. He assumed that Brandy, or the cleaning drones had played art critic and unmade his battered masterpiece. As he left the room he was met by Larry, who was buzzing around excitedly.

"Tho Bawth, what happened in there?" Larry asked.

"Don't you know? You're part of the Gateway." Traven replied.

"Jutht because I'm part of it doethn't mean that I know all that Brandy doeth. When you get down to it, I'm really a theparate thystem. Oh, the'll let me know thingth that are important, but only what thee feelth ith important."

"Sorry, I just assumed," he said, trying to dry his still damp hair by running his hands through it and then rubbing the wetness on his pant legs.

"Thee was a meth and how do I thay it? You're thtill walking." There was a bit of pride in Larry's voice as if he was a proud father awaiting a report card that he already knew was good news.

"She surprised me and I accidentally hit her with my paint brush."

"You got in a firtht hit?" Larry stopped dead in the air. "That'th impothible."

"Oh thanks a lot," said Traven, feeling insulted that even the floating metal ball had no faith in him.

"What I mean, Bawth," said Larry, trying to soften his comment, "thee doesn't get thurpristhed, at leatht not ath long ath I've known her."

"Why not?" asked Traven.

"Because thee'th that good. You may not believe it, Bawth, but I think you've imprethed her."

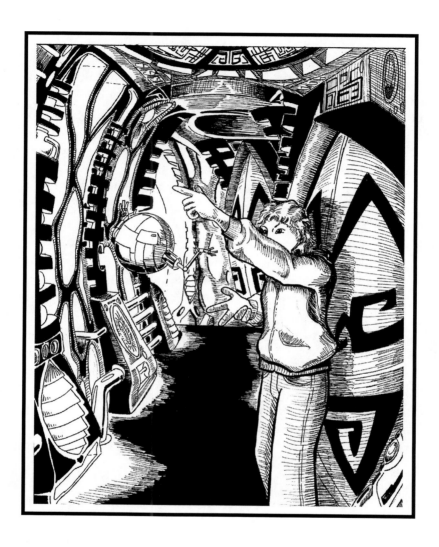

"You mean I've pissed her off. Christ, she's going to beat the hell out of me." Traven stopped and slumped against the light blue vein-like walls of the Gateway's hall.

"Lithten, if you won't tell her," Larry looked left to right as if afraid that someone might hear him, "thee athked Brandy for your painting."

"My painting? You mean the one that we were both wearing?"

"Yeth." Larry beamed.

"She probably wants to set it on fire and I'm next." Traven started walking again.

"Then why would thee have it thent to her room?" Larry's words stopped the boy again.

"She has a room?"

He had never really thought about it. Why wouldn't she have a room, he got one easily enough. The place had started to seem like a hotel for the bizarre. He mentally chastised himself for thinking that like a cat, she would find a warm heating vent to curl up next to.

"Why would she keep it? That's just weird."

By this time the two had come to the practice room. Before the door opened Larry let out what sounded like a desperate plea.

"Let me know what happenth."

"You sound like a little old lady," Traven said as the door opened and Larry flew off.

Thealand stood in the middle of the room wearing one of the headsets that were used to create things in the Gateway. In front of her were three AODs. They looked like human bruisers, the kind where school portraits and mug photos were interchangeable. Immediately Traven guessed that the pay back for the painting incident was on its way. *I bet she hung the painting up to remind her not to drop below a certain level of bitchiness,* he thought. He entered the room and she looked toward him with an almost half smile. He noticed for the first time that her almost smile was a crooked one. The kind that Elvis had, although on her it looked good. He wanted to ask her to say, "Where's my jelly donut," with an Elvis accent, but he knew that would be push-ing it. Was this almost smile of hers a smile of revenge or was she finally going to treat him as if he wasn't one of the animals she enjoyed hunting?

Her hair was damp and back in a ponytail and her clothes had either been miraculously cleaned or replaced by new ones. Her eyes were slightly red from the chemicals used to remove the paint. The green in her eyes had become more intense from the laughter inspired crying, the way eyes sometimes do after some-thing traumatic has happened.

"Well," he said in a huff, "now what?"

She ignored his bad attitude and proceeded with the lesson. Not once did she lose her half smile, so in Traven's mind this was going to be bad.

"Today," she said, "we are going to start with multiple attack-ers." She took off the head-phones and positioned herself in the middle of the three AODs. "The one behind me has a knife, the one in front of me a gun, and the one to the side of me a club. Watch and learn pup." She took in a breath and said, "begin."

As the man lifted the gun her hands shot out and crossed each other at his wrist. This made a loud crunching noise and the gun dropped to the ground. Her right leg shot straight back and the cracking of the knife wielding man's spine echoed in the room. She then pivoted as the man with the club swung down at her. She dodged, grabbed his wrist from the over swing, and holding his wrist tightly in her right hand, used the flat of her left hand to make the man's elbow bend the wrong direction.

"Any questions?" she asked, dropping the thugs broken arm.

Her half smile became a full smile. This was the first time Traven had seen her full smile, that is without being covered in paint, and it threw him off. She was hot when she was angry, but with a smile she could pass as a completely different person; warm, beautiful, and very confusing. He realized he was staring at her.

"Yeah, how do I do that? I mean the elbow thing we've covered, but how do I back-kick someone without getting a knife in the leg. I can't even tell you what that trick with the gun was."

"Reset one," she said, and the AOD with the gun stood back up.

For the next fifteen minutes they worked on disarming the gun with both hands. First slowly then faster. The next fifteen minutes they worked on blocking the gun with one hand and crushing the throat with the other as an option. He learned the kick to the knife man was all about speed, though both tricks that worked on the gun worked equally as well on the knife as long as they were attacking from the front. The man with the stick went down easy. By the end of the session, Traven was performing at fifty percent the speed that she had. Even at fifty percent of her speed, he felt like he was moving quicker than he ever had. Then she called "stop," and then "done." The AOD's disappeared into the floor and the room was empty except for them. Thealand stretched. Her stretch was stunning and for a skipped heart beat it took his breath away.

"Don't worry pup, you'll soon be able to protect your curly hair."

This was the closest thing to giving him hope she had ever said.

"Really?" he said, raising an eyebrow, "I thought I was both weak and doomed."

"Oh, I originally thought you were, but after taking the opportunity to hit me with the paint cans when I was down, I now believe that you might have hope. I mean, you know what I'm capable of and you did it anyway, that took guts."

He found her reasoning backwards to everything he had ever been taught. In the old cowboy movies he had watched with his father it was cowardly to shoot someone in the back. Hitting a person when they were down really seemed like a character flaw by human standards. Was her race really so much different than his in what they thought was right?

"Why did you keep the painting?" he asked hesitantly.

She cocked her head as if she wondered for a moment how he found out.

"To remind me not to underestimate my adversaries, and for a large blue gray mess it's not that bad."

First he had gotten hope and now a compliment, it floored him.

"Thank you," was all he could manage to say.

"You only painted half, I painted the other half of it," she reminded him. She hit him in the arm, much harder than he would have liked for a sign of affection. He asked her if she wanted to get a cookie and she declined admonishing him about the crap he fed his body. They left the room and went their separate ways, but for the first time he had felt the gloom from his life starting to lift.

Chapter Seven

It Ain't Noise Pollution, Mama

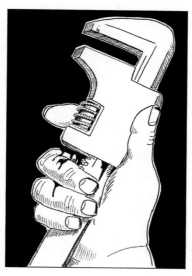

They practiced hard the following month and Traven's fighting skills got even better. His speed improved, but the closest he got to Thealand's was fifty-three percent. Thealand was an Atrill and their natural reflexes meant that they would be better suited for learning combat than the average human or even many other beings throughout the universe. Larry tried to inform Traven of the other reason's why her people were so talented at the art of battle, but his lisp had distracted the weary and overworked boy to the point were he told him to print up his theories and he would study them later.

Thealand told him that while he achieved greater speed he was at a plateau and it would take countless hours to raise his speed any further. Each increase would become harder and harder to achieve the closer he got to her speed. Still, she showed him hundreds of moves and by the end of the week, three attackers were no problem.

When she turned the AODs ability level up it was like starting over again. Like before, she tried to be patient, which clearly wasn't her strong point. She took the time to review both moves and options till they reached an acceptable form of perfection, at least for a human.

The following week also led to many discoveries about Thealand and the history of the Keeper of the Gateway. Thealand had taught the former Keeper and he too was a slow study. He was horribly clumsy at first because his scientific mind controlled his body. The body defended itself better when it did it naturally without over-analyzing the situation. She described it as a right brain action opposed to a left brain. The left brain was the logical, labeling side whereas the right brain was spatial. It was a Zen process where if you questioned your ability too much it would cause doubt and lead to failure. It was Mo-pa's teaching that improved both Docheen's speed and discipline, and it appeared to be working for Traven as well. The meditation and slow movement conditioned him to use his body as quickly as his mind would allow. The final goal would be to allow the body to react on instinct before the mind would have to tell it anything. She said the former Keeper would have been nowhere if it wasn't for Mo-pa. She also added that her race was very right brained, so much so that it often disregarded the logical left side. This was part of the reason that her people were in the mess that lead them to the brink of destruction. A mind needed both sides to be strong so that it could see the outcome of its actions. This made quite an impact on Traven, leaving him to wonder *if he spent too much time building his right brain would time suffer for his lack of logic.*

With Thealand, he picked his questions carefully and made sure not to ask too many unimportant ones. Though they were getting along well as far as the training was concerned, she would still get cross easily. Glimmers of her pre-paint fight attitude would surface any time he tried to get her interested in music or a conversation about anything mundane. He was beginning to be able to read her moods and Larry told him that reading moods was the first step in understanding women. Traven laughed hard at Larry's wisdom and when Thealand wasn't around would call him, "the Doctor of Love," suggesting he should write an advice column for the love lorn. At one point Traven asked Thealand what the other Keeper offered her as payment for her training. She explained that her planet was at war and she was one of the generals in charge of the rebellion. The former Keeper supplied the weapons for her side to win. The down side of the deal was that the new government soon became as bad as the previous one. She was even considered a criminal for speaking out against the party that she had once helped to install. Due to her role in the rebellion and the work she did helping those that opposed the new government, she had many friends. These friends sheltered her from the police and the military. Traven had a hard time thinking of her as someone who had to hide from anything, but she assured him that sometimes it's best to pick your battles. Traven finally asked her about her turtleneck shirts. Without hesitation she pulled down the collar to reveal a six inch scar caused by a knife blade. She said it is also important to both pick and know your friends. When Traven suggested that the med lab would be able to fix it, she was adamant about keeping it as a reminder of the lesson learned.

"In this way," she stated, "you don't repeat your mistakes."

As the week came to an end it was time for a break. He had spent nearly three months away from earth, the longest he had ever spent in the Gateway. Both he and Brandy felt it was important for him to go back home for a while to readjust to his former life so it wouldn't be forgotten. Thealand went back to Fecha and said that they would meet again in a week to resume his training. The amount of time that Traven wanted to wait was up to him. He gave her a signal device so that if anything went wrong she could pop into the Gateway at a moment's notice. It was a small blue box which was a one shot ticket that would allow the user to return from their planet the moment something became seriously wrong. For safety's sake it was also keyed to her genetic code making it useless to anyone else if it was lost or taken from her. Larry re-explained to Traven that time in the Gateway flowed on his timeline and time outside of the Gateway existed all at once. He told him the moment anyone other than Traven left the Gateway their life was completely written. Their life could only change it's course when Traven wanted to see them next and interacted with that time-line. It was because of this that once the blue box was activated, it would throw the user into the landing area with less than a second passing for Traven. The user might have waited years and could possibly return as an elderly version of themselves.

If Traven went back into the other line before and he had last seen the person, and interacted with him it would rewrite everything that had already happened for him and quite possibly leave a rather large mess. Thealand seemed to comprehend the idea but Traven was still a little lost. He wondered if someone other than the Lispy "Doctor of Love" had explained it would it have sunk in? Thealand said her goodbyes and she was gone. Traven waited a full minute to make sure nothing had gone wrong and when she didn't reappear in any form or age, he left to get himself ready.

Traven had his hair trimmed, which caused him great mental pain. A robot cut his hair while Larry read Traven the notes from when he last set foot on his Earth. He put back on his old clothes which felt too large. He had lost a lot of weight and they hung off his body leaving him swimming in his blue jeans and cotton t-shirt. Larry remade them a bit tighter, but left the old size tags on. Traven said his mother would surely check the sizes, if something seemed wrong. It was her hobby to constantly assess his looks and clothing. It was as if the detective novels she constantly read became the real lifes bane of the boys existence, making him the teenage mystery in need of solving. The decision to replace all of Traven's wardrobe was a bit tricky. They left the Gateway door open as he loaded his new copies that were only slightly baggy and frantically threw the old ones back through to be disposed of later. This plan would hide some of his weight loss until he could make it look like he was starting to working out. Weight fluctuations would be a big deal to his mother, and being too skinny would get him a quick trip to the doctor's office to find out what was wrong with her growing boy. He smiled when he realized that he might even have to ask his Mother to take him shopping, she would be in paradise, that is, until she read the tags.

School was the same but at one point he found himself going to the wrong class. Fourth hour gym had become third hour to him and the gym teacher looked at him standing there dressed in his full gym uniform and asked him if he was high.

His drama class was one of the few classes he enjoyed. It didn't seem like the work was too hard and Traven really wasn't what you could call shy in this kind of situation. The word ham could have been thrown around with little argument. The current assignment was a pantomime to a piece of music that they had picked out. Traven's piece of music was a dark Alice Cooper track from the album Da Da. Traven sat in his assigned seat drawing and had completely forgotten about the assignment. For him the assignment was given three months earlier and should have been written on the calendar when he last entered the Gateway. He was so engrossed in his design of a single mask that combined the two comedy and tragedy faces he had managed to block out that his name was being called. The drama teacher leaned over his shoulder to grab his attention.

"Dear master thespian," which is what his teacher called all of her students, "while your drawing skills are impressive you are currently missing your cue."

Traven looked up in a panic.

"Uh, you mean me?" he stated less than gracefully.

His teacher pointed to the stage crossly to answer his question. As the music started playing his mind quickly ran through a list of things that he might do. As he recognized the tune he remembered his distant yet sketchy plan. By the time he hit the stage his plan would be to try and show the transformation of a man into a Werewolf. He had pretended many times to turn into a Werewolf, from a very young age when he saw his first Lon Chaney, Jr. movie thanks to a careless baby-sitter. Even his second grade Halloween costume was a Werewolf, although everyone thought he was trying to be a bear. He started to call to the room for the spotlight to be dimmed and then foolishly realized that he wasn't in the Gateway. He sprinted to the back of the room and whispered something in the ear of the student running the spotlight. The teacher rolled her eyes not once, but twice as he stopped to whisper something else into the ear of one of the other students that he knew. By the time he took the stage again the teacher was impatiently tapping her foot on the ground. The music started for a second time as Traven sat in a meditational position on the floor. The room was dark and his body started to twitch. First slowly and then quicker. His head rolled side to side, looking as if he was in a trance or a drug induced state, this changed to a look of discomfort and then pain. His upper lip pulled up to show his large teeth and he growled low. His eyes became wide and wild as he stared at his hand that he tightened and forced into something that looked like a deformed paw which the spotlight held. Traven arched his back and a deep growl that was as loud as the music ripped out of his throat and a long bead of drool dripped out of his mouth soiling the floor. The sound that he made would have made any rock singer proud and the saliva would have impressed any true punker. He flipped his body in the air and landed on all fours. Raising his head massive gobs of drool were now dripping from the edge of his mouth. The squeamish girls let out little comments of disgust and even though he was having the time of his life he realized that this performance would lessen his chance of getting a date from any of them. This fact made little difference, he never stood a chance with them anyway and, more importantly, he was in the moment. The student on the spotlight turned the focus of the light wide. Traven bolted from the stage running the room partly on his legs and partly on his hands. He made a point out of bumping into any object that he could with his shoulders sending empty desks

flying everywhere and startled students out of the way. Some girls let out screams as some of the boys let out howls of approval, or indifferent mocking barks. The only one that didn't move was the second student that Traven had whispered to at the desk. In an over-acting response, he faked terror as their eyes met. The boy ran from Traven as if he had become the prey. Traven chased him around the room bouncing off of walls and over people till the two boys both ended up on the stage. The stage was the spot where he launched the kill. The boy fell to the floor and struggled as his mock murder was acted out. The boy had stuffed pages from his notebook into his shirt and Traven sent them flying into the air as if parts of this boys flesh were being torn asunder. The paper floated softly to the ground as the music ended. A final howl to tell the lighting man the show was over and the room went black.

The students went wild as the two boys took their bows. Even the teacher was impressed and though she went on to comment that a pantomime was supposed to be silent she said she would not deduct any points. She did however make him straighten up the room and made a discouraging comment about drooling on the stage. He smiled in reply. He didn't even mind the chore, he had caused it so it seemed fitting that he fix it. The teacher didn't even complain about the desks flying here and there where most would have had a fit. As he moved them back to their places he thought about the fighting form he would take one day when he learned to shape shift. Docheen's was cool, but in Traven's heart he knew his was going to be a Werewolf. Traven felt great and even thought that if the rest of the day would go like this he would take more vacations in the Gateway to recharge his creative juices.

Lunch was familiar, Brian and Matt arguing, Willie drawing, and girls walking past them to Brian's commentary. The food, as always, was awful and most shunned nutrition for the peanut butter fudge squares which could be eaten or thrown at people and objects. Most threw them at the ceiling or walls and would take bets as to how long they would remain stuck. Traven was retelling his success in drama class and the world felt right. This could have been his best day in the history of his public education, that is, until the school bully, Jim Salante, came from behind him and was about to whack Traven in the head.

Training sharpens your reflexes he told himself as he sat in the office. The expression on everyone's faces as Jim lay on the ground clutching what used to be his nose, seemed completely surreal. Jim had even muttered something about getting him after school as they hauled them both down to the dean. Traven knew this was an idle threat and was more worried about the fact he could have killed this bully instead of crushing his nose. Because he had no history of trouble they gave him only a one week suspension. Jim's parents talked to Traven's and both boys were to be punished at home. The sad thing about this was that Traven knew his father would live up to his agreements, while Jim's would most likely look the other way.

Matt had run to Traven's side as Jim was laid-out on the floor and, foreseeing what was to come, told him not to forget about the concert that night. He said they'd wait to the last moment for him to show up at Matt's house. It was directly after that, that both he and Jim were escorted to the office.

At home the mood was tense. Traven's father was a short man of very few words. When he talked it was usually best to listen or at least nod if you didn't understand what he was trying to say. Opening his mouth during these talks usually lead to Traven digging a bigger hole for himself than he was already in so he reminded himself to keep it shut. This day the message was clear and simple. One more screw up and it would be off to military school. Traven thought, *Oh my God, I'm only in my third year and I have one and a half more to go. The Vegas odds on me not screwing up are very bad indeed.* Then, the words he knew were going to be spoken came out of his father's mouth.

"And forget any plans you and your friends have made. No contact for the entire week."

"But I paid for the ticket already," Traven protested, forgetting his own rule about interrupting his father, "and it's tonight..." his voice trailed off as he realized he had started digging. His father's look was enough to end the conversation.

He thought about taking his friends into the Gateway and never coming back, but knowing his friends it wouldn't be long before one of them would try to date Thealand, and he still wasn't sure how he felt about her. He did know one thing for sure, he didn't want his friends giving him a hard time about Thealand kicking his butt.

Traven went to bed as usual, listening a long conversation between his parents about what to do with him through the thin walls of his room. That night he slept restlessly until dawn. When he finally did fall asleep it wasn't for long as the next sound he heard was that of a vacuum cleaner which ripped into what little dreamtime he had finally achieved. His mother was standing over him with her ever-present cleaning tool, which usually functioned as his alarm clock on the weekends. She didn't believe that a young boy should sleep a free day away and told him it was time for him to get up. He wanted to call for his Coke and cookie but knew that talking to the sky would get the "Are you on the drugs?" questions again. His father had arranged a marathon of chores, both to punish and to keep him out of any further trouble. Only when his Dad sent him to get a wrench for the lawn mower did he disappear into the basement and reappear in the Gateway.

Brandy was waiting for him as he entered. She was in her usual beautiful form but looking rather cross.

"So, y'all sneaking away to a concert, are ya?" she questioned. Larry flew up from behind her.

"Good punch," he said, as Brandy shot the little metal ball a dirty look. "Oh... I mean, tho I heard."

"Just going straight against your parent wishes? The word "no" don't mean a thing to you now does it?" she crossed her arms and tapped her glowing foot on the floor.

"Look, if I return the second after I leave it's like I never left. As long as Dad gets his wrench no one will ever know," he said, writing the word "wrench" next to the time he left Earth on the calendar. "Shouldn't I get some perks from being a master of time?"

Brandy was visibly unhappy about his choices, but for reasons she didn't share she came down off her soap box.

"Yo' the Boss," she said through gritted teeth, absentmindedly rubbing her necklace with the split triangle, "Where and when would you care to be?"

"Fifteen minutes before they're going to take off for the concert would be fine. Behind Matt's garage would probably be the best entrance place."

With that and a mechanical thumbs up from Larry he was gone. Larry turned to Brandy and said. "Oh, come on now, who doeth he remind you of?"

Brandy started to melt back into the floor, but before she was completely gone she paused.

"Shut up, Larry."

Traven arrived right when and where he wanted to be. Matt and Brian were playing the worst game of basketball that any two white boys could play. Their version of basketball entailed wearing Colorado boots that limited their already slight jumping abilities. Chasing each other with a broom or kicking wasn't against the rules either. Traven turned the corner and watched his friends before he made himself noticed. He had placed himself behind a large pile of dirt that Matt's father had dug out of somewhere. Matt's father was always working on the house spending hours hammering nails and pouring concrete. Sadly, even with all the effort, the house never seemed to change much. It took Traven by surprise that he had missed this place, basketball games, piles of dirt and all. Brian was talking faster than he was playing.

"You can't touch the Master, fool. He's wind, he's air, he's the hand that writes and quickly moves away," he said, stealing a line from a song.

"He's a master fool that rips off Dio Lyrics," Matt said, stealing the ball from Brian, "and fools lose."

Matt made the shot, but like nine out of ten throws either one made, it wasn't close to being in. They both watched the ball bounce off the backboard over their heads and down the steep incline of Matt's driveway.

"Well, go get it," said Matt.

"Screw you, Clutch Cargo lips," Brian returned. "You get it."

"No way man, you get it."

"It was your shot, I would have sunk it... dingus."

"Hey your..." Matt started on what would have been a fine, "your momma joke" when he saw Traven and stopped dead in his sentence. "Dude," he said, running up to him and slapping his hand. "You made it, cool. You are all full of surprises today."

"Man," said Brian punching Traven in the shoulder and then sarcastically jumping back quickly as if Traven might hit him. "That punch was righteous. What made you do it?"

"I don't know," he said, which was the truth. "I just kind of reacted."

"Yeah, reacted on his big ugly face. He totally deserved it," laughed Matt.

"Yeah the only one of us he doesn't hassle is Willie, and that's because Willie laid him out in the middle of Math class in eighth grade," Brian said, thinking back to the day. "Man that was hilarious, Jim hits Willie in the back of the head. His favorite move, you probably remember it. Anyway, Willie stands up, puts both hands together, swings them like a bat into Jim's stomach. When Jim doubles over Willie brings both hands down on top of Jim's head. The dickweed is laid out on the floor and Willie looks up shocked and says, " I learned that from Star Trek."
They all laughed.

"Decent," said Matt, stretching the word and nodding in approval.

Though Traven laughed he also realized how much violence had recently been infused into his life. He wondered if he would become like one of those Vietnam vets who suddenly starts attacking people and a shiver ran down his spine. Since the idea was not comforting, he tried to change the subject.

"So where's Willie?" Traven asked.

"He left me holding a spare ticket, man," Matt replied.

"You knew he was going to do that."

"Same excuse too," said Brian, "got some work I have to do for Mr. K."

"I think Mr. K. takes credit for his work," Matt said, giving in and going for the basketball.

"Yeah probably," said Traven, "I'm not sure I've ever seen Mr. K. draw anything. I mean if you teach it you should be able to do it, right?"

"Who knows what they teach teachers?" laughed Matt, tossing the ball in his yard. "Hey, we'd best be going."

They piled into Matt's old Buick and drove off with the sounds of Ronnie James Dio blasting through the suburban air. Brian had called shotgun, which meant he got to ride in the front. Traven hated the back due to the fact that the speakers were there. Anyone near the speakers heard nothing until the car had reached its destination.

Oak River was an outdoor amphitheater in the middle of a large field of grass. There was no river or oak trees to be seen so the name amused Traven and his friends. They would yell out things as they drove like, "There's an oak," or "There's a river, we must be close." Usually this banter would start in the driveway; it was where they always went to see concerts. It was close, lawn seats were cheap and the sound was not too bad, though the venue had a strictly enforced eleven o'clock closing time. If you were lucky, and the concert didn't sell out, they would open the pavilion seating halfway through the show. This would not be the case tonight. The crowd was excited and the usual drinking and illegal substances were mostly contained to the stoners in the parking lot. Once inside it was more about what you could smuggle in to enhance the show. Beach balls were popular and much easier to get in if they were deflated. Once you were in people would blow them up and send them off into the crowd until someone from security nabbed them. Tonight, frisbees were almost as popular and very hard for security to track. They watched as a young girl caught one in her face and, without even asking if she was all right, her boyfriend sent the frisbee back into play.

The opening band took the stage as the crowd cheered or booed according to how cool they thought the opening act was. Traven and his friends cheered, the band Twisted Sister, was one of their favorites, though not really appreciated by everyone. At one point in the evening the band's lead singer picked a fight with a guy in the second row. Dee Snyder was a monster of blond curly hair, torn leather clothes, thick clown like eye shadow, and six inch platform shoes. He was at least seven feet tall on stage and looked like a muppet created for the wrestling circuit. When he dove from the stage into the crowd the audience went wild. His mass of hair bounced up and down and only those near-by knew what was really happening during the fight. When he climbed back onstage he shouted into the microphone, "Yeah, that's what I thought!"

The band finished off their set and after a short break Dio entered the stage. The stage had become a medieval playground. The drums rested high in the air on a fake volcano. The keyboards sat in a tower of a war-torn castle, and an eighteen foot tall mechanical dragon breathed fire and smoke and shot lasers from its eyes. Even with all that Traven had been through he was awestruck, and found himself thinking he could make a stage like this one. When a diminutive Ronnie James Dio with a voice like a bomb belted out the first song, the crowd was in his control. In unison the people sang, threw their fists up in the air to the heavy beat, and looked like a force of nature to be reckoned with. Willie would be sad indeed that he missed this night, given his love of fantasy. The time passed quickly as one song turned into another. The band quit exactly at eleven o'clock to avoid any fines and the boys sat in the parking lot waiting for the traffic to thin out.

"Unbelievable!" said Matt. "That dragon was way cool!"

"Choice," said Brian, "but Queen was better."

"Will you ever shut up about Queen?" Matt and Traven said in unison.

"Front row center, man. Beat that!"

Brian had gone to the Queen concert without his friends and on somebody else's ticket. From that point on, all concerts were weighed against the event that Traven and Matt hadn't seen. Traven enjoyed hearing his friends fight; at least on Earth his friends only fought verbally. It had been too long without someone to share a laugh with and far too long since he hadn't had to spend an evening blocking a punch or meditating. A smile came over his face that only faded when Traven stepped out of the car.

After the concert, Traven had his friends drop him off near his parent's house. He found a shadow to disappear in and reappeared in the Gateway. Changing his clothes to clean and slightly better fitting doubles, he left his concert shirt behind for future use. He yawned like a seal, shook his head and reappeared back home. When his father yelled he was deep in thought and starting to panic that he had missed something. He grabbed a wrench and proceeded to his assigned duty.

Timothy John Vaulato

Chapter Eight

School By Proxy

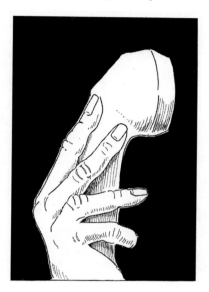

The week of suspension seemed to drag. Traven's parents picked up his homework, which to his surprise seemed much easier than before he became the Keeper. He wondered if he had become smarter from all the tutoring or if this was the first time he had ever applied himself? His mother had always told him he was smart, but what are mothers supposed to say? Math was still difficult and the one subject that his father loved to help him with the most. Showing his work was his downfall. Traven thought, *If I get it, what difference does seeing the work make?* His father, on the other hand, made sure that he always wrote out his steps. Upon doing so, he always had another method that he said would be a better way to get the same answer. The average time to do the math homework would take Traven twenty minutes. Doing his math homework with his father, three hours. He started jogging and lifting weights. The interest in exercise made his father quietly proud. Traven had never been interested in sports, though his parents did make him try t-ball when he was younger. The coach, sensing his lack of interest, made him the catcher. His father did enjoy sports and was rather disappointed when his only son didn't share his interests, and turned instead to music and art. Traven started exercising as an answer to those around him about his increased muscle mass and weight loss. Jogging was the better of the two, though his father would follow slowly behind him in the car to make sure he wasn't up to anything. At night when his parents where asleep he would sneak back to the Gateway, but only for a few hours. He wanted to get his suspension over with and by the time it took to truly be bored without cable TV, his suspension was served.

Returning to school was strange and uncomfortable. He was, after all, the student that started a fight in the middle of the cafeteria. Within the week he was gone, the story had grown quite out of control. The most bizarre elaboration had Traven beating Jim's head on the table with paramedics having to shock his poor victim back to life. Part two of the story had him taking on a dean's assistant and driving to Canada in a stolen car. The thing that he found the most annoying was everyone's questions. Traven retold the story as briefly as possible. "He was going to hit me, I hit him, the end." Jim, on the other hand, became quite the author and his version had Traven saying things about Jim's mother and girlfriend, even though the girl in question wasn't his girlfriend. There was even a version that had him threatening Jim's little brother, whom he had never met, let alone knew existed. Jim contended that it was a lucky punch and there was no way a dork like that could take him on in a fair fight. He also went on and on about his plot of revenge, that is, after he had heard about Traven being sent to military school if he ever got in trouble again. The boy with the bandage on his nose went out of his way to yell things at Traven whenever there was a big crowd around. Traven ignored him remembering his father's threat, while in his head he chanted, *Vegas odds, Vegas odds.*

A Lifetime In Time

In English class, he got to hang with Brian. Well, kind of, the teacher had put them on opposite ends of the room to keep their private conversations to a minimum. Normally this would make a class drag, but as fate would have it the teacher put him next to a girl by the name of Beth. Beth reminded him of Thealand, at least physically, but with Beth you could have a conversation about something other than dying worlds or how to cripple somebody. He never did get up the courage to pass her a note or even talk to her outside of class. She seemed to have her own clique to hang out with, and to have a girl talk to him without using the word "dork" made him happy enough.

Today's writing assignment was to interview an old person. Someone in the autumn of their years the teacher said. Not only did she want them to interview the person, but she also wanted the interview written up and presented to the class. *I don't know any old people* thought Traven. Well there was Mo-pa, but interviewing him would be like trying to interview a Cal-leash. No, that wasn't going to be possible, Mo-pa was a man of few understandable words. His family wouldn't be going to see his grandparents anytime soon, and his grandparents broken English made it difficult to talk to them over the phone. The only other nearby old person that he knew was Mr. Tracborn, his neighbor, and the only time he ever talked to him was when Mr. Tracborn was threatening to call the police. A stray frisbee had landed on the sidewalk by his yard and Mr. Tracborn trea- sured his space. No, that wasn't an option either he decided. By the end of class, he was still idealess. Brian hopped two rows of desks so they could engage in the tradition of watching Beth leave the room.

"Any ideas?" asked Traven.

"Plenty," Brian replied, staring at Beth's very tight jeans. "But I should really get the guts to ask her out first."

"Yeah, you and me both," Traven laughed.

"Dude, that's gross."

"Not like that. I mean... that's not what I meant."

"Yeah, two great guys like us and not an ounce of courage between us. Hey, I hear there's this guy in Oz and..."

"You know she probably likes football players or popular guys," said Traven cutting him off.

"Hey, I'm popular."

"Yeah with yourself."

"Not fair," said Brian as they entered the hallway.

"Look, even if I got up the guts to ask her out, if she said "no" I'm stuck sitting next to her the rest of the year," he said with a small pout.

"No guts, no glory," Brian said, in his deep manly voice that he used when he felt the occasion was fitting. "Hey, maybe she'll ask one of us to that Sadie Hawkin's dance?"

"Fat chance," Traven replied, and then suddenly switched the subject. "So, what are you going to do about the assignment?"

"I'm gonna make up a story about an old drunk in the neighborhood. I'm going to call him Wishbone, Wishbone Jones. He's gonna have an old raspy voice and say stuff like, I drank so much I wish I could still get a bone. He'll live in a cardboard box by the railroad tracks and eat road kill."

"That will go over well."

"Hey, she bought the story about my aunt being a professional psychic."

"I think she was just happy you handed something in."

They both agreed that that was probably the case and went to their separate classes.

After school Traven sat in his room sketching a self-portrait for art class. Looking in the mirror he drew the contour of his eyes, and then his nose, lips, ears, and then the dreaded task of drawing hair. More and more details went down on the paper till once again, he had overworked the drawing. This happened every time he tried to draw a real person instead of a comic character. When he drew somebody real he would pre-age them. Most of the time they'd look ten years older, but today, even though he knew the drawing had gone south, he kept at it. More lines,

more wrinkles, darkening the eyes and making them look deep set, like his grandmother's. The hair got out of control too. He kept making it longer and longer, as if when he was finally old enough he could wear his hair as he damn well pleased. When he stopped drawing, he sat back and gave the picture a good hard critical look.

Not bad, he thought, *if I was seventy.*

It was a moment of clarity for him. His English assignment had solved itself through his drawing. After all, how many people had it within their power to interview themselves. Just before Traven waved his hand there was a phone call. This caught him off guard as his mother whipped open his door to announce that Brian was on the phone.

"Dude," said Brian, "you'll never believe it, Beth just asked me to the dance."

"Yeah, that's great man," he said, feeling his heart sink into jealousy. "That's just great."

"She called me!" Brian said, almost as if he wanted Traven to confirm the date that was too astounding in his own mind.

"Isn't the dance tonight?"

"Yeah, oh crap, what am I going to wear?"

"Something sleeveless?" Traven said sarcastically, which Brian took no notice of.

"I do have that clean up and look good for your court date suit," he said, balancing the phone and digging through the closet.

"Kind of last minute, don't ya think?"

"Timing is important, my man. She was just making sure I was free, she probably had to clear it with all of her friends that wanted to ask me."

"Wake up, dude," said Traven, knowing that Brian was going to be impossible to deal with now that he had a date with the girl of their desires. "You are so dreaming."

"I can't believe it!" Brian's voice rang like a small boy at Christmas and then once again his voice deepened. "It must be my manly abs have been driving her crazy all semester."

"Or your Mick Jagger lips," Traven offered through gritted teeth.

"Yeah that could be it, my... hey, I don't have Mick Jagger Lips!"

"What, did you give them back?"

"Hey man, as I said no guts..."

"What guts did it take for you to say yes?"

"Ok," Brian admitted, "none at all, but you have to admit it's pretty cool."

Traven realized he was raining on Brian's parade and softened a bit.

"Better than the Queen concert?"

"Well," came the deep voice, "that remains to be seen."

They continued talking though Traven didn't remember much of the conversation. He was happy for his friend, but would have been much happier if he was going with Beth and someone else had asked Brian. He looked down at the drawing and remembered that he had something more interesting than Brian's love life to review. He quickly made an excuse to get off the phone and told Brian to call him tomorrow and let him know how things turned out.

In the Gateway the reaction to Traven's idea was less of a celebration than a trial.

"What, are y'all crazy?" yelled Brandy, "not only is it a bad idea, it could be the worst of all possible ideas, on a long list of ideas that has the title, the list of worst possible ideas."

For some reason Mo-pa hung in the background looking nervous, as Traven tried to defend himself.

"Look, what's the point of having control over time and space if you can't use it to your advantage?" he stated as his defense.

"I declare," she fussed stomping her foot on the ground, "nothing good ever comes out of knowing one's future, not in any way, shape, or form." As she continued stomping the glow from the bottom of her bare feet became noticeably brighter.

"Are you telling me that Docheen never looked into his own future?"

"A Keeper who looks into their own future is rarely satisfied."

As she pouted, Traven wondered why she didn't say Docheen as a singular instead of making him sound as a plural, but as she broke into her next statement he remembered his argument and tried to put aside confusion to stay on track of his defense.

"One of Docheen's rules is to not see into your own future!" she stated loudly. The glow from her foot became so bright that it started to cast shadows on her legs. "The future is so elastic that everything y'all do will change the outcome. It cannot make no sense to see something that can never be."

"Well then," he said in a calm voice, "that would be perfect. If I know for a fact that the outcome of my life will not come to pass as I see it, it's just a trip into a fairy tale that will never truly happen. Besides, it will make my teacher believe that I interviewed someone real instead of making it up."

"No! Forget ya teacher and concern yourself with the problem. If something good is to happen to you, you will try to make it happen anyway, and there are too many variables to make it happen the same way. It then becomes a game of where and when do I need to be to get it right. I saw Docheen obsessed with what he thought reality should be and he never got it right, not in a million years!"

"You remember your latht trip you tried to take with a home-work benefit," interjected Larry, "you almotht got eaten."

"But I am a better person for that experience, Larry." Traven sounded cocky but the memory of the bear did bother him.

"Shut up, Larry," said Brandy, as she resumed her prosecution. "Time in the Gateway moves forward from your current timeline. What you do from the moment y'all are currently living rewrites what the future will be, not just for yourself, but for everyone. Let's say ya go and try to meet yourself as an old man, it would be as if ya never took another step out of the Gateway. You would have been dismissed as a missing person. Your parents would have been shattered and might taking up drinking or whatever would have eased the pain. Maybe they would have spent their entire lives trying to find you, only to die alone in a nursing home never knowing what had become of their dear child. Is that the image y'all want to take to bed with ya? Do ya honestly want to see the destruction of the people that gave you birth?"

"Well there's an ugly thought," he said, pondering a future where he disappeared completely.

"See, it's just not worth looking for a mess of trouble." Brandy's voice became calmer, and then the stray thought of a teenager's rambling set all hell into motion.

"It's too bad I can't find out what my life would have been if I never inherited the Gateway."

Before Brandy could stop Larry it was too late.

"Oh, that you can d..." as Larry stopped his lispy electronic reply, Brandy made the ground jump up and swallow the little silver basketball. Mo-pa quickly left the room.

"What the hell, Brandy? Am I the Keeper or just some damn kid you get people to beat up on for your amusement?"

"There are things that you are not ready for!" she yelled. "Y'all can barely handle time travel let alone messin' in other realities!"

"And who gets to determine what I'm ready for? You? The last time I really thought about it, you worked for me. You all work for me. At least Larry has the sense to call me Boss, even if he can't say it right. He doesn't spend hours bitching at me like a Mother Hen either. If being the Keeper is supposed to be so great, why am I the one without any control? I'm starting to believe that being the Keeper just means I get to spend the rest of my days throwing a wooden ball around, and getting my ass kicked by cat girl. If that's the prize I'd just as soon off myself right here and let you burst!"

One of Traven's biggest problems in his life was the ability to say incredibly hurtful things when pushed. It took a lot to get him to that point but once he was there you didn't want to be down wind of one of his blow ups.

Brandy lost all color to her form and became metallic. Her eyes became lights and what could be called seams appeared in the areas where her body would bend. In short, she looked like one pissed off robot.

"Fine!" she said in an electronic tone. "You go get what you need and I'll send you to see an old you. How about the very day of your death, so you will know what that is like too?"

"Fine," said Traven, not wanting to back down from her challenge.

He stomped out the door and down the dark hallways of the Gateway. Twice he had to call into the air for more light. It was a sign that he had gone too far. He was already sorry for what he had said to Brandy and to everybody in the Gateway. He was just glad that Mo-pa and Larry weren't there to witness his temper tantrum. As he entered the clothing room he realized he had no idea of what to wear. He didn't really want to ask Brandy and he even felt bad calling for Larry, that is if the little silver ball had found his way back from wherever Bandy had sent him. He figured to go with clothing that had been around for a while and hopefully still would. In the wardrobe room he searched through the racks. Blue jeans would possibly still be around. To Traven they seemed like they had been around forever. He picked black T-shirts and simple cowboy boots, because in his mind they seemed to be beyond the pressures of stylistic change. Looking through the coats he found a worn dark green army trench coat. It looked like something out of a World War Two movie but the tag on the hanger said 1981. All the clothes had dates so you could blend in to wherever or whenever you were going. Realizing that the clothing had dates, he followed the long rack to it's end. The pole disappeared into a wall right around 1985. The rack after that had a strange number that wasn't from any math class he had ever taken. Instead of the next step in the evolution of fashion the rack contained rags, and then costumes from what he guessed was a strange version of Pocahontas. Could Brandy be so petty as to make the right clothes disappear? Instead of asking, he assumed she was and he wasn't about to ask for help after their blow up. Then, an unsettling thought came into his head and distracted his fashion quest. Brandy had said she would send him to his death bed. What if the other him died young? What if he had a crippling disease, what if he wasn't even on Earth?

At this point he knew he had to talk to Brandy before he left and he knew he had to apologize, but he didn't want to make himself seem more incompetent by not even finding something suitable to wear. He put on the coat and it looked as if he was a child playing dress up with the sleeves flopping over his hands and almost reaching his knees. After putting the clothes in the machine known as the sizer they fit like a glove. He was impressed with the once giant coat. He liked the way it billowed behind him when he walked. He liked the deep pockets. He even liked the color. It was a dark green that in twilight would be mistaken for black and would blend into most foliage. He realized he was starting to think like Thealand.

As he walked through the halls, he tried to think of how to apologize. Nothing that he could think of sounded quite right. The halls remained dark and only when it became next to impossible to see in front of him did he ask Brandy to give him more light. He followed his path back to the landing area. Suddenly he realized that he had been walking considerably longer than the time it took to get there. Brandy must have been lengthening the hallways making it harder to leave. He stopped.

"Listen Brandy," he said, "I'm sorry about what I said. I don't want to see you burst or blow up or do whatever it is that you would do. It's just that I don't feel like everyone's giving me the entire story. I mean I'm supposed to have power, but I feel like a puppet and a punching bag. I learn why you guys are having me do or not do things long after I've been doing them and it just makes me... I guess a little untrusting."

There was an uncomfortable silence and then suddenly part of the wall opened up to reveal the landing area. Traven walked through. Larry flew up.

"Thee wantth to know if you're thtill going," he said, looking around to see if the floor or wall was going to swallow him again.

"Yeah, I guess," Traven replied in an unsure voice. "You all right?"

"Oh yeah, Bawth, thee jutht thent me to the edge of the Gateway."

"Yeah, what's it like?"

"Hard to tell when your moving that fatht, but I think I thaw theveral townth, a thity, and I went through an ocean."

"We'll have to explore those when I get back."

"Are you thure about thith?" Larry asked.

"No, not really, but now it's not a matter of a homework assignment. I just need to know what my life might have been. Did things work out ok? Was I a bigger loser without the Gateway than I am now?" he said with a slight laugh. "Where and when am I going?"

"The year ith 4007, the plathe uthed to be called Glacier National Park."

"Glacier National Park? Cool, my family went on vacation there a couple of..." and then Traven stopped dead in his tracks. "4007? How the hell is that possible?"

"You can athk that quethtion when you get there. It will take you a good hour to reach your deathbed."

The word deathbed gave Traven a chill.

"Wait a minute," he said, "can't I land closer?"

"No, there'th a block. That meanth you will have to come back to where you arrived to get back here. Thee thaid that there ith enough time."

"Well that's kind of her," Traven said sarcastically.

"Look, thee'th really upthet," he said in a worried lisp.

"I'm sorry for what I said." Then he addressed the room. "I'm sorry, but I feel I should do this."

"Be thafe," said Larry.

"Should I take a weapon?" Traven asked.

"I meant mentally," Larry replied.

"Oh."

The door opened at the far side of the room. Checking for his Calleash Traven stepped through into his other life.

Timothy John Vaulato

Chapter Nine

The Mirror

Traven stepped into the fresh mountain air. It was summer and the view was breathtaking. The dark blue mountains reached to the sky and the sun gleamed from their snow capped tops. The mountains did remind him of Glacier National Park but all the telltale signs of human existence were gone. No roads, no cabins, no souvenir stands, and not one forest ranger telling people how to read a compass. A mass of gray clouds floated in the distance assuring him that the customary mid- afternoon shower would be coming. He remembered camping here with his parents and the smell of the pine trees after the rain.

"Well, if this is the future at least we didn't blow up the Earth," he said quietly.

The one thing he clearly did not remember from his vacations was the giant castle. He knew castles were big, but this one looked like a city. It grew from the rocks plopped down in the middle of the valley as if they had decided to join in a common purpose. A stone dragon was part of the north side and the center tower almost touched the clouds. From the dragon's mouth poured a river that fell to a lake on the castle's edge. Something inside told him that was the place to go. He vaguely remembered drawing something similar to this castle for his seventh grade art class, but it was nowhere near this cool. This recognition lifted his spirits slightly and he headed for the castle trying to come up with questions that he would ask the elderly him.

After the first twenty minutes he saw a group of riders upon large horses. The riders were thin and graceful, clothed in deerskin that resembled fancy Indian dress. Though they didn't pass near, they eyed him over their shoulders and a few did double takes.

By the time he reached the castle there were more people. Most took no notice of him. They went about their business, shoeing horses, practicing archery, their children playing games. None of them acted as if he was out of place. For a moment he wondered if he had become invisible. A group of them painted pictures of the lake and the people boating on it or bathing in it. Off on the hillside some flew kites of brilliant colors and strange designs. A few, mostly the older ones, looked at him questioningly. This let him know that he truly wasn't invisible, just being ignored. Still, no one made an attempt to talk to him or interfere in any way with his journey. As Traven looked closer at the people he noticed that they were dressed similar to the riders, but more if the American Indians took design lessons from the Italian Renaissance. The only thing that made them different than humans were the pointed ears.

"Has the Earth been inhabited by elves?" he mumbled, trying to make sense of his other future.

As he walked through the entranceway, he noticed that high on the castle were hundreds of propellers, or small wind mills. As some turned others stopped until the wind shifted, and then they would resume their duties.

The castle doors were ornamented with carvings that must have told a story of great importance. One of the things that threw him off was a stone relief of a mobile home loaded for what appeared to be the longest vacation in history. The carving showed that the vehicle was clearly over loaded, with suitcases and boxes tied to it's frame. It was worn by age and the modern subject matter combined with its mere presentation made it feel surreal. Sadly, he had to pull himself away from the carvings because he knew his time was limited. Entering the main hallway took his breath away. He saw thousands of intricately carved doors, a seemingly never ending system of hallways, and in the center a large hearth that contained a fire the size of a small truck. A copper vent above the fire went straight up twenty feet and then branched into hundreds of directions. The people had laid out clothing to dry near the fire and others used the smaller stone ovens built around it to bake. A few ovens on the far side were being used to blow glass. As he marveled at the scene he glanced up past the venting and decided that the inside was even bigger than the outside. Looking closer at the foundation Traven realized that the inner structure looked like a giant stone tree with branches spreading out from the center to the ceiling or to the walls supporting each level. With mouth open and eyes wide, anyone near would have correctly read his expression as dumbfounded.

An old man approached him. He was stocky and about the same height as Traven. His one eye was normal while the other was replaced by a red jewel. Part of one ear was missing and where his jaw should be was a piece of steel which gave him a strange voice when he spoke.

"You're looking for him," he stated, approaching Traven.

Taken aback by the first person who spoke to him he tried to reply.

"Uh... I am? I mean, I guess I am."

"He said that you would be coming. He told everyone to let you be, but you look a little lost."

"Lost and overwhelmed," Traven admitted nervously.

"Well, just take the main staircase to the top and you'll find him, but mind you, he hasn't been doing well these last few years and, to be honest, I don't think he has much time left."

"Then I guess I should be quick," Traven said. "Thank you."

He started climbing the stairs and told himself that this was not a sightseeing trip.

"If I only had more time," he said, "I could spend days here."

The reality of his words angered him. He was the Keeper, he should have all the time he wanted, but now he found himself having to rush to his own deathbed. His opinion of Brandy was sinking. She was the one that was limiting his trip, *wasn't she suppose to listen to him?*

He was sweating quite a bit by the time he reached the top and took a moment to catch his breath. It was dark and he strained to look at the shadowy door; behind it was the person he would have been if he hadn't become the Keeper. The sides of the door were as elaborate as the others, but this one was at least twelve feet tall and the carvings were abstract, with the exception of a demon-like gorilla figure on the top. He almost let out a shriek when the figure jumped from its perch and landed beside him.

"Good, you're here," it said, in a surprisingly normal voice for it's odd shape.

Traven refocused his eyes and took his hand off of his Calleash which he had deep in his pocket. The creature was a little less than three feet high, walking around on its hands and feet, which were the size of cast iron frying pans. Each hand had four fingers, and each foot, four toes. Every digit on this creature tapered into thick black claws. Its eyes were a bright red with two thick ridged bone like brows where eyebrows should have been. Its skin was green and its long, more gray than brown hair was tied back in a ponytail.

"My oh my," it mused, "you look just like him when we first met."

"Were... I mean are you close?" Traven questioned.

"My best friend," said the creature. "My name is Spider."

"Pleased to meet you," Traven said, shaking Spider's massive hand by holding onto a single finger.

A Lifetime In Time

"Look, you'd better get going," he said, with a smile and a nudge. "I wouldn't want to keep... a... the both of you waiting."

Spider climbed the wall like his namesake and perched himself back on his guard post. Taking a deep breath Traven opened the door.

The room had more windows than should have been possible for such a large space. Crystals of different sizes caught the light and projected small rainbows randomly around the room. Mice sized fuzzy creatures scurried from place to place, some of which were moving books, others grouped together to carry a large serving tray with a pitcher and two glasses. At the back of the room was a forest of instruments, some of which Traven recognized as guitars, others were unfamiliar and he had no idea what they did or how they would sound. All of the instruments were covered in a thick layer of dust which told of years of neglect. Strings were left to rust, and it seemed as if more than one had been smashed, with the scattered pieces telling the story of their abuse. The books were countless and stacked haphazardly on shelves or in piles on the floor. An old man sat upright in a giant bed. He appeared to be writing in a very old, large book. He summoned Traven over to take a seat in a chair by the bed. Traven sat down and the man continued writing as he spoke.

"I lost my calluses," he said in a creaky voice.

"Pardon?" Traven replied.

"That's why I don't play anymore."

"Excuse me?"

"The guitars," he clarified, and then held up a finger to silence Traven so that he could finish writing his thought.

Traven stared at the old man that did look incredibly like the drawing he had tried to do for his art class. Though he felt awkward and very young, his heart was lifted by the old man's hair, which was down to his waist, as white as the snow, and defied any signs of balding.

"Finally," Traven thought, "I get to have long hair."

The man finished his last thought and shut the book. He turned to Traven and spoke.

"So here we are," he said, looking the young him up and down.

This left Traven feeling uneasy, like his meeting with Docheen.

"Well, well, I was a good looking boy, wasn't I?" crackled the old man. "I suppose you want the story don't you."

"The story?" questioned Traven, who for a moment almost forgot why he was there. "Yes, I guess I do, but how did you know I was coming?"

"Tea, with ice right?" asked the old man, avoiding the question.

"You don't have Diet Coke, do you?"

"Not in two thousand years boy. Try the tea."

The old man waved his hand and the furry little creatures poured the drink and added the ice.

"I'd offer you some mead, but you're not old enough yet." He laughed at himself as if he was sharing a private joke until a cough stopped him and he continued. "There's a bottle on the shelf, make sure you take it when you go, it was a particularly good year." The old man opened the book's front cover and looked at page one. "I brought out my diary. You see my memory isn't what it used to be and this gives it a nice jolt as I yammer on. I suppose you would like me to start at the beginning."

"Yes please," said Traven, checking his glass for residual hair from the small creatures that made his drink. The old man took out a pair of bifocals from his pocket and began.

"The world as you know it ended near the end of my Junior year of high school. No bombs, no fighting, just a release of a virus that wiped out ninety-nine point nine percent of the population."

Traven almost dropped his drink.

That's this year, he thought, as the old man continued.

"I would learn later that our government had been testing the virus and that it had gotten out of their control. Luckily or not luckily for us, Matt's father was a paranoid son of a bitch and had constructed a bomb cellar under his house complete with a ventilation and filtration system. Have you noticed all of his digging?" he asked.

Traven admitted that he had. Matt's father was always tinkering with some gadget. He was constantly showing him inventions that no one really knew what they did, but they humored him because he let them hang out at his house. They always joked that Matt's dad was secretly a spy.

"Crazy old bastard," he laughed, trying to suppress a cough, "forced us into the shelter at gun point when the news started reporting massive deaths. Locked the door to make sure we didn't get out. He didn't care if he survived, but he sure wasn't going to let his only son die. We spent three months in a ten by ten room. Sure there was lots of dried food and water, but three months without a bath and let me tell you, we were ripe. Matt was always a little unstable after we got out. I miss him, I miss them all. It's a hell of a thing to outlive most of your friends, not to mention family. There's very few left that remember the beginning. No one to turn to and say, hey remember when we saw Dio, or any other band for that matter. Anyway, Matt became a different person after the world ended, I guess we all did. We emerged to find the remains of Matt's father, it wasn't a pretty sight, but he did what he felt was right to save not only his son, but the rest of us. In the three months that we spent in confinement was enough time for the virus to burn itself out. It most likely did long before that, but Matt's dad had installed a time lock, so having no say in the matter we learned the art of poker and played for those damned dried noodles that you added hot water to. Brian won the most. I guess that the world died slowly or to put it better, they had the time to secure nuclear power plants, at least the ones on our side of the globe. We never had a worry about radiation, not that there was anything we could have done about it if it was there. We would find pockets of people here and there that had survived, but very few. Willie kept us alive. The virus was a designer bug that affected only people, so there were plenty of animals to hunt, and luckily Willie knew how to hunt and clean them. Later, a man named Lynx provided most of the story. He was the only one who had an immunity to the virus, provided by the government's inoculation experiments. How it worked he never said, but he was a hired assassin, paid to protect the virus. He said he was the leader of a group know as the Steel Tear. I know he was there when the virus broke, but he didn't like to talk about it all that much and kept many of those details to himself."

The afternoon rain clouds darkened the sky, stopping the crystal projected rainbows and throwing the room into gray shadows. As if on cue, the fuzzy creatures quickly scurried around and somehow lit candles. The raindrops hitting the tall windows provided a background rhythm to the story.

"After we had collected ourselves and the few stragglers, I convinced our group to head to the mountains. We went there for the hunting and I always felt bad eating dogs, even the wild ones. Living in a modern ghost town was really a downer and a constant reminder of what we had lost. We packed up our collective junk in a parade of mobile homes and headed to an old lodge not far from this site. It was McDonald lodge, which we quickly changed into our home. We even took on different names or nicknames to also try to forget the past. If not for a few well placed shots by Willie, we would have starved that first winter." The old man started to cough and took a long drink from his glass. He looked out to the horizon as he spoke.

"In the spring I had my first encounter with the Daliteen and the love of my life. The Daliteen were a race of elf-like people with incredible life-spans. A group of about two hundred of them had fled their world through a dimensional rift to Earth. Their world had been attacked by a group of creatures known as the Drackeen which made their planet uninhabitable. Like Lynx, the Daliteen had an immunity to the virus, though it was natural. They had arrived two hundred years before the virus, and sensing that they would not be accepted by this world they hid deep in the woods until they realized that the time of the humans was over." The old man started coughing again. It was a violent cough that shook the bed and made a few of the strings on the old guitars chime. The furry creatures ran to his side and stood at attention. Traven looked around as if to find some way to help him, but the old man just put up his hand again as if to signal him to wait. The coughing ceased.

"I met my wife on the shores of the lake. She was bathing in the cold water as if it was a warm tub. I was entranced by her beauty. She had deep brown eyes, waist length brown hair, and stood only five foot two. Even with her short stature you could find no better fighter. I had accidentally made myself known and during our first encounter she almost killed me, but something stopped her. I would like to think it was my eternal charm. What began from that moment was a strange relationship of two people trying to learn each other's language. There was a connection between us, something that kept us meeting by the lake every other day. Maybe when you're destined to be with someone your heart knows and you just listen. We had to meet in secret. Her father, Silver Mane, was the leader of the Daliteen and wasn't fond of humans at all. In fact, my race dying out was the answer to his prayers. He tried to dispose of the humans as he found them and a human and his daughter in love was unthinkable." The old man pulled his cover tightly around himself for warmth, though Traven could sense no difference in the room.

"At one point Silver Mane found Lynx's woman, or was she his wife?" he looked at Traven as if he should have the answer. When his face registered nothing but confusion he nodded as if he understood that the boy had no idea.

"I lose bits you know," he admitted. "Anyway, the bastard made short work of her. Lynx found her as she lay dying. She was a pacifist, kind of religious I was told. But unlike most, she was the kind that practiced what she preached. They had met after the virus and maybe it was her faith that changed him, at least for a while. She made him promise her that he would not kill Silver Mane. Being a man that was strong in his word he did not take revenge, at least directly. That's when he sought me out. He saw an opportunity and trained me in his ways of fighting and killing. When things came to a head, I let Silver Mane live though I would kick myself later for doing so. As time passed I was made a blood brother to the Daliteen, which accounts for my long life. Their blood has powers. I had five beautiful children and became the leader of both the Daliteen and the humans." He stared deeply into Traven's eyes, and Traven felt the cold that the old man must have been feeling.

"At this point," the old man said, "there are no full blooded humans left. Oh, some half breeds live among us, and there may be scattered tribes left in Europe, but none that I know of. The age of man is over."

Traven took an unsteady drink as the furry creatures refilled his glass.

"I learned the ways of magic from the Daliteen and old Earth books. It's all about the mind and faith, you know."

Traven thought of Mo-pa and his training to open his mind. Was the old man trying to tell him that the two were the same? Being afraid to interrupt the story he said nothing.

"I have been many things in my life, a warrior, a sorcerer, a leader, but the thing I miss the most is a husband and a father. I've lived far too long. I have managed to outlive not only most of my friends but my family. Losing my wife was the end of my world, but to see my children go into the ground... took my soul."

There was a sharp rasp in the old man's voice and then he lay motionless. When Traven looked up the old man was gone.

He sat there for about an hour crying. When his tears stopped he tried to collect himself. He went to the shelf and took the mead as he was told. Traven toasted the old man and stood for a moment of silence. He re-corked the bottle and then went to the body of the man he could have been. He carefully lifted the heavy book from off of his chest, put it under his arm, and said good-bye. The fuzzy creatures ran frantically around the bed not knowing what to do and slowly disappeared from existence.

Traven didn't remember much of his trip back to the landing area. The expression on the creature known as Spider kept invading his mind. There was such sorrow and pain as the green beast went sadly into the room to say good-bye.

By the time Traven had reached the departure point the afternoon rain had become a heavy downpour. He took one last look at the castle, circled his arm and went home.

Chapter Ten

Blueprint For Salvation

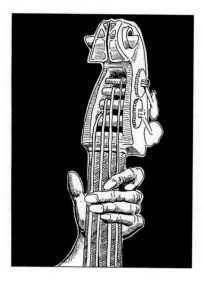

Traven entered the Gateway with tears in his eyes, a bottle of mead in one hand and the record of his other life under his arm. He walked straight past Larry who besieged him with a thousand questions. Traven said nothing and went to his room, closing the door in Larry's face. He laid in his bed for hours wondering if the same fate would befall his world as did the one he just visited. Would Matt's dad force him and his friends into a bomb cellar? Matt's dad was always building things and inventing stuff. Was there a bomb shelter at Matt's house? More importantly, was almost everyone he knew marked for death? Even with the outside of his tree house bedroom simulating the dark of night he couldn't turn off his brain and fall asleep. After fifty minutes of tossing and turning he gave up.

He went to a practice room and threw his Calleash around. His aim was ok, but he was having trouble getting the Calleash to return after striking multiple targets. He could tell that his skills with the Calleash were improving, but at this moment the mess in his mind was undermining any advances in his newly developed skill. He was surprised that Mo-pa didn't show up. Mo-pa was always around, but now that Traven needed to talk to someone human, he was gone. Was Mo-pa human? The question presented itself for the first time. He finally was convinced that Mo-pa was real, but he never had bothered to ask him if he was from the Earth. Maybe he wasn't. There was even the brief thought that Mo-pa may be a shape shifter like Docheen was. Traven decided he would ask the old man if he was human the next time he saw him. After an incredibly bad throw an idea struck him.

As Traven raced through the halls, Larry followed him, although this time he had given up the questioning and just went along for the ride. He had been waiting outside the practice room door like a metal puppy. Into the music library the boy and his robot went. Traven rifled through the shelves looking for any indication that the world as he now knew it would continue beyond 1985. He found nothing in the section that tied with his timeline. Not a single Earth album had a date that went past his current school year.

Other places he had visited had whole catalogs of each of their musicians. Every performer he had seen on Dirgewhere had a complete compilation of their music and usually an obituary of when they passed into the great beyond. Earth music seemed to stop in 1985 without fanfare, without a last blowout concert. He threw down the album he had been carefully reading and addressed the air.

"It's gonna happen isn't it?" he said. "My world parallels my other life."

There was no answer. He looked left to right expecting a reply.

"Damn it Brandy, answer me!"

In the corner of the room her body formed. She could pass for human again, unlike when he left, but there was a mechanical undertone to her southern voice.

"Y'all went looking for trouble," she said. "Now you've found a mess of it."

"So that's your attitude," he barked. "Almost my entire planet is going to die and all you can say is that I went looking for trouble?"

"Planets and races come and go," she stated flatly. "Only the forward motion of time remains."

"My world is going to die!"

"All worlds die. What do you think you can do about it?" she said crossing her arms.

"You said everything I do affects the outcome of the future, if that's the case I damn well mean to change it!"

"This is exactly what I warned you about." All trace of her human voice were gone and her eyes started to glow.

"So when were you going to tell me?" he said shifting the conversation. "Or were you just going to let me find out when I was locked in a bomb cellar?"

"You would just wave your arm and be here," she pointed out.

"And then what," he screamed, "watch oblivion on the television? No way!"

There was a long silence as Traven looked intently at the floor. Brandy regained her southern accent and spoke softly.

"Then what are you gonna do?" she asked again, though she sounded more like a teacher pushing a student to give an answer.

He waved his hands as if trying to change the air and the world. His frustration showed in his voice and it cracked slightly.

"I... don't know?" His body and head seemed to slump forward in depression. "Can I see the future? I mean, do I have to go there or is there a way to access reports, or future TV broadcasts?" *I don't want to pop into a world dying of the plague,* he thought. Plus the thought of seeing his parents die wasn't appealing either.

"Yes," said Brandy, "Larry will take you to the library."

Brandy started to leave and Traven stopped her.

"Brandy," he said, as she tried to disappear into the floor. "I'm sorry for what I said before I left."

"Ah know," she replied, in a tone that indicated that she had finally accepted his apology.

"Why do you want me to let the world go? I mean, I'm supposed to save Thealand's planet, why is this any different?"

She walked closer to him and directed his face to meet her now normal eyes with her hands.

"Thealand's planet is a business deal. When it's over, you are finished mess'n' with it. It's no longer your concern. Earth is home. It's personal, Honey, and it's going to get messier than you can ever imagine. I'm afraid y'all will come to look at Earth as your responsibility, like people do with their children. I was with Docheen for over a million years, in that time he eventually learned nothing lasts forever. There is a time when parents have to let their children make their own mistakes, no matter what the outcome. I know ya have to do what you feel you have to do, but that does not mean I have to like it. You are going to make choices that you have to live with. These choices will make you question who you are and what y'all are truly capable of. It may come to a point where you may not like what you have become. Ah might not like what you become. But, you are right, I work for you. I will be here when you need me." With that, she called for Larry and disappeared into the floor.

Larry lead him to the library. It was a dark room illuminated by what seemed only to be television screens that floated in the air. In the middle of the room was a chair with a keyboard floating in a comfortable position over the seat. Larry explained that all Traven had to do was ask the library for a place, event, date or subject matter and the screens would scan all media. Words like *book, newspaper, radio or television*, coupled with *slow, fast* or *hold*, on the media desired would enable him to select the information he wanted. The keyboard was there for his comfort and could be used to arrange his information the way he wanted.

A Lifetime In Time

He could also eavesdrop on events and people as they would play out, depending on his actions that he had already taken and how they affected the timeline. It could not, however, show him anything based on the speculation of what he might do. He turned to Larry.

"Does Santa have one of these?" he laughed, as Larry replied by rolling his eye.

The information he found was all bad. The world died in plague starting on May 19th and was pretty much finished within the month. The virus was airborne and attacked the body's immune system. The very young and very old were the first to go, followed quickly by the rest of the world. He then went to review the people responsible. He watched hour after hour of meetings and events that led to the virus creation. Government officials and scientists thought they were helping to make a safer world. The virus was a weapon that could kill the enemy, leave their property standing, and prevent the loss of our own troops. The concept was nothing less than the total destruction of whatever foe they decided was a threat.

Traven wrote the names, history, and addresses of all involved. He tried to catalog the dates and events. The information was staggering and he only took breaks to pee or get another Diet Coke. Hours later his eyes were starting to burn and his back was sore. He realized he was no closer to stopping the event than when he started. The random thought of stopping the births of the people responsible did cross his mind and the thought scared him. No, there had to be a better way. He wasn't a murderer no matter what verbal jabs Brandy gave him about Docheen. He felt confused and frustrated.

He then remembered when he tried to create his bedroom. He just needed time to think and plan. Larry had appeared with another Coke.

"Larry," Traven questioned, "can an AOD function outside of the Gateway?"

"Thure," he replied, "they can be made with their own internal power thource that will latht for quite a while depending on how

long they are turned on, but they do act a little thtrange in com-parithon to real people."

"Excellent," he smiled.

He then asked the library for information about McDonald Lodge. He told Larry to pack him a suitcase with clothes and huge amounts of money from around 1917, and to prepare an older looking male AOD. He said the AOD didn't have to talk, just do what he asked it to. Traven changed into period style clothing as did the AOD. He found the clothes constricting and dorky and even the AOD looked uncomfortable. He packed a walkman tape player, a head set, tapes, and the diary of his other life into one of the suitcases; his sketchbook, clothes, and Diet Cokes into the other.

"Going thomewhere?" asked Larry.

"Going to where I can clear my mind. When I have a plan I'll be back."

Traven and the AOD walked to the landing room. On the way Traven stopped off to have the AOD remade with a sickly look-ing color to its face. They left the Gateway and appeared in what would be Glacier National Park, 1917.

Traven went into McDonald Lodge and convinced the pro-prietor to rent one of the best rooms to him and his sickly father whom he was looking after. The AOD was perfect in its role. Management balked at first saying the lodge was full until Traven showed them the money and paid them in advance for the next 80 years. With that, no more questions were asked and Traven and his so called father became the beloved royalty of the Lodge. The AOD functioned as his cover story and would play the role of his imaginary father while he was there. Traven called him Father the few times he let the AOD out of the room. The rest of the time he would make him stand in the closet in a sleep mode to conserve its energy. He told everyone that his father's name was W.B. Jones, after Brian's story about the homeless man. Traven took up the name John Byrne Jones after his favorite comic art-ist. When other guests would ask he would say that his father's health was failing and that his mother had died in a freak horse riding accident. The story even continued to the point that his make-believe father was an inventor and owned the patent on the salt shaker.

Life at McDonald Lodge was in its own way very pleasant. The lodge was built with large redwood trees and the center went three stories straight up. Even with its size it felt cozy, with large chairs and a fireplace that you could have stood up in if it wasn't lit. Other than the stuffed animals that he felt sorry for, it was his ideal vacation spot and he laughed wondering if any of the current staff would be around when his family stayed there when he was only fourteen. The diary had much of the first chapters taking place in McDonald Lodge after his other self had fled from the city with his friends. Once upon a time this had been his home.

Traven would take meals in the small restaurant and started to enjoy foods other than cheese burgers and cookies. Breakfasts of big pancakes, thick ham, and sausage dripping with syrup from the pancakes seemed to take on an almost seductive quality. It had him getting up early, even though he read the reports on the virus and took notes through most of the night. Other than meals, hikes, and jogging, he spent most of his time in the room.

When his research became too much he would switch his reading to the thick book of his other life. This would usually happen late at night when no one was around. Traven would sit by the dwindling fire of the main hall and try to imagine the things that happened in the book. It was bound in an animal skin that he didn't recognize and tied with hair that he could only guess belonged to the important people of his other life. It was very worn and even had pictures that the other him had drawn. He found himself constantly returning to the drawings of Thunder, the girl he might someday love and the children he hadn't had.

Thunder was a Daliteen with waist long dark brown hair and deep brown eyes. She had a small slightly up-turned nose and a body that Traven thought he might have seen once in a nineteen seventies Playboy magazine that he had stolen from his uncle.

When he found himself fantasizing about the pictures he would quickly tell himself that this dream girl was yet just another girl that wouldn't ask him to any dance.

At night the restaurant had music. Three young black men played for the all white audience. There was a piano player named Charles, a horn player named Tubs, and a Bassist named Robert. Of the three Robert was the only one who would talk openly to Traven. The other band members seemed afraid of being seen in a conversation with a guest or possibly even someone who was white. Robert spoke to him of the nobility of the Bass, and on a few occasions, slammed the guitar as being too soft to compete in real music. If anyone else would have insulted Traven's favorite instrument they would have been in for a fight, but Traven was amazed at how well Robert played and was not about to argue with someone this good. The music they played was early Jazz but with an aggressive edge that made it exciting to his rock and roll ears. He was fascinated with both their playing ability and the sound they could produce and would spend hours staring at Robert's hands as he played, praying that someday he would be that good on the guitar.

The band was not allowed to stay at the Lodge, even when Traven complained and his AOD father mimicked him with hand gestures to the management. Robert quickly took him aside and told him that that's not the way it is for him and his people. Traven had a hard time coming to grips with this and only quieted down when Robert told him that the band was in danger of losing its job if Traven made too much of a stink. During the band's set breaks, Traven and Robert would sit outside looking at the lake and the shadows of the mountains against the night sky. Traven revealed to Robert that someday the world would change and that skin color wouldn't be as much of an issue. Robert just replied that he hoped he'd see that day.

One day after a long jog and a successful practice session deep in the woods with his Calleash, Traven found himself standing at the front desk, face to face with the former President of the

United States, Theodore Roosevelt. He was a friendly older man, who immediately commented that a strong body helped perfect a strong mind. He asked Traven if he was in training for competition and was even more impressed when Traven told him he wasn't and it was just something he did to keep fit. As the weeks went on "Teddy," as Mr. Roosevelt let Traven call him, told him story after story of his life. When most older people talked Traven usually zoned out, but Teddy was different, his life was an epic. Even if he hadn't become the President, the life he led was befitting of a movie. Stories he told of being a soldier and riding horses into battle had Traven mesmerized. Teddy even told of his sickly childhood, and how he overcame his shortcomings through grit and determination.

Always within 40 feet of Teddy were two giant bodyguards who were assigned to the ex-president. This bothered Traven, but then he chalked it up to the dues you have to pay when you're the former President. And really he thought, *How much different was it than having the Gateway always watching?*

When Traven admitted that he didn't really fish the old man woke him up early the next day and took him out to the lake. Traven made him and his bodyguards wait outside the room as he got ready, afraid that they might see the endless notes and timelines scattered all over the room. Worst of all was the fear that they might find the AOD napping in the closet. Traven found the AOD creepy and the less that he had to look at him, the better he felt. Keeping him turned off and in the closet at least let him get a good night's sleep. Without incident Traven and Teddy left the hotel and headed to the lake.

That day Traven learned how to cast a fly and how to clean and cook a fish. He thought, *If Thealand could only see me now she might be proud of my low level hunting skills.* To Mr. Roosevelt, the wilderness was the most important asset the world had to offer. Teddy went on and on about the land, his hunting trips, and eventually his children. The bodyguards had their own boat and Teddy constantly berated them for not fishing correctly. At the end of the day they had their meal of fresh trout and caught the band to end off the evening. Traven introduced the ex-President to the trio and quite unexpectedly he spoke openly to them and told them any time they were near his stomping grounds, they were welcome to stop by and visit. When Traven hit the pillow that night he felt much better about the world.

The next morning Traven reviewed his notes and had finally formulated a plan. The key to his problem was a man by the name of Lynx. Lynx was a professional assassin and one that the government paid well to make sure no one would ever find out about the virus. He was one of the few people that was ever inoculated against the virus. If Traven could get to him maybe there was a chance he could help him save the world. An assassin saving the world was a long shot at best, but it might be the only option without wiping those responsible off the face of the Earth. If this was his best plan, he thought he had better get back to the Gateway soon and set the ball in motion. He decided on one last jog before he said his goodbyes.

The jog was exactly what he needed to bring his mind into focus. The sight of the mountains, the smell of the pine made him almost envy his other life. As he ran along Going to the Sun Road, he decide to cut across the tundra at Logan's Pass to get an even better view of the mountains. He was far above the tree line and checked each direction to make sure the coast was clear. The young Keeper removed his Calleash from his satchel bag and practiced with the hard wooden ball on its returns. It was strange to him that after all the time he had spent here without Mo-pa nagging him that he would still feel the need and desire to practice. It had become part of his daily routine, like brushing his teeth. After a strong twenty minutes of throwing he was starting to get the hang of the return. Maybe it was the mountain air that was inspiring him or maybe he was just getting better. Then in his head he heard a voice.

"How are you doing that?" it said.

It was a clear almost in the back of your head whisper, the kind where you question if your mind invented it or if you really heard it. He stopped the Calleash abruptly and scanned the area for the source of the sound. As he focused hard on the surroundings a small figure bolted from behind one large rock to another. Though he didn't see it, the sound made him turn in its direction. Traven dashed toward the sound not really sure if it was human or animal. Over rocks and thin foliage it's trail danced, disappearing for a moment and then making a giggling sound only to confuse Traven on what he had heard. He tried to use the skills Thealand had taught him about tracking, but as he got close to a trail the sound would pop up in a completely different part of the terrain. Though he never got a clear look at it he decided that it sounded distinctly feminine. Then there was a silence. The tracks had completely disappeared off the edge of a cliff. He questioned himself if he was really looking at its tracks at all. The clues were small and the rocks made it next to impossible for a novice tracker like himself. He waited for what seemed to be a very long time. The cold mountain air started to chill him now that he was not moving and after a while he started to wonder if the event had happened at all. He took a deep breath and tried to reach out with his senses, but to no avail. The cold crept into his skin and he decided that maybe he had spent too much time reading and rereading his diary. It must be that his imagination had gotten the better of him.

He laughed at the thought of himself freezing in the cold chasing what was probably nothing more than some really large rock varmint. Heading down the mountain he remembered the stories of all the sailors that had seen a manatee and mistook it for a mermaid. When he was clear out of sight a young girl with pointed ears and dark brown hair pulled herself up from under the edge of the cliff. She chuckled to herself as she went along her way.

When he returned to the lodge something was amiss. He looked up to see people gathered around his room. The bodyguards were in the doorway and someone was inside moving in the shadows. His tired muscles sent him quickly up the three flights of stairs. The guards tried to stop him from entering. Much to their surprise he quickly disabled them and left them in a lump on the floor. As he turned he was greeted by Teddy's somber face. Teddy looked at his bodyguards as they lay in a heap.

"I knew they were over-paid," he said gruffly, and then his face quickly turned back into one of remorse. "Listen son, I'm sorry, but there's no easy way to say this. Your father has passed away."

Traven pushed past him and into the room to find the AOD laid carefully across the bed.

"I know times like this are hard my boy, but these are the very times we have to be strong."

The bodyguards slowly tried to stand.

"Can you get rid of them?" Traven said, pointing to the guards.

Teddy turned and shooed them away.

"Come on, you heard the boy, get out before I fire you. Go to the restaurant and have a drink. Rethink your vocation before I do."

They left, and then Teddy chased the onlookers in the hallway away and shut the door. Traven was now sitting on the edge of the bed wringing his hands trying to figure out what to do. Gently, Teddy sat beside him.

"I know you two were close..."

"We're not close," Traven confessed, "personally I think he's rather repulsive, it's the way I had him made."

Teddy looked shocked and tried to regain his composure.

"Look, you don't know what your saying. It must be shock. Let me fetch a physician."

"Teddy, he's not dead, look," Traven said, and then commanded, "activate."

With this the AOD sat up and walked over in front of them to await his next commands. Teddy jumped back flabbergasted.

"What? What is going on here?" he demanded to know in a deep-bear like tone.

There was something about the Roosevelt voice. The voice that once commanded a nation had never lost its ability to command people. It could have been this factor coupled with Traven's isolation from his friends that caused the difference. It could have been the secret that he urged to share, or it could have literally been the weight of the world that made him break his silence.

"It's difficult to explain," he said, and then like a Pandora's box his story unfolded. "I am the Keeper."

"The Keeper of what?" Teddy asked, trying to remain calm.

"I am the Keeper of the Gateway. The Gateway allows me to travel in both time and space. It allows me to see what might happen and what will most likely happen. My so-called father there is really nothing more than a cover story to explain to others why a boy of my age has large amounts of money. His presence lets me travel without too many questions."

"Look son, I have been in war and I know death when I see it. Two seconds ago this man was dead," Teddy huffed.

"This man has never truly been alive. He's what you could loosely call a robot, an advanced mechanical man." With that Traven told the AOD to go stand in the corner on its head and spin, which it did without question.

"Balderdash," bellowed Teddy, "I was and am still privy to the latest inventions and information. There is nothing that should even suggest what you are telling me to be true."

"Not now," Traven said, "but in the future, not even my future, but in someone's future it's all very real."

"So you are telling me you can travel time like in one of those H.G.Wells books?"

"Yes, that pretty much sums it up." There was a moment of silence as Traven contemplated what he had said, and Teddy tried to grasp what he had learned.

"Why are you here now?" asked Teddy. "Does it have something to do with me?"

"No," Traven replied, feeling that he was somehow insulting the former president by not being here to meet him. "I have a problem that I have been trying to sort out."

Traven went on to explain about what he had found out about the future and how even the great America would end if he didn't do something about it. The two sat down with the book and Traven explained it the best he could. After an hour, sharing a couple of Diet Cokes and showing Teddy how his walkman worked, Traven started packing his things.

"Son," said Teddy in a fatherly tone, "I am having a hard time trying to fathom your story, but the one thing I have learned, to my great pain, is that my government would be very capable of leading the world into Armageddon," he stated sadly.

"You can't blame the entire government for the actions of a few," Traven said, trying to reassure him that the whole of the government wasn't to blame. "From what I learned only a relatively small group are really responsible. Unfortunately, the resources at their disposal are vast, and they also don't foresee the outcome of their actions."

"Do you think you have a chance?" Teddy asked.

"I don't know, but I have to try." Traven gave his bags to the AOD, waved his arm in the air and sent him through.

The expression on Teddy's face of seeing the AOD disappear into thin air was one of utter amazement.

"I should be going," he said, making sure that he hadn't left anything behind. "I just wanted to say it was an honor spending time with you and that I'll do everything I can."

As the two shook hands, Teddy started to shake his head vigorously.

"Wait," he said pointing to the spot where the AOD had just disappeared. "It's not every day that you see a man or mechanical man rise from the dead... or see him disappear in an act that would make any vaudeville magician proud. Your story seems to hold true merit," his voice started to boom through the room as if he was addressing the masses. "I believe in the underdog and that one man can make a great difference and rise to greatness. Your foes seem to have the advantage on you as you have stated, perhaps I can level the playing field."

Traven raised an eyebrow to which Mr. Roosevelt took some minor offense to.

"Listen son, just because I'm no longer the President does not suggest that I am a man without means. As you stated only a few truly run things, as it is in your day, it has always been. It will take some time, but that you seem to have in abundance. I have spoken to the desk clerk and he informed me that you have paid for this room for the next eighty years. All I ask is that you check back in three years, at that point you will see what kind of help I can offer."

"Thank you, Mr. President," Traven said with a smile.

"It's Teddy to you, Mr. Keeper. I might be betraying my government, but the needs of the people and the land have always come first in my book and always will."

"Thank you again, and my real name is Traven."

"It has been a pleasure to meet you, Traven."

"The pleasure has been all mine."

Chapter Eleven

Where Lines Are Drawn

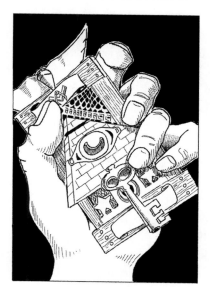

When Traven arrived in the Gateway, Brandy was waiting. Her body was completely silver and floating three feet off the floor. Both her eyes and the soles of her feet were glowing bright and for the first time so were her fingertips. Traven thought that she was not unlike the robot from the old Metropolis movie.

"Do you know what you have done?" she said, pronouncing each word as if she had been taught to speak from a child's electronic toy.

He ignored her anger and spoke as if he was oblivious to the weight of his recent actions.

"I have probably sent an old man down a path that will allow him to be considered insane and looked upon as a kook for the remainder of his years."

He turned and scribbled a few notes on the calendar wall of the landing room, and checked the clock that showed how much time he had stayed away from his first life on Earth. It had been a long time and knowing himself he knew he wouldn't return to a normal life until he fixed things.

"If you are lucky he will be considered a kook. Have you even considered that you may have become the most valued prize that mankind has to fight for?"

"What do you mean?" he asked, confused by her statement.

"If people believe him, they will want the power over time. They will search for you the way people look for lost treasure and the things that humans do in the search for wealth and power are dark things indeed. You have made yourself a target!"

Her voice contained none of its southern charm and as her arms waved in exclamation the trio of necklaces became entangled in each other.

"Look, he has no witnesses, he has no proof, and really I don't think that Teddy would set me up," he said, wondering if she was really trying to scare him, or if this was just another attempt to teach him a lesson.

"Greed and power cannot be trusted," she said, as her body moved like a puppet in the hands of an unskilled puppeteer.

"Why don't I go down to the library and see the outcomes of my actions?"

With this she seemed slightly pacified and finally lowered herself into the floor. Her normal voice returned.

"That might be one of the more intelligent ideas y'all have ever had," she said smugly, as she straightened her necklaces.

Traven entered, followed by a very quiet Larry who was carrying a drink and cookie. Brandy formed behind him as he set upon plowing through a series of video scenes eavesdropping on the former President. Like searching through videotape it took a while to hash out what Teddy had set in motion. From what appeared on the screen he had made contact with several secret sections of the government to grant the boy special clearances. These clearances would be unchangeable as long as the secret sections still had power, and deemed him an asset, or as Brandy had stated, a useful prize. Now the government or parts of it knew about him. They still didn't know who he was, but on the strength of Mr. Roosevelt's reputation and one misplaced can of Diet Coke, they were willing to give him the status of an agent working outside of the confines of the United States government, answering to only himself.

Traven also discovered that these sections owed Mr. Roosevelt a favor for throwing the last election by inventing a third party which took votes away from the party that would have won. Traven guessed that Teddy was all he bragged to be, and from his actions most likely deserved his face on Mount Rushmore. According to Teddy's deal, a sealed package was left in Traven's rented room at McDonald lodge. Inside the package was a badge that gave him unlimited accesses to all government information, buildings, and bases. It also gave him the authority to act as he felt was in the best interest of the Earth, without prosecution, that is, at least by the U.S. government.

"Does this mean I'm my own double knot spy?" Traven said with a grin.

"This is what I was afraid of," Brandy said, "they know about you and just because some of the government now holds you in questionable high esteem, or even in fear, it does not mean that others won't be looking for ya. If not for the powers of time and space, but to have free access to your government's information. People kill for that everyday."

"I already have access to information that people would kill for," he pointed out, waving at the library screens.

"Yes honey, but no one needed to ever know about it. Y'all screwed up and gained nothing. If one part of the government knows, then others will know. It's a strong bet that information will fall into the wrong hands, and someone will come looking for you. Damn it, Traven, you have all you need here in this room!"

Traven got out of the chair and walked to the door.

"Where are you going?" she asked, punctuating every word like an angry parent.

"To get my badge," he replied. "I want to see if there's a secret decoder ring in the package."

Traven left Brandy and Larry in the room alone.

"Who does he remind you of now?" Brandy asked Larry in a menacing tone.

Traven appeared in his room in McDonald Lodge, the year was 1974. The room hadn't been cleaned in a very long time. Dust covered everything like a layer of snow. It reminded him of Fecha with its ever present gray brown soot. He hadn't thought of Fecha in a while. He thought of how he missed Thealand and his promise to her and her people.

"Well," he mumbled, "one planet at a time."

He tore through the dusty envelope, and all it contained was a gold badge with a familiar symbol. The symbol was a pyramid with an eye floating over it. As he looked in the empty envelope for more information the door swung open. Standing in the doorway was a government agent. His suit had a laughable seventies cut to it with a very wide lapel and wide tie. His hair was almost as bushy as Traven's. A thick mustache covered his upper lip as if he had gotten some bad styling advice from Fu-Manchu. Traven drew his Calleash and just about as it left his fingertips the agent spoke.

"Wait!" shouted the agent. "Please, sir, I mean you no harm!"

Traven stopped the Calleash as it was about to leave his hand. The agent put his hands in the air as if a gun was being held on him.

"They said you wouldn't come. They told us that this assignment was a cake walk," he said, with a wide eyed amazement and a smile. "You can't imagine the paper work I'm going to have to do."

"Who sent you?" questioned Traven.

"Well sir, through the years agents have been posted outside this room awaiting your return. We have been put here by the request of the person that wanted you to have that badge. If you can tell me who that is and answer another few questions I can give you the rest of the package."

"You mean Teddy?" Traven questioned.

"I'm sorry sir, I need more confirmation than a first name."

"Roosevelt... Teddy Roosevelt," Traven clarified.

"That is correct. My name is agent Nixon and, no, I'm not related. Can you tell me what you may have left behind after your visit?"

Being that he had just seen that mistake in the library video screen the answer came easy.

"A can of Diet Coke," he replied.

"Excellent,"he said, checking the answer off on a pad of paper. "What bit of the future did you share with the former President?"

"Do you mean predictions or objects?"

"Objects."

"We listened to some tunes on a walkman."

"A walkman?" asked Nixon.

"A portable tape taper."

"You mean like an 8-track?" he asked, becoming way too interested in the answer. "You guys had those way back then?"

"No, it's a lot better than an 8-track," Traven replied, thinking back to his childhood and his cousin's bulky music collection. "It's more compact, better sound quality, and doesn't cut out in the middle of a song just to finish it on another track."

"Really?" he asked in awe of the concept.

"Yep," Traven nodded. "Ninety minutes of music straight from your favorite records."

"How can it be portable, they have to be really large, right?"

"No," Traven said, measuring the air to show the size, "just a little bigger than a cassette. Heck you can listen to them when you're jogging, I mean, if you're into jogging."

"Oh, so it plays cassettes!"

"Yeah," Traven said, realizing that the whole conversation could have been shorter with the right word choice.

Nixon looked left to right as if he was checking to see if anyone was listening.

"Could you get me one of those?" he asked sheepishly.

"Is that on the list of questions?"

"I'm sorry, forget that one. There's one more... your name."

Traven was hesitant, wondering if this was a set up. With his Calleash tightly grasped in his hand he spoke.

"Traven. My name is Traven."

"Wow," said agent Nixon, "I am honored to meet you sir... May I?" he asked, pointing to his coat, to which Traven nodded a yes.

The agent pulled a yellowed letter sized envelope from his jacket pocket.

"He wrote this a week before he died," he said, handing the letter to Traven. "I just wonder where they'll assign me now?"

Traven opened the letter and put its contents into his back pocket. Walking over to the desk he took some blank paper from the drawer, drew a one eyed smiley face on it and folded it into the empty envelope. He then took a very old jar of rubber cement from the desk and resealed it.

"Well agent Nixon... I hate to see you do a ton of paper work," he said, handing the yellowed envelope back.

"What are you saying, sir?"

"Lets say this just never happened," Traven winked.

"Sir, I couldn't do that..."

Agent Nixon was cut off by Traven waving the badge in front of his face.

"So, does this work, or not?"

At first Nixon had a look of fear and then a smile spread over his face.

"Yes sir, I guess it does. Its been an honor to meet you sir, it's like finding out Santa Claus is real."

With that the agent returned to his post, shutting the door quietly behind him. Traven took one last look at the room, doubting he would ever return and remembering his time with the man he knew as Teddy. He waved his hand and disappeared.

Larry was the only one to meet Traven when he reappeared. He filled Traven in on Brandy's mood, which was as he expected; bad. At least this time he didn't have to verbally spar with her. Larry also informed him that very little changed in his timeline because of the pop he left behind. In fact, in 1982 it was mistakenly opened and drained by a thirsty guard that had no idea of its importance, but found it refreshing anyway, though rather flat. He had ordered Nixon not to tell, and to the man's credit he kept his mouth shut an entire six months. Then one night he went drinking with some fellow agents and they started one up-ing each other with work stories. So, to say the least, Nixon won the most impressive story contest and then spent the rest of the year in solitary. The badge seemed to be a useless prize.

They both went to the library to research the man known as Lynx. They found that not only was he a freelance assassin, but he was the man other assassins had nightmares about. His abilities placed him as the head of the Steel Tear, a group of professionals that could be hired when anyone had the cash and needed to be sure that the hit would go down without a hitch. The Steel Tear were a mystery to all common folk, but a whisper of great fear amongst the underground. Thanks to the library, Traven traced the organization back to the iron age when most appropriately they were known as the Iron Tear because the discovery of iron was changing the balance of power throughout the lands. Lynx became the leader in 1962 when he defeated the previous leader and took the throne.

Lynx had a sordid and difficult history. His father was killed at Pearl Harbor when the Japanese bombed his ship, "the Arizona." Lynx's mother, not wanting to raise a half breed Indian child on her own, left him in the care of relatives on her reservation. She disappeared through most of his life and the few times she returned were uncomfortable. He was abused by his relatives and last saw his mother at her burial in 1952. She had died of a drug overdose.

With Lynx's incredible natural fighting skills he became the youngest enforcer organized crime had ever seen. He would later sharpen these skills beyond that of the lead street thug under the training of an old Chinese man who taught self defense as a cover to his less honorable activities. The man would describe the gun as a weapon for the loud and clumsy. This led Lynx to develop a dislike of the gun as a weapon and focus almost every hour on his hand to hand ability or more graceful weapons. When the young assassin turned sixteen his teacher introduced him to the Red Claw, a feeder group of assassins to the Steel Tear. After that he quickly worked his way up the ranks and eventually to the top.

Traven had the screen pause on the face of the man named Lynx. It was a hard face that looked even older than it was due to his life and the dark deeds he had done. The lines in his face were deep and his hair had already turned completely silvery gray. The hair was long, stopping a foot from the floor when he was standing and tied back with seven silver bands. His eyes were almost catlike, and on each side of his face he grew two long mutton chops that came almost to his chest, stopping at the edge of his nose and leaving his upper lip and chin clean. This strange facial hair gave him the look of his name sake, the look of a lynx.

His fighting abilities would have impressed even Thealand. He could kill a person in the time that it took a heart to beat. He had the ability to move around a room without being noticed, as if he was almost invisible. During a few of the assassinations that Traven viewed from the safety of the library, he felt that he was watching a horror flick, the kind where you're yelling at the hero to run because you know the killer was there, yet the victim was oblivious to his predicament.

After watching countless battles and assassinations, Traven decided that it would be for the best if Thealand accompanied him on this meeting. Besides, he was supposed to meet with her anyway. As he straightened his notes he ran across the outline of the planet Harken. Harken was destroyed by the Drackeen and that was what originally lead the Daliteen to the exodus of their planet, according to the history the other him had written in his book. He wished he had more time to read the book and find out about his other life and what the Drackeen really were. He had read most of the book haphazardly when he was at McDonald Lodge, but his main concern at the time was forming a plan to save Earth and he really didn't focus on the how's and why's of Harkens destruction, just his other life with a girl named Thunder. It dawned on him that the

Drackeen should also be stopped. If for no other reason but to save the people that were the ancestors of his other life's true love.

Brandy was right this was getting messy. He knew in his heart he would need help and a lot of it.

"Well," he mumbled, "one world at a time." He waited for a reply or cryptic comment to come from a suddenly forming Brandy. When none was given he tried to make sense out of what he had become. *Maybe this is what the Keeper does?* he thought, as he rolled his Calleash on the back of his hand, *Maybe he balances the scales and gives the world, or all worlds a fighting chance.*

It sounded noble, at least in his head. He wondered what Docheen did with his time, he couldn't have spent all his time in the bordello, the AOD girls were just too creepy.

Switching clothes to that which blend into Fecha standards he went to get Thealand.

As he appeared in the sewers of Fecha there was a great rumbling. As before, an unseen hand dragged him into a protective cove and pressed a button. As the waters blasted past the plastic cocoon Thealand removed her hood and spoke.

"About time," she said.

"Waiting long?" he asked.

"Not really." She looked at him hard and even sniffed him a bit. It was as if she could tell there was a greater worry on his mind.

"Hey, I took a bath," he protested.

"Not recently," she replied. "You look different."

This was true, his hair had grown longer. The lines around his eyes from lack of sleep had started to make him look older than he really was.

"Just tired," he said, as he tried to stop a yawn.

"It's been more than a week for you hasn't it?" she said, as the air blew the tunnel clean.

"Yeah a bit," he admitted sheepishly.

"Well, I hope you were enjoying yourself."

She sounded slightly cross at the thought of Traven gallivanting around while she had a planet to save. She hit the button for the plastic screen to rise although a fairly strong breeze was still whipping through the tunnel.

"Why does it do that?" Traven asked, waving his hand in the direction that the sludge and wind had traveled.

"You mean the flushing? That's all we have left to keep us alive."

The confused look of Traven's face made her roll her eyes. Frustrated at his naiveté she continued her explanation.

"We hold the sewage in large containers until there's enough to flush. The action of the flushing activates the kinetic power absorbers that are lined along the walls."

She ripped a small piece of the walls lining off and handed it to Traven who took it although he was disgusted at the thought of touching something that had just been drenched in fecal matter.

"This is how we produce the limited energy that we live by. At the end of the tunnels there are the growing units. We grow fungi, mushrooms and such, introduce synthetic vitamins into them and that's how we get our food."

"No wonder you enjoyed hunting so much."

Traven looked at the piece of lining in his hand. It was part electronic weave and part hardened plastic. Against his better impulses he slipped the lining into his coat pocket, thinking he'd just make a new coat later and wash and study the piece in a better light.

"Aside from the gross out factor, it does sound like a great idea," he observed. "I mean it's a complete cycle of growth and decay."

"It would have been a great idea ten years ago when we had suns. At this point it's only crumbs for the dying." Thealand started to walk away as Traven just stood there. "Are we going, or what?" she said over her shoulder.

"Thealand, we need to talk," Traven said, as a cross look came over her face.

"This isn't going to be one of those, I think I'm falling in love with you" speeches?" she said crossing her arms, "because I really don't have the time to deal with that kind of crap."

Traven was taken aback, he knew he had feelings for her, but this wasn't the time or place for that discussion. On top of his misunderstood feelings weighed the diary of his other life. He knew that somewhere out there was a girl that at least one reality of him had loved beyond measure. Would he meet that girl? Would he fall in love with her if he did? Would he risk that possible love and future by falling in love with somebody else? Besides, did Thealand really just shoot his feelings down? All these thoughts took less than a split second and he responded by shaking his head, waving his arms in the air.

"No, no, I just have a favor to ask you," he said, trying to recover the moment.

"Oh," she said, giving him a quick unintentional look of rejection and then moving on. "What?"

"I need you to help me save my planet."

He tried to explain what had happened over the time he had last seen her, the diary, the badge. On and on he talked realizing that by her body language he was making her upset.

"You mean you have the audacity to ask for my help before you fulfill your promise," she said. "Your world might mean something to you, but it means nothing to me! We have a deal and you have to keep it."

"I will, but my world is going to end in less than a year."

"And mine might end in less than a month, who has the greater need?"

"I just have to stop one event and then I can get back to figuring out how to save your world, which is a much bigger problem. Look at this place, two hundred years of abuse or more. Even Larry says that I would have to go back centuries to even start to correct the mess it's in now. If I change the past nothing will be the same. You might not even be you or even ever born."

"It doesn't matter, my people must survive!"

"So must mine!" he yelled.

"Yeah and if you go get yourself killed who will be there to save us then?"

"Well if you come with me maybe I won't get myself killed."

"That's your problem. At least the other Keepers knew how to honor a promise."

She reached into her pocket and threw the instant transporter he had given her earlier at his head. Catching it in midair he threw it back at her. As she ducked it bounced off the wall and skidded across the tunnel floor.

"It's our problem," he yelled, as she turned and started to walk away.

"Gurassa!" she screamed, which Traven took as an insult and wondered why it didn't translate. "Don't bother to come looking for me till you're ready to honor your promise."

She disappeared into the darkness of the tunnel leaving Traven alone in the half light wondering if he should go after her. He finally decided that he had done enough damage for one day and with a heavy heart returned to the Gateway.

Timothy John Vaulato

Chapter Twelve
The Grim Reaper

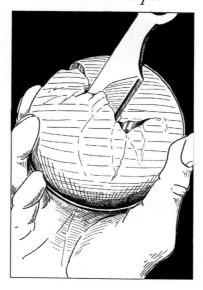

Traven took some time in the Gateway to mull over his most recent argument. It seemed to him that everywhere he walked he would be screaming at someone to justify his actions. He thought that someone, anyone, would look at him trying to save the Earth as a valid pastime. Other than Teddy, most of the people he talked with were dead set against him interfering with the flow of events as they appeared they would play out. Because of Brandy and Thealand, his teenaged mind replayed the old phrase, *It's a chick thing*. He then started to worry that Brandy might be able to read his mind even though Larry had said, "Thee motht thertainly couldn't do that."

He had hoped that Thealand of all people would sympathize, but he realized that her concerns were with those that she loved, not a planet of humans. He wished that he knew how to save her planet first, but unfortunately the only plan he had at the moment was to save Earth. If he could get to the one person who could walk into the Government base that would start Armageddon and get him to switch sides, Traven might be able to save his planet. Lynx was the key to the whole plan. He was the one that could gain access to the virus containment area without infection. He knew the codes that unlocked the room and maybe even more importantly Traven wouldn't have to open a door from the Gateway to the containment area. The idea of just opening a door to the virus and dropping the bomb off was nixed. The virus could escape into the Gateway infecting Traven and Mo-pa and in a worst case scenario evolve into something much more deadly than what would occur on Earth.

With a few suggestions on the operating techniques from Brandy the library proved to be even more powerful than Traven could have guessed. When asked to show specific areas of a given place and time it was as if there was a hidden camera in the room manned by an invisible director, editor and sound crew. It could even trace the history of people and objects throughout time. With these newly discovered features Traven tried to track the history of the virus. The screens showed that the virus never existed before in the history of Earth or the universe. The components that they could analyze were not even naturally found on Earth. Traven thought that this was more than a little suspicious, so he tried to trace its creation. There was no creation just a very deadly petri dish containing the mysterious elements for the end of most human life on Earth. Traven watched the screen as the dish appeared as if by magic. As he slowed the image and rewound time, the library video showed a point of static and then the dish was gone.

How is that possible? he thought, as the screens continued moving forward, playing a vision of a man in a lab becoming radically sick as the dish lie open in front of him. It wasn't there before the static or before he became sick, just at the moment he dropped to his knees. As Traven wondered how or who could have set this in motion the screens showed the lockdown on the room where the man in the lab coat took his last breath.

He asked Larry about the static on the screen and was informed that static happened from time to time. Some planets were more likely to have static when their timeline was at an important juncture and the moment would have a massive domino effect on all future events. The static represented a fork in the road and would also be a turning point that would share static in other realities as well. There were other less dramatic reasons. It could also form when humans used what they loosely define as magic, or certain technologies could also block viewing. Certain weather conditions could also make it difficult to view parts of the timeline. Traven asked him about what could have happened during the static and why the dish had components not found on Earth. He said, that there are many things on Earth from other planets. Some things had arrived over the years with travelers or falling asteroids. As for the dish itself, it was probably placed there by someone during the static. Traven felt that something just didn't sound right. But at the moment his obsession with saving the Earth from the spread of the virus was more important than placing blame.

Traven switched the screen and studied Lynx's fighting style. He moved silently like a big cat and pounced with no remorse. The few who had ever set eyes on him rarely lasted long. Even most of the people in Lynx's organization, "the Steel Tear," had never seen his face. His orders were given out by a handful of his generals that feared him the way most children fear the monster under the bed.

Traven's plan was simple, open a door below the assassin and let him fall into the Gateway. Then spill all the information about what was going to happen and not to be killed while he was talking. He knew the plan wasn't great. He also knew that Brandy wouldn't approve, but sending him a letter wasn't going to persuade Lynx that Traven was anything other than someone who probably needed to be killed for knowing his mailing address.

Traven tried to rest, to get in a good night's sleep before attempting this game of Russian Roulette. He found sleep was next to impossible. When he tried he would think of the upcoming meeting or his fight with Thealand. When the brief moment of sleep did come he would dream. The dream would quickly become a nightmare of him smashing Docheen's heartstone and then the image of a world where his friends were dying in front of him. Toward the end of the nightmares, he walked alone in a field barefoot. One poorly placed step left him trying to scrape off what he believed was dog crap on any nearby object. It wouldn't come off and in his fixation a man appeared from nowhere and offered his assistance. As Traven tried to decline the man's form changed into a giant cat and gutted him with one fell swoop of an enormous claw. Traven woke up covered in sweat and shaking. It only took two of these dreams to make him finally get dressed and head to the Landing area to set forth the moment when Lynx would tumble into the Gateway and outside of time itself.

As he walked through the hall Mo-pa stepped out of a doorway apparently looking for him.

"You are troubled," stated the old man, clutching a pizza to go box.

"Yeah, I guess that would be an understatement," Traven said, glad to see someone, but hoping that this too would not end in a fight.

"I know that many disagree with the actions you are about to take." Traven nodded his head as if to state the obvious. Mo-pa continued, "It takes a brave man to stand alone in his convictions. It takes a wise man to ask for help and it takes a strong heart to do what is right, even in the face of adversity." The old man dispensed his wisdom, patted the boy firmly on his shoulder, and turned to walk away. Remembering his earlier question Traven called after him.

"Mo-pa?"

The old man stopped.

"Are you... human?" he asked, drawing a smile from Mo-pa's wrinkled face.

"Let us say we share some common beginnings," he replied, and with that he disappeared down the corridor.

"Well, as always," Traven said, "I know no more than I did before."

As he entered the Landing area Larry awaited. He was holding a new trench coat that had a brown metallic shimmer to it.

"What's this for?" asked Traven.

"Well, after the thewers I knew you would want a new coat. Thisth one ith a little different than the latht one."

"Yeah, I would says so. What's up with the color?" he asked, taking the jacket and trying it on.

"Ith really body armor. It will take the abuthe of most weaponth you currently have on your planet. You'll feel the impact, tho don't get thot at close range or you'll break boneth. Would you like a helmet?"

"Well, wouldn't that be a sign that I'm not operating in good faith?" he asked, admiring the length in the landing area mirror and giving it a spin.

"Not in my book," Larry replied.

"Thanks, but this should do fine, after all I'm just dropping him into the landing area," he said, tying the belt tightly at the waist.

"Don't thank me, thank Brandy. Thee thought of it," said Larry, "and I am quite thure he will be rather upthet when he landth."

"Thanks Brandy," Traven yelled toward the ceiling. "She's not talking to me again I take it."

"Women, who can figure them," Larry said, hoping not to get shot through the Gateway again. "Where do you want the opening?"

"The Steel Tear base is the location. When Lynx is meditating in his room is probably the best, at least from what I gleaned from the library. I already fed the information into the main. If the opening is large he won't know what hit him."

Larry nodded and Traven tensed long enough to get a brief glimpse of Lynx's body landing. In the second it took Traven to recognize that there was a body, Lynx recovered and threw three short handleless knives. Traven's reactions were quick. His Calleash had stopped the blade aimed at his face, nearly cutting the hard wooden ball in two. The other blades hit his chest and abdomen knocking the wind out of him but failing to cause fatal wounds thanks to his coat. Lynx moved toward him even as he threw the blades and at that moment all hell broke loose. The floor and the walls sprung at him at the speed of thought, as if they were alive. They bound his hands and legs and a branch of plastic steel shot into his mouth to gag him. Traven frantically tried to catch his breath, not understanding what was going on. Brandy formed in front of them. Traven had seen Brandy upset plenty of times before, mostly because of himself, but this was the worst. She was beautiful as ever, but now in a demonic version. It was as if the bride of Satan was computerized. Moving veins from the walls of the Gateway stripped Lynx of all hidden weapons and dropped them thoughtlessly to the floor. She approached him and signaled Traven to keep his mouth shut. Lynx stared defiantly at her glowing eyes.

"I am the Gateway," she said, in a frightening electronic voice. "My powers are limitless. I move faster than thought and can make you feel every death you have ever caused. This boy is under my protection, attack him again and hell will seem like a welcomed relief."

In the background Mo-pa held up the broken Calleash he had snatched from Traven's hand and offered a challenge with his elderly burning eyes. Brandy dropped Lynx hard on the ground; he immediately stood up.

"Remember," said Brandy turning away, "I am always watching." And then she disappeared. Lynx turned his burning gaze toward Traven.

"I'm sorry about that, she can be a little impulsive. If you would just walk this way."

Traven signaled Lynx to follow him and the two proceeded through the halls of the Gateway without a word. Every thirty feet Brandy would reform to remind Lynx that she was the one in control. She would then disappear only to form again a bit further along the hallway after they had passed her. Traven felt uneasy.

It was like being at school with the class bully behind you in the hall, but this time the bully might kill you.

In the library Traven had another chair created, but Lynx refused to sit so the chair disappeared.

"I am sorry for abducting you," he said, "but with your skills it wasn't like I would have stood much of a chance to plead my case without you killing me first."

"Some god favors you child, for the mere fact that you still live." Lynx's voice was cold and sounded like nails on a blackboard. Brandy formed in the back of the room and waved as if she was taunting him.

"Uh... yes, I... guess so." he stumbled. "I need your help."

"I don't help anyone, but into death," he whispered. There was a strange sense of pride in his voice that Traven found disturbing.

"It's about the virus."

"Get rid of her," Lynx said, pointing to Brandy.

"Her body can disappear, but she is always here whether we see her or not."

"I tire of her face," Lynx said, as Brandy smiled wickedly at him with more teeth than Traven thought possible for a head to contain. "You have my word bitch, I will not kill him till he has had his say."

"You will not kill him," she stated as mere fact instead of a challenge, "not in this time or any other."

"Brandy!" Traven yelled. "This is not getting us anywhere. Please... go. I know you're here and believe he does too."

She flashed her teeth once again and melted into the floor. The walls seemed to move with her tentacles as Lynx paced ignoring his immediate danger.

"I will ask the questions child, you will answer. Don't believe for a moment that your life isn't already forfeited."

Traven couldn't believe that Lynx had still planned on killing him. Didn't Brandy scare him? She scared Traven, but there was no trace of fear in the assassin's eyes. Traven rubbed his chest where the blades had hit him and as Lynx leaned toward him, his breath was cold as if his body was incapable of producing heat.

"Who sent you?" he asked.

"I sent myself."

"You do not appear to have the ability or the intelligence to find out about the virus, let alone my location. Explain yourself," he growled, as the tentacles perched at the edge of his head.

"I'm what's known as the Keeper. I travel time and space and I'm trying to stop the destruction of the world. It will end in a days time because of the virus."

Lynx chuckled a frightening laugh.

"Insanity and a death wish," he scoffed, "how entertaining."

"Look, I can prove all that I'm saying."

"I am not a fool child, but I am curious. How did you get me here?"

"We opened a portal in time underneath you... you landed."

Lynx scanned the room and tried to assess the truth in Traven's words. Then a hesitant question popped into Traven's mind.

"You don't think I was trying to kill you... do you?" he asked.

"With a boche ball? Hardly."

"It's a Calleash, it's a non-lethal weapon," Traven clarified, "and Brandy is only protecting me from you. Your death is not in anyone's best interest."

"There you are wrong. My death would be celebrated by many," he almost smiled. "Life is always perched at the doors of death."

"Ok..." Traven said, thinking that Mo-pa should be having this conversation instead of him, "but why would I want to kill you? I don't even know you."

"It is true, you don't have the body language of a predator and if you were sent by my people, they pick their lackeys poorly. On the other hand, if the bitch wanted me dead I would be already, wouldn't I? Or perhaps it isn't within her, so called, infinite powers."

"Why would your people try to kill you?"

"We're assassins, it is what we do. You could be working for a rival country. One that wants the virus for it's own."

"Sorry, that's not it."

"It could even be they have convinced you that you are doing what you believe is right and deceiving you as well for their own gain."

Lynx's conspiracy theories verged on paranoia and for a brief moment Traven wondered if his life as a Keeper was a hoax. If it was, it was certainly more trouble to provide him with this role than it would be to find a virus of their own. The Gateway was a far more powerful weapon than any virus even if it wasn't real. Robot's, med labs, and the armor were most certainly real, and in the wrong hands could be used to control the world. The thought of someone being in the Gateway that would be willing to use its abilities for evil outcomes brought a shiver.

"That's crazy," Traven said in defense, "next you'll be telling me that you know who shot Kennedy or where Jimmy Hoffa is buried."

Lynx smiled.

"How is it that all here speak Navaho?" he questioned. "You are surely not of my blood."

Lynx was still trying to make a connection. Maybe it was something from his sordid past, but his loose threads were not satisfying him. Traven had forgotten about his ability to speak all languages and was surprised that Lynx would hear him speaking something other than English. Would everyone hear him in the voice they had been raised with? For a second he thought about his grandparents. Would they hear him in Italian? He had better find out before his next visit.

"Language is one of my gifts that I got from becoming the Keeper. In the Gateway we all hear the language we were raised with." For a moment he wondered what Mo-pa's native tongue was. "Look, I'm telling you the truth, the virus will bring about the destruction of the Earth. Millions will die."

"Truth is a funny word," Lynx whispered with a dark tone. "Truth is only truth to the person speaking it. The history books are full of truth, but only the writers truth. When the white man won it was a victory, when the Indian won it was a massacre. I don't believe in the truth of others."

"This room has the ability to show you what is currently going to happen if we don't change things. All I'm asking for is one chance to show you." Lynx looked at the tentacles.

"One."

Traven let the screens show the world over the dates that the Earth would die. Image after horrible image appeared on the screen as he explained the events that would take place. He showed Lynx the meetings that Lynx had already had with the powers that be. He showed him the human error that was soon to end the world, and then what would happen to Lynx after the carnage. Lynx's face was like stone.

"What is your point child?" he said.

"My point is that you're the one person who can change it."

"With all this Gateway's supposed powers, you can't prevent this?"

"Not without dropping a bomb on the base and even that won't ensure the virus won't become airborne. I could go back and stop the people responsible from ever creating it, but that doesn't mean someone else wouldn't accidentally stumble on it like they did in the first place. This virus was a mistake as far as we can tell. No one knows how it works or why. If I drop the room containing the virus into the Gateway it could mutate into something even worse, and being that we're connected to the webs of time it could end up everywhere. We can't risk that. Even the antivirus solution they have given you was made as a mistake while trying to recreate more of the same virus. No, this virus has to be stopped at the source, before it can reproduce itself. That's why we need you."

"I'm not interested," said Lynx.

The fight with Thealand was still fresh in Traven's mind. While he understood her reasons, he couldn't understand how you could show someone the end of their world and they wouldn't offer to help stop it.

"Why the hell not?" he asked.

"I am a professional, my word is my bond."

"But the world will end!"

"I will survive, I have already been guaranteed that, as long as I don't stick a knife into you," he said with anger. "Alive or dead, people carry the same weight to me."

There was a long silence as Traven's mind tried to grasp at straws, and then one presented itself to him.

"I was told once to offer someone anything they want to train me. What is your price to help stop this?" he asked.

"My price has already been paid. I work for the people you want me to kill." He folded his arms and looked very bored.

"Look, I said stop, not kill," Traven said, being reminded exactly of who he was talking to, and trying to make sure he himself was being understood. "Well if money isn't an option, what about your life?"

"Are you threatening me, child?" Lynx asked with a laugh.

"No Sir, not at all. What if you could change any event in your life? What if I offered you the chance to do something differently? What if you could relive a moment or change a mistake? That's all I'm trying to do in saving the Earth. I'm trying to change that one mistake that will bring the world crashing down. I need your help to fix it. Maybe I can help you fix something, anything. It's your call."

At that moment Traven felt like a used car salesman of fate, trying to sell a car that no one wanted to buy. To his surprise Lynx paced the edge of the room deep in thought, as if he might buy into this mad scheme.

"Anytime, any place?" Lynx questioned.

"Yes."

"Pearl Harbor?"

"You mean your father?" Traven asked.

Lynx stared at Traven as if this was something he shouldn't know.

"Oh come on," Traven said, "if I can find out about the end of the world, I can certainly check up on the one man who can help save it."

"I would have thought you would have learned to defend yourself before approaching me."

"I have trained," Traven admitted, "I'm just not that good of a student."

Traven called up the image of Lynx's father. A navy man on the wrong boat, at the wrong time, fighting to save his ship at the very moment a torpedo would claim both his ship and his life.

"There it is," Traven said, a bit stunned that he had found the scene so quickly, "the moment you want to change."

Lynx stared hard at the screen almost as a child seeing something that would scar him for the rest of his life. He then had Traven show him other random events through time, as if to check the library for it's accuracy. The events seemed to have no connection to each other, but in Lynx's mind, they passed the test. Traven also found that there were two shooters at Kennedy's death. Maybe Lynx's paranoia was just.

Lynx cleared his voice with a growl. "How do we do this?"

"I don't know," Traven replied, "do we make it that he never becomes a Navy man, or do we grab him as the attack starts?"

"He met my mother because he was a Navy man," Lynx stated.

"Ok, well if we save him what's the guarantee that he won't get killed later in the war."

"I can make sure of that," he said with an ominous tone.

"There's another problem," Traven pointed out. "If I save your father, your life will be completely different."

"Your point?" Lynx asked.

"You will not be who you are now. It's not that I'm trying to talk you out of this at all, but I do need the Lynx that is the assassin, not the Lynx that might end up as an investment banker."

"What will happen to me?"

"I don't know, we are writing the timeline as we act. You might be killed in a car crash in 1960."

"I'm willing to risk it."

"I need to talk to Brandy," he said, realizing that he didn't prepare for this offer.

"Can you repeat his death scene," Lynx asked, throwing Traven off of his quest.

"Why?"

"I need to study my options."

"Oh... ok."

Traven reset the screen to loop the event and left the room.

After a briefer than normal lecture on what a bad idea the plan was, Brandy informed Traven that there were several things that could occur. Nothing would change for the Lynx that was currently outside his own timeline. That is, until he had been put back at the moment Traven had dropped him into the Gateway. He could move throughout any timeline without effecting who he was now. Upon putting him back three things could happen.

The first was that Lynx could replace himself as the Lynx that knew his father, never even remembering the events that had occurred during his current life as an assassin.

The second possibility was there would be two Lynx's walking the Earth, the one that knew his father, and the assassin that he was now. This was a dangerous outcome because the timeline isn't fond of anomalies and it might try to choose the dominant being and erase the other.

The Third option was that Lynx would enter a world knowing all that he knew now, but would physically replace the life he had knowing his father and remembering none of that time spent with him.

The options seemed bleak. To Brandy's frustration she had to explain the options several times for Traven to understand them, and when it came down to it, he finally wrote them down in his sketchbook.

Traven then asked Brandy if she thought he could trust Lynx. Her only reply was that Lynx had never broken a deal he had entered into. Would he break his deal with the government to take the one he was being offered?

As Traven was about to go back to the library he asked Brandy why she had threatened Lynx and lied to him about her powers even though her powers did not extend past the Gateway. Her reply was that he didn't know that and shouldn't.

In the library, Traven read the options to Lynx who never stopped watching the loop of his father's death. When he failed to reply Traven asked if he understood him, thinking that maybe he read the list wrong. All he said was that when you make a deal with the devil there is always a price to pay.

Timothy John Vaulato

Chapter Thirteen

Duck And Cover

The plan to save Lynx's father was simple, at least it seemed that way to Traven. The first porthole he would open would be on the ship, the Arizona, December 7th, 1942. Lynx would be fifty yards away from his target. Then a second porthole would open exactly five seconds later and three yards from where Lynx's father was standing. Lynx would run the distance, knock out his father and they'd place him on the shores of Pearl Harbor an hour later when the air strike was over. The last door would be left open as to not break the rule of threes that Docheen had set down long ago. Traven still wasn't sure why this was, even after Larry had explained it, but it seemed like a good idea not to tempt fate anymore than they already were.

Not getting hit by a stray bullet was a consideration, so they mapped out the flight patterns of each bullet that would fly on the deck, even though Lynx said that it wouldn't matter. With the exception of a request for a handgun that would fire a single Japanese zero's bullet, they were set.

Larry brought them the gun and asked Lynx, in a very timid electronic voice, if he would like more bullets. Lynx's non reply was answer enough.

The portal opened to Pearl Harbor and a brilliant blue sky, stained with dark plumes of smoke rising from the battle beneath it. The sound was deafening, with the mixture of planes, bullets, and the cries of men in pain and panic. The smell of fear drenched the ship, along with ammunition, oil, sea air, and burnt bodies. Lynx focused past all distractions. He ran the deck as if he was in real time and the events that surrounded him were slowed. The assassin moved like a ballet dancer, trained on a uneven floor. His footing never faltered. He leapt over several servicemen whose attention turned for a only a brief second to this very strange acrobat. An unarmed man was of little concern in comparison to the metal flying around them. Approaching his father from behind, he hit him in the neck and his father's body effectively turned off. Before his father started to fall, Lynx had scooped him up and disappeared into the landing area of the Gateway, as bullets rained down on the spot they were just standing.

In the Gateway, Lynx laid his father's unconscious body on the ground and for a moment sat in silence studying the man he never knew. Nobody spoke until Lynx turned to Traven and said, "Now."

The young Keeper acted without hesitation, requesting another portal to open on a sandy beach a quarter of a mile from the fighting and an hour after the brunt of the attack was over. As Lynx lay the body of his father on the sand, Traven thought how ironic it was that the one person who could convince Lynx to save the world was a man Lynx had never met. A man that wasn't even alive in 1985. Maybe by saving his life they had changed that fact. With no emotion Lynx drew his gun and shot his father through the foot with the bullet that he had requested. He screamed out from the pain only to be knocked out a second time by a nerve pinch. His blood flowed and the sand soaked it up like a sponge. Lynx removed his belt, which was no more than

a simple black sash and used it to slow the flow of blood by tying it around his father's ankle.

"What the hell was that for?!" asked Traven, shocked at this sudden violation of Lynx on his own father.

"He'll walk with a limp," said Lynx, "but he will not be able to serve."

Traven finally understood the importance of the gun.

They returned to the Gateway without fanfare and were met by a silent Brandy. Lynx said nothing to Traven which by now was what Traven had come to expect. Larry offered to supply Lynx with a room and to show him where he could get a bite to eat. Lynx said they should go after the virus right away, but Traven replied that he needed sleep and that they needed to confer on the plan to attack the government base when they were rested.

This was only partly true. Traven was tired after the day's events, but was mostly just sore from the two knife hits he received earlier at the hands of Lynx. There was a question in Traven's mind about the saving of Lynx's father, and the one place that it could be answered was in the library.

Traven sat in the library chair and called up the altered images of Lynx's life. His father did survive and was sent stateside. He stayed with Lynx's mother, who did not die of a drug overdose. Both of his parents were instrumental in starting the Navy's code talker program and fought to keep the agreements the government had made with the American Indians. Lynx had a fairly normal childhood. He went to college and spent time as a hippy in the sixties. He even attended the three days of peace known as Woodstock. Traven found himself being jealous of the Lynx who was at the greatest event in the history of rock and roll until he realized that he too could go to Woodstock, and that Queen concert that Brian wouldn't shut-up about.

"Well, maybe when this is over," he muttered.

In the altered Lynx timeline the assassin had become a Professor of Native American studies and a human rights activist. The walking machine of death even had a proper name, "John Oleson."

The difference one person could make was astounding. There was a greater understanding and respect for the Indian people due to John's teachings. Traven totaled the list of people that had been affected by this different Lynx and it was a long list indeed. He then checked to see how the world was effected.

Thanks to the new Lynx life, students studied the American Indian more in depth than they had in Traven's history classes. He wished he remembered it, or had been there, but the young Keeper's memories tested as unchanged. The outcomes of his changing time were mostly good. He thought of the movie, *It's a Wonderful Life*, and listened for a bell to ring, jokingly wondering if he would get his angel wings. After all, that's what was supposed to happen, at least on film. Even though he was proud of what happened today, he knew he shouldn't get too cocky, if the world ended this one event would seem trivial at best. Traven's lack of sleep was starting to take over and he still didn't know what would happen to Lynx once he was placed back in his time stream when they were done. That is, if they both didn't die in the process.

He went to his room, took a brief dip in his stream, toweled off, and was asleep the moment he crawled in bed. The next time Traven opened his eyes it was to a blurry version of Larry, zooming about his tree house room in a panic.

"Bawth, Bawth!" buzzed Larry. "Wake up, they're fighting!"

Traven tried to focus his eyes on a clock by his nightstand. The clock told him that he had been asleep almost nine hours. *Hey, that's not bad,* he thought, *I don't usually sleep that well.* Then his mind finally realized what Larry was saying. He jumped out of bed and made a mad grab for his pants.

"Who's fighting?" he asked, with visions of Brandy in his mind ripping pieces of Lynx's body off and redecorating the Gateway in a vibrant red.

"Lynkth and Mo-pa," Larry replied. "Hurry!"

"Mo-pa?" said Traven stunned. "Why would he be fighting Mo-pa?"

"Mo-pa egged him on, he wouldn't let the cracking of your Calleash go. I think they have thome thort of religiouth thignificanthe to him."

By this time Traven had most of his clothes on and was hopping toward the door of the tree house trying to wedge a sockless foot into a tennis shoe. He couldn't imagine Mo-pa picking a fight with anyone, let alone the greatest assassin to ever walk the face of the Earth.

"Let's go," he said, running with a limp, still not having gotten the entire shoe on his foot. Traven ran as fast as he could following Larry's lead, trying to figure out what he was going to do when he got there. Lynx could kill both of them he figured. How could he break up this fight and why wasn't Brandy stopping it?

What he witnessed inside the practice room confused him even more. The two men were indeed fighting while Brandy was watching the fight with great interest, as if she was watching a sporting event. The practice room itself seemed alive, with target posts forming and disappearing from the floor, the walls, and the ceiling. The two men dodged the posts and took turns trying to hit each other. Lynx moved as he did on the ship's deck, as if the rest of the world was in slow motion except him. He easily avoided the posts, as did Mo-pa, but he had the added problem of trying to avoid the two Calleash that Mo-pa had set into play. Mo-pa would use the posts to his advantage bouncing his attacks with the Calleash from unexpected angles. It almost seemed as if he knew where the posts were going to form next. Maybe he sensed them after so many years spent in the Gateway. For an old man that didn't have long to live, Mo-pa was doing better than Traven would have dreamed possible, leaving him spellbound by this battle dance. He tried to talk to Brandy, but she hushed him with a finger to her mouth, as if she was afraid she might miss a moment of it. Against his better judgment Traven stood still and became a spectator. He then noticed that there was something different with Lynx, something that he had never seen before, it was an ever so slight smile. He strained his eyes to make sure of what he was seeing. It was not the kind of smile Lynx had when he had been threatening Traven. Not a smile out of cruelty, but a smile of what might be actual enjoyment. Traven didn't know what to make of the entire situation. A Calleash grazed Lynx's head. Not enough to hurt him, for it only whisked his hair, but for some reason this was a sign for the two men to stop. The smile faded and was replaced with an intense look of respect. They bowed to each other and the room went back to its static state. Mo-pa walked from the room also with a slight smile, but more obvious than Lynx's, and winked at Traven as if he just proved to them all that he still was a warrior. Lynx said nothing.

"Will someone tell me what is going on?" Traven said in frustration.

"A gentlemen's disagreement," Brandy replied, still looking metallic and frightening, but not as much as the day before. "Men," she said as if the one word would explain everything and then melted into the floor.

"We could use him," Lynx spoke, offering up his first suggestion.

"He can't survive long out of the Gateway," Traven replied, not bothering to inform Lynx as to why.

"What are our resources?" questioned Lynx. "Or is this mission a force of one?"

"Two," clarified Traven, "and the Gateway can provide limitless resources."

"One," restated Lynx, to imply that Traven wasn't really going to be any help in this attack on the government. This angered Traven, but he said nothing.

"Come on," said Traven, "let's discuss this in the banquet room. Larry can you patch a Library screen into the banquet room?"

"Thure thing Bawth," said Larry, and before he could leave, Traven also requested the files he had made about the government base.

In the banquet room, Lynx scanned the area as if he was casing the hall for a robbery.

"Nice room," Lynx said, admiring the weapons and then turning his gaze on the bear skin on the wall, "big bear."

"Damn thing almost ate me," Traven said under his breath and a chill went up his spine remembering his encounter.

He laid the files out on the large wooden table. The files were the size of five Chicago phone books. He unfolded blueprints and the timeline for the day that provided the best window for their attack.

"What about the metal bitch?" Lynx said.

"What?" said Traven, taken aback by the question.

"The friendly one," Lynx said sarcastically, as Traven then realized who he was talking about.

"Oh," said Traven, wondering how to cover for the fact that she too couldn't leave the Gateway, for in fact she was the Gateway. "She's not very subtle."

Lynx raised an eyebrow as if he didn't really believe Traven, but he let the answer be. Larry then flew into the room with a tray that contained a Diet Coke and two large calculator sized gizmos. Each had a small screen and several buttons.

"Thanks Larry," Traven said grabbing his Coke and tossing one of the gizmos to Lynx. "These are virus bombs, they were created by the Gateway. Although we don't know exactly what the virus is, these are made to destroy every known part of every virus throughout the universe and the history of time." Traven went on to explain. "They also detect the virus and its levels and when you push the button they activate, eliminating it in the given area."

"What happens to the person who activates it?" questioned Lynx.

"Well, yours stops at the point of killing the virus as long as it's outside the body. It must be used in a rather small area, basically the containment area that the virus is being kept in."

"And yours?" Lynx asked.

"Mine is the insurance," said Traven, with a worried look on his face. "It wipes out all virus's inside and out of the body, all computer memory, and all human memory."

Lynx's face became stern and Traven continued.

"There are several problems with my bomb, which is why I don't want to have to use it. First of all, mine will destroy everyone's memory and leave a small city of drooling idiots. Secondly, since it kills all viruses, even the ones that your body uses to fight off other viruses, leaving those exposed to its rays highly susceptible to disease. In many ways it does what the virus we are trying to get rid of does, except that it will only effect the people in a half mile wide area and it won't proliferate like our target will. The effect of my bomb can't be carried in the wind or by touch, or bodily fluids, but in the x-rays that the bomb gives off."

"Have you thought about selling it to the government?" Lynx asked.

"No," said Traven, miffed at Lynx's question.

"It is what they're trying to create. It is what they think they have. Why not profit on it and give them a safer version of their weapon?"

"Look, I don't trust that government cheese goes to the right places, I'm not going to trust them to use it wisely."

"Not a very good businessman are you?" Lynx observed.

"I have no reason to be."

Traven was surprised in the terseness of his statement. He was still very much afraid of Lynx, but he wasn't about to add to his government's ability to enact world domination. There was a long silence as the two looked at each other. For a moment it looked as though Lynx would launch another insult at the boy, but his face softened ever so slightly and he spoke.

"I've been trying to figure out your angle, child, but to your credit you do seem to be what you appear."

"And what's that?" Traven asked.

"Idealistic and naive. Don't misunderstand me, your attitude is charming, but once you've done this deed you will quickly grow up. At one point I thought that you were an agent of the devil, now I am certain you are but a pawn. You may want to question the things that are going on around you and if they are what they seem. The devil can take on many forms."

"What are you trying to say?" Traven asked.

This was the first time Lynx had spoken at length about something other than killing him, and now he sounded like the anti-Mo-pa.

"How do you know that the world isn't supposed to end?" Lynx said.

"So what if it is?" Traven replied, "how can saving the world be wrong?"

"If the dinosaurs didn't die the human race wouldn't have come into being. Maybe you're stopping the next step in the bigger picture. More importantly, who convinced you to do so?"

Lynx leaned back in his chair almost relaxing, which was an unfamiliar pose for him. Traven knew what he was getting at. He was trying to say in a round about way that Brandy was pulling his strings and Traven was the puppet dancing. Traven knew the more you say no to a child the more they want whatever it is they're not supposed to have, or do. Could Brandy really have been using him for a different purpose? What if Docheen wasn't dead? What if it had all been a great scam to get him to do their dirty work? But why would they need him? They could do whatever they wanted with the Gateway, they certainly didn't need a child to carry out any secret agenda. Traven sat for a moment. The thought wasn't going to leave his head, but even if he was being used to save the Earth for some other purpose, he was still saving all he ever knew and for the moment that was enough.

"Look, maybe I am being used," Traven said. "But it doesn't matter. Billions of people will die if I do nothing. For good, or bad, I can't let that happen. If someone is pulling my strings, so be it. I will do what I feel is right."

"You have changed already," Lynx said. "That commitment might make you useful."

Traven was mad, but didn't really know what to say, instead he pointed to the blueprints and tried to shift the conversation.

"I've fulfilled my end of our agreement, are you honorable enough to fulfill yours?" he asked.

"Certainly," Lynx replied, "after all, according to our meddling, I now haven't made the first one." Traven sat back and hoped that this was the loophole that Lynx was looking for to switch employers. His eye made an involuntary twitch as he hoped that no one would offer him a better deal.

"Then let's get back to the plan and save the philosophy for when we are finished."

With that the two returned to the blueprints and charts, and counted how many men they would have to bypass to get to the virus.

Timothy John Vaulato

Chapter Fourteen

Got My Threads, Where's My Date?

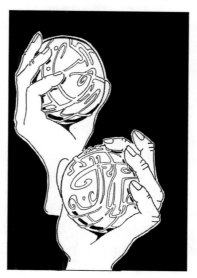

Five days passed in the Gateway. During this time they laid the ground work for their assault on the government base that housed the virus. Traven and Lynx reviewed their plans and covered various simulations of what could possibly take place in the government stronghold. The training room was found to be invaluable in planning the different strategies that would change as people made different choices in how they would respond to the attack. Lynx made it clear that he wanted Traven to be no part of the plan. Traven held fast to the idea that he had to be present in case things went awry. He believed that he was the only hope in case Lynx failed, or there was a miscalculation. The master assassin had never made a mistake in the past, not as far as the library could tell. He was like a machine and to him the young Keeper was just one more thing that could make it more difficult to achieve his mission.

The insurance bomb that Traven would carry would most likely kill ninety-eight percent of the occupants of the base. Though he was less than comfortable with this thought, he knew that the fate of the world hung in the balance and he wasn't about to let the lives of 1900 men affect that. Being an idealist, this change of vision was exactly what Lynx had warned him about. Tough decisions were going to have to be made if things didn't go as planned. Was he tough enough to make them? Only time would tell.

The responsibility weighed heavy on his mind and he prayed that he would make the right decisions. Though religion wasn't something he took a liking to, he wondered if God was really watching from on high. From his history classes he remembered how the white man had killed the Indians in God's name and how countless others had done similar atrocities. He wondered if there was a God at all, or if God was something people created to control others with the fear of retribution. *How could people kill in God's name? Wasn't God supposed to forgive all trespasses, even the really bad ones? Did that extend to killing in war time? What if Lynx was right? What if the end of life on Earth was supposed to happen? What if it was part of God's plan and more importantly what if Traven was trying to stop God's divine destiny for the Earth?*

This left Traven feeling uneasy. Even questioning God's existence left him feeling like he might be struck down, or at the least would bring bad luck upon himself. One night he decided to ask. He stood in the middle of his room and addressed God, hoping that Brandy wouldn't consider him foolish.

"God, it's me," he started. "I know I don't go to church unless I'm forced or act like everyone says that you're supposed to. I know that I don't talk to you often. I try not to ask for things that I feel are selfish or even foolish. If I fail a test it's my fault, not yours. This I feel I understand. Now I find myself in a situation where my actions will effect everyone on Earth. Since you're God you must know this, so I'll get to my question. Am I making the right decision? I don't want to kill anyone, but I know that I might have to. Is it your plan that the world end? I know in one reality it did, was that what's supposed to happen? I know that you, according to what I've read, once destroyed the world with a flood. Which by the way, they make baby toys of the ark and I always thought that was really weird. Why would people want to start off a child's life with images of the destruction of the world? Anyway, I guess I'm looking for a sign to tell me that what I'm about to do is right. I guess that the leaders in every battle want to come out the winner, they probably ask for a sign too. There can be only one winner. Do you choose or do you just let it play out and tell the others later if they screwed up or not? I think this might be a situation where a sign could be useful, not that I'm telling you what to do."

Traven stopped for a minute to try and come up with a decent wrap up to what he already felt was a very poor attempt at a prayer when a loud cymbal crash came from the stage. He jumped five feet in the air and when his feet touched the ground he turned around not to see the image of God or some burning bush, but Brandy. She had deliberately knocked over the crash cymbal on the stages drum set and was smiling mischievously back at the frightened boy.

"Sorry," she said, "I had to, the moment was too perfect."

"Damn it, Brandy!" yelled Traven. "Do you always have to be watching?"

"Well, in the spirit of the moment and without sounding too blasphemous, Ah see all. If not like God, then how about Santa?"

"Will you cut it out," Traven said, visibly angry and flustered, "or at least not look like the bride of the devil."

"Sorry," she replied, "that was just to scare Lynx. If he wasn't human Ah would have picked a different little stereotypical image to try to induce fear." Slowly she changed back into her normal form. "Look sweetie, finish your prayer, such as it is, and then we all can talk."

"Could I have a little privacy?" Traven huffed.

"Honey for better or worse we are bonded, yuh can't get rid of me anymore than Ah can get rid of you." She lifted the cymbal stand back into place and sat down on top of an amplifier. "I promise, I'll keep my mouth shut."

Hesitantly he turned his back on Brandy and continued.

"Sorry God," he said, "If you could just give me a sign it would be a big help... Amen."

Traven waited for a minute in the total silence of his room. Another minute passed by and he strained to hear anything, even a whisper. During the third minute he just hoped Brandy wouldn't knock over another cymbal. Finally, in his head he gave up. His shoulders slumped forward and Brandy took this as a cue.

"Not easy is it?"

"What?" he mumbled.

"The question of God, faith or religion."

"Do you believe in God?" he asked.

"Which one?" she returned, as Traven walked over and pulled up a seat next to her. "Almost every culture on Earth and in the Galaxies has a God, or Gods. Some are supposed to be good, some are supposed to be bad. In the worst case scenarios bad things happen in the name of good Gods."

"All right, is there a God?" he asked, thinking that she might have the answer.

"When cultures are in their primitive stages they create Gods to explain the unexplainable."

With this statement she created a three dimensional cartoon in the air to illustrate her point. The cartoon changed from the history of the cavemen to the Egyptians, to the Greeks. She continued.

"When they advance further they develop science which explains the things that used to be only in the realm of God. Then God switches into the idea of the soul, which usually is talked about in the same breath as good or evil. Good and evil are abstract concepts that can be measured in tangible outcomes. For example, killing millions of people that never raised a hand in violence to you would be seen as an outcome of an evil act, while teaching someone that could not provide for himself how to provide and become self reliant would be considered good."

The cartoon turned more real to show the holocaust and then a child being taught to hunt and fish thousands of years in the past. Finally a child from Traven's timeline learning to read and count formed.

"The concept of God is a complete abstract," she said. "There is no way Ah have ever seen to prove the existence of God. If there was, God would become a science and science tries to operate on fact, not faith. Faith can be powerful, it can accomplish things that would normally be beyond the person's abilities. People of strong faith, good or bad, use it to reach their goals. Some of them have to believe or they start to question their own intentions. They can use it to feed the hungry or just to obtain power. For them faith in something works."

"What about religion?" Traven asked, realizing this was probably the most he had ever heard Brandy talk outside of the subject of time or his mistakes.

"Well, in my observations, religion, like politics, works well on paper. The problem with both is the human factor. Humans, like others throughout the galaxy, are flawed by their emotions and desires. That usually is what leads them to do wrong or even follow someone else's interpretation rather than questioning for themselves, and once they've screwed up, they're caught in the makings of their own mistakes. At that point they usually run back to the paper of their belief and ask for forgiveness. Asking for forgiveness makes them feel better, but if they don't try to understand how their actions led them astray, they tend to repeat their mistakes."

There was a moment of silence as Traven stared at the ground and tried to assess all that had been said.

"That doesn't help much, does it?" Brandy asked, as the cartoons disappeared.

"Well, it's left me with more questions," Traven admitted.

"Questions are good. They help exercise the mind and not every question is meant to be answered, just pondered upon." Brandy stood up and shook her long dress straight as any normal girl might have. "So yuh didn't like the bionic devil bitch look?" she asked.

"Well, it was scary," Traven said, standing up as well.

"Ah still got it," she smiled with pride and then melted back into the floor.

Brandy stayed in her usual form. With Lynx about it was as if there was a common enemy that they had to worry about. She didn't trust Lynx and because of this she spent more time focusing on Traven's well being than on the follies of the decision he had made to save the Earth. As breathtaking as she was and as much as Traven enjoyed looking at her when she wasn't yelling at him, he was troubled by what Lynx had said. She had warmed up to Traven as if she was a mother wolf protecting her cub and the thought of her setting him up as a pawn for a greater scheme bothered him deeply. What if Lynx was right? What if Docheen wasn't dead and this idea of Traven as Keeper was just a ruse to get him to do Docheen's dirty work? These ideas seemed insane when he thought about them, but he thought about them nonetheless.

Brandy had Larry take Traven to the Armory. The Armory wasn't that much different than the room that created the AODs, with the exception that these press forming vats created armor and weapons instead of people replicants. Larry helped Traven create an outfit that would protect him on this mission. They first created an impenetrable suit of armor, but it's bulk limited his movements and the timing for the attack hinged on both Traven and Lynx being able to move quickly. What they ended up with Traven would affectionately call his, "double knot spy suit." It was lightly padded to stop the full force of bullets, but they would still feel like bee stings.

The first helmet did nothing to help his vision, so it was revised. It was almost like having a thick ski mask on. Brandy was very unhappy about this for it didn't provide the protection that she felt was necessary. She almost demanded that the helmet be remade. On it's second incarnation it looked very much like the

A Lifetime In Time

comic book character Iron Man, except in black and white. Traven took the drawing from his sketchbook that he had done in drama class of the combined comedy and tragedy faces and had them recreate it a third time. The mask finally met with Brandy's approval. The face plate was thick enough to stop almost anything. Brandy commented on the irony of wearing a comedy/tragedy mask to a storming of a government base. Traven didn't quite get what she was trying to imply. Larry had suggested that they add long dark wavy hair to the back of the helmet so it looked like he was wearing only a face mask. Brandy agreed, though Traven questioned why they would want to do such a thing. Larry said that it would throw off the investigation that would be sure to follow, that is, if they succeeded in their mission. In this way the government would at least be looking for a person with long dark hair that should have belonged to a pirate.

"What about Lynx?" Traven asked, "Shouldn't we create a suit for him?"

Lynx declined the offer almost scoffing at Traven's outfit. Traven pointed out that Lynx would not be known by the people on the base since they have altered the timeline. But when they put him back into his timeline, and if it came down to a future investigation, Lynx's face was rather unique and very identifiable. Lynx declined a second time saying he'd take his chances, although he did allow the room to create him his own outfit. There was nothing special about it, just a standard black body suit with multiple pockets that would have looked normal on most army mechanics. He immediately took a knife and cut off the sleeves.

Lynx said that he was good enough not to need training wheels, though he did ask to have his hand weapons returned to him and silently delighted in designing a few others that the Armory quickly made real. Traven had remembered what Thealand said about being good enough that her long hair and earrings were not an issue. Could Lynx really be that good that bullets weren't an issue? Was Lynx better than Thealand? Traven missed her. He wished that their last meeting hadn't ended in a fight. He asked

Larry if he could do research on Thealand's planet and what options they had in trying to save it. Larry said that he certainly could, but would send one of his doubles to do it because it was better if he focused on helping Traven not be killed so that he could have the chance to save her planet.

Boy, they don't openly offer up information, do they? Traven thought. He could have had Larry figure out how to save Earth while he practiced guitar. Traven asked what other super-hero-like clothing they could offer. Combat boots and gloves were suggested.

The boots had the ability to increase both your jumping range and your stride, as long as the battery lasted. The boots could pull power straight from the Gateway, which meant that they would work nonstop, but to do this a portal had to be left open to supply the power. This idea was considered too risky because of the virus. The boot's battery would last thirty minutes which was about twenty seven minutes more than they had planned to even be on the base. The boots in combination with the gloves would also allow the wearer to climb almost any surface like a spider would, you just had to have the body strength to lift yourself. After an afternoon of getting used to the boots and gloves Traven wished he had taken up rock climbing as a child, because his body was sore. He laughed inside thinking this is how Spider-man must feel.

The gloves felt like a second skin until he made a fist. Upon making a fist they instantly turned almost solid like stone. He could deliver a brutal punch and a second after find his keys in his pocket or tie his shoes. He also found that when he stiffened his hand the finger tips turned razor sharp. They were perfect for making deli sandwiches or opening brand new record albums.

Brandy also insisted that he wear the coat he had been given when he first met Lynx. She said that it would help to lessen the feeling of the bee stings that any bullets would have if the occasion arose. He complained at first but, being a teenage boy, all it took was a look in the mirror to tell him that the combination looked cool.

He felt like a dark super-hero and even with the weight of the world on his shoulders, he was enjoying the training and the preparation for their mission. Lynx kept him from getting too into the idea of being a hero by pointing out on many occasions that Traven was really the lame side- kick. Lynx was the man, and the man was getting anxious.

The time had finally come. He put on his double knot spy suit and headed for the landing area. Carrying his helmet under his arm, he wondered if the long fake hair would get in his way, he knew he wasn't as good as Thealand. In his mind he tried to psych himself up for the day's task. He started half humming, half singing a song from his favorite childhood television show.

"Spidey-dum, Spidey-dum, friendly dum dee dum Spidey-dum." He started to walk a little faster to the landing area. "Spins a dum, dum dee dum, catches thieves just like... argh!" he screamed like a little girl as Mo-pa pulled him into one of the rooms off the hallway.

"Mo-pa, you scared the sh..." he started to say, as Mo-pa cut him off.

"Silence," Mo-pa commanded, as he led him further into the room.

The room was almost dark with a smooth stone altar in the middle of it. The only things disrupting the darkness were four plates that seemed to be on fire. Each plate rested on the corner of the altar and in the middle sat the broken Calleash that Lynx had cracked. Traven said nothing, feeling as though he had stepped into a church in the middle of mass. Out of habit he bowed his head as Mo-pa lifted his arms and spoke in notes instead of words. Traven understood the meaning due to his gifts as the Keeper. Mo-pa's speech was about the circle of life and the ability to navigate life with a clear purpose and goal. There was lots of beautiful imagery which sounded nice to Traven, but its symbol- ism and deeper meaning were mostly lost. When Mo-pa finished he shocked Traven by lighting his own hand in one of the plates. With no expression of pain he brought the flame down to the broken Calleash which also started to burn. He stepped back, brought his hands together, extinguishing the flame and bowed his head in silence. The Calleash burned brighter and brighter. Suddenly the room was a giant light bulb itself with the Calleash as the filament. It was so bright that Traven lost his sight for a moment. When his eyes finally focused the room was no longer dark. There were two Calleash were the old one used to be. They were darker than the old one though slightly smaller with faint red lines in geometric patterns. Mo-pa motioned to Traven that they were his for the taking. Traven picked them up gently and bowed to the altar, and then to Mo-pa.

Mo-pa put a finger to his lips to indicate that the moment was still happening. He pointed to the door and Traven left without a word. Entering the hallway he pocketed one Calleash and examined the other. It felt harder than his first one, but lighter. It really seemed too light to throw for any real distance. Without thinking Traven threw it at the side of the hallway and to his surprise it smashed a hole out of the wall three times it's size and returned to Traven's hand before he had realized what had happened.

"Damn..." Traven said in awe. "That was just way too cool."

Just then Larry flew up and followed him down the hall.

"I thee you have your new Calleash," he said.

"Yeah, two of them," Traven replied, staring at his new weapons that now seemed rather lethal. "Hey, how is it I'm the last one to know anything around here?"

"You have to be in the loop, Bawth," Larry replied.

"How am I going to use these without killing someone?" A concerned look overcame his face. "Maybe we should wait a day?"

"I don't think Lynkth ith going to go for that."

"I know, he wanted to do the mission the day he saved his father." Traven took another throw. This time the Calleash returned without causing any damage. He wondered if he was really ready, not just for the mission, but to be able to control two Calleash at the same time. "He sees me as a liability," Traven said sadly.

"Liability?" Larry lisped. "Why, you're almotht a thuperhero."

"Almost may not be enough," he frowned.

"Trial by fire, Bawth," Larry beeped, "ith not like you believe you have a choithe."

"Yeah, I guess..." Traven paused, "that I'm operating on faith."

The two entered the room. Lynx was waiting, seeming calm and collected. Brandy formed out of the floor and asked Traven to go over the plan one more time.

Traven said the plan was to open a doorway down the hall from the containment area. The doorway would close in case something went wrong so the virus would not escape into the Gateway. They would be close enough that Lynx could knock out the guards and type in his passcode. If he wasn't fast enough the guards would sound the alarm and activate the flushing procedure. The flushing procedure would cause the hall floor to open dropping them thirty feet into a sealed room below. With Lynx's speed no one felt that this would come to pass. Traven would use a monitor that was built into his bomb to scan for any men who would be coming their way and any stray virus particles. Lynx would gain access to the containment room. Once entering the containment room he would set the bomb and they'd be good to go. There were four hundred men in the base alone and fifteen hundred on the outside. Luckily there would only be thirty men in the wing of the virus containment area. They covered the list of names from the library and there was no one Lynx recognized as a problem. He made a brief complaint about not being able to use lethal force. Traven held his ground. He then asked if he could use lethal force at least on the operations commander. Traven had no idea why he would want him dead, but decided that this was not the time for questions about who Lynx liked or disliked.

General Gillette was the commander in question. He ran the entire operation and he was a bull from hell who followed military procedure to the note when he felt it fit with his plans. The rest of his time he ruled his men with an iron hand that would make any dictator proud. From the screens in the Library they saw that he once shot one of his own men for disobeying an order. Traven had no interest in meeting the General.

The entire plan had been reduced to two minutes thirty-eight seconds.

"Welcome to D-day, y'all," Brandy said, as she walked to Traven and tied the belt on his coat. She nodded an ok. It was time to go. Lynx shook his head in disgust.

"No kiss on the cheek?" he smirked. Brandy snarled at him and the two walked through the portal.

Timothy John Vaulato

Chapter Fifteen

D-Day For The Blind

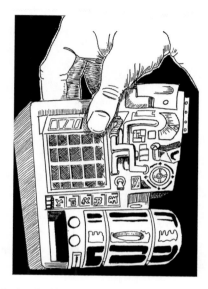

They entered the hallway for the containment room. Traven pulled his monitor out as Lynx attacked the servicemen. By the time their two bodies hit the floor Lynx was punching in the code. Traven's monitor bleeped and indicated that a person was approaching, much faster than someone should have been able to move.

"We have company!" he yelled. His hands felt wet under his gloves.

"How many?" Lynx asked, still entering the code.

"One, but he's moving fast, too fast."

The door at the end of the hall opened and a boy not much older than Traven, wearing all black, like an assassin, came barreling toward him with a speed that was on par with Lynx. He stabbed Traven in the chest with a knife. As he was being stabbed he noticed the boy was Asian with shoulder length hair. The thrust of the knife knocked Traven against the wall, hard. The coat held, as did the spy suit, but the hit was in the exact same place that Lynx tried to stab him when they first met. A moment of fear spread over Traven as he realized that this was most likely another member of the Steel Tear.

Lynx and the boy countered blows with machine-like precision, as Traven tried to pull himself off the ground. *What kind of person can stab you with a force that's greater than a bullet?* he thought. As he reached for his Calleash the boy who was fighting Lynx managed to block Lynx's attack and simultaneously hit the flush button on the code panel.

"Damn you, Mersan!" Lynx growled, as he and Traven dropped to the sealed room below.

The floor closed behind them leaving a young assassin to wonder how his adversary knew his name.

Lynx landed on his feet as did Traven, though his special boots threw him back up at the trap door. It was already closed. He grabbed the wall and stuck to it. Lowering himself to the floor he tried not to step on the bodies of the unconscious servicemen that fell with them.

"Who the hell was that!?" he asked, rubbing the sore spot in his chest.

"Mersan," Lynx replied, with no additional information.

"Ok, who the hell is Mersan? You said that no one on the list was going to be a problem."

Traven's voice was frantic, they had not planned on someone with skills on the level of Lynx in any of their simulations.

"He must be using a different name, he is... he was to be my replacement."

"Come again?" Traven said, starting to panic.

"All Steel Tear leaders pick the one who will succeed them. I had raised Mersan to replace me. I knew that one day he would be good enough to beat me."

"What exactly do you mean by beat you?"

"Kill me," Lynx said in his creepy cold-as-ice voice. "The new leader of the Tear must kill the old."

Traven shook his head in despair.

"Great little country club you got there, Lynx," he said, and then he noticed a pattern. It was the same way he had become the Keeper. "What do we do now?" he asked as more of a plea for help than a question.

"Your bomb?" Lynx said.

Traven shook his head again to say no.

"Can you beat Mersan?"

"Yes," Lynx said, not hesitating.

Then he handed his bomb to Traven. Traven gave him a questioning look.

"I'll take care of Mersan, you plant the bomb."

Lynx pulled a black marker from his pocket and wrote the code numbers to the containment room on Traven's sleeve. Traven thought for a second about the virus infecting him and was afraid.

"Plant the bomb? I don't even know how the hell we are going to get out of here?" Traven's hands flailed as if he was an excited pizza maker, as Lynx grabbed two grenades off the bodies of the servicemen.

"That side will lead up a secret back hallway. Three rights will place you into the hall we just fell from. It will now be heavily guarded as all the halls will now be. Don't be afraid to kill them, or you will have to use the other virus bomb and many will die. Don't touch anything in the containment room and you will most likely not become infected. The room has tested low since they gave me and the few others the antivirus. I'll head up the other side and take care of Mersan and whoever else I find." Lynx handed Traven two grenades. "Pull the pin, count to five, throw them at the wall and duck."

Even through Traven's mask Lynx could read what was going through the boy's mind. It was the fear and the dread of having to take someone else's life. Lynx thought back to his first kill and softened for a brief moment.

"You wanted to be a superhero," he said, pulling the pins. Traven pulled his pins as well.

"I did not!" he said angrily, "I wanted to be a Rock Star!"

They threw the grenades at opposite walls which exploded with the force of a million of Pete Townshend's guitars smashing on the stage at once. Before the dust settled they had run to their destinies.

Lynx dispatched the servicemen with blows to their pressure points as Traven had requested. In this new timeline he found it ironic that he, the most lethal man to have ever walked the Earth, had now never taken anyone's life. Even with this thought he knew the truth. He was a killer and not even a trick of time would change that fact.

Traven encountered heavy fire as he made his first turn. The bee stings of the bullets were considerably lessened by the combination of the coat and the suit. He stood in the hall and let the men empty their clips on him.

A voice at the back yelled, "hold!"

As the smoke from the guns cleared Traven stood with a Calleash in each hand. The emergency lights cast his body in a silhouette and with the points on his mask he had the appearance of a demon. He wished he was as imposing as he appeared. In the spilt second that the men had realized their efforts had been in vain the Calleash were thrown. Each Calleash bounced from wall to head with a devastating effect. While the balls did their ricochet dance Traven ran up the walls to the ceiling and over the men who could not tell where the attack was coming from. Traven dropped to the floor behind their leader, and paused for a moment when he realized it was General Gillette.

"Bastard!" Gillette yelled as he pointed his gun.

As a reflex of Thealand's training Traven blocked the gun and hit him hard. The older man fell to the floor and the last two soldiers standing were dispatched by the returning Calleash which found their way safely back into Traven's hands and then into his pockets. Mo-pa would have been proud.

A Lifetime In Time

The second right was a clear hall which made Traven more nervous. The speakers that had been blaring an alarm were now informing the base that it was in a lockdown status. He thought this was good, at least they weren't going to have to fight the entire army, just the ones on the inside. Cautiously he stepped toward the next right from which he could hear the sound of battle and men screaming in pain. No less than thirty servicemen lay on the ground, some with needles in different pressure points, others trying to set bones that had been dislocated from their sockets. This made them look vaguely like Plastic Man caught in mid stretch. The cause of these injuries was never in doubt. Lynx had beat him back to the containment area hallway and was fighting toe to toe with Mersan.

"You're good, old man," Mersan said, blocking a kick and flipping off the wall to return.

"Good?" said Lynx, who was clearly insulted. "Who was your mentor?"

"Inbrognio fell before me," Mersan said with pride.

"Inbrognio?" laughed Lynx, "he was old when I was a pup."

"How do you know him?" Mersan asked, with great disdain in his voice, "I was the only one allowed to set eyes on him."

"Child, I beat him twenty years before you."

Lynx connected his foot with Mersan's rib's. The young boy stood up without showing the pain Lynx had inflicted. Though all of his ribs were broken along his right side, he wasn't about to give up. At that point the tables turned and a bruised General Gillette pointed his gun and fired directly at Traven's head. Sensing the attack Traven turned into the shot, his Calleash never having the chance to find his hands. The bullet hit Traven's mask and bounced off towards Mersan's face. As Traven flinched realizing that he was both alive and unhurt he saw from the corner of his eye Lynx's hand moving in a blur. Lynx caught the bullet in mid-air and sent it off in another direction. All movement stopped as Mersan peered wide-eyed at Lynx who gave him a wicked smile. The General spit red, wiped his bleeding lip and leveled a gun at Traven again.

"Fast bastard, fast and tricky. You should have been working for me." Gillette paused to spit more blood from his mouth. "In three minutes," the General said calmly, "this entire base will be flooded with nerve gas. The gas will melt through your precious mask and strip your flesh slowly like water on a sand castle. You boys have failed. The codes are changed, you'll never get your hands on that virus."

Mersan's face relaxed as if he was making his peace with his impending death, while Lynx's was unchanged. The general scowled at Traven. Traven had only one option left and it was definitely not the one he had wanted to rely on or he would have tried it in the first place.

"Protocol 847," Traven said, almost in a rehearsed monotone. "Section T. R. A. Code O-N. Paragraph's R. A. and E. Keyword F. Fargo. This operation is under my jurisdiction General, please step down."

General Gillette's face became white.

"That is a myth," he replied with anger.

"It is no myth, General," Traven responded.

"Were is your proof?" said the shaken general.

Traven reached into his jacket's inner pocket to produce the badge that Teddy Roosevelt had procured for him. The golden eye and pyramid shined brightly in the fluorescent lights.

"This is no joke, General. We have less than two minutes to save your men and the world. Do you follow orders or only give them?" Traven said with a strength of will that he could hardly believe.

The General's face was contorted with hatred, as he picked up a base phone and established the verbal protocols to call off the nerve gas.

"The code, General," Traven demanded.

The general walked to the end of the hall where the room containing the virus was held. He punched in the fail safe numbers and the door opened. Traven threw the bomb that was meant for Lynx back to him and Lynx proceeded to complete his mission.

"There will be a day of reckoning, boy." The General hissed.

Traven showed the general the other bomb.

"This would have been a day of reckoning for everyone in a five mile area, General. Your virus would have been a day of reckoning for the entire Earth."

"You know we'll just make another, you've done nothing here but make an enemy you won't be able to shake."

"Your virus was a fluke, you can't recreate it. Hell, you're not even sure why it does what it does. This project is over. Try thinking about early retirement. With your spare time you could get a job in a video store, they're going to be huge."

A bright glow shown from the windows of the containment area. Lynx came through the door with a smile Traven had never seen on his face, a sincere one. Traven checked the virus levels with his bomb. All was clear. A defiant Lynx walked to the General and removed his bars and ribbons without any confrontation. Lynx then walked over to Traven and pinned them on his jacket.

"Your success," Lynx said, with great distaste toward the general, "are built on the deaths of thousands. This boy's success was made of his own accord."

Traven was taken aback by this display and wondered if Lynx was just trying to get in another dig on the General or if he truly meant what he had said. A confused Mersan just stared at them as Traven waved his hand in the air and they disappeared.

They arrived in the Gateway to smiling faces. Lynx turned to Traven.

"Job in a video store?" Lynx said quietly, and then gave in to a slowly building laughing fit. He only stopped to yell something that Traven guessed was an Indian victory cry. Brandy gave Traven a big hug.

"Ah am glad to see that we both still exist."

"Did it work?" he asked.

"Ah am checking the library, and y'all did it. You saved your world."

Chapter Sixteen

Aftermath With A Bottle

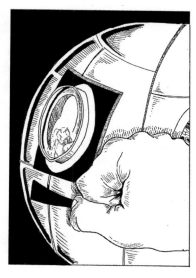

There was a small celebration in the Gateway after the success of the mission. Traven created his favorite bands to play the background music. It turned out that Lynx was a fan of the band Rush. Traven would have never guessed this about the one time greatest assassin of the world and was even more surprised when he caught him mouthing the lyrics to the songs. Everyone was in a good mood and for a moment, even Brandy seemed to let her guard down. They broke out the bottle of mead Traven had received from his encounter with his other self and then toasted the Earth and those that had made the victory possible. Lynx lifted his glass several times to the failure of General Gillette. Traven had not yet developed a taste for the sweet brew but the others seemed to enjoy it quite a bit. Traven noticed that when the bottle reached a halfway point it would mysteriously refill itself. He chalked it up to his other self's comment about being a sorcerer and figured he would ask Brandy about it at another time. Between the mead and the victory, Lynx seemed to soften. At one point he took Traven aside to admit, with very few words, that he had been wrong about him going on the mission. He told Traven that he needed to be careful with the power that he now controlled. That kind of power was a dangerous blade to walk upon. Lynx said he was proud to have fought beside him.

Traven wasn't sure which was better, to win his respect or to have not screwed up in the eyes of Brandy. He decided that, while both were important, the real success was saving the Earth and those he cared about. He felt better than he had in a long time and even this gave him a sense of worry. It seemed as though when great things happened they usually were followed by something very bad. He decided that he would check the library before he left just to make sure all was well. As the celebration wound down he noticed that both Mo-pa and Lynx had become rather sloppy from the mead. They started displaying tricks that they could perform with their weapons of choice. Calleash flew through the air as did knives, stars, and other weapons Traven had no names for. When Mo-pa's Calleash almost smashed the mead, Traven grabbed the bottle and decided that it was time for him to go to bed.

Lynx wanted to return to his timeline, but Traven convinced him to wait till morning. This would allow Traven to find out the best place to return him to. He couldn't send him to the Steel Tear stronghold. What they had done in the time stream had already made it clear that now none of that group knew their former leader. By saving his father, he had now never been their leader and the idea of putting a semi-drunk assassin into a hive of assassins, didn't seem wise. Lynx grudgingly agreed and both he and Mo-pa headed off to explore the Gateway's areas of recreation.

Traven returned to his room, took a bath, and still feeling a little itchy from the thought of the virus, switched into his t-shirt and blue jeans. His tennis shoes felt great, worn, dirty, and broken-in. The closest thing to perfect comfort he could ever wish for. He put the bottle of mead on a shelf next to the diary and headed to the library.

When he entered the room, Larry and his clones were doing research. Traven had asked them to find a way to save Fecha and they seemed to be working hard, that is, for a bunch of metallic balls.

"Great party," said Larry.

"Yeah, it was fun," Traven agreed, feeling a little buzzed from the mead. "What's up?"

"Thingth don't look good," Larry lisped, "The Atrillth have done irreparable damage to their planet and on top of that, the ruling faction will launch a final cleanthing attack to get rid of what they conthidered the 'undesirableth'. Bathically that amountth to the entire planet. They won't even thave any of the military of lower ranking."

"What's the outcome?" asked Traven.

"Well, they thought they could hide in bomb thelters and wait out the blatht to emerge to a planet all their own."

"Can they, I mean will... or did they?" Traven hated trying to figure out the appropriate tenses when talking about things outside of the Gateway.

"No, by the time they realithe they have dethtroyed their othone completely they will be dead." Larry's body mimicked a chill.

"Can we go back before the damage and stop it?" Traven asked hopefully.

"Well, if you do, you would have to go back theveral hundred yearth to even have a minor effect on the pollution the warth have created. By doing that you would throw all of their timeline into thpeculation. Thealand might have never been born or in the worse cathe thenario, the planet might have been dethtroyed much earlier. You wouldn't know till after you did what you had done, by then it might be harder or next to impothible to ficth."

Coming off his recent victory Traven knew that he shouldn't be cocky, but it was tempting. He would like to just go in and fix the mess by beating up some people and be done with it. The cost of this action would be unpredictable till he had done the deed. Larry interrupted Traven's thoughts with a warning.

"Bawth, the problem ithn't jutht the planet, the Atrillth are their own wortht enemy. They haven't much ability to forethee the outcometh of their actionth. In many wayth they're like humanth but worthe."

"Hey!" Traven yelled. "Human standing here."

"Just thating an obthervation, Bawth."

"Well, what are my options?" Traven asked.

"If you overthrow their government, the planet can only thuthtain life for another three yearth. That action might get you out of your deal with Thealand."

"Three years and a world dies? That isn't an option, Larry." Traven said bluntly.

"Ok, the next betht plan I've been able to come up with ith to get everyone off the planet."

Larry became momentarily distracted by one of his clones who approached him with what seemed to be some sort of silent information.

"Is that possible?" Traven asked.

"Pothible, yeth, eathy no. We have to find a thuitable planet for them to move to and then we have to dethide who thayth and who goeth."

"What do you mean who stays and who goes?" Traven asked, openly offended by the comment.

"Well Bawth, to put it gently, they dethtroyed one planet and the bet ith good they will dethtroy another. Leaving the ruling faction behind would put the devathtation of another planet on hold, if only for a while."

"You mean no matter what they'll destroy the next planet as well?"

"For thure? No, but the chance is good. Look Bawth, you only have to thave them oneth, after that they're on their own. Your obligationth are done. Ath Brandy thaid, children must thometimeth be left to make their mithtaketh." Larry could tell that this didn't sit well with Traven. "I'm thorry Bawth, I can only give factth. While I can thugar coat thome thingth, I am not programmed to lie."

"I wouldn't want you to, Larry."

Traven felt that the choices were bad and making these decisions were like playing God. Could he really be that cold? Certainly the Atrills had no problem in killing each other, but that didn't give him the right to deal out death to people whose politics he didn't agree with. Was Larry right? Would these people destroy another planet? That hardly seemed fair either.

"When will or did they destroy Fecha?" Traven asked, as Larry conferred with one of his clones.

"Twenty one dayth from when you latht thaw Thealand," he stated.

"Then shouldn't she have appeared in the landing area the second after she left?" Traven asked, remembering the oneway device he had given her in case something went wrong.

There was a silence from Larry as if he was trying to carefully choose his next words.

"Well, Bawth, that'th a bit complicated."

"How so?" Traven asked, fearing an answer that he wouldn't like.

"When thee left we thcanned the library for any uthe of the blue box. Being that the planet wath doomed we athumed that you would be going back to get her before it blew up."

"So... somewhere before boom, Thealand is pressing a button and nothing is happening?"

"Yeth, but when you get her thee will have never prethed the button."

"That's not the point," Traven said, becoming clearly upset. "The button is suppose to work. That's what I told her, that's what should have happened!"

"But, Bawth, if you bring her back at the moment her planet diesth and then we have to thend her back three weekth prior to that moment to rally her people, there will be two Thealandth running around."

"Does that mean the one that pushed the button would have never pushed the button in the first place?"

"Yeth."

Even though he was still upset, Traven felt a small bit of pride that he at least understood what Larry was talking about. "I suppose two Thealands being mad at me would be worse than one," he said, tapping his fingers upon his forehead. "But, I don't like it, Larry. I don't like it one bit. It's like I lied to her."

"In truth, Bawth, you are the only person in time that hath the ability to change a lie."

Traven pondered on Larry's statement, wondering if there wasn't another deeper meaning. The pride from the moment before washed away as he decided he couldn't read anymore into the comment and really needed to focus on the bigger problem.

"Well, I have to talk to her, I have to explain what's going to happen," he said changing the topic.

"Bawth, thee motht likely knowth. Not much happenth on her planet that thee ithn't aware of. I would even gueth that's why thee didn't want you to go off to thave Earth in the first plathe. I've never know her to thtay out of a fight without good reathon."

"Well, she certainly played it cool," said Traven, trying to stifle a yawn. "Larry, I'll meet you in the landing area, please get my clothes for Fecha."

"If I may make a thuggestion?" said Larry, as Traven's tired eyes turned back to his little round friend, "you're very tired, probably thore, and in need of thome thleep, at leatht for clear thinking, if not for anything elthe. Why don't you take a few hourth or even a week to get thome retht and tie up loothe endth."

Traven thought about Lynx's need to be returned to his time stream and how he wanted to check up on General Gillette's threats. The general wasn't a high school bully that talked big, he was big and could be a whole lot of trouble. The general had seen Lynx, and Traven wasn't yet sure what was going to happen when he was returned.

"You're right," said Traven, "I need a nap."

"And a cookie?" offered Larry.

"Yeah, a cookie would be great, one with frosting, I'm celebrating."

Before Traven left he asked Larry to look up information about the General and the best place to put Lynx in his new time stream. With cookie in hand, Traven went to bed.

The next morning Traven showed up for practice with Mo-pa, but the old man wasn't there. As Traven waited he tried out his new Calleash and was amazed at their ability to make him seem even better. Multiple targets were no longer an issue and for a while he was lost in this incredible new skill they provided. They almost always came back after he threw them, unless the throw was ridiculously bad or in the wrong direction. As he wondered how many of these tricks he could pull off with a normal ball, a most disturbing thought came into his head. *Last night Mo-pa and Lynx left the celebration together. What if Lynx and Mo-pa got into another fight? What if Lynx killed Mo-pa?* The old man had never missed a practice before. True, they had not talked about a practice at the party, but he was nothing if not consistent.

"Larry," called Traven and before he finished, Larry was beside him giving him a slight startle.

"Yeth, Bawth?" Larry said.

"Have you seen Mo-pa or Lynx?" he asked.

"Not thince the party," Larry replied.

"Can you scan for them?" Traven asked, as Larry sat still for a moment.

"They're both on level 3X9," he replied.

"And that is what?" asked Traven.

"Ath memory therveth, I believe that it ith a thity comprithed of the galaxy'th finetht drinking ethtablithmenth." Larry replied.

Traven shook his head in disbelief.

The boy and his servant headed down several hallways and three elevator drops arriving on a city street littered with AOD's that seemed to be having the time of their lives. Drinking, laughing, and dancing in the streets, these AOD's were very passable as real. Larry told Traven that the AOD's would pass as real in any bar, but put one in any library and they would be arrested as slobbering drunks. Traven couldn't understand why people would do this to themselves. Sure the mead tasted all right, but it wasn't a Diet Coke and, for that matter, the warm feeling that it left wasn't something that he would like to feel turned up to ten. After bumping into several people and other glassy eyed creatures, they stopped in front of an establishment known as the "Full Moon Bar." Inside the bar it seemed even darker than the street. Traven's eyes had to readjust to the smokiness of the room. There were few people and an old blues tune, *"All Night Long,"* by Muddy Waters, was playing from the jukebox in the corner. The song certainly set the mood and without thinking, Traven found himself tapping to the beat. The jukebox was giving off what little light there was on that side of the room. Lynx was asleep on the pool table, his body covered by shadows as Mo-pa sat at the bar staring into a half filled shot glass. Traven pulled up a bar stool next to the old man.

"I didn't know you drank, at least not like this," Traven said, with a bit of revulsion in his voice.

"I don't often," said Mo-pa, with a bit of a slur, "it's bad for you."

"I thought it would be bad for your medical condition?"

Traven sounded as if he was the disappointed parent of a teenager who had made a questionable decision.

"The Gateway has changed my system," Mo-pa burped. "While I am still dying outside of this place, poisons and viruses don't effect me for long."

"Too bad I didn't know that before the mission," Traven frowned.

A Lifetime In Time

"I offered my assistance, but Brandy felt that it would be unwise." The old man finally pushed his half-full shot away from him and, as if on cue, the bartender took it.

"What happened to him?" Traven said, pointing to Lynx who was being scanned by Larry for any signs of life.

"He challenged me to a drinking contest," Mo-pa said, standing up and looking as if he was starting to sober as they spoke.

"And you didn't tell him about your abilities?" Traven asked.

Mo-pa smiled.

"In life," he said, "you have to laugh when you can."

The quiet of the bar was broken by the sound of Larry getting an unfocused but somewhat accurate punch by Lynx.

"Why are people alwayth hitting me, thooting me or thending me to the cornerth of oblivion?" Larry lisped, in frustration.

"I'm glad you woke him up rather than me," Traven smiled.

They walked cautiously to the great assassin to offer assistance. Lynx waved them away and then tried to stand. The weight of his body betrayed his legs and sent him crashing to the ground where he continued his once undisturbed sleep. Traven looked to the ceiling and called out.

"Stretcher."

Traven made sure Lynx was delivered to his sleeping quarters and that Mo-pa also went to bed. After closing the door he turned to Larry and, shaking his head, said, "Sot's... dangerous sot's."

"I don't want to be around when Lynkth wakes up to that hangover," Larry said, and Traven agreed.

Traven and Larry went to the landing area with Traven's Fecha clothes. Brandy formed from the floor and was almost beaming.

"So now y'all know what's it like to be the mother hen around here."

"Couldn't you have cut them off at some point?" Traven asked, still disgusted at their behavior.

"Sometimes you have to let the grown ups, as well as the children, make their own mistakes," she said, tossing her hair like a snooty princess.

"Well this child here is going off to hopefully not make another mistake," Traven said, adjusting his outfit.

"You'll be fine, I have been keeping an eye on your destination and as long as you don't leave her apartment complex, or disturb the neighbors, I don't see ya running into any trouble, other than an angry Thealand."

"That's trouble enough," Traven stated, having trouble with the clasps on his Fecha styled garment.

Brandy touched him lightly on the shoulder and when that didn't get his attention she tapped him more forcibly on his head.

"I am proud of you for keeping your word," she said.

"Why wouldn't I?" Confusion spread across his face as Brandy took a deep breath.

"Power corrupts. The position of Keeper gives ya power that can easily be abused. Not everyone who had left an argument like the one you and Thealand had would have the desire to set things right. I just wanted you to know that while this makes you reckless and a danger to keeping both of us alive, it also makes you honorable. Ah would rather risk my existence for that, than the alternative."

There was a sadness in her voice. It seemed that it wasn't from the fear that Traven might get the both of them killed, but from something in her very long past. Traven wanted to ask her if Docheen had become less than honorable, or if he, at some point, had just become evil. Even the question that Lynx had brought up, the thought about him being set up by Brandy, or even Docheen snuck into his brain. *Was it possible? Was she feeling guilty?* He had so many questions he had wanted to ask her, but his mind wasn't clear on how to say them, at least not without losing any sense of coolness he might have picked up in the last few days. He decided that clarification could wait and if he got anymore distracted he would completely forget what he wanted to say to Thealand.

"Uh... Thanks," was all he could manage to say.

"Articulate as always," she replied. "Be careful." And with that she melted back into the floor.

Timothy John Vaulato

Traven reviewed the notes that they had taken the night before, put on the weather mask and stepped on through to Fecha.

Chapter Seventeen

The Cat And Her Litter

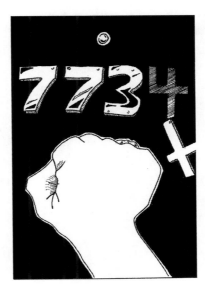

Traven stepped into a hallway that looked like almost any other large government housing project. The walls seemed to be made out of some substance that could very well pass for concrete, but darker and rougher in texture. The floor was a tatter of torn carpet and broken glass. Though dirty and stained, this hallway seemed to echo his muted footsteps. There was a stench of urine and the walls were wet in areas all around the same height. He tried to step lightly. The lighting was much dimmer than would be allowed by any inspector on Earth and he guessed that cat people probably didn't need much illumination. The highlights off the metal numbers on the apartment door made them readable. He was in the right place. Muffled party sounds came from another apartment behind him. As he gagged from the stench, all laughing and music stopped. The hall became quiet with a heavy sense of foreboding. He raised his hand to knock on the door in front of him, but before he could, it slowly swung open. This gave him pause; as he went through the door he checked for his Calleash. Two steps into the darkened room he realized, to his dismay, that he couldn't get to either Calleash through his thick garment. Before he could rectify the situation, he was under attack. Four small bodies pulled him to the ground. One was at least half his size with the others in descending mass and height. They jabbed him in pressure points and hit him with hard objects until he realized he was helpless. Different swear words rang loudly out of his mouth until the lights came on. A fifth attacker stood poised over him, pointing a gun that was too large for someone of her age and size.

The girl with the gun was shorter than Thealand, but Atrill without a question. Her thin white body was clothed in hand-me-downs that were too big and hung loosely on her young frame. Her lips were as black as the tip of her nose and her hair was a scruffy mismatch of white and black patches which would have made a fine chessboard for drunkards. Purple eyes stared over the rim of yellow tinted sunglasses and showed no trace of mercy. Thealand stepped between the young girl and Traven. She then motioned for the others to cease their attack. Traven's eyes focused and his attackers came into view. Counting the one with the gun there were five in all while the other cat children stood at the ready holding household appliances which had worked quite well as weapons.

"What the hell!" said Traven stunned, "are you babysitting the children of the damned?"

"It's not babysitting," said Thealand coldly, "when they are your own."

A deep breath sucked into Traven's chest.

"You have five children?" he said in shock. "You can't be much older than I am."

"Six all together, and I am older than you are, pup," she said, as the children snickered. "Of course, most of my people do start very young." She shot a look of disappointment toward the oldest girl who just rolled her eyes. Thealand motioned for the children to

stand by her side and like trained soldiers they lined up in order of height.

"Amazing that you have the time to fight with each other," Traven said from his reclining position.

"He does have round ears," said the smallest child.

"He's a shaved ape," said another.

"My oldest is Annie." Thealand put her arm around the tallest girl who was still pointing the gun. Her eye's glued on Traven as if she was dissecting him. "To my right is Tox, and the triplets are Nix, Mucha, and Lele, and now that you've met my family you can leave."

Traven tried to pick his beaten body off the ground and on the second attempt he succeeded. The children were tough, in fact he was less sore from the raid on the government base than from these children hitting him. He wished for a moment that he had worn his double knot spy suit. He took a deep breath.

"We made a deal and I'm here to keep my end of it," he said, trying to puff out his chest and stand confidently as if the attack hadn't hurt him.

"Well, from the looks of you, I didn't teach you much," she said turning away. "Consider our contract broken. Now get out, you've already compromised our position."

"Look, what you taught me kept me alive yesterday, if it wasn't for you my world would be dead and so would I. I mean to keep the agreement and save your people."

"You were suppose to save my planet too, but that doesn't matter anymore. Just get out."

She walked over to the small window and peered into the dark red Fecha sky. Traven noticed she had several wounds that had been carefully dressed; one to the side of her head which was partially hidden by her hair. Another wound was on her cheek and her wrist also seemed to be wrapped. He quickly glanced around the room. It was a contrast to the barren hallway. It was small and clean though it was sparsely decorated. On the wall hung pictures drawn by children of trees and worlds where the sun shone bright. One he guessed was a crude depiction of Thealand training him. He couldn't understand why he was being thrown out, or why she was now releasing him from their deal. He knew this wasn't right. He knew she normally wouldn't act this way and he wasn't about to give up.

"Your planet's doomed, but your people are not, at least not all of them."

"I said get out!" She started to raise her voice and a worried look spread over the faces of the children. "You can't be trusted and your presence here is putting us all at risk."

"Damn it, Thealand!" Traven said matching her volume. "Three weeks and this planet is going to be a smoldering rock."

"Don't you think I know that!?" She said, her eyes starting to tear.

"Hell, I don't know what you know or why you're behaving this way!"

Before anyone could say anything else, Annie pulled a smaller gun from her back pocket and discharged a shower of sparks and volts of electricity. The other children jumped back in horror as did Traven. When the light show was over Thealand lay unconscious on the floor. Annie looked up and gave him a challenging stare.

"She'll be out for hours," she said. "When Mother is worried she doesn't make the best decisions. It seems to be an issue with most of our people, they let their emotions dictate their actions. I, however, do not have that problem."

Traven wasn't so sure. Two of the children went to make their mother comfortable while the others stood by as back up. He wondered if he was the only one left in the galaxy who hadn't taken a shot at his parents. He was also amazed that a girl this young spoke as if she were a jaded adult.

"They have my brother," Annie continued, "since then Mother has tried without success to save him. She is having one of her panics. Last night they almost got her, they almost got us."

"Did not," mumbled one girl.

0

"Come on Annie, we took them easy," boasted Tox, until she gave him a glare. "Well mostly," he rephrased, as she continued.

"The government is closing in on us and if you look out the window you will see that the lady from next door has already alerted them."

Traven stepped lightly over the unconscious body of Thealand and the children tending to her. Looking out the window he saw this was true. Several vehicles lined the street with flashing lights and more were arriving.

"She said that you could get us out of here," Annie said re-cocking the gun. "She also said that you couldn't be trusted." She leveled the gun at Traven's head. "I want my brother back. You get us out of here and then we go to get him."

Traven shook his head in disbelief.

"All you had to do was ask." He waved his arm in the air and directed the children through. They disappeared into the Gateway as he and Annie grabbed the limp body of their mother and carried her through the porthole.

"Stretcher!" he yelled, for the second time in his life and dropped his garment on the landing area floor.

Quickly the cleaning drones retrieved his garments as Larry's clones arrived in full force.

"Get me Lynx and the location of the child," he demanded.

"His name is Kovacs," clarified Annie, in an almost monotone voice as she watched the clones load her mother on the stretcher. Brandy formed from the floor and gave Annie a dirty look. The other children jumped back in fear. Their sister gave them a signal that it was all right.

"Neat trick," she said, sounding unimpressed.

Brandy turned to Traven ignoring the impudent child.

"Ah have rarely found myself at a loss for words," Brandy stated. "But, instead of the titanic yelling, which Ah am holding back, I will tell you that you have only been gone ten minutes and Lynx is still very much intoxicated." Her eyes started to glow when she looked in the direction of the young girl.

"I don't care. I said bring him here," Traven said, also holding back his anger. It wasn't directed at Brandy, but at what was unfolding around him. He couldn't believe that the people Thealand stood against would go as far to use a child as a hostage.

"And what is your plan?" Brandy asked, as Annie interrupted.

"The plan is to save my brother."

Brandy's stare was this time accompanied by the floor springing to life and securing Annie's hand's, feet, and mouth. Traven ignored Brandy's timeout on the young Atrill.

"I'm going to turn the greatest assassin Earth has ever known, drunk and pissed on these people, and save the boy as all hell breaks loose."

Traven was handed his double knot spy outfit by Larry and proceeded to put it on as Mo-pa attempted to calm the children.

"This plan is not rational," Brandy said sharply. "Why not drop him into the Gateway the way you did Lynx?"

Traven thought for a moment and gave her a very determined look.

"My uncle once told me that nobody's beyond a spanking," he said. "I hope to teach them a lesson they won't forget."

Annie tried to say something through her living gag, but it wasn't understandable. Two Larry clones helped a wobbly Lynx stand in front of them. Even drunk, Lynx cut an impressive figure. The children's eye's grew to the size of saucers and whispered heatedly amongst themselves as Lynx pushed the Larry clones away.

"Kitties are talking," Lynx said, raising an eyebrow.

Brandy put her hand to her head in disbelief.

"How do you feel about beating the snot out of some very bad men?" Traven asked, as a large smile slowly spread across Lynx's face. "See," Traven said, putting on his coat, "we're good to go."

Larry flew up to Traven and filled him in on the boy's location and the people guarding him. Brandy released Annie, who calmly pushed her glasses back in place and muttered a quiet word of dislike for her momentary captor.

"This is irrational and insane," Brandy said, "and it breaks Docheen's law of three's."

"We'll leave the portal open," Traven replied, rolling his Calleash on his hands.

"That means you'll have to be the last one back through," Brandy pointed out, with her arms folded and a strong pout starting to form on her face.

Traven glanced at the read outs that Larry had handed him.

"Look, there are seven men on the inside..." he said, and then was abruptly cut off.

"Seven well-trained men," she corrected.

"Is kitty girl joining us?" Lynx slurred.

"No!" said Traven.

"Yes," said Annie, without raising her voice. "Kovacs will not come to you."

Traven thought for a moment and decided that the girl could handle herself. She was right, why would her brother trust two funny looking humans?

"All right, she goes. Get her a coat."

"I don't need a coat," Annie said.

"Look, if I get one of Thealand's children killed in the quest to save another, she will kill me. You'll wear the damn coat or you can go back to being a statue." Traven was becoming enraged and at that moment he questioned the sanity of ever having children.

"Coward," she replied.

Before Traven could answer her accusation Brandy interrupted.

"Let me get this straight," Brandy said, losing her color and her eyes glowing brighter, "a drunk assassin, a teenaged girl, and you are going to pop into a hostage situation, save the boy and reemerge unharmed?"

"Am I the Keeper or not?" he barked.

Brandy's scowl was her only reply.

"Good. Keep the portal big, I might have to throw him through."

A protective coat appeared in the arms of one of the Larry clones and begrudgingly the girl put it on. Traven quickly, and in very simple words, explained to Lynx what they were going to do and what needed to be done to save the poor kitty boy. Lynx's face became a mask of death and his eyes dark shadows. Traven didn't know if this was because a child was involved and Lynx sympathized because of his abused childhood, or if Lynx just had a fondness for cats. The look reassured him that even a drunk Lynx was a force to be reckoned with. Lynx reached his hands into the pockets on his thighs and when he pulled them out two eight inch knife blades had locked into his metal wrist bands. Traven didn't know if it was the alcohol that Lynx had drank or if the large man had tapped into some ancient Indian spirit of vengeance that made him run ahead of them through the portal screaming, but it froze everyone in the landing area for a moment. Within a second two very damaged Atrill bodies came skidding into the room, both dazed, confused, and bleeding. Brandy turned to Traven.

"I will deal with them, you had better go," she said, as Mo-pa could be heard in the background asking the children if they had ever thrown a Calleash.

Traven put on his helmet and he and Annie ran through. Annie quickly grabbed her terrified and beaten brother and escorted him back into the Gateway. Of the original guards none were left standing and more poured through the door. Lynx dispatched them as quickly as they came. Several of their guns were cut in half by Lynx's blades and Traven stood for a moment feeling as if there was no real reason he was there at all. He felt as he did when Lynx and Mo-pa had their sparing match, just a spectator. Then he realized what his purpose was. It was to convince Lynx to stop. There was a lull in the fight for too many bodies lay motionless blocking the door. Lynx screamed furious that his flow of opponents had slowed. He turned with a crazed look toward Traven, who, without a second thought banked a Calleash off the wall and while Lynx traced it's path bounced another one off his head. Lynx's body fell toward the floor. Before he hit, he was in Traven's arms.

"Damn, he's heavy," Traven mumbled, as he dragged Lynx through the fallen bodies and the portal sealed behind them. Again Traven yelled for a stretcher and looked up to see two Atrills suspended in the air by Brandy's tentacles.

"And what should I do with our guests?" she asked, pointing to the cat men.

Traven bit his lip to stop himself from suggesting that they be skinned.

"Put them in a cage next to the bugs that eat people," he said, "and make sure they can see the feeding."

Chapter Eighteen
I Need A Vacation From This Vacation

The next twenty-four hours were the most interesting look into the workings of a dysfunctional family that Traven had ever witnessed. Thealand woke up angry, the anger was directed at her own daughter for having shot her with the stun gun. Traven didn't see much of the argument, only the aftermath. Annie walked stiffly by him as he entered the med lab. Her eyes were intense, trying to control both anger and tears, as the rest of her face was as non-emotional as ever. The side of her face was cherry red as if a hand had made unwelcome contact with it. He asked her if something was the matter, if there was anything he could do. She ignored him and just kept on walking. Traven was slightly upset that he wasn't there to see Thealand wake. Partly because he had a million questions for her about her family, but more because he couldn't conceive what she would have said to her own child after she had been shot by her. From the looks of Annie's face there hadn't been much talking, just reacting. As Annie said, the Atrills tended to respond with their emotions.

Traven was with Mo-pa at the time of their confrontation. The old man and the cat children were having the time of their lives. He had taken them to a room in the Gateway that Traven had never seen before. It was a winter room, fresh with snow that was meant for packing. Its hills were designed for the greatest sledding one could ever hope for. The landscape could have been designed by Dr. Seuss with it's incredible peaks and angles that weren't possible on Earth. It looked as if tidal waves had frozen to become snow. The best part of the room was the fact that it was a less than chilly, seventy-two degrees. Traven enjoyed his first true snowball fight in years. Practicing with the Calleash had turned him into a deadly snowball warrior. He found himself holding back so as not to hurt the children physically or injure their pride. Quickly he found out that pride was not an issue. The children were very intense and competitiveness seemed an inbred trait. They ganged up on Traven and attacked him from all sides, sometimes quicker than he could anticipate. Being in the snowball fight he lost track of time and he didn't think Thealand would wake so soon.

He had sent those who needed it to the med lab. As Kovacs was being nursed back to health, he assumed that Thealand was sleeping off the effects of the stun gun. Lynx was also recovering from a hit to the head, or too much alcohol, the real culprit being anyone's guess. Traven made sure that the med clones would take away both his concussion and the impending hangover. He guessed that he might have been able to take away Lynx's intoxication if he had thought of it before they attacked the kidnappers.

Two government bases in two days on two different planets, he thought, *I hope this isn't becoming a trend.* Traven was also secretly hoping that Lynx was too drunk to remember being hit by the Calleash and he did not look forward to facing him when he finally came to.

Traven watched Annie head down the endless hallways to the Gateway and then he proceeded into the med lab. Thealand was talking to a shaken, but much better looking Kovacs. The med lab had taken care of both their wounds and now only Lynx was still unconscious. Thealand looked up at Traven sternly and then asked Kovacs to go find his brothers and sisters. The boy went to the door and paused to offer Traven a look of concern.

"So, you let the little snot shoot me," she said, in an incriminating tone that directed his full attention to her.

"I didn't know that she was going to do that," Traven replied sincerely, "and I'm guessing, neither did you."

Thealand gave him a look that was first betrayal, then softened into one of frustration.

"She always was the most head strong of the lot," she said, hopping onto the med lab cart and stretching out as if she might just go to sleep.

"How are you feeling?" Traven asked.

"Like a bad mother," she replied with a sigh. "I love them more than anything, but sometimes that just isn't enough."

"So..." Traven said hesitantly, "where's Dad?"

"Whose dad?" Thealand asked, confused by the question.

"Their dad," Traven clarified, with a waving of his arms.

"God, I don't know." Thealand said, trying to stretch a kink in her neck. "Which one in particular?"

"How about your husband?" Traven asked, feeling as if his question had not been phrased correctly.

"A husband?" It was now Thealand's turned to be shocked. "Who can afford one of those?"

"Whoa..." Traven interjected, "what the hell are you talking about?"

"Pup," Thealand said, with a tone that an adult uses on a child who should already understand a really simple concept, "did you grow up knowing your father?"

"Yeah, doesn't everyone?" Traven said. "Or at least, don't most?"

Thealand laughed and a large smile spread over her face.

"Why don't you tell me how families work on your planet," she said, starting to be amused by the conversation.

"Well," Traven paused, trying to analyze the marital customs of Earth in his head. "A man and a woman fall in love."

"Same here," Thealand interrupted.

"And if they love each other enough they get married," but before Traven could continue Thealand cut him off again.

"People almost never get married on my planet."

"Why?"

"The government levels heavy taxes against those few oddities that try," she said, as if this concept was bizarre and immoral. "Besides, what kind of man would stick around to watch you raise children? They're really not cut out for that responsibility."

Traven took a step back and nervously started to pace the room.

"Lots of them would on my planet, and in a perfect world, the men don't watch, they help raise the children."

"Really?" Thealand said, as if she didn't believe him.

"Well, a lot of couples get divorced too, and some stick around until the children are older and then get divorced, and some stay married until death does them part," Traven tried to assure her.

"Why would you want the same man to stick around?" Thealand seemed engrossed though confused with this conversation. It was as if this was one of the most radical and insane ideas she had ever heard. "I mean, don't get me wrong, men have their uses, such as they are, but raising the children is hard enough without having to deal with a needy man underfoot."

"Okay then, how do you afford to raise children?" he asked, with a raised eyebrow.

"Oh, the government taxes all males. They leave them about 30% of their income and the government uses the rest to provide food, health care, and shelter. Well, that's what they say it's for, most of us have our doubts. It's supposed to work like this: the more children you have the bigger dwelling you get and the more food. You're also supposed to get a bigger allowance for clothing and education, but your options are limited with both."

"You're a welfare mama?" Traven said, with a slight laugh and complete disbelief that one of the greatest fighters in the universe might be buying dinner with food stamps.

"What's a welfare mama?" she asked, sensing this wasn't a compliment.

"Oh, that's a whole other part of my world that would really take too long to explain. Are the men okay with this arrangement?" Traven said, trying to deflect from his last statement.

"I guess, it's been that way for hundreds of years." For the first time Thealand wondered if there were any men that didn't like the arrangement. "I mean, men get to come and go as they please, sit at bars drinking and watching sports. If there is someone who doesn't like it, they don't speak up."

"Who runs your government, men or women?"

"Both. Usually it's run by the military. Men try to get the position of Leader, but they're usually too distracted, they'd rather fight than think, but there have been quite a few men in the past, and far too many in the last couple of regimes. Women usually only seek power if they have no children, or are past the age of child bearing."

Traven pondered this system of government for a moment when Thealand gave him a sly smile.

"Maybe you should try living on my world for a while," she suggested. "No responsibilities and you don't even have to interact with your children."

Traven's face turned to an expression of disgust. How could someone not want to be part of his children's lives? It was true that this happened on Earth all the time, but it wasn't something he could grasp, and what was her comment about his children? Did she really think that he had children? He hadn't even worked up the courage to ask a girl to the movies, let alone steal his first kiss.

"No, thank you," he said, "besides, your planet doesn't have much of a lifeline left."

Thealand's expression became very serious.

"We're going to have to do something about that," she replied and then suddenly broke from the subject matter. "Hungry?" she asked.

"Starved," Traven said and the two set off to find food.

They made small talk along the way. Traven filled Thealand in about him saving the Earth and she almost looked impressed. He then explained about Lynx and how together, with her daughter, they saved Kovacs. Thealand seemed upset from the conversation and made a few disparaging remarks about her own daughter. While Traven could understand that she wasn't happy about the way Annie had gone about saving her brother, she still had saved her brother nonetheless. He thought Annie's ruthlessness would have impressed her mother. They arrived at the Chicago Street room and entered the pizza joint. Mo-pa was there feeding the litter of cat children who appeared as if they had just discovered the greatest treasure in the galaxy. Traven laughed when he saw that all but Nix had managed to drip greasy cheese on themselves. The children rushed to their mother and begged her to try this new discovery. After several choruses of, "please, please," she rolled her eyes and gave it a try. Traven laughed as Thealand found it hard to chew all the cheese that a true Chicagoan has come to expect from a real pizza. Her children excitedly jumped up and down saying things like, "Ain't it the best Mom?" and, "Can we stay here for good?" Trying to talk with food in her mouth she admitted that it wasn't bad and she proceeded to explain that they would be staying, at least for a while. The children all gave up a bombastic cheer of approval and only stopped when Mo-pa told them that now they must go for ice cream. Though they had no idea what this was, they had come to trust their dark skinned, round eared, tour guide and followed him out the door. They left to the yells of Thealand warning them not to eat too much. Kovacs was the last one out and, for a second time, he glanced back at his mother and waited until she shooed him on. Traven ordered another pizza and two Diet Cokes from the zombie-like AOD waitress. They grabbed a table near the neon lit window. Traven was surprised how much the cat children were like children from his planet. The only difference was that their natural appearance made them look like they were dressed for Halloween.

Thealand watched as her children paraded down the street and into the ice cream parlor. A sadness came over her face.

"They never have experienced anything like this," Thealand said sadly.

"Pizza and ice cream?" Traven asked.

"Fun," she stated flatly. The two of them watched from the window as the children made a game of piling insane amounts of ice cream upon oversized cones. "Oh God, they're going to get sick." She started to rise when Traven stepped in.

"So, how come you never told me about your family?" he asked, taking a drink of his Diet Coke, trying not to sound hurt.

"You're a man, men don't care on my planet, they just move on in a week or at the most a month. Besides, like most men, you probably don't even know how many children you have out there."

Traven froze inside. She did think that he had children. He didn't know how to reply, luckily Thealand continued talking.

"Their lives shouldn't be what they have been. Annie has watched over them and kept us together as a family, kept us alive. She has been their mother when I wasn't around, and even when she was far too young to have that kind of responsibility."

"She's done well," Traven said. "and she is still too young."

"What do you mean?" Thealand asked. "Most girls her age are starting on their second child."

"Second child!?" Traven said in shock. "She can't be more than thirteen."

"Thirteen and a half, I was at least a full year younger when she was born." Thealand watched Traven fall off of his chair and land on the floor with a thud. Thealand laughed, "Oh come on now, pup, surely at that age you must have..." The shock in Traven's eyes betrayed him. "Wait a minute, you didn't, and you haven't." She started to laugh harder.

Traven thought about lying, like boys in his school often did about girls, about how far they had gotten with them. He didn't like their bogus stories, they always sound like lies, no matter how well they told them. Traven didn't like to lie; besides, it was clear at this point that Thealand could see right through him. It was almost as if she could read his mind. Embarrassed and feeling his face turn red, he got back in his chair dreading her next words.

"Well," she said, playing with the straw in her drink, "why not?" and she quietly awaited his answer.

Traven squirmed in his seat and prayed that this moment would just magically pass, that maybe if he wished hard enough the question would have never been asked.

"I don't know," he said, searching for another answer than, *I haven't had the chance.* Luckily his brain didn't release that part of his confession.

"Religious reasons?" she pushed, trying to understand him.

"No, I just hoped I'd be in love, maybe with the person I would spend my life with. It's different on Earth. On Earth there is a commitment that goes with doing that. Maybe not for everybody, but at least there is for me."

"You are a curious pup and now I do mean, pup," She said, emphasizing the word.

"I thought pup was a comment on my age."

"No, I always meant it as an insult on your maturity." She took a big sip of her drink and was surprised by it's pleasant taste.

"Well, thanks a lot," he said, chewing on the end of his straw.

"Look, while you may never hear the end of this," she teased, "your ability to follow through on your commitments makes you more of a man than any on my planet. Even Kovac's father, whoever he is, wouldn't have made such an attempt to save him. Some take more time to be ready than others, and time you have in abundance. If it makes you happy, wait. Only you can decide your course."

"Crap," said Traven, "now you sound like Mo-pa."

"He does leave an impression and speaking of, I need to round up my children, one of them is somewhere in the Gateway hating me. I need to talk to her," and with a slice of pizza for the road they left.

Timothy John Vaulato

Chapter Nineteen

This Is My Stop

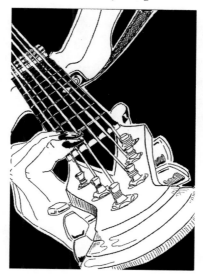

Lynx woke with one demand that he delivered in an ice cold whisper that made Traven very nervous.

"Show me what happened."

"Pardon me?" Traven replied, confused.

"Show me what happened," Lynx repeated, his face dark and angry.

The assassin stood up and walked through the med lab door as if it was he that owned the Gateway. Traven followed behind him with a great sense of foreboding. He couldn't understand why Lynx seemed so upset. Was he mad that Traven had knocked him out? He knew he was no match for Lynx sober and Lynx knew it too. Surely he didn't really feel that he had bested him? Was the world's greatest assassin upset that he killed a few cat people after Traven had given him an alternative to every death he had caused? Was saving his Father just a way to stop the killing he had done, or did he really just want to save his father? Traven had come up with many questions, all of which he was afraid to ask.

As they entered the library, Brandy was waiting. She, as always, had been listening and in response to what had just occurred, used the monitors to review the saving of Kovacs. Before either Traven or Lynx could speak, she had the answers.

"Ya managed to hurt most them severely," she stated, replaying the scene on the monitors. "With their advanced medical abilities all but two will recover before the planet is destroyed. In truth, even in your drunken state, y'all were holding back."

Traven now wondered if Lynx was upset that while being drunk he might have performed poorly and tarnished his own reputation, which by what they had done to change the time stream was at this point nonexistent anyway. Brandy cocked her head and studied Lynx with her slightly glowing but questioning eyes.

"When the planet is destroyed, everyone hurt, maimed, or nearly killed will be dead, regardless."

Lynx's face was unchanged but his mouth spoke six very intense words.

"Return me to my time stream."

Brandy cocked her head in the other direction and answered him calmly.

"Certainly," she said, as Traven started to protest her reply.

"Wait a minute, we don't know what the outcome of putting you back will be," he said.

Lynx and Brandy walked past the boy. She signaled him with a wave of her hand not to stop what had been set in motion. He felt helpless. He felt as if they should spend a little more time studying the ripple effects that might occur by putting this man, who was now a time anomaly, back into his time stream. They walked in silence to the Landing Area. When they arrived Traven turned to Brandy and asked in a hushed voice, "What the hell is going on?"

"The man wants to go home," she said, as if it should have been obvious.

Brandy asked Traven for the okay to open the door. He nodded. The destination would be where Lynx would have been in the timeline if he was raised with a father. The time was the second after he had originally entered the Gateway. Traven tried to speak before Lynx went through.

"Lynx, I..." but before he could say anything else Lynx chastised him.

"You got more out of me, boy, than we had agreed. Don't cross my path again," and then Lynx disappeared.

Traven stood for a moment stunned, trying to grasp what had just occurred. He felt as if he had just lost a friend. When he thought about their tense friendship he wasn't sure why he was upset. Clueless to the workings of his own emotions he turned to Brandy.

"Explain?" he said.

Brandy said nothing for a moment and then gave a slight smile.

"The workings of organic beings have always been a mystery to me."

"Why was he..." Traven grasped for a word to explain his question.

"Pissed off?" Brandy said, finding the word that Traven had lacked. "Ah am not entirely sure. Maybe he felt that rescuing Kovacs wasn't part of the bargain, but when someone wants to go they should have the right." Traven, perplexed by the outcome, looked at Brandy, but decided that he wasn't going to get any answers from her.

"I want to know what happens to him."

"Now?" she asked, which threw Traven off.

"Can we?"

"Now that he's back in his own timeline we can most certainly track and catalog his actions; in fact, the outcome of the rest of his life," she replied, "but I think you had better clear your little ole head first. Yuh seem a bit tense."

Traven shook his head and headed back to his room.

When he arrived he found Annie on the stage that bordered the far side of his massive bed-room. She was trying to figure out one of the many guitars that lined the stage. Being surprised that she was in his room, he climbed up to join her.

"It's a guitar," he stated, motioning to the instrument in her hands. "It's for making music."

She gave him a look that conveyed this was not a satisfactory answer so he picked up a guitar that was nearby and plugged it into a amp on a soft setting.

"See, you hold it like this."

Annie mimicked his actions with the guitar she was holding.

"You hold down the strings in different combinations to create different chords, or you play single notes to create a melody." Traven demonstrated.

Annie had no problem in recreating his actions. Traven noticed that she bit her lip in the same fashion as her mother did when she was thinking.

"Not much of an instrument," she said, "its barely audible."

"Hold on," Traven went to the amplifier that Annie's guitar was connected to and turned it all the way up, "try that."

Hesitantly, Annie strummed the guitar and the amp let out a frightening yell. Her reaction was priceless. She immediately threw the guitar to the ground and jumped back ten feet holding her hands over her ears.

"Hey!" yelled Traven, "don't go all punk on the guitar."

He walked over to her amp and turned it off. Then he proceeded to the amp that he was plugged into and turned it down to a lesser volume to the one that made her jump. He motioned for her to come back from her spot of safety. He proceeded to give her an impromptu guitar lesson.

"As I was saying, the notes create melodies," and with that he played a riff from Rush's *Closer to the Heart*, "and the chords can be used to create rhythms."

She folded her arms and raised an eyebrow.

"And then what?" she said, unimpressed.

"Well, if you get together with a few other people you create a band and make music." He raised his head to the sky and

266

said, "Band, Rush," and with that the members of the band Rush formed from the ground and took their place at their instruments. "Play Closer to the Heart," he said to the AODs. It was the only song Rush played that he could do the rhythm line to without totally screwing up. He mouthed the words to a four count intro and the band began. They played well, as they were programmed to and though Traven knew that his roll as a second guitar wasn't really necessary to the song, he still loved to play with the big boys, even if they weren't the real Rush. The song ended quickly, around 2 minutes and 52 seconds. When they stopped Annie squinted her eyes at him.

"Can you play anything more... aggressive?" she asked.

Again he looked to the sky.

"Band, Black Sabbath," and with that the AODs turned from three into four and they played a rather garage band version of the song *Paranoid*. When he was finished he handed his guitar to Annie and picked the one off the ground she had thrown down. After tuning it he introduced her to the power chord and the two of them joined Black Sabbath for the second version of Paranoid. Annie played incredibly well for someone who had never held a guitar before. They spent the afternoon playing every song Traven knew he could play without major difficulty. To his relief, Annie's fingers had started to hurt and they took a break.

"So, that's music on your planet?" she asked.

"Oh no, there are tons of different kinds," he said, turning to the sky again, "band, gone." The stage was clear. "Come this way."

Traven led her into his tree house bedroom and introduced her to the incredible stereo system that he once only imagined in a drawing. He explained to her about the different types of music on his world and why he liked them. Some of the music reminded him of places he had been and even times in his life, whether those times were good or bad. He told her that the music was a way to keep or relive those memories or sometimes just to let off steam. Lastly, he played her a few pieces from Dirgeworld; he admitted that some music took lon-ger to grow on you than others. Annie tended to like the heavy music, even Alice Cooper, though when Traven explained the stage show that went along with it, fake decapitations and chop-ping up plastic dolls, she found it confusing and in some ways down right silly.

"So, this is all yours?" she asked.

"Yeah, I guess so," he pondered. "It feels more like I'm just living here than own it," he said sitting down next to her on the bed. "Have they made you a room yet?"

"I slept in some room last night," she said, "but the screams of the guards that you captured from Fecha kept waking me up."

"My God," Traven said in shock, "you slept in the bug room?"

"I didn't want to chance them getting out."

"The bugs?"

"The guards," she said, rolling her eyes.

"Well, there's not much chance of that," he said, suddenly painfully aware at the stupidity of his bug comment. "I'd be more worried about the bugs..." but before he could finish Annie had leaned in close and had started to kiss him.

The kiss was passionate and forceful and Traven found that he was kissing her back. He ran his hand down her back and the other through her hair. Everything seemed like a dream and just as quickly as it started Traven's brain gave a quick but powerful, *What the hell are you doing?* to his subconscious. Though he didn't want to stop, the thought of Thealand kill-ing him was enough incentive to break him from his actions. He pulled away in shock. Annie pushed her glasses back up to their place on her nose.

"What's wrong?" she asked.

"Uh, I've got to go," he said nervously.

She stretched her body back on his bed.

"I'll wait," she said, fluffing up one of his pillow.

Dumbfounded, Traven stumbled out of his room and down the halls of the Gateway to the library, finding it difficult to walk.

He plopped himself down in the library chair and closed his eyes.

"Diet Coke," he said out loud and for a change Brandy appeared holding the cold refreshing beverage, causing him to jump as if he was guilty of a crime.

"Well, well, now who's playing Romeo?" she said, with a great big smile and handing him the Coke.

"You know," he said, with anger growing in his voice, "it's bad enough you eavesdrop when I'm trying to pray, but do you have to watch when my friend's daughter kisses me?"

"Poor baby," she teased, "ya know it's unavoidable and I believe it takes two for the act to happen. Ah don't recall you complaining."

"Look, I had no intention," Traven protested.

"But she did and from what I observe still does."

"Brandy, she's like, thirteen. I could be arrested!"

"Oh sweetie, in ten years a four year difference won't matter," she stated coyly.

"Look, my life-mate is out there somewhere..." but before Traven could continue Brandy cut him off.

"According to some book from another life," she said in a huff. "This is exactly what I warned you about. You can't keep running your life by that book."

"The book has been right so far," he pointed out.

"That doesn't mean that everything about the book is right. You have changed the time stream already. Your true love may not even exist in this reality."

"But what if she does? Can I risk that?"

"Can you risk putting your life on hold for something that may never be? If you spend all your time waiting for the future you lose the now. You will never learn to appreciate the moment. At that point ya lose your life. Y'all will become a slave to the concept of, what might be, and that's not being alive, Dearheart."

Traven buried his head in his hands in frustration.

"My first kiss and it's from a thirteen year old cat girl."

"A day ago you would have been all right with the idea of your first kiss being from a somewhat older cat girl."

Traven looked at Brandy in shock hoping that she wasn't about to tell him she could read his mind too.

"Oh, come on now!" she said, "I've seen the way you look at her. Even Larry could tell, and his programing is not all that exceptional. Here, let me play devil's advocate," she said smirking at his predicament, "was your first kiss really that bad?"

"No, it wasn't," he admitted, "but what Thealand's going to do to me will suck the big one."

"Ah wouldn't be too worried about her," she said, "we girls can talk, but what you do have to worry about is the thirteen year old back in your room and what you're going to tell her."

"I don't know." His shoulders slumped heavily and his mind drew a blank. "I didn't even know that she liked me."

"Maybe she doesn't," Brandy said, giving him a whack on the shoulder, "maybe she's just trying to get back at her mother."

"Well, thank you for the conspiracy theory," he frowned.

"Just pointing out a possibility. She wouldn't be the first woman to use a man to get her way."

"She's hardly a woman."

"On your planet and in your culture no, but you already know what Thealand has said. By her world's standards she's all grown up, and then some. Maybe y'all are the first male that has ever shown her any kindness. Some girls love that type, the kind of man who pays attention. Why, you could be the man of her dreams. Maybe Thealand even told her about your world. Girls love foreign types and you couldn't be more foreign than anybody her world has to offer."

Brandy was definitely amused by Traven's advanced state of being overly-perplexed. Traven just sat in the chair mumbling to himself.

"Damn, damn, damn, damn," he repeated under his breath.

"You know," Brandy observed, "I thought I sent you to go clear your mind."

"My mind couldn't be more clear if you put it in a blender and sucked it out with a straw."

He knew that this was untrue, his mind was full. It was full of his first kiss which he did enjoy or at least parts of him did. It was also full of the various reactions that Thealand might have upon finding out. Even with all of this he felt guilty, not only for what he had let happen, but to the life-mate he had never met. He felt he had just betrayed someone. In Brandy's eyes that life-mate may not even exist. Brandy was right, his mind was not clear in the least. Finally, after a few minutes of deep thought Brandy interrupted.

"You know it wasn't any easier for Docheen," she said.

"What do you mean?" he asked, surprised that Brandy had even brought up the former Keeper.

"Oh, he had his lovers."

"She's not my lover," Traven pointed out quickly.

"No, but she probably wants to be," she added. "Have you given any thought as to what will happen when you go back to your room?"

"I'm not going back."

"Well that is less than brave, for the recent savior of the Earth, that is. As I was saying, Docheen would fall in love or like and then whatever little miss of the moment would have him wrapped around her finger, at least for a while."

"And then what?" he asked, hoping for some words of wisdom.

"Well being the Keeper is a rough lot in life. You will out-live all of those you love. Ah guess in time he learned to accept the moment and then distance himself when he felt the moment was over. I would have thought he would have given up on a mate all together, but I suppose if you don't have the moment ya just have an eternity of loneliness."

A slight sadness came over Brandy's face.

"Didn't it bother you that he had all these girls?" Traven asked.

"What do you mean?" she asked back.

A Lifetime In Time

"Didn't you get jealous? I mean, you did say that you loved him."

"I said I loved him in my own way," she clarified. "I'm cute when I want to be and I can give powers to people that they could never have dreamed up on their own, but I know I am the genie in the bottle, not the princess for the prince on the white horse."

Traven realized that he was pitying Brandy and as Brandy realized it too she switched the topic.

"Would ya like to see what mess of troubles Lynx is sloshin up?"

Traven leaned way back in the library chair.

"Why not," he said, "could you bring me a cookie?"

"One cookie, coming up."

The screens flickered with their eavesdropping on the new life of Lynx.

Timothy John Vaulato

Chapter Twenty

Two Bodies One Life

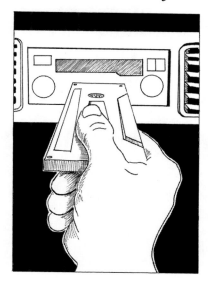

Lynx entered his timeline next to a modern suburban home complete with a two car garage, and several rather appalling lawn ornaments. The Gateway had placed him where he should have been in his life if his father had never died and thus he had never become an assassin. He stood next to a tall oak tree, and less than twenty feet away was a man with a large headset radio cutting a pristine lawn. He quickly became part of the tree as was his training and observed the other him. The man dripped with sweat and busied himself with the chore of changing the bag of lawn clippings that had been let go for far too long. Lynx had no new memories of his father, except saving him from his death and he retained all memories of every man he had killed though he had now never done the deed. He watched the man intently for but a few moments and realized that he needed to distance himself from his current location and come up with a rational plan. As a shadow he slipped into a nearby car and as if the ability to hot-wire a vehicle was as quick as turning a key, he was gone.

"Can we fast forward this movie?" asked Traven from his seat in the library.

"We certainly can," Brandy replied and the highlights started to play on the library screen.

Throughout the afternoon Lynx went to several drop boxes that the Steel Tear kept in every large city in case of emergencies. The money he was able to acquire in a single afternoon would have kept the average person set for years. He then drove up to an inner city garage and exchanged his stolen car and a few dollars for an old mustang with a top of the line stereo system. They even sold him with unattractive but passable clothes. A room at a safe house, where no names were asked or given, provided him lodging. With no appointments on his agenda, he found himself at a loss for purpose. While wandering the streets he found a record store and bought some cassettes for the tape player in his car. Driving became one of the most liberating and freeing times of his long and complicated life. As he drove he thought about the events that were now unfolding on the government base where he and Traven had saved the world. For the first time in his sordid life he had become a hero; it felt both odd and uncomfortable. As the days passed he would occasionally be hit with sharp pains and his body felt as if it was becoming liquid. When this happened his mind felt that it had become a television screen placed on a blank channel. As the pain subsided it would clear to show him the world he had now chosen. The pains were infrequent, but they were getting stronger. After two days he decided he needed to know more about the other him. In the late afternoon when the house was sure to be clear, he made a reconnaissance mission to learn what the new truth of his other life had become.

He disturbed the air with no more impact than a summer breeze leaking through a closed window and found himself standing in a modern suburban living room. None of it looked familiar and it certainly wasn't what he would have chosen for a dwelling. Nevertheless the evidence pointed to the fact that in his new reality it was his home. Pictures on a baby grand piano had showed a different him. He stared at the photographs as if to get a better clue of who he now was. His face in the photographs was similar but thinner, almost younger looking with a short haircut and no sideburns. The most striking difference was the easy smile that spread across this stranger's face. This man wore his smile proudly in the company of his loved ones. These people that held the other Lynx tightly in their arms stirred no recognition in the world's greatest assassin. In a wedding picture, a woman, whom he assumed to be his wife, wore traditional Indian garment though she was a blonde white woman. In another photo two children with Lynx's and the woman's mixed features were held in his arms. He followed their growth through the different photos, birthdays, school plays, and grammar school graduation. An older girl with darker skin and bleached blonde hair; a younger boy who had a love of baseball. Bookcases upon bookcases gave the room a feeling of a library branch that specialized in political science and Native American studies. Certificates of merit hung on the walls which were not taken up by shelves. This Lynx had a Doctorate and many humanitarian awards. The irony left him with a smirk.

It appeared to Lynx as he searched for clues that some things were triggering memories of his childhood. Indian artifacts that contained the flavor of his upbringing on the reservation were prevalent in this abode. Lynx almost completely turned his back on his heritage with the exception of parts of his clothing, (which he had left in the Gateway) and his hair. Lynx had donned his black work suit complete with weapons for this mission out of habit. He did not expect to need them, but consistency is what had made him the professional he was. A sound triggered his defense training. It was not the sound of an attacker, but the sound of a car. As the doors of the gray Buick slammed shut the woman from the photos and the two children walked into the house carrying their shopping bags and school items. Lynx's years of training allowed him to almost become invisible within the surroundings. As the strangers that were his family entered, the woman shouted to her children to get busy on their homework. The children disappeared into their rooms though it could be clearly heard that the girl had ignored her homework in the favor of the phone. The woman started making dinner after plopping a Roy Orbison tape into a boom box in the kitchen. As the music played Lynx studied her, wondering what qualities the other him saw in her. She was not unattractive, she seemed to handle her kitchen knife well, as the peppers were diced with skill. But, she was too blonde, too soft of muscle, and her eyes carried no edge to them. There was no trace that she had any fire of life, no hint of the ability to fight for self preservation. No streak of danger. No, these eyes appeared only too willing to nurture, too needy, too caring for his current liking. Her singing to the music grated upon him, but she did know the words if not the key. What kind of love had he missed? What could she have said or done to attract his attention upon that meeting that lead to her being the wife that he had no memory of? What had developed in his tastes then that he did not have now? She turned and wrote a note on the refrigerator to remind her daughter that she had a math test in two days, that her clean gym outfit was in her backpack as well as the money for an up-coming field trip. She dotted her "i's" with hearts. She continued with dinner, shoving her dish in the oven and when the tape clicked to it's end she turned it over. She took a deep breath and then her eyes focused on the phone.

"You'd better not be on the phone, Teresa!" she yelled over the music and then returned to her meal.

The phone rang. She smiled and turned the music down.

"Oh, hi Bob. Sorry, that was Teresa, I have a hard time recognizing her without a phone to her face. How's the University treating you?" she said, still not allowing him a word in edgewise. "You wouldn't believe it, but our neighbor's car was stolen right off the street in front of his house the other day and..." her voice stopped abruptly and then a tone of concern appeared. "Slow down, what do you mean arrested? What do you mean, you think he was arrested. By who? If they weren't police then what the hell were they?"

As Lynx listened from the other room he felt he knew what was happening.

"Ok, ok," the woman continued, "how can I get in touch with him... what do you mean you don't know? Damn it, Bob, where did they take my husband?"

As Lynx listen to the conversation he knew what had happened. General Gillette had most likely run his photo through the computers and matched his face with his other self. *Damn the child,* he thought, *he was right to use a mask.* Lynx's other self was an activist and well known to the government that they managed to anger in their attack on the base. It was clear to Lynx that General Gillette now held his other self responsible. In short, the man was trying to make good on his threats. As the heated phone conversation continued onward, Lynx slipped out of the house and into his Mustang. As a freelance agent he had done many questionable acts for the government. This knowledge now allowed him to know many of their secret bases and holding areas. He knew exactly where his other self was being kept and had every intention of dealing with General Gillette in his own special way.

"Y'all want some popcorn with this movie?" Brandy asked Traven, as he stretched in the library chair and watched the events unfold.

"Popcorn?" questioned Traven.

"It's only proper," she replied.

"Yeah, that would be cool," Traven said, surprised that Brandy could actually eat junk food, or any food.

As Brandy handed him a fresh batch of hot, buttered popcorn, the young Keeper asked the library to fast forward to when Lynx got out of the car. Rush's *Flight by Night* cassette blared as Lynx stopped the vehicle. He checked his weapons as he stepped out of the car. The Gateway had replaced the ones he had used against the attack on the base. When the Gateway had done this he was unsure, but once again he wondered if this had been done as a gift, or if he was now a puppet for the Gateway's greater scheme.

The holding area was in the middle of nowhere and Lynx knew not to drive to the front door, though he was tempted to crash his car into the building for the element of surprise. *No,* he thought, *there might be a need for a hasty getaway.* He hid the car in a grove of trees a mile away and moved through the night like a wolf on the prowl. The holding area appeared to be a deserted house. That was a deception, the real cell was deep underground in an abandoned mine tunnel. He sent five highly trained guards to the land of dreams before any alarm could be sounded. He waited for the base's elevator to come up with their second wave of defense to check on the disturbance.

Five minutes went by when Traven asked for a fast forward from the library screens.

A swarm of nondescript vehicles pulled up to the house. The elevator doors opened and the army elite wearing gas masks fell to the ground as Lynx gave them bruises that some of them would feel for life. He ducked a storm of bullets from the outside troops as he opened the floor of the elevator and disappeared into the shaft. Knock out gas flowed into the compartment above him. He used his discipline sticks from the back of his outfit to slow his decent. Almost magically, he entered through the crack in the doors on the holding cell level. Twenty armed men kept their guns trained on the thin black line of darkness when to their dismay they realized Lynx was already behind them.

"How does he do that?" Traven mumbled, with his mouth crammed with popcorn.

"Hush up and watch," Brandy said, as Traven looked up to see she was indeed nervously eating fistful's of popcorn too.

The fight lasted less than sixty seconds, reminding Traven of the images of Docheen in the training room, but without a tail and a

second set of arms. Throwing jaxs came out of the handle of the discipline stick and nailed five of the men with a single throw.

"Wow, I wonder what he could do with a Calleash?" Traven pondered out loud as Brandy scolded him with a loud "Shh."

Pressure pins hit pressure points, razor disks severed arteries, leaving the men to stop their fighting to stagger away and try to save themselves from bleeding to death.

"He's still holding back," commented Brandy.

"Shh," said Traven, and then thinking to himself, *that's holding back?*

The men lay unconscious on the floor, or running down the hall in search of medical assistance. Lynx threw two more jax's disabling the security camera's.

In a darkened room John Olsen sat tied to a chair as General Gillette turned his attention to the drugged and beaten man.

"Who is he?" the General demanded, now pointing to a blank security screen. John lifted his weary head with great effort.

"Obviously someone you pissed off," he struggled to say.

The General hit John hard with the butt of his gun.

"Get on the horn," the General said to one of the other interrogators, "we need back up immediately."

A frightened look spread over the man's face as he picked up a nearby phone.

"Sir, the lines are dead, sir."

"Well, yippee ki aye ladies," the General said in disgust, "get ready to dance."

The sound of the men cocking their guns almost made John stir. In a whisper, the second interrogator turned to the general.

"We still have men outside, sir." He pointed out trying to sound hopeful.

"There's only one door in and out of this room," the General said, "Keep your eyes on the door and wait my mark. We're gonna nail that, son of a bitch!"

The room went silent, until the General realized that the only heavy breathing he could hear was his own. He slowly started to back-up toward the wall until his heel pushed up against something soft. He glanced down and recognized the bodies of his men. Quickly moving forward he pointed his gun into the base of John's skull.

"Show yourself, you bastard," again there was silence. "I know this man means something to you or you wouldn't be here."

The General started to apply pressure to the trigger when the silence broke.

"General, I'm not here for your hostage," Lynx said, his voice seeming to come from all directions at once, "I'm here for you."

Sweat broke on the General's brow. He looked into the darkness of the room that was dimly illuminated by the one light they were using for their interrogation.

"Who are you?" he asked, eyes shifting from left to right.

"I am your worst nightmare. I am your greatest dream. An assassin that cannot be traced, an assassin that cannot be stopped. The perfect soldier, for every dirty little act you've been given the money and ability to act on."

The weightlessness of the general's hand told him there was something very wrong. As he looked down he came to the realization that not only was his gun now missing but so was his hand. In one clumsy panicked motion he removed his tie and used it to slow the pulsing flow of blood that was coming from his stump. The General's voice cracked and betrayed the fear that now raced through his body as fast as his blood pumped through his arm.

"Why... why are you doing this?"

"You have used the Steel Tear for years General," Lynx said, his voice echoing loudly in the general's ears. The General staggered and started to go limp. His legs buckled dropping him onto his knees.

"Do you remember a group of young hit men you sent in front of the troops back in Nam?" came the question from the darkness.

"Nam?" he muttered, "that was years ago."

"Yes it was. The group was spectacular. They soften up the enemy so that your poorly trained men could move in and establish order."

"Yes," stuttered the General. "They were good, but none of them survived."

"No, there's one. One who watched as his comrades died. Every assignment was more impossible than the last to get out of until you reached that point where you felt that the information they possessed was a liability to your position, so you put them in between the enemy and your own troops. A brilliant move, General, but paybacks are a bitch. Every person you've had killed to further the interest of your career, every person that was in the wrong place at the wrong time that you rolled over or was brought to their knees for your benefit has felt the way you do now. Hundreds, thousands have died in your wake." Lynx stepped forward making himself known and stared into the General's eyes. "You are a foolish amateur. I am death. I am your target. Catch me if you can."

The general passed out and hit the floor with a loud thump. Lynx stood and directed his gaze toward John. Blood trickled down his chin as he sat still unconscious in the chair. A pain shot through Lynx that was undeniable and knocked him off his feet. As his eyes regained their focus he realized that John was feeling it too.

"What the hell is going on?" Traven asked, as the popcorn fell out of his mouth. This time instead of shushing him, Brandy tried to explain.

"Time is starting to realign," she said almost distantly, as if this was a plotline she had seen too many times before. "It's trying to decide which one of them should exist."

"Well hell, let's pull him back into the Gateway!" Traven said, as if he was stating the obvious.

"Wouldn't matter now, it's been set in motion, it can't be stopped." She brought her finger to her chin as if to ponder. "Ah have seen this happen before, one of the outcomes of putting someone back, as I had warned. If we had put him back in a slightly different moment there would have remained two of them, though our Lynx never would have been the dominate life, just a stranger in a world where there was already a man that lives a life that he should've had."

"What happens now?"

"The timeline will purge one of them or combine them. If our Lynx disappears there will be no loss to the continuity of the timeline. If the other one goes our Lynx will exist without knowing the family he might have made. The last possibility is there will be a hybrid Lynx that shares the memories of both."

"Well we just can't sit here and do nothing!" Traven said, demanding action.

"It's too late, Dearheart," she replied, "unless you go back and stop yourself from ever making a deal with him. It would be difficult since most of your time together was in the Gateway. You would have had to drop yourself a note at school and then even if it worked you would have to start trying to come up with another plan to save the Earth because it never would have been saved."

She looked at him as if she wanted to say more, to tell him about the possibility of fractured timelines, or even birthing other realities from his actions. As he shook his head in disbelief she decided that he wasn't ready. "He's a big boy," She reminded him, "he knew the risks."

As Traven looked back up to the screen Lynx had already grabbed John and somehow got him out of the holding area and into the woods.

"Fast forward," he said.

The scene slowed as Lynx reached his hidden car. Another jolt of pain hit both men and they fell in a heap on the ground. Lynx was the first to rise and looking toward John he realized that John's pain wasn't over. John's face pointed toward the stars and scream after scream bit into the dark of the night. In the interest of not being discovered Lynx tried to administer a nerve pinch when his other self slowly melted into thin air as if he was nothing but streams of water and mist.

"Holy..." Traven was in shock, but Brandy nodded her head as if this was the normal chain of events in the flow of time. "What's going to happen to him now?" he asked.

The screens answered, responding as if they were showing a trailer at the beginning of a movie.

Lynx spent months driving the back roads of America, never staying too long in any one place. At times he would come back to spy on the family that John left behind. None of John's memories transferred to Lynx, he now had no life save that which he made for himself. No past left to call his own. John's family would spend years and most of their money trying to locate their lost loved one.

Lynx felt that John's family should never be bothered by the government that had abducted him. Lynx even broke into a few other government bases with little to no fanfare and wiped out records that connected John and John's family to any other future investigations. For fun he even wrecked General Gillette's credit line through the base's computers.

Gillette searched for Lynx and spent much of his time jumping at shadows and trying to learn to use a prosthetic hand. The government forced him into a form of early retirement, but even from his desk job as the head of forestry he misappropriated funds and used them to search for the man that took his hand.

As the years passed, Lynx spent most of his time as a recluse. When he wasn't digging up information on the Steel Tear, he drank. He found out that almost all of the people he had been assigned to kill had been dispatched into the great beyond by other assassins, mainly Mersan.

Mersan also searched for the one man who he had not beaten in combat. This became an obsession for the young leader of the Steel Tear. Five years to the date Traven and Lynx had attacked the government base Mersan caught up with Lynx inside of a bar in Montana. Lynx knew Mersan was coming, he chose to be both unarmed and drunk. The fight was over quickly leaving Mersan feeling unfulfilled and cheated of a glorious battle.

Lynx was dead.

"This sucks!" Traven yelled. "It can't end this way."

"Life's not a movie, Sweetie," Brandy finished the last remnants of the popcorn. "We all make choices. Lynx has made his."

"Well this movie can have a different ending!" Traven said, throwing his drink across the room. Brandy gave him an incriminating look.

"Before y'all get too cocky youngster," she said, with her eyes starting to glow, "your world is better off without another assassin in the mix."

"Well at my last assessment, he hasn't killed anyone and he saved Earth."

"No, you saved Earth. Lynx went along for the ride."

"We can't just let him die!" Traven screamed. "If he wasn't with us, then he would have stood against us and I wouldn't be standing here now."

"The man told you to stay away!" Brandy yelled back. "Not to mention the threat that he'd up and kill you if he ever laid eyes on you again."

Traven paused. Brandy was right. He did say not to cross his path again, and all that implied. Traven's mind reeled in thought. Could he convince Lynx not to give up on the life that he had left, or would he kill Traven before Traven could open his mouth? Brandy broke his train of thought.

"Anyway, y'all have a bigger problem than the outcome of Lynx's decisions."

"Oh yeah, what's that?" he asked.

"I believe there is still a thirteen year old girl waiting for you in your bed," she smiled.

Timothy John Vaulato

Chapter Twenty One
Field Trip

Traven left the library with too many questions on his mind. The least of these questions was Lynx, and even he seemed like a gigantic moral issue that could leave Traven once again playing God. He had already gone down that path by saving the Earth, but spending time thinking about his effect on the time stream did frighten him. Brandy told him that Lynx's fate could hang in the balance indefinitely depending on when Traven had finally decided what, or if, he wanted to do something about it. Could he just leave the man that helped him save the Earth to give up his own life, or could he persuade him that there was a reason to keep on living? More to the point, would he be able to help him without Lynx killing him on sight? Then the bigger and more immediate problem of Annie crept back into his head. He had an aggressive and permissive thirteen year old in his bedroom. He just hoped she was sleeping and wouldn't wake in the morning trying to put the moves on him. Brandy had brought up several reasons as to why Annie had kissed him and most of them didn't sit well with Traven. *What if she was just trying to get*

back at her mother? Traven did not want to be in the middle of that family squabble, especially that family. What if she really did like him? Did he still have feelings for Thealand? Thealand, being the mother of six children had definitely set him back. He knew he wasn't ready to be a surrogate father and he wasn't really sure he was even ready for his first date no matter what his hormones told him.

He decided he would stop into the Chicago street room to think. One of the buildings was an old coffee house. Though he wasn't really fond of coffee he decided that at the least it would be a place to think, and he wouldn't have to return to his room to deal with Annie right away. The coffee house was dim and was surprisingly full of AOD's. A man on the stage toward the back of the shop played an acoustic guitar and harmonica on a strange looking device that Traven would learn later was a harmonica holder. The young man's voice sounded oddly like the noise that killer bees made. Even with the young man's unique singing style Traven found him interesting. The lyrics of his songs were sometimes funny, most of the time powerful and even angry. As the waitress poured Traven a cup of coffee, which he quickly dumped huge amounts of cream and sugar into, the man on the stage sang a song called, *In My Time of Dyin'*. Traven wondered what his hero, Alice Cooper, could do with such a song. Halfway through the song in walked Thealand. She was eating another piece of pizza and quickly spotted Traven. He tensed as she pulled up a chair and sat down across from him.

"What the heck is this?" she asked, trying to talk with her mouth still half full of pizza, "he's awful."

"I don't know," Traven replied, "I was kinda digging it. What are you doing up?" He quietly said a prayer that she had not talked to her daughter.

"I put the children to bed and realized I was still hungry," she said, grimacing at the man on the stage, "I saw you come in here from the pizza place and figured that you would come out soon. I could hear his squawking from the other side of the street." She yelled over the music and pointed to the stage. "When you didn't come out I decided to brave the ruckus and come in to get you. Do you really like this?"

Traven thought for a moment and replied.

"Yes, I think I really do." Traven flagged down a waitress.

"What is his name?" he asked her.

"Bobby Zimmerman," she replied.

"Never heard of him."

Traven pondered why this man was vaguely familiar as the waitress left. Thealand wiped her mouth on a table napkin and leaned way back in her chair resting her feet on the table.

"I've been thinking," she said, "and I believe I have devised a cunning plan."

"Uh oh," Traven smiled, as she threw a crumpled pizza stained napkin at his head.

"My planet, as you have so eloquently put it, is doomed, so the next logical step is to find another one. I believe we have been to such a planet."

"Ok," he said, "where and when."

"Topacies."

Traven's blank stare made her frustrated so she attempted to clarify herself.

"You know, the planet with the floating rocks. We trained there, it's beautiful, unspoiled, and has plenty of wildlife."

"But does it have enough to support life?" Traven asked.

"We can always ask the library," she smiled.

Her plan wasn't bad Traven agreed, but the thought of her people destroying another planet made him cringe.

"We only saw parts of it," he said trying not to get her hopes up.

"So we go in the morning. We have the Gateway whip up a few sky sleds and we check it out."

"Well, I've never been on a sky sled, whatever that is," Traven admitted, "but it does sound like a plan."

"Good." Thealand got up and started to leave. "Oh, and by the way. Be gentle with her," she said awkwardly, and then regaining her composure. "She acts tough and is, but in many ways she's emotionally quite young."

The coffee Traven was trying to finish became lodged in his windpipe causing him to cough it out in one loud gag. Luckily, he was able to direct his head to his side and didn't embarrass himself further by coating the table. The sound was loud enough that the AOD's became silent and turned to the hideous noise. The musician on the stage even stopped his song as if to see what was the cause of this sudden interruption.

"What?" was all Traven could manage to say through his choking.

"I can smell her all over you," she said, raising one eyebrow.

"But we didn't..." he said, in an almost pleading voice.

"I know. But, she's my daughter and I love her. Just be gentle."

Thealand left the coffee house as Traven thumped his head on the table. An AOD waitress filled his cup of coffee and as if on cue, all activity resumed.

He decided for better or worse he had to go back to his room. The room was dark with the projection of stars and a brilliant moon on the ceiling from a Rocky Mountain summer time sky. He followed a trail of small puddles up his tree house stairs and into his bedroom. Annie lay fast asleep in his bed. Her hair was wet from what he assumed was a nighttime swim. Her clothes were neatly piled on an old chair in the corner. He did not want to guess what she had on under the covers. Moving quietly he pulled a blanket and pillow from the closet and curled up on the floor next to the bed. A difficult hour and a half later, he was asleep.

Traven awoke in the morning with the strangest sensation. A warm small body was spooning his back. He quickly jumped up, his clothes sticking to him from a night of restless sleep. Annie opened her eyes and gave him a questioning look.

"I, uh," he fought hard to find words that could allow him to retreat from this awkward situation. "I have to go on a mission with your mother," he blurted out.

"Then let's go." Annie stood up letting the covers drop to the floor. In modesty, Traven turned away letting her get dressed and trying to stifle the urge to run from his bedroom, or to look. Suddenly two hands came from behind him and caressed his chest.

"Do you find me repulsive?" she asked in a monotone voice.

"Not in the least," Traven said, turning around and gently pushing her away from him. His eyes danced frantically from the ground to her now clothed body and then focusing on her face. "It's just that I don't know you. I know your world is different, your mother explained it to me. On my planet most of us take our time to get to know someone." He ran his fingers through his hair. "This is all just too quick for me."

Annie almost smiled.

"Well, I guess you'll just have to get to know me," she said, coolly kissing him on the cheek and walking out the door.

Traven stood for a moment just shaking his head and followed Annie to the hallway. She quickly strutted in front of him and outdistanced his stride. *Was she running away? Should he catch up to her? Was he supposed to?* The thoughts in his head confused him. She wasn't his girlfriend, why did he suddenly feel like he should be near her. Did one night on his floor with nothing happening make him somehow attached? She disappeared down the hall as if she knew exactly where she was going. He slowed his pace. *Damn it,* he thought, *Thealand is going to smell her all over me.* He slouched back against the hallway which was brighter than he was used to. It seemed as if most of the blue coloring had left and now it had become white. He wondered if Brandy's mood had been uplifted by the sudden influx of new people now living in the Gateway. She certainly was enjoying his pain due to the new drama of his love life. He thought about his new life as the Keeper and let out a sigh. How long had he been in the Gateway? How long had it been since he had last seen his time stream? The answer alluded him. It had not been a boring ride, of that he was sure. He had managed to meet a President, become a semi-superhero and save the Earth. He had developed several crushes, one on Brandy, and two on cat girls that had a tendency to beat him up, and point guns in his face. How did he really feel about Annie? Was this really the beginnings of a crush? Sure she was cute. Sure she was bold and even a little dark in her workings, and she even liked to play the guitar. As these events unfolded he hadn't even taken the time to consider the possibility of her as a girlfriend. She's thirteen he kept telling himself. He was only seventeen, but Brandy was right, even on his planet in ten years it wouldn't make a difference.

"Oh god," he said to the walls. "What if I'm eighteen. I've been in the Gateway a long time, maybe I've missed a birthday."

He started thinking about his friends and school, even a trip home to see his mother and father might be a nice change of pace. Suddenly Larry flew up.

"Long time no thee," buzzed Larry.

"Yeah," replied Traven, "where have you been?"

"Well, thith morning I've been creating sthky sthleds for the landing area, the retht of the time I've been thaying out of the way of you and your lady."

Traven rolled his eyes.

"Nothing is going on between us," he said firmly.

"Thee thpent the night in you," Larry pointed out.

"Why can't you and Brandy get a hobby?" Traven said, pointing his head to the ceiling as if he were addressing Brandy as well.

"Bawth, believe it or not, you are our hobby," and with that Traven started walking.

"What are you going to do about Thealand?" Larry asked.

"She already knows Annie has a crush on me."

"And you thill have all your limbth, very imprethive." Larry almost gleamed with pride.

"She said it was all right, just be gentle," Traven said shaking his head. "What mother says stuff like that?"

"What!?" Larry's voice jumped three volume levels, "you have a green light and nothing happened? What were you thinking?"

"Look," Traven snapped, a bit shocked that Larry had started to sound like he was one of his horny friends on Earth. "It's none of your business, and besides aren't you a robot?"

"Robot ath charged," Larry confirmed. "We live vicariouthly through otherth."

"Whatever... somewhere out there there's a girl I'm supposed to marry and spend the rest of my life with."

"Bawth, don't believe anything you read and only half of what you thee. Life ith to be lived in the moment. Even you can't be a hundred perthent thure of the future."

"You sound like Brandy," Traven said with a pout.

"Thome of my betht programming cometh from her."

"Does that make her your mother?" Traven asked as they entered the landing area.

Brandy formed to Traven's right side and gave him a dirty look.

"No," she said in a cross tone, "Ah am certainly not the little fellow's mother."

In the middle of the landing area Thealand and Annie were having a heated discussion. Traven's heart sank hoping that it wasn't about him.

"What's that about?" he whispered to Brandy.

"I'm sure it's about you, Sweetie," she replied with a smirk.

Traven just shook his head and walked toward the squabble.

"It is about you," Thealand stated loudly.

Damn it, Traven thought, *I forgot about her hearing.*

Thealand continued, "she wants to come with."

"And?" Traven said, and suddenly wondered why he would want Annie to tag along. Thealand shot Traven an angry glare and turned to Annie.

"If something were to happen to me..." Thealand started only to be cut off by Annie.

"If something were to happen to you it would most likely happen to him as well." Annie said gesturing to Traven. "And if something happens to him this whole place goes boom, correct? After that I believe there would be no children to watch."

"How much did you tell her?" Traven asked Thealand.

"Too much it appears," Thealand huffed as Traven then turned to Brandy.

"And how much does she know?" he said, pointing at Thealand and scolding the Gateway herself.

"Lots," Brandy replied, "she has to protect us you know."

"Well then," Annie said, "two protectors are better than one."

Annie hopped onto the sky sled and motioned for Traven to join her.

The sky sleds looked like two jet ski's with large sleek garbage can lids on the bottom of them. Grudgingly, Thealand motioned to Traven to join her daughter on the back of the vehicle. Traven gave her a look of slight dismay.

"Do you know how to fly one of these?" Thealand asked.

"No," he admitted.

"Well she does... get on."

Thealand hopped on her sky sled as Larry flew up between them.

"The library thayth there ith a problem with Topacieth," he informed them. "The future on the planet cometh up unclear."

"Why?" asked Traven.

"Well, it could be that the planet'th future ith at a crossroads. Thith doeth happen from time to time. A timeline ith thubject to blurring when it's future ith under a point of unthertainty and becauthe of that, the time thtream is blurred. The other pothibility ith that there ith a moment of great trouble and reathon ith the thame."

"Well do we stay or go?" Traven asked.

"A blurred outcome ith not uncommon," Larry stated.

"Docheen traveled into them all the time," Brandy offered. "Blur does not necessarily mean unsafe. If the planet was being destroyed or didn't exist, those would be solid outcomes and ones we could see. Most likely, there's a magnetical storm a brewin somewhere on the surface."

Brandy patted Traven on the top of his head like she would a small child.

"Y'all see trouble just get back here immediately."

Annie shot Brandy a look of intense dislike.

"You know there was a time when you wouldn't let me into a situation like this," Traven reminded Brandy pushing her hand away.

"I know," she replied. "Ah must feel that you have matured somewhat."

The three adventurers donned their helmets.

"Hold on tight," said Annie, as Traven reached around her, "and don't worry, I'll be gentle. At least as much as I know how to."

A knowing smile spread across her face as they rocketed into the wilderness know as Topacies.

The two sky sleds zoomed across the Topacian sky. Thealand activated a communication switch in the handle of her sled and her voice came out loud and clear in Annie's and Traven's helmets.

"I did some research last night in the library," she said. "The planet's about fifty five percent water with strong metal content and some violent magnetic storms. The storms tend to charge the floating rocks. If you notice, there is always a dominant rock that has a greater charge and the other go in varying orbits around the main rock. In times of less storms the orbits go slower and the rocks themselves lower toward the ground and can even settle."

"That explains the big grooves on the planes underneath," Traven guessed, thinking that his Earth Science teacher would have loved to see this place. "What does all that electricity and magnetic activity do to things living on the planet?" he asked, as a brilliantly colored bat creature with a long neck and pancake-like head flew past them.

"The library stated that it shouldn't have any long term effects, or hurt any future generations, that is, as long as you don't pitch a permanent tent under the floating rocks' orbit. We're really just here to run a few more precise tests just to make sure of it's habitability and to get a look at the real-estate." Thealand paused. "Annie, what do you think of it." Thealand's tone seemed odd, as if she was seeking approval from her firstborn.

"I believe the term is cool," she said, momentarily glancing back at Traven.

"Keep your eyes forward," he requested, not feeling at all well with Annie's racer-like driving style.

Their sled dodged back and forth between the floating rocks using the magnetic pull on the sled to drive toward them and quickly shoot out in the other direction.

"Be careful, Annie," warned Thealand.

"Yes, Mother," she replied, without the customary whining that most teenagers would insert when having a conversation with their parent. The truth of the matter was that Annie was most of the time a very obedient daughter and in some ways followed her mother's directions as a soldier follows the commands from his higher-ups.

As they broke over the ridge below them they saw a herd of large grazing animals. Some were the size of school buses, others, which Traven guessed were the young, would barely fit into his parent's one car garage. They were covered in hair and only the direction of them walking and the giant rhino-like horn gave a clue as to what part of them was the front. The sight of the two sky sleds made the herd stampede. Annie buzzed the group with her sky sled herding them in different directions as if in another life she might have been a cowgirl out for a joy ride.

"We're not planning on eating them, are we?" Traven asked.

"I don't know," Annie replied. "Mother, are they edible?"

"Oh, I'm sure their quite tasty, but we're not here to hunt."

"Check," and with that Annie broke off her pursuit.

"What are your brothers and sisters doing today?" Traven asked, trying not to imagine himself falling off the back of the sky sled.

"I believe the old one was going to show them how to play something called ping pong." Annie banked hard to the left to avoid the first tree that they encountered. It must have been ten stories tall, spindly, and looked like it had managed to survive a life of hard winters and brutal summers. Several of it's pink and yellow-green leaves were torn off in their wake.

"Oh, that's good."

"My driving?" questioned Annie.

"Well, your driving has made a heck of an impression on me," Traven said through gritted teeth, "but I meant the ping pong. Everyone loves ping pong."

"Good," said Annie.

"What's good?" asked Traven. "The ping pong?"

"No, that my driving is impressing you," she said with a laugh, her voice almost becoming sweet.

They followed a dry riverbed that also showed scars from giant rocks which had once touched down. Annie picked up speed. Traven held on even tighter for fear that he would be thrown off the back of the sled. The faster she went the tighter he gripped. She seemed to either be enjoying his embrace, or his fear. Either way, she wasn't about to slow down.

Her waist felt thin and strong without an ounce of fat on it. Traven still worried that he would have been better off with a seat belt. As the riverbed turned into marsh they spied hundreds of frog-like creatures. The largest were the size of large German shepherds with an extra eye in the middle of their foreheads. A few sat comfortably on the edge of the muck where the sludge met the sea, soaking in the last rays of light from a setting sun. Others were half submerged in the slime and would only pop out to feast on what appeared to be small birds that were feeding on even smaller unseen insects. Traven remembered them well as the beasts that Thealand had made him hunt and clean. As they slowed their sleds to take in the twilight of this possible new home they saw something that was clearly out of place. On the edge of the muck where the frog creatures sat walked a humanoid form. Annie handed Traven an advanced set of binoculars from a compartment in the sky sled. They seemed to be no different than thick sunglasses and as Traven focused these enhanced set of eyes he once again was reminded of Docheen's fighting form.

The being he was watching had an ax blade on it's tail. The difference from Docheen's tail was that this creature had a strange syringe-like needle at the very tip above the two blades. Other than that and its overall shape, everything about this creature was completely devoid of anything human he had ever encountered.

The creature seemed to be made out of constantly changing geometric forms that shifted almost naturally as it walked. With some steps it had one eye, with others it had two or even none. It would leave spaces between its changing shapes and Traven could see through it and then quickly it would solidify and then change again, rarely appearing the same way twice. It lowered its head intensely scanning the surface of the muck. Its feet were wide like snow shoes and it used them most effectively to navigate the slime as if it were going out for a daily stroll. Suddenly the creature's feet changed and became long posts that plunged deep below its form, beyond the muck and into the more solid ground that was underneath. It's body dipped for a fraction of a second and then became still as if it was waiting for something.

"What the hell is going on?" whispered Traven, to which there was no reply.

Suddenly it's arm elongated and plunged into the slime. In a flurry of green muck and dirty water the arm reemerged holding one of the frog-like creatures that was screaming in pain. Traven sucked in a deep breath of shock as the geometric man plunged the needle end of its tail directly in to the base of it's prey's spine. The frog creature started to shake violently and large egg-like boils formed all over it's body. The eggs were clear, half in the skin the other half bare to the sky, with shadows of dark snake-like babies swimming inside of them. As the boils erupted, crawfish-sized line children wiggled out into the muck and devoured anything that could move. Choruses of screaming frog creatures destroyed a once tranquil setting and as Traven and his bodyguards floated dumbfounded, a large mechanical egg lifted itself over the horizon.

Traven's mind couldn't even register the size of the floating goliath, but from the binoculars he could tell that the patterns on the giant floating egg were the same as the creature that had just unleashed the total genocide of the peaceful frog creatures.

"Damn it!" yelled Thealand, "that thing's just a scout," and without another word both Thealand and Annie jerked their bikes and headed off in the opposite direction at top speed.

"It's not that I don't appreciate the quick and hasty retreat," Traven yelled over the howl of the screaming sky sled engines, "but does anyone have a plan?"

"We get the hell out of here," Thealand yelled back.

"You know," Traven yelled, "that sounds like a really good plan. I'm in."

As Traven looked back over his shoulder he realized that a flock of pancake headed bat creatures were trying their best to follow them. Noticing that something wasn't quite right with the flock he focused the lens with one hand and held even tighter on to Annie with the other. For a second he thought he heard Annie purr with approval. With the lenses focused he saw that the flock were not pancake headed bats but the same kind of nightmarish creature that had planted eggs in the frog creature only these were spawned from a different beast. Geometric shapes moved and changed on the creature but now the creatures were merging with one another to create a bigger faster version of what they had taken the form of. With each new addition into its growing body it was getting closer.

"Weapon!" screamed Traven.

"Under your seat," shouted Thealand.

Not wanting to see this creature in any more detail he let the glasses fall to the ground below and with the same hand felt around for something useful. When it was in his grasp his face turned into a mask of hopeless dismay. It appeared to be some sort of hand weapon that looked as if it was a cap gun for a five year old.

"Bigger weapon!" he pleaded.

"We don't have bigger," Thealand yelled back.

"What the hell is this thing going to do?" he barked in frustration.

"Set the lever on the right side to the blue dot," commanded Thealand, "this will allow you to release all the the energy at once, but don't you dare miss."

"Is this an electrical blast?" he asked, turning the switch with his nose.

"Yes. Why?"

"Would it be enough to effect the floating rocks?" his voice cracked as if he was just starting puberty.

"Unknown, but it is far more powerful than it looks. Again, why?" Thealand was clearly getting cross with him.

"I'm shooting at the main rock and praying!"

"Damn it, why?" she yelled, "you can't waste it!"

"Do you have one? Traven screamed, ignoring her question.

Thealand quickly felt under her seat.

"Yes," she replied.

"Shoot the main rock," he said.

As Traven looked back he noticed that on the horizon the giant mechanical egg was starting to glow and bolts of lightning where blasting off it toward the ground and to places beyond the horizon.

"Not until you tell me why!" Thealand didn't like following orders from anyone, let alone someone she could best in a fight.

"Look, I don't have time for this!" Thealand's silence urged Traven to explain. "We're blasting the main rock super charging it and letting the things be crushed as the smaller rocks come crashing toward it."

"You mean crashing toward us," Thealand stated grimly.

"I'm opening a portal as we circle the rock," he said, starting to aim and realizing that there wasn't much of a way to miss. "Thealand you'll have to be the first through."

She said nothing and turned her sled to the biggest floating rock.

"Brandy and Larry had better be watching," Traven said, being

A Lifetime In Time

amazed that for the first time he didn't care about his privacy. "There might be a lot of debris about to enter the landing area."

The Beast was almost upon Annie's sled and geometric bodies and arms started to form out of its head and reach toward them. Annie cut a short and tight circle at the top of the main rock as Traven concentrated on opening the portal and then speeding away to allow Thealand to enter first. The two sleds confused the beast for a fraction of a second as Thealand discharged her weapon and flew at full speed up and then flipping down toward the invisible opening to disappear. The plan was working. The smaller rocks started to move rapidly toward the main one. Suddenly the beast shattered into a plague of smaller humanoid shaped beings jumping onto the main rock and methodically climbing and stretching toward the portal as if they could sense it was there. They had lost all interest in the sky sled and moved quickly until Traven shot the main rock with a second electric charge as the sled climbed the side coming within inches of the geometric men.

There wouldn't have been time to turn the sled back into the portal Annie would tell Traven later, which is what prompted her to turn around grab him in both of her arms and throw them from the bike. They plummeted 30 feet into the portal as it sealed itself behind their falling bodies while the floating rocks decimated the geometric men and the main rock itself.

A cloud of dust and debris landed with the two teenagers as a large air bag cushioned their landing. Toward the edge of the room Thealand's sky sled sat smoking from the abuse. Traven's legs were numb and tingling from the great acceleration and this most recent dance on death's door step. As his mind tried to quiet itself the edges to the air bag slowly floated gently down toward the floor. He realized that he was holding Annie tightly in his arms and once again almost as if it was beyond his will they were kissing.

Thealand pressed a button on her sky sled causing it to turn into dust rather than keep smoking. She turned Brandy giving her a worried look and then back to Traven and Annie who hadn't let go of their embrace. She offered a slight smile at the sight and then noticed that Brandy's face contain nothing but stone cold dread.

"Ah hum," Brandy said clearing her voice, "when all y'all are finished, there is something we need to talk about."

Timothy John Vaulato

Chapter Twenty-Two

Things That Could Be Confused With Truth

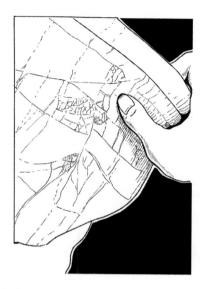

They walked down another long hallway, wondering what news Brandy had to announce. Her floating stride gave little indication of her mood, though the tone in her voice was serious. Traven's mind was once again jumbled with the thoughts of what he had just encountered. His near death experience was still making his heart beat strong enough to be a constant reminder of the day's events, not to mention another kiss with Annie. *Had she started the passionate lip-lock or had he?* The question had made him uneasy, for he could not remember who had made the first move. All he knew was that part of him had enjoyed it and her taste was still fresh in his mouth. *Damn it,* he thought, *are all relationships this confusing?* His brain then halted though his body still embraced the motion of walking, *Did I just call this a relationship?* With a scream of panic in his head he knew from that moment that things were not going to be easy.

They had followed Brandy into another of the many rooms within the Gateway. This room appeared to be decorated in a Japanese style, which in the center had a carefully raked rock garden. Traven knew that this tranquil setting would most likely contrast the bad news that was sure to follow. Brandy waved her hand in the air and a screen that resembled one of the library's monitors formed from the wall. Brandy stood silent as Thealand, Annie, and Traven took their places on the hard wooden floor. No one had said anything about Annie and him kissing and, though he had almost died, the public display of their emotions was the thing that was foremost in his mind.

Brandy started her lecture and images of the strange creatures he had just encountered appeared on the screen.

"The beings that you encountered on Topacies we are calling Puzzle Men," she said, as if she had rehearsed this speech before. "Out of all the encounters you could have had, over the infinite possibilities of places and beings you could meet, this is the worst possible encounter and the one that we all have dreaded from the start."

"What do you mean we?" asked Traven, becoming slightly paranoid from all the warnings that Lynx had given him about being a puppet and wondered why Brandy had chosen the plural instead of the singular.

"I mean me," she clarified, "and every support system in the Gateway that has tried to lead you away from them. Larry being one of the others, and his doubles, not to mention systems that y'all have never even seen function. We have all tried our best to see into the different time streams and keep you away from ever meeting them."

"Why?" asked Traven, questioning Brandy's actions while knowing at the same time that he would have been much happier if he had never met these so called Puzzle Men.

Brandy took a deep breath as if to punctuate the seriousness of the moment and her accent started to fade.

"In over a million years of traveling the webs," she said softly, "we have only encountered one adversary that had the potential to cause us direct harm and it is them."

"What makes them so different?" he asked.

"Because they are looking specifically for me," she sighed, staring deeply at Traven. "In nature everything has a predator, the Puzzle Men are mine. They were designed to tear through the webs of time by finding the weak spots or scars. The weak spots are created by a Keeper traveling to the same point over and over again, this is why the rule of three's was created. Although a spot usually heals itself if left alone, occasionally a scar is formed. Think of it as a discernible mark left by repeated travel into one destination, the Puzzle Men seek these out. They land on the planet, create as many Puzzle Men as possible and then they join to form a series of transport eggs."

She pointed to the image on the screen of three constantly changing mechanical eggs.

"The transport eggs requires a huge amount of energy to try and locate the Gateway and to make the jumps through the webs. It so far has failed to find me and has located instead other weak spots or scars to transport the Puzzle Men to. They are self creating for many reasons. When they strip whatever planet they land on of all life and resources they use the energy which they have converted into their own bodies for fuel to power the next jump. Only about twelve of the Puzzle men seem to make it to the next location, the others are destroyed or more correctly burned as energy in the process. Then they start all over again and will continue this process until they find a path into the Gateway."

"Why not attack them when there are only twelve?" Traven asked, finally feeling he should break into her science lesson.

"There is a block, stopping us from locating them. The block covers the time before they are born and enough time after they jump so that they become hidden from us in the natural static of time. Anyway, the point is moot, we don't know how to defeat them."

"Why do they exist?" Traven asked.

"Why do any of us exist?" Brandy replied smugly. "That's really a philosophical question."

"No, not really," Traven said, with a sound of cold accusation in his voice. "Docheen created you, correct?"

"Yes," she replied, "of course."

"Then what, or whom created the Puzzle Men?" He felt as if Brandy was only giving him half of the story. "The Puzzle Men are not natural predators anymore than you are a natural part of time."

Both Thealand and Annie gave him a look of surprise at his forwardness. There was a long pause before Brandy would answer.

"It is unknown as to their origin," she stated.

Traven looked hard into Brandy's eyes. He felt as if he was being lied to, as if she was trying to avoid the real answer to the question. Could all of Lynx's warnings have possibly been right?

"Then explain this," he said, in a quiet but demanding voice, "why do they look familiar to me."

Thealand and Annie's eyes became wide, astounded by Traven's comment.

"Ah have no idea why they look familiar to you," Brandy said, cocking her head to one side as if she too was as confused as Thealand and Annie.

Traven wondered if this too was a lie, but continued onward with his interrogation.

"Why do they have the same tail and tail blade as Docheen had in his fighting form and why do they shape shift? Docheen was a shape shifter too, right?" he knew the answer.

"Docheen's tail, while in his fighting form is a very useful weapon," she stated. "You will find that many races and life forms have also developed this appendage because of it's ability to protect and devastate. As to their ability to shape shift, it is a trait of advanced beings, a skill that can be learned as we intend to teach you. Sometimes it's an inborn ability that can be passed down from parent to offspring."

"Why did they come to Topacies?" Traven quickly huffed. "We never broke the rule of three's there and to my counting I don't think I've been there more than a handful of times all together."

"Docheen traveled to Topacies quite a bit," Brandy reveled. "In fact, he believed that it was an almost mystical place, between the floating rocks and brilliant sunsets. Though he never broke the rule of three's it is very likely that he had gone there enough to create a scar on a location if not the time stream."

Traven became enraged.

"You mean to tell me that by going to a place over and over again I make it a target for the Puzzle Men to destroy!?" he yelled.

"Well..." she said, clearly not wanting to give Traven the answer that was sure to come, "yes you do, but it's not just you. Those who use what your people loosely define as magic can also create weak spots by traveling different dimensions or times."

"Well, what the hell," he said, standing up and pointing a finger at Brandy, "have I just doomed Earth by living there?"

"Well, the Earth hasn't been traveled to as much as Topacies had," she said, trying to remain calm.

"You said that Docheen was quite fond of Earth and traveled it extensively." Traven was starting to pace the wooden floor of the room as Thealand and Annie remained riveted to the unfolding drama.

"Docheen knew that leaving a scar or a weak point on Earth was possible so he just started living there. He would be gone months at a time, he also never returned from the same spot he landed. When he found these measures cumbersome he created an open door that ran with his timeline. After a year, or so it was discovered by a maid and caused a big mess. In the end he created the Chicago room and others like it so he would not have to jump back and forth and scar the time streams to get his favorite pizza, cup of coffee, or ice cream," she said, waving her hand as if to tell Traven to calm down.

"When I opened a portal to the Gateway during our fight with the Puzzle Men they locked on to it as if they could smell it, why couldn't they have found Docheen's open doorway?"

"They didn't exist at the time of Docheen's door, though he always worried that something like them might come to pass," Brandy said, knowing that this was not an answer that would calm Traven's anger.

"When the hell did they come into existence?" he demanded.

Brandy fell silent and then slowly lifted her head and stated in her most monotone voice. "The moment you became the Keeper."

She bowed her head again as the silence of the room became unbearable. Traven just stared at Brandy becoming angrier and angrier, feeling as if any trust between the two of them had just completely evaporated.

"And what the hell did me becoming the Keeper have to do with their existence!?" he yelled. There was a longer silence. All eyes focused on Brandy. The wait for an answer seemed to stretch into minutes and then Traven broke the wait. "Damn it, I asked you a question!"

Brandy never looked up, but then she said in an almost meek and uncharacteristic voice.

"I can't tell you."

This was the final straw for Traven. He picked up a beautiful Japanese vase and sent it smashing through the paper and wood framed wall surrounding the garden. He turned to Brandy and growled through the grinding of his teeth.

"You can tell me when you realize that you are suppose to be working for me. 'Til then, I don't want to hear a word out of you."

He turned his back to the room and left, leaving Thealand and Annie dumbfounded.

Traven stormed into the practice room and put on his double knot spy outfit. He stood in the middle, put on the headset that created the room to whatever desired shape the wearer could imagine and suddenly the biggest China store the Earth would have ever seen flowed into existence. Porcelain finery and blown glass vases accompanied figurines along isle after isle of glass shelving. Traven said to the sky, "Black Sabbath, *Children of the Grave,*

loud," and then placed his helmet onto his head. He reached into his pockets and screamed as his Calleash left his hands. They flew through the air like canonballs powdering the porcelain and glass, saturating the air like a twisted sadistic snowfall. The sound was deafening even over the music. He continued to retrieve the Calleash and sent them flying again not interested in what his skill was, but basking in the amount of damage he could produce. As the room became quiet with the ending of the song he stood in a dangerous drift of broken glass with a thick haze of powdered debris hanging in the air. His breath was heavy and his pulse beat rapidly. He screamed loud and long as if he was trying to wipe the day's events from his soul. The scream was followed by the stillness of the room as he bowed his head under the weight of what he felt was the betrayal of his friend. Then a familiar voice spoke softly.

"Clean," said Mo-pa, and the wreckage Traven had just accomplished sank into the floor. A strong breeze pulled the haze of powdered glass from the room and by the time Traven had removed his helmet everything looked as it had before. Mo-pa stood on the side of Traven with a look of great concern on his face.

"Things have not gone well, have they," he stated.

He looked at Mo-pa as if he too was an enemy.

"What do you know about Puzzle Men, Mo-pa?" he asked, throwing down his helmet which made a loud crashing noise on the floor. The old man bowed his head as if he too was harboring a secret.

"I see," he said, "you feel as if you have been lied to."

"Well, what would you call it?" Traven yelled, in a tone of voice he had never taken with his teacher. "I suppose you have some incoherent bit of wisdom to confuse me with?"

"When you were younger," started Mo-pa, "your parents didn't tell you everything about life because you may have not understood it from where you were standing. A child needs only to know love and belonging until they are ready to start out on their own. When they finally do they find out that the world is not always the safe and protected place they once stood in."

"Are you calling me a child again?" Traven said harshly.

"No," said Mo-pa, "I am only making an analogy, I mean no disrespect. When you were a child food was placed before you and you never questioned it. The food you ate was once alive, a life that had to end for yours to continue. One day you realized it, and most likely accepted it without a second thought, and without thinking of yourself as a killer, even though you have taken the life of another so that you can survive, even if the life was taken indirectly."

Traven's mind quickly flashed back to the distorted images of the smashing of Docheen's heartstone and wondered if Mo-pa was trying to reach him on several levels.

"Maybe," Mo-pa continued, "life holds other secrets from you to protect you until you are ready to accept them or understand them fully. This is not uncommon, this just is the flow of life. Just as the river flows into the sea, the water must travel to its destination before its becoming."

Mo-pa turned and started to walk away. His speech did little to stem the flow of Traven's anger and as he reached the door of the practice room Traven yelled back at him in a most sarcastic voice.

"Well, thanks a lot Mo-pa!," he yelled. "Tell the sea she can find me when she wants to talk. 'Til then, this little river will just be busy flowing all over the place."

As Mo-pa left Traven put back on the headset and created a glass factory.

Timothy John Vaulato

Chapter Twenty-Three

Reading Is Fundamental

Traven worked his way through the smashing of a glass factory, a luxury car dealership, and a sleek office building inhabited by killer robots from an old fifties B-movie. He was surprised that the robots remained black and white like the film he had watched while the office was in color as any office in the real world would have been. He guessed that was because the images the room had read were from his mind. He was also surprised at the power of his new Calleash. When thrown at full force they were devastating, ripping through walls as if they were paper and even smashing through the cars and robots as if they were made of glass. This was the first time he had thrown them with his full force, because until now he was always using them against living beings. The power was exhilarating. Images of Thor, the Thunder God's hammer popped into his head as the Calleash made quick work of a Cadillac's engine block, and he wondered if these Calleash were the top of the line or if Mo-pa had only taken him to the next level of his training. He also wondered if they would be of any use against the Puzzle Men. He hadn't even thought to use them as they were on the sky sleds. *Probably for the best,* he decided, I *don't know if they'd return while moving that fast.* Though it hadn't been said, the Puzzle Men meant that he may not be able to go home. If they could target in on all the places with scars where Docheen had walked it might already be too late for Earth.

The soundtrack of the day had ranged from Black Sabbath to Iron Maiden and then with Jimi Hendrix's, *Purple Haze.* When he requested the Who's, *Won't Get Fooled Again,* he created an endless forest of guitars. As he raised the first guitar over his head he realized that he couldn't do it. *For God's sake,* he thought, *what were people thinking when they smashed perfectly good guitars?* He ended the program, kept the guitar and left the practice room dripping with sweat.

He found he had been in the practice room much longer than he had thought. Most of his day had disappeared in a blur of destruction. He was tired, sore, and hungry. He made his way to the Chicago room and back into the coffee shop he had been before. It was packed as it was last time and looked very much the same. The singer was the same AOD as last time, but now older and playing a different set of tunes. The song *Shelter from the Storm,* rang out over the audience and for a moment Traven just drank in the words of the song. Whoever this Mr. Zimmerman was he had an incredible way with words almost as if he could do with lyrics what Jimi Hendrix could do with notes. He stood by the back wall of the small room until the song was finished and a set break followed. Traven glanced across the room for an empty table and noticed that close to the stage sitting by herself was Thealand sipping a cup of coffee. A waitress tried to refill her cup and was sent away by a gesture of her hand. As Traven sat down he noticed he almost startled her. She held up her hand to indicate for Traven not to speak and she quickly removed two large earplugs. Traven smiled and set his new guitar gently on the edge of a chair.

"Wow, that's better," she said, putting the ear plugs into her pocket, "I almost didn't smell you over the cigarette smoke and the coffee. Boy you are ripe."

"What are you doing here?" Traven asked. "You hate this."

"I figured you'd end up here eventually," she said. "That is, when you finished destroying the car dealership."

"Oh, you saw that?" he said, almost embarrassed as the waitress filled his cup.

"Both me and Annie watched you for quite a awhile. She's pretty hung up on you, y'know."

"I know," Traven admitted.

"Well pup?" she asked with a raised eyebrow.

"Well what?"

"Well, how do you feel?"

"I don't think I'm supposed to have these conversations with a girlfriend's mother," he stated in an annoyed tone.

"So, she's your girlfriend?" she smiled, pondering the blackness of her coffee.

"No... I, I don't know."

"Then why do you keep kissing her?"

"She kisses well," Traven said becoming extremely flustered, "and I really shouldn't be having this conversation with you."

"No, you should be having it with her, but let's get back to your feelings. It's been a lifetime since I've had the chance to talk about anything other than saving my planet, I'm rather enjoying this."

"I can tell," he grunted, "and I don't know my feelings," Traven admitted and then took a deep breath. "Believe it or not, I've never really had a girlfriend."

"You don't say?" The tone of sarcasm was at least slight in Thealand's voice, which Traven found almost comforting.

"All right, let me see if I can sum up my life for you. The day I became the Keeper I sat in my desk at the last period of the day when they hand out flyers for the upcoming events at school. They handed out a piece of paper that said there was going to be a Sadie Hawkins dance. That's where the girls are suppose to ask the boys they like to go to the dance with them, sometimes they call it turn around."

"Don't girls usually ask the boys to dances?" Thealand asked.

"Well, sometimes I guess they do, but I think it's more rare on my planet. Anyway, when I got this piece of paper I didn't think, 'cool I wonder whose going to ask me,' I thought 'cool a piece of paper to doodle on.' A girl liking me isn't something I have any experience with, and I've never really tried to ask one out, I guess I'm fairly gutless."

"You went up against an army and saved your world, that's not what I call gutless," Thealand pointed out.

"That was easier," Traven said almost without thinking and then paused to try and clarify. "I had no choice, I either saved the world, or all the people I love would have died a sick and ugly death."

Thealand laughed.

"You amaze me pup. You run into a hail of bullets, but are afraid to date my daughter. Don't you like her?"

"She's beautiful, smart, mysterious, tough, and likes to play guitar, what in the world isn't there to like?"

"You tell me."

"She's too young."

"Too young?"

"She's thirteen."

"Not a problem in my world."

"It's against the law in my world."

"Law?" Thealand paused, trying to wrap her mind around the fact she wasn't talking to someone from her planet. "You are not functioning in your world anymore, or don't you see that?" she said, flipping a sugar packet at him like a teenager shooting a paper football.

"The age thing is a big difference in everything I've been raised to believe." Traven slumped back in his chair and rested the full weight of his head and his problems on his hand.

Today, Thealand wore her smile more easily than he had ever

seen and she pulled her elbows up on the table resting her face in both of her hands.

"Remember when you pissed me off?" she asked.

"Which time?" Traven said rolling his eyes.

"When you had come to me to tell me you needed my help to save your planet."

"I remember it well. It wasn't one of our better moments."

"After I threw the transporter for the Gateway at you, you threw it back and left."

"And?" Traven said trying to comprehend where Thealand was going with this replay of their fight. She reached into her vest pocket and pulled the transporter out.

"I went back for this," she said waving the device in her hand. "It took a while to find, your throw was awful."

"Why did you go back for it?" he asked, as visions of it not working shook his mind.

"Well, you may or may not believe this, but I was worried about you."

"Why? You said that I had just cheated you out of our deal."

"Pup, women will react to things that aren't always the cause of the real problem. Kovacs had been kidnapped, my world was, and is, going to be destroyed, and you had just said that you had no feelings for me. While the fear for my child and of my world being destroyed were the main reasons, the personal rejection is probably what set off my temper tantrum. My daughter constantly informs me that our emotions are a weakness in our people."

"What are you saying?" he asked, almost knocking over his coffee.

"That age doesn't stop feelings from being feelings. You have qualities that make people, even girls, like you. Surprise! What I'm trying to say is that you're foolish for not dating my daughter."

Traven tried to collect himself and worried that now he might become the babbling idiot he believed himself to be.

"You had a crush on me?"

"In a small way, yes," she said matter-of-factly. "Nothing in comparison to what my daughter feels."

Traven just sat dumbfounded staring at her.

"Why is it so amazing? We trained, we fought, we even managed to create a painting together. Those kind of situations tend to draw people close, but don't worry, it takes me less than a week to get over my crushes."

"What about your daughter?" he asked.

"Well, she is an Atrill... we don't mate for life, but I must admit I've never seen an Atrill girl pine for a boy the way she is for you. In some ways I believe she's fascinated by your culture's belief in an everlasting love. On my planet girls don't normally act like this. When a female finally admits it to herself that she's interested she immediately becomes the aggressor. I believe you missed my moment of truth by about a second when you left after our fight. To have a female Atrill following you around like a puppy is unheard of, but then again Annie never was a normal child."

Traven felt compelled that he should keep this purging of the truth rolling.

"Thealand," he said, "I found this book when I was traveling..."

Thealand jumped in and cut him off.

"You mean the book that tells you how a you from another reality lived and loved, right?"

"Damn," Traven said finally knocking over his coffee and losing his cool. "Why is my life an open book? This is worse than living with my parents!" he said using napkin after napkin to wipe up his mess.

"Because, believe it or not, we all do care for you, even if our actions might indicate otherwise. I'm sure the decisions your parents make might make it seem like they are your worst enemies at times, but as a parent I can assure you that's not how we think even though it might feel that way. As for the book... I can't tell you if your road is right or wrong. We Atrills live for the moment because the moment may never come again."

A mindless waitress walked past the table and without missing a beat tossed Traven a towel to help him finish cleaning his mess.

"Where is Annie?" Traven asked while scrubbing.

"I believe she is in the library," Thealand replied.

"What's she doing in the library?" he asked, handing the towel back to a different waitress as she made her rounds.

"Well, you said that you two should get to know each other. I believe she's doing research."

Traven's jaw dropped as his head once again hit the table with a thud and staring into the coffee stained old oak he asked the question he was afraid to hear answered.

"You mean she's watching my life?" he mumbled.

"Don't worry, pup," Thealand said as she started to rise from her chair to leave, "from what you've told me about your love life she's probably napping by now. I'll see you in the morning, we need to discuss a new plan to save my planet. Oh, and by the way, try not to hate Brandy, she may look like the devil sometimes, but she's really more of your guardian angel."

As Thealand started to walk away Traven called for her over the noise of the coffeehouse and the guitarist tuning.

"Thealand?" he yelled.

"Yes, pup," Thealand said pausing her exit.

"I had a crush on you too," he admitted in a most shy and uncool tone.

"I know," she said, "it's nice to hear you admit it. Oh, and by the way, take a bath, even my daughter won't get close to you smelling like that."

Another song floated out amongst the half light of the room as Traven tried to lose himself in the words. He was tired of having to guess everyone's intentions. He wanted to just go home and take a break from being the Keeper, a break from being the savior of worlds and a break from the stress of a love life that he wasn't sure he could handle. As the song ended he sniffed himself and realized that a day's worth of sweat was not the most attractive scent he had ever worn. He finished his coffee and left.

His room was dark save for the stars in the sky, indicating that the faux night had begun. Assuming that Annie was asleep in the library due to the watching of his pathetic life, he decide to dive into the pond and try and scrub the day,s stink off of him. Small voiceless versions of Larry appeared to bring him a towel and disappeared with his dirty clothes. The night sky was beautiful and he sat at the edge of the pond trying to remember what his life used to be like. *What would his parents think about him now? The student with the very questionable grades who saved the Earth. Would they look at him differently? Would they just try to get him a room in a mental ward? What would they say about a thirteen year old girlfriend?* In his heart he knew the answer to that one. *Oh son, don't you think she's a little too young for you?* Not to mention the questions about her ears. *Well on the upside,* he thought, *maybe she would just shoot them with her stun gun. After all, electric shock worked for Grandma.* The thought of a Thanksgiving family dinner with his parents joining his strange crew in the Gateway made him laugh. Then his thoughts turned to the other days events. *Could he defeat the Puzzle Men? Someone had created them to destroy the Gateway, but who? Why were they created the moment he became the Keeper?* Brandy knew the answers, but wasn't about to tell him. *What was she afraid of?* Traven felt one of those overwhelming brain freezes coming on and decided it was probably better if he just went to bed. As he entered the darkness of his room he heard the sound of someone turning pages. His body tensed from the unexpected noise.

"Light," he commanded the room, only to be cut off by the voice of Annie.

"Candlelight," she corrected and the candle lit.

In the glow he was greeted by the sight of Annie wrapped in his sheets reading the book from his other life. She squinted for a moment as if even the candlelight was too bright for her eyes.

"What are you doing here?" he said, as he quickly went into his closet and threw on a sweat shirt and a pair of jeans to hide his body.

"You know one of the things I like best about the Gateway?" she said avoiding his question. "No shoes are required. Being barefoot is not something one can do on my planet with its state of decay."

"I said, what are you doing here?"

"Reading," she smiled flipping a page.

"In the dark?" he asked while desperately looking for a comb.

"Yes," she admitted, taking her eyes off the book. "Well, with the exception of the show you just put on outside. We Atrill's have great vision in the dark."

"Wonderful," he frowned. "I thought you were in the library?"

"I was. Most of it was very tame and kind of sad, that is until you got into the Gateway."

"The library lets you see what has happened in the Gateway?" he asked, surprised by this revelation and finally giving up on his quest for a comb.

"Yes, I must admit I didn't really understand the whole smashing of the heartstone thing, but there was some great comic moments when you had to find clothes."

"You saw that too?" Traven whined. "Did you really have to watch that?"

"Twice... well, three time's actually," she said readjusting her glasses. "Oh, you did a nice job saving your planet."

"Thanks, now I have to find a way to save yours," he said, sounding sad, like someone who was unprepared for a test.

"I'm sure you will."

"I find it odd that everyone has faith in me but me," he said, slumping against the edge of his bookshelf.

"A fool is someone that has too much faith in themselves, and while you sometimes act foolish, I don't see you as a fool. "

Traven stared at her for a moment and for the first time realized how cute she really was. Sure she was a tom girl, but that sense of roughness made her easier to talk to than any of the girls that he had tried to talk to at home. She continued just as his mind tried to fill in the blanks that the sheet was covering.

"I came up here looking for you and found this book."

"How can you read it?" Traven said, becoming very confused. "It's in English."

"Well, after walking into far too many strange rooms in this place I asked the Gateway to redesign my glasses." She handed them to Traven and he put them on. All the words on the page of his book changed through the glasses making them appear as if they had always been written in Atrill script.

"Wow, how come I never got a pair of these?"

"You can't read Atrill," Annie replied, making Traven wonder if she meant it as a joke or not.

"I meant one that does English," he said, staring at his Alice Cooper concert poster on the wall. "Your language looks cool."

"I'm sure if you asked her... "

"Brandy and I are not talking," he said, cutting her off and directing the comment to the sky.

"I guessed as much," she said turning the page, "but you can't stay mad at her forever."

"Why not?"

"She's part of you. As much as I disagree with my mother, I know that we are not only related, but function as part of a family. Family means you don't always get along, but you still have that bond."

"Are you saying that Atrill families don't break up?"

"We might spend years apart, but we do keep the lines of communication open," she said lowering her glasses to look at him better. "Are you saying humans don't?"

"Sometimes no."

"Well there's a strike against your race." She pushed her glasses back in place and returned to her reading. Suddenly she stopped. With her eyes widening she called him over. "Look at this." As Traven looked at the drawing in the book of his other life he read the word, "*Drackeen.*"

"Yeah that's supposed to be the creature that chased the Daliteen to Earth," and then his speech started to slow, "after it had destroyed the Daliteen's home planet Harken." With this realization he looked carefully at the dragon-like monster that had been drawn hundreds of years ago in a different reality.

"Look closely," Annie said, "at the texture of its body." As Traven looked at the drawing he had looked at many times before he recognized that its form was made out of the same geometric shapes that the Puzzle Men had. Why hadn't he remembered this sooner? Maybe it was because the drawing didn't show the creature's movement or maybe it was that the times before when he had read the book he was too involved in saving the Earth from the virus and had no reason to look for the Puzzle Men.

"Oh my God," Traven said aloud, "how is that possible? Brandy said that they were created the day I became the Keeper." He paused and thought hard. "Wait, the Puzzle Men must be able to hop not only in time but in realities as well."

"Would the hopping in time also mean they can destroy futures that already have happened?" Annie asked.

"As I understand it, being outside of time means everything that can happen all ready has, until I step into the timeline and screw up that outcome. Which would mean that..." Traven stopped unable to grasp the threads that he had been weaving, "okay, I'm not sure what that means but, I think they could unwrite all history." He paused again, something just wasn't right. "I thought I was the head of the time flow. They shouldn't be able to screw up the timelines," Traven said trying hard to wrap his mind around the concept.

"It would appear that you might have competition." Annie scanned the book for any more useful information. "The other you worked extensively with magic, maybe that's what brought them to that Earth? Maybe the scars in time are messier when they are created by magic. It could be that they discovered the scar left by the Daliteen making their escape to your planet."

"Did you pick up anything on how the other me defeated them?" Traven asked, his voice becoming hopeful. "If the other me defeated them shouldn't they be like... gone?"

"Maybe only one came through the scar. It seems like one alone could breed enough trouble by itself, and no," Annie said bluntly, "there's nothing here about destroying it. The passage reads like bad poetry, not a cookbook for salvation." Traven fell back on the bed in frustration. "You realize that the Daliteen would already be living on the Earth in your time stream?" she said.

"What do you mean?" Traven asked, propping himself up on his elbows.

"According to this book they arrived roughly two hundred years ago, that is from the time stream that you live in on your planet."

"No," admitted Traven, "I never spent the time to do the math, it's not my best subject." He looked at Annie as if she was trying to give him a clue as to a secret that he hadn't yet grasped. "How much of that book did you read?"

"Most of it," she admitted. "The question is, do you save Harken from the Puzzle Men to stop them from coming to Earth, or do you let it be destroyed so that you can be with your life-mate?" There was a sadness in her voice and a hint of accusation. A look of great pain washed over Traven's face. What Annie had just told him was that there was a great possibility that the woman he was supposed to spend his life with was alive and well on his own home planet. A planet that he may not even be able to go back to because of the Puzzle Men. Could he let the Puzzle Men do to Harken what they had done to Topacies? Would he sacrifice an entire planet and God knows how many lives so that he could meet the girl of his dreams?

"No," he said in whisper, "somehow I'm to blame for the Puzzle Men. I can't let them do to Harken what they did to Topacies and in my reality there's no, 'Traven the wizard,' to count on stopping them." The two sat for a while in silence and then a smile spread over Annie's face. "What's the smile about?" asked Traven.

"Well," she said slyly, "by my calculations, that means I've got about two hundred years to get to know you before you meet your life-mate. I'm thinking that's probably enough."

Timothy John Vaulato

Chapter Twenty-Four

Hard Truths

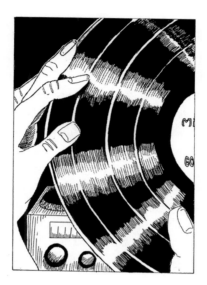

Traven and Annie sat up talking through most of the night. The topics were wide and as scattered as the colors of Easter eggs on the Sunday hunt. What to do about the Puzzle Men bled into Traven's glimpse into the future of his so-called other life. Annie had read almost the entire book of his other life and took pride in pointing out the improbabilities for being able to achieve a similar future now that he had saved his own world. Traven thought that with the Puzzle Men out there the Earth he saved may not be safe for long.

Finally they talked about Annie's life. The story was sad. Her planet was a mess and a horrible place to grow up in. Her schooling had stopped at age ten as was customary on her world. Even while she was in school her mother had given her responsibilities that few children on Earth would have been able to deal with. The raising of her brothers and sisters, the protection of the family, and to involve her in the cause of saving her planet and her people from themselves. At times she looked like a young girl, one that he would have stared at in Junior High from across the school cafeteria. At times like this it was hard to see the young soldier, the one who could have only traveled a road meant for someone twice her age.

Finally the conversation turned to more pleasant topics as they both drifted off to sleep as the Jazz of Charles Mingus played on the stereo. Traven had started listening to Jazz because of meeting Robert the bass player, and had grown a new appreciation for the role of bass in music. Before he mistakenly thought of the bassist as the spot where the weakest of the guitar players had to go, now he had come to view it as the point of control.

In the morning, Traven woke to find Annie gone. For a moment he panicked, then quickly got dressed, found the comb that eluded him the night before and set off through the Gateway. Thealand had Larry track him down and the two met in the coffeehouse. This time the musician was gone and the night scene had left the room. Larry informed him that daylight was only present during three hours of his day's cycle in the Chicago room. He gave him the option to change that if he wished. Traven marveled on how the environment smelled completely different in it's morning hours, without the stale after-taste of smoke and as if a dew had been brought in from the countryside. He told Larry that the night atmosphere was just slightly more comfortable, but that nothing needed to be changed; besides, there were bigger problems to worry about than the time cycle of the Chicago room. Thealand told him that she thought she was becoming rather fond of the coffee and he admitted that he too thought it was a nice change from his oceans of Diet Cokes. Annie had found Thealand early in the day and presented the idea of their people being relocated to Harken. "After all," she said, "in some reality the planet had already been obliterated. If our people move in and take care of the Puzzle-Men we would be welcomed with open arms."

It appeared that Annie had spent some of her morning gathering data on Harken. As Traven and Thealand reviewed the phone book-sized document on the home of the Daliteen it became apparent that this idea held great merit. The planet was large, relatively unspoiled, a low population, and had both an adequate food supply and water to support the number of Atrills that Thealand said would need refuge. In the back of Traven's mind he remembered the warning that Larry had given him about the Atrill's ability to destroy not only their own planet, but any future planets. The only thing he didn't understand is why Thealand would be willing to lead her people to a world where they guessed the Puzzle-Men would show, and he tried tactfully to discover why.

"Harken is not the deal we made," he pointed out.

"Are you telling me that you don't want our help?" she fussed, clearly insulted.

"No, I'm not saying that at all, it's just that I'm surprised. It kind of is like taking your people out of the frying pan and putting them into the fire."

Her face became very serious and her tone deadpan.

"If I've learned nothing from the Gateway I at least understand that what effects the whole of time effects the galaxy. Sooner or later they will come calling for my people as well, and I'd rather have the powers of the Gateway on our side if it comes down to that."

He nodded that he understood. They toasted with their coffee cups and then Traven headed to the practice room only to find another surprise. Mo-pa had all of Thealand's children, including Annie in training. Each one had been given his own Calleash. They paid close attention to the master of the ball and as they threw Traven realized that they were doing far better than he had done when he had first started. Annie gave Traven a smile as she showed her ability to nail not just one target, but two. Traven hoped that Annie being better than he was, right off the bat, was due to her being an Atrill and not because he was just pathetic when he first started.

When the session was over Annie approached Traven and had the practice room create two wooden staffs with padding on the ends. Without a word she threw a staff toward Traven and the two began to battle. For her small size she was incredibly strong and several of her hits sent Traven flying across the room. By the third time he picked himself off the floor he knew he had better stop thinking of her as his friend but as a real opponent. The staffs whizzed through the air and the sound made Annie's brothers and sisters stop their giggling and stare in silence. Annie blocked an awkward overhead attack, but it was a deception and Traven pivoted under her staff and smacked her in the face with the other end of his weapon. This knocked her to the ground and as she lay there with her brothers and sisters in shock, she just smiled.

"I think Mom was more impressed when you didn't leave her an opening," she said, and with that she swung both her legs around as hard as she could and brought Traven to the ground with her. His staff fell from his hands and the two started rolling around on the ground as if it had become a high school wrestling match. She straddled his chest and either she had clearly gotten the upper hand due to her skill or he had let her as an excuse to get this close. As their lips met Mo-pa ushered the smirking children from the practice room with promises of ice cream. When she sat back up Traven wondered what on Earth he was doing. She was really too young for him no matter what he felt, and before his Earth sculpted morals started to protest, she smiled a beautiful smile and spoke.

"Want to see what I've learned?" she asked. The question scared him, but, once again, before he could speak she jumped to her feet. "Topacies's last hour." She commanded the room and the room became the familiar nightmare that they had both shared. The beautiful landscape of Topacies was a darkened vision of Puzzle Men and the giant floating egg. Traven wondered if his fear of them being together wasn't vastly preferable to what he now saw before him. "Freeze," she said, and all motion but theirs came to a halt. She began her explanation. "I found that the Gateway doesn't have the ability to monitor the Puzzle Men with the exception of when you are present. Even though it locks

A Lifetime In Time

on your eyesight the reception isn't good. The Puzzle Men send off some sort of blocking signal that hampers eavesdropping and produces a fair amount of static or blur that can be easily mistaken for other natural static. The practice room pieced the rest of the environment together from my description."

"You have one heck of a memory," Traven said, thinking that if he didn't know that he was in the practice room he would have surely been fooled, "but why?"

"To defeat the enemy one must know the enemy and one must have a starting point." She then looked to the sky and said, "weapons." Three large heavy tables appeared before them with weapons ranging from the primitive to the futuristic. Traven picked up a crossbow that was cocked and ready to fire. Annie grabbed an M-16 and pulled the bolt back as if she had seen every Vietnam movie Earth had ever made.

"Even if these weapons have any effect on these Puzzle Men there's no guarantee that they would even scratch the real Puzzle Men. The Gateway doesn't know what their weaknesses are or so she says." Traven stated while demonstrating that he could put on a sword sheath with one hand.

"That isn't the point," Annie said calmly while checking the sight of the gun. "The point is to visualize your victory, to catalog your moves so that you have options. My people, at least the successful ones, believe in pre-visualizing your goal and thus making the goal a reality." Traven looked at her skeptically. "If nothing else, if we win it's a morale booster." She then showed Traven that she too could put on a sword and sheath with one hand. "Begin," she said quietly and the room reactivated. Puzzle Men moved quickly to surround Annie and Traven. Traven let the arrow from the crossbow fly. The shot would have been straight into the middle of its head, but the geometric shapes that made up it's skull shifted just enough to let the arrow pass through and hit the Puzzle Man behind the first one in the chest. The wounded Puzzle Man looked down at the arrow and then pulled it out of him as if the wound was no less disconcerting than removing a piece of lint. Annie's bullets ripped through the one closest to her making the sound of breaking glass as Traven threw his now useless crossbow at the one he had originally intended to shoot. The bullet riddled Puzzle Man reformed without even pausing as the one Traven had targeted sucked the crossbow into it's body and used what parts it could to increase its mass while spitting the rest out through the empty spaces in its body. It was like watching a pencil sharpener throw up. Traven drew his sword as his opponent came closer and succeeded in cutting off its arm. This small victory took three heavy hits and two blocks, one to its tail and the other to its other arm. Annie focused her shooting tightly on specific areas of its head and body. This slowed the creature, but still it pieced itself back together as if a giant unseen child was rebuilding it with white legos. The severed arm broke into smaller pieces and crawled back to its home as the creature tried and nearly succeeded in stabbing Traven with its tail. Traven remembered what the tail had done to the frog creature on Topacies and executed a hasty retreat to the weapons table where he met up with Annie who was down to her last clip of bullets. Ten Puzzle-Men had formed a circle around them and their options were diminishing. Traven grabbed three grenades and pulled the pins with one hand. "Duck and cover!" he yelled as he threw them as if they were Calleash into the three closest adversaries. Annie pulled the futuristic section of guns down under the table with them as they took cover. The Puzzle Men sucked the grenades into their bodies and exploded in a shower of puzzle pieces that rained down onto the table and the surrounding area. The pieces lay dormant for a moment as Annie showed Traven which buttons on the guns to press. Like mice the pieces of the Puzzle-Men scampered across the ground to join into the mass of the other approaching Puzzle Men. Traven and Annie jumped from the make-believe safety of their table and let loose a stream of high powered laser blasts on the closest

Puzzle Men. This seemed to stagger the Puzzle Men but after a moment they adapted and even started to feed on the blasts.

"How strong are these freaks?" screamed Traven, as Annie yelled to him over the battle.

"It's only making them stronger, flip the blue switch on the gun."

Traven flipped the switch which changed the blast from an energy laser to a solid light concussion beam. This seemed to have the desired effect. While the Puzzle Men would still pull their bodies back together it at least created the breathing room they needed to think and prepare their next move. Traven wonder how many battles Annie had seen in her life. She was only thirteen, yet she was more composed than he was, at least outwardly she seemed to be almost enjoying this.

"Ideas!?" yelled Traven, as more Puzzle Men came to join their brothers from over the horizon. The pieces from the broken Puzzle Men started to form into one long snake-like beast who's body was creating an ever-tightening circle around them.

"Just one, children," Thealand's voice came from behind them. She carried a sleek organic shaped rifle that should have been too big and heavy for a human of her size. The blast was a massive blue light that hit the snake-like creature and froze it solid. As the oncoming drone Puzzle Men tried to join the frozen snake beast they found that they could not. Thealand continued blasting away at any Puzzle Man that came over the perimeter. The three misfit warriors held their own until their guns started overheating. First Thealand's overheated and became the biggest bomb that this battle had yet to see. As she threw it over the frozen remains of the now dethawing giant snake she screamed, "Down!" Without a second to question her orders, Traven, Annie, and Thealand hugged the ground for dear life. The blast lit the entire area in a bright blue glow and when it was finished hundreds of Puzzle Men stood frozen and the ground had become a sheet of frost. Traven shivered as he looked up. A slight prayer of hope suddenly dissipated when he realized that the inner edge of the snake beast was thawing and trying to reestablish into another form.

"Damn it!" he screamed as he leapt on top of the frozen edge of the great snake and threw his gun to the ground. Reaching into his pockets his Calleash went flying at the frozen drones. It was one of the best throws that he ever had made. The Calleash bounced from Puzzle Man to Puzzle Man destroying their current frozen forms like two never ending grenades set loose in a giant pinball machine. As the Calleash returned to his hands he heard Thealand's strong and commanding voice.

"End and clear!" she said as the battlefield faded and the practice room returned to normal. The three of them lay on the floor trying to slow their breath.

"Nice throw, pup," Thealand said once she steadied herself.

"For all the good it did," he replied, sucking in a big gulp of air while glumly staring at the ceiling.

"That was..." Annie said still trying to breath, "enlightening."

"How can you say that?" Traven's voice became angry and then it lost its edge as he said, "We know no more than we did before." He laughed slightly realizing that the phrase came out of his mouth in an almost sing-songy way and the last time he had said those words he was talking about Mo-pa's philosophy. "How are we ever going to beat those things?"

"Pup," said Thealand rising to her feet, "We are going to beat those things, not just because my people need a home, but because you're the Keeper."

"Why do you people keep making me out to be some sort of savior? I'm a seventeen year old human who would rather be playing a guitar." He propped himself up on his elbows and gave her a hard look.

"I call you that because of your actions," Thealand said, "and because I've seen you grow over these months. Now you're not the boy who talked me into a tutoring job anymore you're the Keeper."

"I've helped to save one planet, with a lot of help, nothing more."

"If I was to place anyone else in your position I don't believe they would have made the choices you have."

"It's not the choices I've made that I'm worried about, it's the damn Puzzle Men. We've learned nothing other than they're next to indestructible," Traven said sitting up.

"Learning isn't about the answers," said Annie. "It's about the journey to the place of understanding. Just because you don't have the understanding today doesn't mean you won't have the understanding tomorrow or that you haven't been taking the steps to that understanding. Every solution creates new problems which will have new solutions. Only a fool believes that there is a neat and clean end to a story, that's why a story is a story and not a life."

"You have been listening kitten," said Thealand proudly, "and besides, we now know many ways not to fight the Puzzle-men."

"Crap me on a bagel," exclaimed Traven, getting up and extending his hand to Annie, "now all the hot chicks sound like Mo-pa."

"What's a bagel?" asked a puzzled Annie.

"You two had better get going," said Thealand, "you don't want to be late."

"Late for what?" asked Traven with a great look of confusion on his face, as Annie gave her mother a secret nod.

"Brandy has something waiting for you in both your rooms," Thealand said.

"She has a room?" Traven looked at Annie as if there was something she should have told him a while ago.

"Of course pup," said Thealand. "We all have rooms."

Chapter Twenty-Five
Rites Of Passage

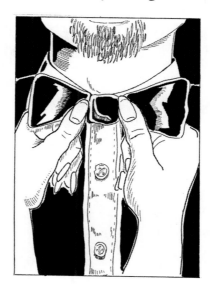

Traven was led to his room by Larry while Annie was escorted off to her room by her mother. Traven was surprised to find Brandy in her usual form waiting for him by the pond.

"What are you doing here?" he asked, as Brandy waved Larry a signal to depart.

"We have decided that y'all need a break."

"Who is we?" he grunted, "and I told you I didn't want to talk to you until you were ready to come clean about the Puzzle Men."

"Ah am not sure how to come clean about them," she said. "It's difficult."

"Why not dig deep and give it a try," he sternly suggested. Brandy took a deep breath and began.

"There are things that you are not yet ready to know," she said, "but how they relate to the Puzzle Men Ah am not sure. Ah can tell you what Ah am theorizing."

"Why do I keep having to hear the, 'There are things that you are not ready to know speech?' It's getting really old."

"Look at it this way," she said starting to pace, "when you were a child you probably would have seen a picture of Alice Cooper in concert and been afraid. As you have grown you've learned to see the tongue-in-cheek dark humor of his performance that you wouldn't have accepted when you were younger. Since you've been in the Gateway your taste in music has grown to include Jazz, folk, and even the music of Dirgewhere. These new tastes would not have developed for many years if you had been living on Earth and not had the experiences that you have had here. Because you have grown mentally you can now accept them, where as before y'all would have most likely stuck to the music that was comfortable to you and your friends. Being the Keeper holds many secrets and what Ah'm looking out for is your growth to give you the information you need without overloading your current mental state or scaring you horribly."

"Look," he said in an angry yet whining tone, "I think I've been through enough and I'm sure I can handle whatever it is."

"All right," she replied, "try this as an example. When did you learn about your creation?"

"As a Keeper?"

"As a person," she clarified.

"What do you mean?" he said, once again being confused.

"Your parent's," she said with a smile. "When did ya realize what they had to do to create you."

"Oh gross," he said in shock, "I don't need to think about that."

"Why not? It's a fact of life, it's natural, almost everyone who has ever walked your planet has got there the same way."

"But they're my parents."

"And that's why you don't want to think about it. You've put up blocks to not accept the reality that you know had to happen for you to exist. In the back of your mind you know it happened, but you're not ready to see your parents in that light, you're not ready to accept them as humans like you and all your friends, even though you know deep inside that they are. Someday you might choose to start your own family and when ya do you might be able to understand the outlook of your parents and maybe be able to understand why they have made some of the choices they have made, even in raising you. Without those experiences you don't see the world from their point of view."

Traven suddenly felt very young and the example was dead on. It was much easier to think of his parents as the enemy at times than to think of them as people who have gone through the same life experiences that he had or would someday go through. This speech did take the edge off his attitude, and after a few moments of silence, and trying to mentally burn the image of his parents trying to create him from his mind, he knew he had to change the subject.

"Fine," he said, "then tell me your theories, on the Puzzle Men or anything else."

Brandy laughed and sat down on the bank of the pond, motioning for Traven to join her she began.

"Let me state that my theories may be wrong."

"That's a hell of a way to start."

"But sadly true. We have no way to track the Puzzle-Men and they have the ability to block us from seeing them. While this isn't something that occurs very often naturally, it's not unheard of in the fabric of the webs. That's why Ah let you go back to Topacies, blockage of the signal isn't a definite sign that it's them and most blocks are not."

"If you can't track them how do you know of their existence?" he asked.

"When they first appeared their blocking ability was intermittent. It must have been a glitch in their system because when we tried to find their creation it too was blocked or missing. In fact, when they destroyed their first planet we could only see enough through their blocking signal to realize that they were a threat. When they formed their first transport egg Ah realized what they were trying to do and that's when we lost complete track of them. Ah hoped they had been destroyed in the jump and because of their inability to be tracked, Ah assumed they had; sadly, Ah now know this was not the case."

"And this all happened when I became the Keeper?"

"Yes it did, but Ah don't know what the connection is," she sighed. "To be honest, Ah wouldn't have even been looking for them if my programming didn't contain elements of self-preservation. Now this is the difficult part," she paused for a moment to scratch her head. "My consciousness was turned off for a time. Ah don't know how long exactly, possibly ninety years or more." As she peered down her face became slack. She focused on her third necklace end. It was an upside down U shape with a broken diagonal line. Toying with it's chain, she wouldn't touch the symbol itself.

"What do you mean turned off?"

"Think of a person in a coma. They're alive, their body functions, but their mind is dormant."

"How the hell did that happen?"

"The Keeper turned it off," she said dropping the necklace end and looking up.

"Why!?" Traven yelled, quickly realizing that his volume was unnecessary and that Brandy was having a tough time telling this story as it was. "I mean, why would he do it?" Concern had replaced his shock and anger.

"Once again, Ah'm not entirely sure, but the one thing I've noticed about the Puzzle Men is that they are composed of some of the same geometric designs that line many of the doorways and the architecture of the Gateway. Because of that and that they are trying to locate me, Ah believe that they might have their beginnings in the Gateway."

"Have you checked the library? Annie told me that it can replay events that have happened inside here."

"Those sections are blank or erased."

"What possible reason could he have had for creating them?"

"Ah don't know? To test me, to test the next Keeper, to give us a common foe to struggle against to bring us closer? Maybe revenge?"

"Revenge?"

"Honey, the workings of the organic mind have always been beyond my ability to comprehend."

They sat in silence as the room started to change into it's twilight mode. Finally, Traven broke the silence.

"How do we stop them?"

"Ah don't know." Though her words were quiet, they had the weight of a million years of baggage. "Ah guess that's something we have to figure out." She stood up and extended her hand. "Still mad at me?"

"Not so much," he replied. "Hey, I know that you don't eat, except it would seem for popcorn, but would you like a cookie?"

"Maybe another time," she smiled, "besides y'all have to get ready."

"For what?"

"It's a surprise."

"I've had enough surprises for one day, thank you."

"Ah think this one y'all will enjoy. Go take a bath and get dressed in the clothes that are set out for you. Larry will take you to the landing area when you are done."

"What's going on?" he asked suspiciously.

"You'll see, but hurry up, we spent a mess of time talkin."

As she left Traven felt guilty about his earlier tantrum and as she melted into the floor he thought, *I guess everyone's got their problems whether you're human or Gateway. After all, I'm not sure I would want to have to break in a new Keeper, especially if he was me.*

After Traven's bath he went to his room to find the sleekest suit he had ever seen carefully laid out on his bed. Traven hated getting dressed up, but there was something strikingly cool about this outfit. It was a shiney blue metallic that gave off turquoise highlights which almost glowed. Slick black shoes, white button up shirt, and a bow tie that he had no idea how to tie. He wondered what Brandy was up to, but decided that he would know soon enough. After he put it on he admired himself in the mirror. *Not bad,* he thought, *but this dangling bow tie bites.* Even with the outfit looking cool he just couldn't get used to the dress socks and thought for a moment about changing them. Before he could make any fashion faux paux Brandy formed out of his bedroom floor.

"My oh my," she said in her strongest southern accent to date, "don't y'all resemble a gentleman!"

"Brandy," he said with a sigh, "what's this all about?"

"Ya find out soon enough, sugar. Now, stand still." She stepped in close to him and tied his tie. "There, perfect." She kissed him on the cheek. "Knock'em dead tiger," and she was gone. Larry flew into the room and circled him checking out the suit.

"Are you in on this too?" Traven asked.

"Yeth Indeed," Larry buzzed, handing Traven a box with a beautiful corsage in it.

"Are you going to fill me in?" Traven asked accepting the box.

"Nope."

"I didn't think so. Hey, this isn't one of those bad movie plots where they dress up the victim just to kill them?"

"Thill haven't got over the bug thing have you?"

"Nope," Traven pondered the flower and finally said with a sigh, "let's go."

As they entered the landing area Larry wished him luck and stayed at the doorway. As Traven entered he was greeted by Thealand who was trying hard to block the body of someone who was standing behind her.

"What's going on?" Traven asked in a tired voice, trying to see around Thealand who kept pivoting to block his view.

"There's someone I'd like you to meet."

Thealand step aside to reveal Annie. For a moment Traven almost didn't recognize her. Her patchwork hair of white and black was now completely black. Her skin had gone from a snow white color to a summer tan and her ears were mysteriously human.

Her once black nails now had become a crimson red as had her lips and she was wearing a champaign pink dress that had a touch of ancient Greek flare to it. She looked taller due to the high heels and even a few years older.

"I'll leave you two alone," offered Thealand bowing out of the room.

"What happened?" asked Traven dropping the flower only to have his other hand rescue it mid-fall. Annie blushed and for the first time in her life experienced shyness.

"What do you think?" she asked, biting her lower lip.

"I... I think you look stunning. Again, what's going on?"

"I had what you could call a makeover in the Gateway's med lab."

"It's not permanent, is it?" his tone was worried.

"No, why?"

"Because you're beautiful in your normal form."

She smiled wide and kissed him hard. When they were done she stepped back and wiped her lipstick from his lips with her thumb. It smeared and she licked the end of her finger to try again. All of her fussing seemed so alien to her personality that Traven had to laugh, and then made it difficult for her by playfully biting at her fingers. This turned into a wrestling match tickle fight that ended as she grabbed both his hands and pressed her nose to his. She looked straight in his eyes and asked, "Would you go with me to the Sadie Hawkins Dance?"

Traven lost count of how many times he said yes and even parts of the plan on how they were going to pull this off. He found himself holding hands with Annie in almost a daze as their shuttle flew through his solar system toward Earth. Brandy had arranged their flight to start at the outer edge of Pluto, so that if the Puzzle Men had followed the opening they would be stuck in deep space and would have no way of creating more Puzzle Men and trying to breach the Gateway. They would return on the opposite side of Mercury for the same reasons. Traven briefly wondered if stranding the Puzzle Men in deep space could be an option to their removal.

They arrived on Earth, landed the small ship on the roof of his school and engaged the cloaking device which rendered the ship invisible to the naked eye. Finding a way down was easy enough, being that Annie had a computerized skeleton key which allowed them access to the roof door. As they stepped into the dance Annie activated a button on her choker necklace that allowed her to understand human language. All eyes turned on them as they were, without a doubt, the best dressed couple at the dance. As the music started, Traven realized that he was still holding the box with the corsage in it. He handed it to her and she asked him to pin it on.

"You know this is not only my first dance but my first flower," she mused.

"Mine too," he laughed, as the band kicked into a killer version of *Brick House*. They danced surprisingly well as if they had spent their time in the Gateway working on their moves instead of preparing for battle. They were definitely lost in the moment and as the songs changed they soon became the center of attention attracting the admiration of the onlookers. *Who was this girl?* his peers wondered in the same breath that had them also wondering what had happened to this dork they once easily overlooked. As they slow danced to Prince's *Purple Rain*, Traven had to tell Annie that it wasn't appropriate to kiss through the entire song. He realized that she could pass for someone older as a human, but still he wished he could be with her in her true form. His life had become a complicated mess by all human standards, but for this one night it seemed that all was right. As the song ended they were approached by Brian and his date, Beth.

Traven explained that this was Annie and that she was from France and couldn't really speak English well. When Brian suggested that a girl that couldn't talk could be the best possible date Beth punched him in the arm and Annie asked if it would be okay if she broke his legs. Traven assured her that he was only kidding and that he would need his legs in the future. Beth took Annie to the punch bowl and continued talking to her in English which she

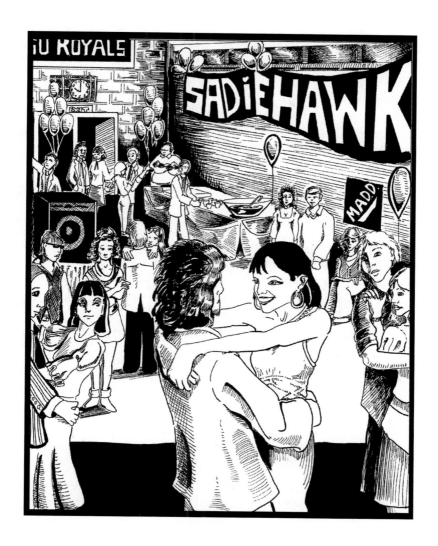

could understand because of her choker, but she replied in Atrill which didn't seem to throw Beth's ability to hold a conversation at all. As the two boys eyed their dates Brian commented on Traven's luck at scoring such a hot looking girl and besieged him with questions on where he met her and where she was staying in this foreign country of America. Traven lied like a dog and sounded quite believable, at least in a high school teenager form of believability. As the two boys talked at length about everything from their girlfriends to the latest concerts, Jim Salante and his bully squad approached them.

"So you finally found a girl pathetic enough to go out with you," he said, as his cronies laughed loud and hollow laughs.

"At least I'm not dating one of my relatives," Traven replied, which caused Jim to defend himself in the form that he was most accustom to, by throwing a punch. Traven dodged the punch and then calmly opened the door to the parking lot. Jim, his cronies and Brian followed Traven into the darkened parking lot, carefully looking to see that the chaperones were not watching.

"Man, your ass is so kicked," boasted Jim. "You can't lay a hand on me without getting shipped off to military school, isn't that right, puss?" Jim got right up in Traven's face and it was all that Traven could do to restrain himself.

"That might be true, Salante, but that doesn't mean that my girlfriend won't put you in a body cast."

Stepping from the shadows and into the light Annie whistled loudly, placing two fingers in her mouth and screeching out a high pitched note which Traven recognized was in the key of B. She walked slowly toward them as if she was a female terminator, leaving Beth behind as a shocked onlooker. Annie turned for a moment to eye the movable bleachers that were used for outside sporting events. With a crescent kick she snapped the first row of seating in two, with a front kick she snapped the second row, and the third and forth rows quickly became sawdust with an elbow and an upper cut. She then turned her gaze on Jim and walked toward them with full confidence as if she had worn high heels her entire life. Jim's cronies parted like the red sea and stepped away as if they were merely extras in a gunfight. She asked Jim in Atrill if he thought today was a good day to die. Traven translated.

"What, you need a girl to fight your battles?" Jim said weakly.

"No, I don't," said Traven, "but the idea of military school doesn't appeal to me. What does it matter who kicks your ass tonight, the outcome will be the same."

"I don't fight girls!" Jim said trying to find a way to back out of his situation.

"You don't date them either," Brian said under his breath being terribly amused at the unfolding drama. Jim yelled a couple of crippled threats as he backed off and disappeared into the darkness, his friends quickly joining him and praising his choice to back down. Annie approached Traven slowly and as he was saying thank you to her, she stopped him.

"You called me your girlfriend," she said.

"That I did, Kitten." He no sooner had admitted it when she knocked him to the hard ground in a passionate liplock. Brian and Beth turned their backs to give them privacy, but after five uncomfortable minutes Brian suggested that they leave this lame dance and head up Lake Michigan to the beach. A phone call and within ten minutes they found themselves in Matt's car, even Willie had come along for the ride. They picked up Matt's cousin Bertha who could keep pace with Brian's jokes and laughed the whole way to the beach. As Traven's friends threw frisbees in the early morning light, he and Annie walked up the beach to find some space of their own. She removed her shoes and spread her toes into the sand and for a moment drank in the feeling.

"I have mastered the weapons of a hundred planets," Annie said in deep and funny voice, "and yet I have never encountered anything as diabolical as high heeled shoes." The both laughed and then sat down on the beach, Annie resting her head on Traven's shoulder. "I wasn't sure you'd agree to come to the dance," she said.

"Why?" he asked, a bit stunned by her statement.

"Well, we're both different species for one. You still believe that you have a life-mate out there somewhere and you keep bringing up that thing about our ages."

Traven touched her chin lightly, directing her face to his. His finger traced the edge of her jaw line up to play with the new curve of her ear. He breathed a slight laugh.

"We might be dead tomorrow because of Puzzle Men or who knows what else. Maybe I'm not destined for a life-mate, or the one that my other self loved, and I don't know what the future might bring. All I know is how I feel, and at this moment I can't imagine being happier with anyone else, anywhere else, or in any other time. Thank you for asking me, it has been an honor."

She kissed him and then purred, nuzzling into his neck.

"I'll be there for you when you face the Puzzle Men, you know," she said in a moment of seriousness.

"That's because you like to blow thing's up," he teased.

"No," then she paused, "well, I do like to blow things up."

"I thought so." Traven smiled.

"No, it's not that, it's because you mean that much to me. I'm willing to be there when you need me. I'm willing to wait if you need time."

"You're willing to kick ass for me," Traven said with a laugh.

"Always," she returned the laugh.

"Those Puzzle Men have no idea what they're up against, do they?" he said.

"No they don't," she replied.

The two held each other tightly as the sun came up over the Lake Michigan and the world slowed and the moment touched perfection. The two kissed a silent promise to take on all odds together and win.

A Lifetime In Time

Want More?

Check Out

www.alifetimeintime.com

For author apperances, updates, orders, contact information and more art.

Tim Vaulato was born in 1966 and lives in the Midwest. At a very young age he started to draw on restaurant napkins to ease his boredom when his parents would drag him out to dinner. Around second grade he became obsessed with comic books and that obsession sparked both his interest in drawing and writing. By high school he was enrolled in art and creative writing classes which were the only subjects that his attention deficient mind could focus on. Entering college his grades improved greatly and after a number of years at the Community College he transferred to Northern Illinois University to major in printmaking and art education. He has been an art teacher since 1991 and has taught every level, Kindergarden through 12th grade, and every subject in the art realm, including jewelry, sculpture, photography, drawing, painting, cartooning and animation.

He has played bass with the band Harlem Klapsaddle, recording four albums and was with the band Wishbone Jones for fourteen years. He has written over 200 songs, and one rock opera. He is married with two wonderful children that have been named after the characters in his books.

Give the gift of adventure to your family and friends.

Check your local bookstore or order dirrect
from alifetimeintime.com

For snail mail
Make your checks payable to :
LoKante & Mooshlock Publishing
P.O. Box 5898
Elgin Il. 60121-5898

$17.95 us.   Copies _____

$4.50 us. shipping per book

Illinois Residents Add. tax $1.17 Total _____

Contact us for special bulk order prices

Name _____

Address _____

City/State/Zip _____

Phone _____ Email _____

Please allow 10 to 15 business days for delivery